"*Inside Out* is tender, romantic and una... ...y. Lauren Dane writes with an emotional depth and authenticity that always leaves me breathless. Simply put, I love her books!" —Lara Adrian

Praise for
LAID BARE

"It's impossible not to love this story. The sex is sizzling, the emotions are raw. Lauren Dane has done it again. *Laid Bare*, quite simply, *rocks!*"
—Megan Hart, national bestselling author of *Selfish Is the Heart*

"I was blown away by Dane's emotionally charged, deeply erotic tale of second chances and redemption. I can't say it enough: I loved this book!"
—Sylvia Day, national bestselling author of *The Stranger I Married*

"A tender love story that wrung my heart with its sweetness. Don't miss this book." —Ann Aguirre, national bestselling author of *Hell Fire*

"*Laid Bare* lives up to its title . . . Dane provides a heated yet entreating second chance at love due to the tender caring in and out of the bed of each of the prime players." —*The Best Reviews*

"A roller-coaster story that will have you crying one moment, aroused the next, and laughing with glee at each triumphant step along the way . . . This is Dane's best story yet!" —*Romantic Times*

Praise for
UNDERCOVER

"Lauren Dane deftly weaves action, intrigue, and emotion with spicy, delicious eroticism . . . a toe-curling erotic romance sure to keep you reading late into the night."
—Anya Bast, *New York Times* bestselling author of *Jeweled*

"Sexy, pulse-pounding adventure . . . that'll leave you weak in the knees. Dane delivers!" —Jaci Burton, national bestselling author of *Riding the Night*

"Exciting, emotional and arousing." —Sasha White, author of *Most Wanted*

continued . . .

"Fast-paced action, steamy romance."   —Megan Hart

"Scintillating! . . . a roller coaster of emotion, intrigue, and sensual delights . . . I was hooked from the first sentence."

—Vivi Anna, author of *The Vampire's Quest*

"Be in line at your favorite bookstore the day it comes out. In other words, it is a Recommended Read . . . one I plan on reading over and over again."   —*Joyfully Reviewed*

"A hot, sexy and action-packed piece of writing that will keep you glued to every page wondering what will happen next. A fabulous read!"

—*Fresh Fiction*

"Wow! This book rocks! Lauren Dane pulls out all the stops with this soul-searing, awe-inspiring read . . . Definitely a must read and deserving of a special spot on the keeper shelf."   —*Romance Junkies*

More praise for Lauren Dane and her novels

"Drool worthy."   —*Romance Junkies*

"This story has it all! There is action, drama, interesting characters, an electrifying story line and hot, passionate sex . . . a truly beautiful and sensual story . . . a truly enchanting series!"   —*Joyfully Reviewed*

"Starts out hot right out of the box, and then keeps getting hotter. Lauren Dane has a knack for making readers feel the passion and excitement of a new relationship . . . it's easy to see why Lauren Dane is such a well-loved author."   —*TwoLips Reviews*

"Lauren Dane has once again created characters that you can't resist . . . the sexual chemistry sparks and sizzles."   —*Sensual*

"From its completely romantic beginning to it's oh-so-sensual end, I loved every word . . . Ms. Dane is definitely becoming a master of the romantic pen!"   —*The Romance Studio*

"Rich and sensual . . . entirely delicious."   —*Romance Divas*

INSIDE OUT

LAUREN DANE

HEAT | NEW YORK

THE BERKLEY PUBLISHING GROUP
Published by the Penguin Group
Penguin Group (USA) Inc.
375 Hudson Street, New York, New York 10014, USA
Penguin Group (Canada), 90 Eglinton Avenue East, Suite 700, Toronto, Ontario M4P 2Y3, Canada
(a division of Pearson Penguin Canada Inc.)
Penguin Books Ltd., 80 Strand, London WC2R 0RL, England
Penguin Group Ireland, 25 St. Stephen's Green, Dublin 2, Ireland (a division of Penguin Books Ltd.)
Penguin Group (Australia), 250 Camberwell Road, Camberwell, Victoria 3124, Australia
(a division of Pearson Australia Group Pty. Ltd.)
Penguin Books India Pvt. Ltd., 11 Community Centre, Panchsheel Park, New Delhi—110 017, India
Penguin Group (NZ), 67 Apollo Drive, Rosedale, North Shore 0632, New Zealand
(a division of Pearson New Zealand Ltd.)
Penguin Books (South Africa) (Pty.) Ltd., 24 Sturdee Avenue, Rosebank, Johannesburg 2196,
South Africa

Penguin Books Ltd., Registered Offices: 80 Strand, London WC2R 0RL, England

This book is an original publication of The Berkley Publishing Group.

This is a work of fiction. Names, characters, places, and incidents either are the product of the author's imagination or are used fictitiously, and any resemblance to actual persons, living or dead, business establishments, events, or locales is entirely coincidental. The publisher does not have any control over and does not assume any responsibility for author or third-party websites or their content.

PRINTING HISTORY
Heat trade paperback edition / November 2010

Library of Congress Cataloging-in-Publication Data

Dane, Lauren.
    Inside out / Lauren Dane. — Heat trade paperback ed.
      p. cm.
    ISBN 978-0-425-23688-8
    1. Self-actualization (Psychology) in women—Fiction. I. Title.
    PS3604.A5I58 2010
    813'.6—dc22   2010017220

PRINTED IN THE UNITED STATES OF AMERICA

10 9 8 7 6 5 4 3 2 1

This one is for my very own alpha male.
Ray, you're my everything.

ACKNOWLEDGMENTS

At this point, I have a cast of characters who support every book I write (I'm lucky that way).

My family—my wonderful husband, who rarely complains about having a wife who uses parts of his real life in her books. My kids, who keep me grounded. My parents, who've been the best example a girl could ask for.

Leis Pederson—thank you for being such a wonderful editor. Each of my books is better for the work you put into it and the effort you make to get me in line.

Laura Bradford—wonderful agent, wonderful friend. Thank you.

Megan Hart—thank you for always being there. And for making me use more commas. Ann Aguirre, Jaci Burton, Maya Banks and Anya Bast—thank you for always being there to listen to me and to give me such great advice.

Mary, Renee and Fatin, who beta read for me even though they all have busy lives—thank you.

My readers—you're all the very best in the world. Thank you for supporting me and my books!

I would be remiss in not mentioning the poetry of Pablo Neruda. Neruda's poetry really communicated to Cope's sense of romanticism and sensuality. It was a thrill to use that in this book, and I hope I've steered some people toward at least a few volumes of his poetry.

1

She arched on a gasp as the heat of his mouth met her neck. His hands, clever, wicked hands, quickly divested her of her shirt, leaving her free to rub against him like a cat. She groaned as he moved away, reaching to grab him back. He grinned. That cockeyed uptilt of his mouth that had driven her insane for years.

"Sugar, don't rush me. Do you know how long I've waited to have you like this?" Cope's voice was rusty, filled with burrs and edges as it washed over her. His hair, gleaming blue-black, caught the glow of light from the nearby lamp.

"Take your shirt off. I want to see." God, how she wanted to see his body. She'd fantasized about him for so long it seemed beyond surreal as he peeled off the tight, black T-shirt, revealing acres of sexy muscles, taut skin and tattoos.

She sighed happily as heat bloomed low in her belly, tightening her nipples.

"Like what you see? *Oh sweet Christ . . .*" He left off on a hiss of plea-sure as she cruised her mouth and tongue up his belly and to the ring in his left nipple. Her hands slid over the ornate Chinese dragon tail wrapping around his left biceps. The body of the dragon dominated Cope's entire back, marking him in a decidedly masculine way. She knew it had taken Brody Brown nearly six months to complete. Worth every moment. It was breathtaking. Beautiful and beyond sexy.

"This tattoo makes me so hot." She nipped his side, and he leaned into her. His skin was salty; the taste filled her with craving and a sense of triumph at finally being able to touch him the way she'd wanted to for so long.

His scent curled around her senses, holding her there: the tang of his arousal, of his skin, the musk of his cologne, the citrus of his shampoo, all little sensual treats she'd picked up from being around him all the time.

Laughing, she pushed him back and scrambled atop his body, straddling his hips. He raised a brow at her, and she briefly stopped, fascinated by the jump of his pulse at the hollow of his throat. She leaned down to kiss him there because there was nothing else to do.

He was getting naked, and his hands were all over her. It was like Christmas and her birthday at the same time. Maybe even a bit of Halloween too, it was so good.

"Do you like bad boys, Ella?" he asked in a murmur caught between a purr and a growl. All while thumbing one nipple until she squirmed, breathless.

"I like *you*. And I like that." She may have squeaked a bit, though she'd probably deny it if asked.

He grinned again as he raised himself up enough to reach the nipple he wasn't already tugging. She rolled her hips, unabashedly delighting in the way the seam of her jeans slid against her clit, giving her just enough friction to make her gulp in some air, but not enough to satisfy.

Only the hands on her would satisfy. Only his mouth. Only the cock she currently ground against, still locked behind his zipper. *Stupid denim!*

"Ella . . ." His voice was tortured, laced with need.

"Please." She didn't know what she was begging for, only that he'd be able to give it to her.

"Ella? Hello?"

She blinked several times and nearly died as she focused on the man standing just on the other side of the counter. *How very special.* She'd just had a fuck fantasy about *him* in the middle of the café at midday.

Piercing blue eyes met her gaze. A grin, god, *that* grin, marked his mouth. Andrew Copeland stood two feet away looking amused by her lapse in attention as well as ten kinds of delicious bad boy.

And to answer the question her fantasy Cope had asked? Hell yes, she liked bad boys. But *his* kind of bad boy. Unfortunately, she'd had a real one, and that had been enough to land her in the hospital and then physical therapy for nearly a year. The mental scars would probably be there forever. Yeah, not so much fun, *those* bad boys.

She swallowed, feeling the burn of her skin as she blushed furiously, but managed to smile at him, because, well hell, look at him! How could you look at all that and not simply smile in thanks to whoever created such perfection?

"Hey, Cope, sorry about that. I was woolgathering. What can I get you?" The counter had never been cleaner than right then as she rubbed the cloth over it nervously, the taste of his skin still in her mouth.

She could easily get lost in those eyes. Everything about him attracted her. For years she'd thought him the sexiest guy in town. *Way* out of her league, but still beyond delicious. Besides, it didn't hurt anyone to objectify him in her head, now did it? Plus he was a total flirt, which made it even easier to crush on him without really taking it seriously. He flirted as easily as he breathed. He'd probably like it if he knew. Not that she'd tell him or anything.

He leaned toward her, his movements slow and easy, but she

recognized the strength coiled in those muscles, knew he was a predator. "You have the prettiest blush. Did you know that? Now, see, if I didn't know you better, I'd say you were having a very naughty fantasy in your head just now."

That voice. Holy crap, his voice was like sex in a jar. Or whatever. But it was hot and sexy, and she heard it lots and lots. Usually when her eyes were closed and she was masturbating. Wrong. Bad, bad Ella! Not the place to think about that.

He chuckled then, cocking his head, and whaddya know, he looked even better like that. Man, she was hopeless. Hopeless and sex-deprived. She was even getting interrupted in her fantasies. How pathetic was that?

"You *were*, weren't you? You have no idea how much I want you to share."

"I don't know you well enough to scar you with my nasty sex fantasies." She winked and turned, hoping he didn't see the blush heating her cheeks at that very moment. "I'll make you an Americano instead."

"Killjoy. If you have nasty sex fantasies, Ella, it would help if you shared them. Unburden yourself and stuff. It's good for you. I'll even share some of mine. You know, so you don't feel so alone."

She choked with laughter and embarrassment. Good thing she wasn't looking at him right then. Or drinking anything. Then again, a drink sounded good. A stiff shot of tequila. Gah, not stiff! Um, yes, a shot of tequila might help.

Trying to get herself back together, she focused on getting his drink. He could tease with just about anyone. Normally, once she knew a person well enough, she could too. But he was different. For years he'd teased her but had kept it gentle. She'd often felt the warm slice of envy at the way he put the moves on women. He was so smooth and sexy when he had a woman in his sights. He'd never looked at her like that. Hadn't ever given her the smoldering gaze she'd fantasized about for years.

Until . . . well, lately it had felt like he'd changed the tenor a bit. Felt as if perhaps he'd glimpsed her as a woman instead of his friend Ella.

Which was stupid, she knew. He teased and was casually sexy, but he couldn't have had any idea she pined for him. He'd probably feel sorry for her if he knew. Their relationship would change; he'd distance himself to keep her from getting her heart broken. And she'd hate that, hate to lose the friendship and ease they had, even if she did want to lick him from head to toe. No, a playboy like Andrew Copeland was totally out of her league. She knew it, and he did too. That's why it worked between them.

He was one of the few people who never looked at her with pity in his eyes. He didn't ask how she was in a pained voice that told her the asker expected the answer to be sad. She was sick of being defined by something that happened to her nearly four years ago.

He let her be. Didn't try to control her under the guise of helping her. Didn't see tragedy when he looked at her. Which only made her want him more.

Cope watched her back, itching to beg her to tell him more. Wanting to hear her voice when she talked about sex—about dirty, fabulously filthy things she wanted him to do to her when they were naked and alone. It was his favorite way to drive himself crazy, thinking about Ella Tipton naked and in his bed.

He was fairly sure she was teasing about the sex fantasy thing, but her reaction was interesting. His cock crowded uncomfortably behind his zipper, awakened, as always, at the very thought of her. No other woman had caught his attention and his imagination the way she did. Which might have been a huge part of his fascination with her. It *was* a big reason why he knew she was different, had the potential to be far more than someone he dated. Ella had marked him already. Her determination, the way she aimed herself at goals and didn't stop until she met them. What wasn't to admire about that? What other woman could compete?

Damn, she was something else. Striking. Short, sleek fiery hair, big blue-green eyes, freckles across her cheeks and over her nose. Her skin was so pale she shone like a pearl. She was perfect in her imperfection. All her features, in and of themselves, were not pretty, but combined, they made her singular, the sort of face that drew the eye. And she had no idea how compelling she was, how people simply watched her move for the pleasure of it.

And funny in an odd way. He got her sense of humor. Offbeat. There was truly no one else like her in the entire world. Her voice made him laugh, sort of high-pitched, like a cartoon sometimes. He knew others teased her over it, but it fit her.

She was intelligent and diligent, loyal and brave. Braver than most people would ever know. His eyes swept to her legs, covered by a long, loose-fitting skirt.

She turned and handed him the Americano, made just exactly the way he liked it. She tucked an amaretto-almond biscotti on the edge of the saucer with a smile. "Made fresh today. I promise it's good."

He handed her the money, and she sighed when he waved away the change. "You deserve it for the biscotti. I need it this afternoon. I've had a long day."

Instead of going to a table, he leaned against the counter and watched her work. The café his sister-in-law Erin owned and Ella ran was quiet for the time being, so he had her pretty much all to himself. He planned to take advantage of that fact.

"Are you all right? You mentioned your day," she said when he must have looked confused. "I haven't seen you around lately." She bustled around the counter area, straightening, cleaning, polishing. Ella was rarely still; this fascinated him, though he couldn't say why. It wasn't a rare talent or anything.

She glanced up at him. "Ben said you were hiking. Was it fun?"

He knew she'd asked after him because his brother had told him. Still, it didn't diminish the silly pleasure that she'd noticed his absence.

"A very good time was had by all, thank you for asking. Me and some buddies—Brody and Ben usually included, but they're both a bit busy this year—hike Hurricane Ridge out in the Olympics." He laughed, thinking of the way Erin's belly had grown, of how she looked at his brother and their husband Todd like they were the best things on earth. "It was good. We were at a high enough elevation that we actually got a bit of snow, which isn't totally unusual for early fall. I've seen snow at the higher elevations in the summer, even. It's beautiful just now. Have you been?"

"You camped and hiked *in the snow?*" She shuddered, and he bit back a laugh. "Um, no, I'm happy to say I've not been snow camping because I'm not insane. I've been to the Ho Rainforest and I've done some hiking out there near Crescent Lake, but I've never camped and hiked like you do. Snow camping is just not a phrase I'd ever utter as a suggestion to how to spend my time. I love to ski, though I have to watch my knees now. I enjoy all that outdoorsy stuff, as long as I can escape it at day's end. As in, hot toddies at the lodge in front of a fireplace, or cabins with high-speed Internet. I'm not much for roughing it."

He laughed, but had the crazy desire to take her camping anyway. He could take her on long bike rides, show her the beauty of the Olympics in the fall. In the winter he was sure he could show her plenty of ways to keep warm, though he did agree with her that a hot toddy at the end of the day inside in front of a roaring fireplace was better than sleeping in a tent in the snow.

"I bet you've just never been with the right person. I promise you, camping is something you'd love with the right guide and gear."

She raised both eyebrows. "It always sounds nice, but then that *crazy* reality comes knocking, and I remember it's sleeping on the ground in a tent with nothing but less than an inch's worth of fabric protecting me from bears and bugs. And random snow? Hmm. Can't wait for that." She wrinkled her nose. "Plus I'm the kind of girl who gets third-degree sunburn even after I put on sunscreen on. Then I peel and have eight thousand more freckles as a result. It's a horrible cross to bear."

She sighed and blinked, the corners of her mouth struggling to stay in place and not curve upward.

He laughed. "I like freckles." He liked *her* freckles. He couldn't say he thought about them much before he'd walked into the café that first time and laid eyes on her and those bewitching spatters of ginger all over that pale skin.

She looked him up and down, putting another biscotti on his saucer when he'd finished the first one. "Easy for you to say, since you have none."

He wanted to lick her. Lick her freckles, taste the salt of her skin, hear whatever sounds she made when aroused, and he had a feeling she made them, though selfishly, he liked to pretend she hadn't made them in a while. His mood soured then. He hadn't seen her with anyone since that fuck brutalized her years prior. Just thinking about her ex made him want to punch something.

"You all right? You didn't talk about your day." She touched his hand, her thumb sliding over a knuckle and then into the indentation between that and the next. His anger slipped away, chased by the waves of pleasure spreading from the place she'd just caressed.

"Sorry. Some stupid work thing I thought of. You're much better to think on though." He flashed her a smile, and she rolled her eyes.

"Don't you have some hussy to harass?" Erin walked in with a jingle of the bells over the door. Erin was his sister-in-law and a friend. She was also about to expel nine and a half pounds of baby, and though he'd never say it out loud lest he take his life into his own hands, she looked it, around the edges anyway.

"I'll have you know I haven't harassed a hussy in years." Cope pushed a stool back so she could sit down, which she did with a rusty exhalation of air.

Ella pushed a glass of juice toward Erin and dared her to come behind the counter. Erin, ever so smart, obeyed, staying seated at the coffee bar.

"You and the gorgeous Ms. Tipton here are the only hussies I harass. Anyway, you look harassed enough for a few hussies. I thought you knew what caused that state." He waved at her belly, and she snorted.

"I do. But it's hard to remember *this* part when you're having *that* part. It's the getting here that's so fun, damn it." Erin grinned as she eyed him. "You look good. Tan and ready for trouble. You Copeland boys are hell on a girl's eyes, you know."

Ella nodded and then blushed when he caught her. He raised his brows at her but was content enough to let her get away for the moment.

He'd danced around her for years, wanting her. Truth be told, he hadn't been ready for her. Not then. He'd had no real interest in being tied to any one woman. He liked women. He liked them a lot, and he liked a lot of them. Back then he'd taken one look and had known a girl like Ella was a relationship type of woman.

And she hadn't been ready for him, either. She'd been with someone else when he'd first started getting his inkwork done at Brody's place, just next door. He'd been no less compelled by her, but she'd been different then. *That* Ella had been vivacious at times. But the light in her had slowly dimmed as the relationship she'd been in had gotten worse. As the man who was supposed to love her had ground her into nothing and finally nearly killed her.

The Ella he'd first known had begun to shine through again. Not all the time, and she'd changed in ways that would alter her forever. She was harder now, stronger, more wary. But no less beautiful to him.

More so, in fact, as he watched her rise from the wreck her life had become and work her way back, never wavering. Her strength was what he admired the most.

Ella Tipton was one of the best parts of his day when he came in to the café. She was the kind of woman a man could be *partners* with. A woman who'd lean on him when she needed it, but not cling. A woman who'd need, but not depend. He found himself thinking about this, that this woman was all the things a man wanted in a mate. More than he'd ever considered before.

The bottom line was that Andrew Copeland was more than halfway in love with a woman he'd never even kissed. In love with a woman who didn't even know how he felt. Then again, he probably could stand to make himself more obvious. He was so used to having women fawn all over him that he had little experience with wooing one. He could flirt like a gold medalist, but he needed to up his game when it came to making this one woman know he was interested in far more than a few nights in his bed.

This woman called to him in ways he couldn't deny. Ella. She was something else, something worth time and attention, a woman worth forever.

And a woman so badly used, Cope wondered if she'd ever find her way back into a normal romantic relationship again.

"I need to go grab the invoice for the dairy guy," Ella said, looking to the door where the big white truck had pulled up. "Be right back. Cope, if Erin gets up for any reason other than labor or a robbery, yell."

Erin snorted and watched Ella go before turning back to Cope, where he'd been watching too. "Well now, jeepers Andrew, I think I recognize that expression. Are you sweet on Ella?"

He raised a shoulder. "Smart-ass. I like the way she moves. That a crime?"

"Not at all. In fact, it's a good thing. I think she's ready for it now.

Though"—Erin looked him up and down with a grin—"I'm not sure anyone could be totally ready for you."

Cope thought it was the other way around. "I'm not that bad."

Erin snorted. "You are a first-rate lady killer. I rarely use that phrase, but you're it. She's been off the market for some time, while you, well, you're Cope." She shrugged. "It's hotter than hell, but even I would be intimidated."

"I'm more than just my dick." He said it a bit more sharply than he'd intended. It hit him though, just then, that for the first time ever that he would care about, he'd be judged for his devil-may-care attitude about women and romance. Still, Erin knew him, and it was silly to think she meant it in any way but the one she brought up. He and Ella *did* have differences of experience.

He softened his tone. "You okay? Should you even be here? Isn't your due date approaching?"

"I've got two months to go. I'm pregnant, not sick. Anyway, Todd is right next door with Brody. They know you're here mooning after Ella, so I was allowed to come over if I sat down right away and drank some juice. I believe the assumption was that you'd also be their eyes and ears over here and tattle should I start tap dancing or cage fighting with the customers. Not that the men in my life are bossy or anything."

He nudged the glass toward her. "Keep drinking it then." He considered whether or how to put the next question. "Does everyone know? About me and Ella? Am I so obvious?"

She took a big drink and flipped him off before grinning. "Ben's your brother and Todd is your best friend; of course they can tell. Ben told me the other day that he'd never seen you look at a woman the way you do her. And of course you're more than your cock. *Pffft.* I've known you for years now, and I've seen you date a lot, but it never seems like serious business to you." Erin paused, searching for words.

"She's serious business, Cope. She doesn't have a lot of people she can count on. There's stress in her family over her insistence on staying independent.

"For the longest time she shied away from all of us. She's only begun to come out of her shell and trust us more. It would have been unimaginable to me a year ago to watch her opening up with us the way she has."

He nodded. Erin was being protective of their friend, but he hoped he could be trusted to never hurt her on purpose. When it came down to it, Cope knew a little something about feeling like you're on the outside looking in. "She is, which is probably why I like to look at her more than I have liked to look at a woman in a long time. She's not a hit-and-run for me."

Erin looked at him over the rim of the glass for long moments before speaking. "I can see that. So then? You planning to make a move? Or just moon at her more?"

"I'm thinking about it. Been a few years now. I've had other women, and she's had a lot to deal with. None of them were what I wanted, what I needed. I get the feeling Ella might be just that. I think the time is right, and I'm done filling my time with women I don't crave the way I do her."

"Years, huh? Very nice. She doesn't stand a chance. You Copeland boys are a threat to the willpower of women everywhere."

"We play a lot, but once we settle down, we're rooted. We love well." He touched her belly, palm flat to feel his niece or nephew move around. "Active today."

She grinned. "I know. I ate an entire box of Hot Tamales. Babe-O seems to dig that. As for you boys and that playing, it makes you all very handy to the ladies you end up with. That's a good thing too." Ella's noise came closer, and Erin changed the topic. "How was the trip? Adrian pouted for the last week because he couldn't go with you guys this year. Thankfully Todd and Ben were too preoccupied pestering me to get too sad about it. Brody's so caught up in all the wedding plans, I don't know if he even noticed."

Cope laughed. "He noticed and bitched about it a bit. But he wasn't that serious. And there's always another time to go camping."

Ella came back through to the café, calling out a hello as the delivery guy came in, wheeling the milk cartons with him. Of course, Cope barely registered a word Erin had said once Ella was in his line of sight again.

"She hasn't been out in a while." Erin shrugged, looking at her nails. "I've been so glad not to have to worry about the café. She'll be getting her degree soon enough, and she'll move on to a different job. I think she's interviewing soon with the place she's interning at now. They seem to really like her, and who else could be so good at helping families who've been torn apart by violence?" Erin's gaze slid to his for just a moment and then away again. "She's already beginning to train one of our part-timers to take over for her as the manager. Even hired on two new part-timers to take over for her and to fill the gap of my absence too. Smart girl, our Ella. But boy, she's always so busy. I'd hate it if she never got out for any fun at all."

Subtle. He rolled his eyes.

"Hey, Brody." Ella waved as Erin's older brother ambled in from his shop next door. He paused to kiss Erin's cheek and rub her belly.

"Sit down, and I'll get you a hot chocolate. Elise's mother gave me the best recipe. I've been using it this week, and people love it."

"Ella, my darling, you're all things bright and wonderful in the world," Brody said with a wink as he hopped up onto a stool.

Erin perked up. "Cocoa? Oh! Me too, please."

"Finish your juice, and I might be persuaded." Ella sent Erin a look before turning around and using a whisk in the ceramic pot she had placed on a low burner. Moments later, the fragrant mugs were on the counter. "One last detail," she murmured, drawing a quick leaf in chocolate on Erin's, dropping a dollop of whipped cream on Brody's and adding a shake of cinnamon to Cope's.

She remembered. Who did he know well enough other than family who remembered silly stuff like that? He said so, and she laughed. "I've been making you coffee for a few years now, Cope. I know how much you love cinnamon. Like I know how much Brody is a whore for whipped cream and Erin loves extra chocolate shavings. I remember these things. I like taking care of you."

She turned before he could say anything. Which was good because she totally sent him reeling. Thankfully, she also missed the elbow to the ribs Erin had delivered.

"How's school?" he asked, not ready to let the contact with her go.

"Good. I'm nearly done now. My internship has been really helpful. The agency has provided me with some excellent training."

"Ah, so you're finishing early? Or going until June?"

She had the longest legs and a very nice ass. Still, he wasn't disappointed when she turned to face him again. "Yep. It took me longer than it would have normally, but they've worked around my schedule and stuff. I'll be finished at the end of this quarter. Or I hope so." She laughed. "If I complete these last classes successfully, that is. I'll have my MSW in December. Maybe I'll do the official walk in June, but the important part is the degree."

"Dunno why you'd doubt yourself. I have faith in you." He meant that. Watching her not just survive what happened to her but use it, rise above it, and empower herself and others with her energy and determination had only made him more attracted to her. "Why wouldn't you do graduation? You worked hard to get here. You need to give us all the chance to cheer you on as your name gets called."

"Thank you, Andrew." He smiled at the use of his given name. "It means a lot to me to hear that." She nodded and smiled at a customer who'd come through the door, and he felt like a toddler, aching to get her attention back.

"And what about you?" she asked when she got free again. "How are things? How's your life? Work?"

He sipped and watched, took a leisurely detour around the curves of her cheeks, noting each freckle. He also noted she sidestepped the graduation comment. "We need to catch up, you're right. What are you doing after you get off today?"

Surprise showed on her face. Luckily, it seemed to be the good kind of surprise. "I have to go by work—my other work—for a few hours. I have a paper due next week, so I need to work on that when I get home."

"I guess two jobs and school sort of cuts into your social life. No time for a pizza then? We can be quick. I realize we haven't talked in a while, and I want to know more. You know, about the program you're in." Not so much with the smooth. She set him off balance in a way no one else ever could. Shook him up so that he couldn't even connect with his inner cool right then. He just wanted to touch her.

Her blush was back, and he ached to brush his fingertips against the swell of her cheek, to feel the heat of that soft skin.

"I wish. Pizza sounds good. But this paper is due next week, and with Erin getting closer to her due date, I want to get it out of the way." She hesitated. "You'll be in here though, still, right? You know, coming by time and again to get lunch and some coffee? We can talk then."

"Couldn't keep me away." He'd have to find a way to get her to go out with him soon. If he didn't snap out of this, he'd be trying to get her to ride with him to Brody and Elise's wedding in two months. And he didn't want to wait two months.

He loved the way her eyes widened with pleasure for just a brief moment before she spoke again. "Good. I don't get out much to see my friends. I'm greedy for it I suppose."

Like he was greedy for her. Maybe, just maybe, it was time to do something about it. To feed that need he had.

2

Ella pulled down the street toward her parents' house. Wariness was a heavy weight in her belly at the twice-monthly dinner she was expected to attend. The weight of their disapproval and lack of understanding of her choices had put strain on their previously close relationship. There lived a wedge between them, and for a long time, Ella didn't have the energy to deal with it, so she'd pulled away emotionally.

It hadn't always been so. Her parents, especially her mother, had supported her through the time she was in the hospital and had even gone to court with her and Erin when Bill had been put on trial.

That had changed though.

She pulled up at the curb before taking a bracing breath. Before leaving home earlier, she'd stood at her open medicine cabinet, looking at the bottle of pills her doctor had given her to deal with the anxiety from the attack. It would have been so easy to give in to the lure of the chemical calm they brought her, easier to keep her emotions tucked away and protected.

She'd realized she was finally strong enough to open herself to her parents in hopes that they could find their way back to each other again and recapture that closeness they'd had before.

She knew they loved her. They just didn't understand why she hadn't moved back home. Her insistence at being independent and getting her degree had been perceived as a rejection of them and their attempts to help. They'd wanted to give her money, but it would have dented their savings, and they needed it now that her father had retired after an injury he suffered on the job. They'd wanted her to live at home while finishing school so she wouldn't have the pressure of paying rent and having to work at the café.

How could she explain that paying her rent, having a job, finishing school, making her own choices to make her way in her life gave her the sense of control she needed after having none for so long? They didn't understand it when she'd made an attempt to say so, to tiptoe around how every day for a few years, someone had made every possible choice for her until she had nothing. Had made her nothing. Bill had told her what to wear, how to look, who her friends were, what party to vote for. Just paying rent with the salary from her job meant something to her in a way she felt impossible to get across.

The small house in the nearby working-class suburb of Des Moines was the one she'd grown up in. Her father had been an ironworker, her mom stayed at home with her and later on, she'd run a day care. James and Moira Tipton were good people in the best sense of the word. They worked hard and raised a family—Ella, the baby, and Michael, also known as Mick, who was seven years older.

Her family had given her all the foundation she needed to build her life from the ashes, and she never wanted to forget that. Perhaps it was time to say that to them.

She let herself in with her keys and hung her coat in the hall closet. The house smelled of garlic and onions and the hint of cinnamon she knew was a result of her mom's apple pie. This was what had built the person she was. Home and hearth and people who loved you and were happy to see you even when things weren't perfect.

"Hey there!" she called as she came through into the family room adjacent to the kitchen where her mother currently stood at the stove. Her father was in his favorite chair, so she leaned down to hug and kiss him. "Hi, Dad."

"Hey, sweetheart." He patted her hand and smiled. "Glad you're here."

She leaned in. "Yeah? That 'cause Mom wouldn't let you have any roast until I got here?"

Her mother hooted with laughter. "She's got your number, James. You've got some color in your cheeks today, Ella. Come and let me look at you."

Her father got up as she did, moving to the table.

Placing her package on the counter first, Ella hugged her mother, letting the pleasure of that simple contact comfort her. No matter the strain she had with them at times, a hug could always make her feel better. Keep that connection despite their disagreements.

"I brought a pie, but that was silly of me." Ella carried the platter of meat to the table as her mom followed with bread still warm from the oven.

"A man can always eat more pie."

"Not if his doctor told him to slow down on the sweets." Her mother shot him a look, and he snorted.

"So, how are things, Ella?" Her father turned to look in her direction as she sat down.

Gah! Dangerous territory right away. He was totally throwing her under the bus to get around the pie conversation. Sneaky.

"Good. Busy, but that's all right. I talked to Uncle Michael day before yesterday. He and Mick were on their way to some remote village. Sounded great. Mick got on for a few minutes. He's met a new woman. She's English, which he knows is risky and all." She grinned at her mother, who tsked and rolled her eyes.

"Why does that boy torment himself with Englishwomen?"

Mick had been married for three years. Rebecca had been an aid worker too, but she'd wanted to get out. To move to London or Seattle and start a family. Mick wasn't ready, and things had fallen apart. Mick took responsibility for it, and Rebecca had been a lovely woman. But they got divorced anyway, and Rebecca was now someone else's wife with a toddler and a thriving medical practice in Virginia.

Four years later, Mick was still single, but this new woman had possibilities. Even better, in Mick's letters over the last eighteen months, she'd found a man who was maturing at long last, a man who seemed ready to start thinking about a family.

"She seems nice, Mom. She's an American; I was just teasing. Her father is English, but her mother is American, and she grew up here in the States." Ella paused to butter the warm roll and sigh happily after the first bite. "So good. Anyway, Mick sounded happier than I've heard him sound in a long time."

"I'll have to take your word for it. He calls you far more than he calls us." Her mother sniffed her annoyance. Mick *did* call her more often because he'd ended up on Ella's side of this divide she had with their parents. He'd understood why it was important to her to do things for herself. Ella figured he called her more often to fill in the gap, make sure she felt connected and loved, even when he was out of the country.

But Mick wasn't her mother, and he wasn't just a few miles away where she could see him all the time and hang out. She'd missed that ease and closeness she'd grown up with. The loneliness of it had been difficult to bear, and it wasn't until the last four or five months that she'd begun to deepen her friendships with what she'd always thought of as Erin's crowd. Now they were her crowd too.

"They're in and out of service for satellite coverage. They don't always have phones in the villages when the team arrives. He calls when he's not out in the field. He knows I'll tell you guys all about what's going on."

Her mother's mouth flattened a moment. "Neither one of you calls enough. Except he's changing the world and you're making coffee. You're wasting your potential and working yourself to the bone trying to do everything when you could just let us help you." Her mother buttered her bread with choppy little swipes. The tension began to build in the room. Slowly stealing the oxygen until the fight-or-flight reflex threatened to kick in.

"I don't want to have this argument again." And she didn't. She wouldn't argue and wouldn't defend her position anymore because they'd said it all, and it was time to move on. She didn't want to be angry over it anymore.

Her father put his glass down and began to eat. "You had a job interview sometime this week, didn't you?"

He remembered, and that made her smile again.

"It went really well. I know them all since I've worked there for the last nine months. I'm already in training for the job, which really gives me a leg up. I'm good with the clients, and I really want this. That has to mean something. I'm not just doing this job until something better comes along. I *want* it."

She studied her father. He'd lost weight since his last back surgery, but his color was better than it had been just a few months before. He'd never be the vibrant man he was before the accident, but he walked with a cane and didn't have to sit every few feet. He was making an effort, and she wondered how many times each of them might have extended a little bit more and the others missed it or were too angry or hurt to respond. Suddenly it all seemed very silly to not just try a little harder.

"You look good, Pop. I forgot to tell you that when I came in." She squeezed his hand.

Startled for a moment, he smiled back at her. "Thank you, sweetheart."

"When will you know about the job?"

She looked back toward her mother. The tension lifted a little bit. "A few weeks or so. They have an executive committee who'll meet to discuss final recommendations, and they have special steps to perform to comply with the grants that partially fund the position. I'm training one of the part-timers at the café to take over for me and hired another two people for staff since Erin won't be back for a while, and I'll be gone."

"Good. Good. Well, so tell us then, what your brother and uncle are up to." Her mother put another slice of roast beef on Ella's plate, daring her to argue.

She didn't.

Instead she filled them in on Mick and her Uncle Michael's recent trips into the Bolivian interior to deliver medical supplies and run clinics in the villages, leaving out the part about the team getting shot at. They worried about him enough as it was.

And for the first time in a long time, when she left, she didn't want to cry.

It had felt as if she'd finally reached the end of a long, hard road and could afford the luxury of pausing enough to look around. She liked a lot of what she saw in her life. She'd spent the last years putting her life back together. Slowly getting herself through one challenge at a time. Each one of those moments had been powerful in its own way. There were struggles to be faced and overcome. She knew she hadn't seen the last of them in her life. But she did look forward to more normal struggles like dating.

As Elise had told her just a few weeks before, she wasn't alone. She had her friends, and that took the edge off a lot of crappy days. She was still smiling as she parked her car in the very well lit space near her apartment building's front door. The stars were out, but the moon hid, glowing through the high clouds shrouding it.

Summer had faded, and early fall was beginning to settle in. It got dark earlier and light later. The brilliant blue of the sky would fade as the rains made the bright red and yellow leaves stick to every surface like confetti. The rain would settle in soon, and like most Seattleites, she didn't mind it. She worked around it and found ways to enjoy the weather because it was simply the price one paid to live in a place so verdant and lush.

One small, dark corner of her heart hated it when it was dark so much. It brought the edges of her fear closer. It was the darkness and the way it could hide things. People. She paused at that last thought, remembering.

She'd been walking back from her car. Had deliberately disobeyed Bill by staying out late with her cousins who'd been visiting from Maine. It had been dark and cold, though her cousin Sharon had mocked Ella. After all, Mainers were made of stern stuff and scoffed at thirty-eight degrees!

She'd been smiling as she hurried toward their apartment. Earlier, before she'd left, she'd made him his favorite dinner. Pork chops, mashed potatoes and green beans. Sometimes such little things could keep him happy, and he'd let her infractions slide.

It was then he jumped out from the hedges at the front door, screaming, grabbing her and dragging her toward the alley. Her heart had raced, more so after she realized it was him and not a stranger. He'd clamped a hand over her mouth then and told her, as she'd trembled and held back her sobs, that if he'd wanted her dead, he could make it happen.

"See what could happen if you stay out after dark? No one would miss you but me. I'm all you have, Ella. Don't you forget it. When I tell you to be home by eight, I'm being generous because it's your family. And then you go and ruin it by making me worry."

As he spoke, he'd pressed her into the brick wall at her back, his hand around her throat. The world dimmed, the darkness at the edges of her vision encroaching more and more until she felt herself let go. For one moment there had been some peace, and then he'd slapped her hard, letting go of her throat.

He'd been conciliatory then, taking her inside, making her tea and coddling her. But she'd never forgotten that lesson, and she'd never been late again.

The dark was a reminder of that helplessness, and so, each time she confronted it, even if she broke out in a sweat at the very thought, she won.

As she shook off the memories, she pulled herself back together again. Mainly she was past it. She had seen Erin's therapist, a woman specializing in survivors of violent attacks. It had helped immensely, and Ella would be forever grateful for Erin, who made sure Ella's insurance coverage would pay for the sessions.

Erin had offered to pay at first. Because she had so much and Ella didn't. Erin's reaction was part of who she was. That had been touching, of course. But it was always Erin's insight, the way she seemed to understand Ella's need to do it herself and the way she helped make that possible—it was that sort of love that made Ella so loyal to Erin. They shared some common history with their past, the violence that had changed them totally. Facing the fear helped. Most days. But the thing about fear was that it ate away at your reason, made you smaller.

It was her mini dare each day to come home to this place. To embrace normal and live her own life on her own terms, even if she was afraid. Her life was her own. She made it, and no one would take it from her again.

This building, this parking spot, her nearby grocery and the Vietnamese restaurant two doors down were her prizes for living and being happy. It wasn't big or new or even grand, but it was home.

The front doors into the small lobby squeaked when she managed to get the lock unstuck. She jingled her keys, balancing the bag of leftovers as she headed inside. Choosing to avoid the ancient elevator, she took the stairs to the third floor, walking the long hall, loving the creaks in the ancient hardwoods and the curves of the often-painted ceilings and doorways. This had been a home in the months after the attack. The walls; the faded, once-glorious carpets in the lobby; the temperamental lock on the front doors.

Two very sturdy locks unlocked, and her door swung open. She checked the entry automatically, still unwilling to say out loud that she lined up her desk chair in the way just to see if it had been moved. Despite feeling stupid, she put the bag down and locked up, including two additional inner locks. And put the chair back.

It was almost like a tic; she felt safe in the building and in her apartment. She knew her chances of being attacked again were very small, and Bill was doing time. She knew these things and slept well at night most of the time. But still, she found herself putting that chair in the hall.

After changing into fluffy sweats and washing her face, she headed to her bed where her tea and a few cookies awaited in the little alcove she pretended was the same as a bedroom. She considered writing in her journal but stared off into space for a while instead.

As she settled back and sipped the tea, her gaze moved around the room. A framed picture sat on the small table in the corner. Taken just two weeks before at a picnic in Brody and Elise's backyard. Brody and Elise, two of her favorite people. That weekend, those two wonderful people were having an engagement shindig of sorts, hosted by Brody's brother Adrian.

Elise was as tenacious as Erin was, and friendship with the woman had been inevitable. She'd been in the periphery of the group, though she'd been invited many times. Had watched Brody fall in love, had watched Elise become part of his life, of his family, and when Elise noticed Ella, Elise had simply been Elise. She'd reached out and in doing so had become her closest friend. Elise and Erin, she'd let in, had felt *understood* in a way she rarely felt with others.

As if she'd been summoned, Elise's text buzzed across the screen of Ella's phone. *Call me if you're awake!*

Yes, a phone conversation with Elise would be a good thing. She dialed in the number, and Brody answered, making her smile.

"Hey there, Ella. You looking for my missus?"

"Yes, please."

"While I watch my lovely lady hop around and jiggle, I'm going to continue to keep you long enough to ask how your hip is doing." He'd nearly finished the tattoo she'd been getting in bits and pieces over the last year and a half. Each new achievement, and he'd add another piece. For a time it had been her secret. Only Brody knew about it. But after a while, she'd told Erin and then Elise. He'd just completed the last major part a few days before, roots and some drifting blossoms at her hip.

Her first tattoo had been small, a silly little four-leaf clover he'd done on her inner arm, near the elbow. Something about it had filled a need inside, the need to mark her progress in an indelible way. It's how she'd truly gotten to know Brody. He'd always been her boss's older brother, friendly, but it never went very deep. He was good at his job, good at listening, and over time she'd poured out her story to him.

She understood, totally, why Elise adored him, why her daughter, Rennie, now *their* daughter, lit up every time Brody came into a room. There were very few men in the universe who could hold a candle to him.

"Good. Soreness is mostly gone, and now it itches."

"Coming along then. If you need me to, I'll check it for you."

"Aw, thanks. But I think you might have more things on your mind than looking at a healing tattoo. You ready for the engagement party on Saturday?"

"I've been ready to marry Elise for a long time now. I'm just annoyed I have to wait another few months."

She heard the smile in his voice and smiled herself. They were good together, a family. Unconventional, just like all the Browns were. But it worked, and it was genuine. They gave her hope that once she put dating back on the menu, she might find something like what they had too.

"Stop hogging her." Elise got on the line, and Ella heard the noisy kiss her friend gave her very sexy fiancé. "I hear Raven is asking to photograph it for that tattoo magazine she works with down in L.A."

As if she'd bare her back from hip to shoulder for strangers to gape over! Raven could do that, Erin, bold, brash women like them. In any case, things were complicated between Raven, one of Brody's exes, and Elise in the best of times. Therefore in the time-honored tradition of girlfriends everywhere, Ella kept her distance when Raven was involved. She actually liked Raven because the woman was totally herself. There was pretty much no bull when you dealt with her; she said exactly what she thought, when she thought it. Which was uncomfortable sometimes, but once Ella had gotten used to it, it made her easy to be around. Well, since she'd finally backed off and accepted and respected Elise's place in Brody's life.

"Ha. Yeah, not so much. I will be really happy when it's finished though. What's up?" she asked.

"Just wanted to check in. You looked tired today. I wanted to be sure you were okay. I would have called, but I didn't know if you were still with your parents at dinner."

"I'm good," she said to Elise and meant it. "I'm making a mental promise to try harder with them. I have a fridge full of leftovers, and now I'm here drinking some tea and trying to wind down for bed."

"Good. Okay, just FYI, we're all going out dancing on Friday night. Girls only. Meet me here, and we'll all get dressed and head out together."

Ella laughed. "Okay then. I thought I was supposed to plan this, and you said not to bother?"

"I decided going dancing would be fun. Erin says we can make it her baby shower too."

"I'll grab some red velvet cupcakes then. That'll be fun. I haven't been out dancing in forever and ever."

"Friday. My house no later than seven. You'd better bring some hot clothes, or I will dress you myself," Elise warned, and Brody chuckled in the background.

"You doing all right? Anything I can help with?" Erin was the official maid of honor, but she and Ella had shared a lot of the duties.

"It's all good. I'm marrying Brody in a few months. What could be better than that?"

Ella smiled, truly thrilled for both of them, and for Rennie too. "You're right. I'll see you Friday."

3

Cope knew exactly what he was doing when he showed up at Brody's door on Friday night. Brody had invited friends over for a guy's night while the women would be heading out dancing. Not a bachelor party with strippers or anything. Brody and the rest of the crew were past that.

He had no intention of sitting around playing cards and drinking beer while Ella was out looking hot and dancing at a club. In a while, he'd make the suggestion that they go out and connect with the ladies to have a unified bride and groom party. The rest of the guys would pretend to fight the idea for all of thirty minutes, and then they'd head out.

The idea that men didn't want to be in the company of beautiful women when they were dressed up and ready to dance and have fun was absurd. He found men who proclaimed to want man caves, without out the presence of women, hard to understand. If the ladies didn't want them along, that would be different. He wasn't a stalker or anything. But from everything he'd ever learned about women, they liked being around their men too.

"Wait up," Ben called as he caught up with his brother on the porch. "You can carry this." He shoved a bag full of chips, dogs and five kinds of dip at Cope.

"Glad to be your pack mule. I hear that happens to you when you get old."

"What? You're smart enough to con younger people into hauling your shit?" Ben snorted. "Hey, listen, I'm going to support you when you inevitably suggest we go and hang out with the ladies, won't I? You can carry some chips."

Oh. Well, yes then. "Sure." He shrugged, and they went into the house. The place had been a single man's paradise a year before, but now a family lived there. Cope liked it better now. He smiled as he thought of Brody's daughter. Rennie's backpack was hung on a peg near the door, her little rain boots lined up under the bench. They'd filed all the paperwork for Brody's formal adoption of Elise's daughter earlier that week. She was a tough little girl, smart, funny, and his friend loved her fiercely. Watching them grow into a family had taught Cope what it meant to truly love another person. He wanted that, craved that connection and rhythm that was so much bigger than him.

The sound of laughing women caught Ben and Cope both as they slowly entered the main family room where Brody sat talking to Adrian.

"They're jammed into our bedroom." Brody tipped his chin in the direction of the back hallway leading to the master bedroom. "Women and skimpy clothes all over the place." He grinned. "I'm a lucky man."

Cope grinned right back at him. "I happen to agree with you. Speaking of pretty women, what about the youngest one? Where's Rennie?"

"Her grandparents picked her up from school. They're keeping her this weekend. But she'll be at the engagement party tomorrow."

"Dude, don't forget to tell them she got an A on her very first essay." Adrian shook his head at his brother. "She was quite insistent that everyone would want to know."

"My kid is smart. Everyone knows that." Brody tried to sound tough, but Cope heard the pride and love in his voice. "She was pretty damned proud of herself. Elise and I told her if she kept it up, we'd go to Disneyland next summer."

A burst of laughter and chattering from the bedroom rose and then faded again. Todd came in the front door with a few more of their friends. Cope half listened to them, taking the beer handed his way, nodding his head. But his attention was focused on that hallway.

The door opened, and the sound level rose enough that the men silenced, their attention snagged as they turned toward the uniquely female noise.

Elise came first, her pale, elegant beauty highlighted by a deep red sweater and a black skirt that came to mid-thigh. The woman had spectacular legs, no doubt. Brody's mouth curved into a smile as he took her in. Envy crept into Cope's heart; he wanted that. Wanted to look at a woman and know she was the one.

Erin looked pretty and damned pregnant in a high-waisted dress with big red roses on it. Ben sighed happily as she headed straight to where he stood with Todd. For that moment, everything was right in their world, and Cope would do his best to continue to attempt to mediate the damage between their father and sister and Ben.

Despite Ben's happiness and success, their father and sister had walled Ben out of their life because his brother had found his happiness with a man *and* a woman. It galled Cope to no end. Ben had been the golden boy, the kid who rarely got in trouble in school, got great grades. He had been a good cop, a good friend and no doubt, he was a great brother. Their father's reaction to Ben's unconventional relationship was stupid, and it had split their family in half.

He turned his attention back to the hallway. Waiting. Anticipation and then a punch to the gut followed as Ella came next, her normally sleek, short red hair tousled and curled. Her face, usually bare of makeup, bore just a bit, enough to line those spectacular eyes. Her lips were stained dark, calling to his gaze, leaving him wondering for the millionth time what she'd taste like.

She wore pants. She usually did. He'd always assumed it had to do with the scarring she ended up with after her ex-boyfriend attacked her. The bastard had had every intention of killing Ella. So, to Cope, just being alive and beautiful, being strong in the wake of such a terrible ordeal, meant she won.

It didn't hurt at all that she had great legs and wore the pants well. Tight, with boots on her feet, showcasing legs that went on and on and on. *Damn.* The shirt, *shit*, if you could call it that, was more of a corset with barely enough fabric to cover her areolas. Her breasts made him lose his hearing for a few moments. She didn't often have them on display, a pity because it wasn't like she could hide their size, even in a T-shirt. Just then they heaved up, mounds of creamy flesh, freckles sprinkled across the luscious curves.

Christ.

"Wow. You ladies look gorgeous." Brody got up, moving to Elise, and no one else existed for the two of them for long moments. Their connection was palpable and staggeringly intimate to see. Cope couldn't tear his attention away for a long moment.

"You guys just going to hang out here all night?" Elise asked, blushing as she broke her gaze from Brody.

"Maybe." Brody grinned and kissed his wife-to-be quickly before turning to his sister. He touched Erin's belly and kissed the top of her head. "You better take care of yourself."

"You can't smoke indoors anymore, so the air will be clean of that. I have no plans to drink, and I have enough energy to sit at the table and watch everyone else dance while I eat a few of the red velvet cupcakes Ella brought." Erin smiled sweetly at her brother. "Anyway, we all know you'll show up in an hour or two, so I'm sure Ben and Todd will take care of me once that happens."

Cope moved nearer to Ella so he could speak just to her. "I like that color on you. Sets off your skin and hair." The shirt was deep blue with just enough purple to compliment her skin outrageously. The breasts helped, in the way breasts always did. But this was more, and he let himself drift a little closer, breathing her in.

Some things were natural; flirting was one of them, and he realized that simply because he'd given up his wandering, it didn't mean he couldn't use every skill he had to lure Ella. He smiled as she drew in a shaky breath.

"Thanks. It was Erin's idea. I don't normally . . ." She waved around her breasts. "You know, show this much boob."

He was sure his grin was wolfish because she was ringing his bell like it was dinnertime. Christ, what she did to him without even knowing it. "Ella, I must dissuade you from that policy. You have beautiful breasts. They're a delightful addition to anything you wear. Trust me, please."

Her laugh was sultry. On a lower register than her speaking voice. Which wasn't that hard, given her normal voice. And beyond sexy. He was sure that was her sexually interested laugh. She'd finally reacted to him as a woman did to a man she was *truly* flirting with. Victory flushed through him, and hope that things could move forward with her at long last.

"I'll, um, keep that in mind." Her lips quirked up in one corner.

"You know, you're like a cartoon character. Like a quirky superhero." *Holy shit*, did he just say that out loud?

Her eyes widened, surprise washing over her features. His heart began to plummet into his gut when genuine pleasure pushed the surprise back.

"Andrew, I gotta tell you, that was one of the most awesome things anyone has ever said about me. Wow." She cocked her head, the grin on her lips zinging through him like a pinball. "Thank you."

He ducked his head, fighting off a blush. "Well, sure." Who knew he was even capable of a blush these days? Damn, he was sweet on her.

Before he could say anything else, the others called to her that it was time to leave.

"See you later." She smiled at him, and he took her hand, kissing the knuckles.

He gave her a look, showing her exactly what he wanted to be seeing later. Her pupils expanded, and she blinked quickly, licking her lips.

"You'd better. I want to get a long look at the tattoo you're finally showing off a bit."

He stood so close he caught the throb of the pulse point just beneath her ear. "All right."

Elise leaned closer to Ella with a grin. "Well now, is it just me, or was there some major chemistry between you and Cope tonight?"

Ella laughed as she fanned herself with the napkin. "He really turned up the flirt on me, didn't he? He's never been like that before, not with me. He's a lethal weapon. I'm sure I acted like a total idiot, but he makes me forget how to speak. Flusters me. I'm sure it's just pity or bored reflex."

Elise rolled her eyes. "Do you *really* think that? Deep down, doesn't it feel different? Because from my perspective, it *looks* different. I've seen him flirt many times. Like, a lot, which, gah, doesn't sound very good, but hold on for the point. Flirting for him is sort of automatic. He's irrepressible that way. But he doesn't really mean it. Watching him with you was *totally* a different thing. He meant it. Whatever he said, Ella, he meant. He did that murmur thing men do when they, well when they want to make you all tingly. God knows when Brody does it, I'm all gooey."

Erin leaned in. "We talking about how Cope totally eye-fucked Ella at your house?"

Ella nearly choked on her drink. "He did not!"

Elise snorted. "He was an inch from you, oh yes, speaking to you in that sex murmur they do. He kissed your hand at the end!"

Her skin still felt the heat and pressure of his lips. "I do not deny that Andrew Copeland has major game. He does. Like a lot. But he sees me as a friend, nothing more."

"Are you huffing paint? He does not eye-fuck women. Looks at 'em, likes to have sex with them, yes, but I've only seen him that focused on a few things in the time I've known him. Never, not once, was it about a woman." Erin sipped her mineral water.

The music got louder, providing Ella with cover. Truth was, he'd been so sexy with the flirting he'd made her wet and achy. She couldn't remember the last time anyone had done that with mere words.

"I'm gonna dance," she said, waving to one of the other women in their group who was motioning at the dance floor.

As it happened, one of her favorite dance songs came on, Whitney Houston's "It's Not Right." Smiling, she headed out, people all around her, the music throbbing, the crowd bobbing. There was no fear, only the joy of moving and enjoying the music.

A man sidled up behind her, and she moved away, hating that aspect of going out dancing. But he followed, so she spun and found herself facing the aforementioned game-haver, Andrew Copeland. Well, all right then, *that* was a totally different thing than some stranger trying to rub his dick all over her in the dark. Her heart jumped and did a cheer with the rest of her body, all for him. Damn, he was ridiculously hot.

She smiled, and he gave her one in return, easing back into the space he'd ceded when she thought he was just some dude trying to cop a feel in the dark.

Women seemed to be drawn to him like he was a magnet. They crowded in, trying to get his attention, but he never took his gaze from her, as if no one else in the world existed for him. If he'd acted any other way, she'd have been uncomfortable on a different level. But those other women didn't matter to him at all, and that made her feel ten feet tall.

Even hotter, he knew how to dance. He didn't crowd her but lured her instead, until she found herself very close. His gaze was locked on hers, drawing her in. She couldn't deal with how exposed she felt, so she spun again, facing away and breathing deep.

Until he was right against her, his body like a magnet as she arched her back to get closer.

Two martinis would be her alibi the next day when she realized what she'd done. Right then, though? Well, she closed her eyes and let the music pulse through her, let go of her fear and just danced. With him, against him, their bodies sliding against each other. His palm slid around her waist, cupping her hip bone a moment before moving around to her belly. The shirt hem had risen, and the heat of his bare skin burned against her stomach.

Every part of her was electrified as pleasure like she'd never felt rushed through her veins. The freedom of the moment, the lack of fear, the delicious sexual tension, the chemistry of music, vibration and movement putting her under their spell.

And she went willingly for the first time in years.

His forearm pressed against her belly and side, so hard and muscled. Whitney's voice rose into the last chorus, and Ella turned, laughing, as it ended.

He leaned in quick and kissed her before stepping back and leading her to the table where the men had joined them. It was just a peck, she told herself, but she didn't stop smiling because she was happy either way.

"You're an amazing dancer," he said to her as she slid into the booth.

"*Pshaw*. Thank you. You too." Thank goodness it was dark and hot in there, or she'd be horrified by her blush.

"What other talents are you hiding?" He got very close as he spoke, his breath on her neck. He'd turned on the flirt again, made her drunk with it.

She laughed somewhat shakily. "I'm really not that interesting, I swear."

"On the contrary, Ella, I find you fascinating. You want another drink?"

On impulse and because he flustered her, she blurted out, "Tell me one thing about yourself no one knows."

He paused, clearly surprised by her question, and then shrugged. "Only if you do the same."

"All right."

"I love poetry." He said it while his gaze danced away for a moment. Was he embarrassed? Did he not know that it made him even sexier?

"Like what?"

"It's getting loud in here. Come with me into the bar. We'll get drinks, and my ears won't bleed."

She shrugged and let him pull her from the booth. Once standing, she turned back to the table, leaning over Adrian to speak to Elise. "You want a refill?"

Cope wanted to punch Adrian in the face for the way he looked at Ella's boobs. Yes, they were right there in his line of vision, and goddamn if they weren't mouthwateringly gorgeous, but they weren't Adrian's to gaze at.

He stepped over just a bit until Adrian looked up and discovered he'd been caught. Cope flipped him off, and Adrian waggled his brows before going back to look. Annoyed, Cope hooked a finger through one of her belt loops and tugged. She turned with a grin and let him pull her to him.

"Ready?"

She nodded, and he sheltered her against his body and pushed through the crowd, keeping people from crowding her too much. Just to be safe, he kept an arm around her waist, liking how she felt.

The volume level dropped back down to only partially insane once they reached the back bar. One arm to either side of her, he bracketed her with his body as she moved forward. It shielded her from the crush of the crowd and kept her against him.

She rattled off drinks to the bartender, who nodded, looked down at her tits and grinned as he went to work.

"Pablo Neruda," he said softly in her ear, partly to answer her earlier question and partly to snag her attention again.

She froze a moment, not knowing what he meant, until she remembered the poetry conversation.

Leaning her head back, she caught his gaze. "Really? I admit I don't know all of his stuff. I had a world lit course a million years ago."

"I'll have to remedy that. Now it's your turn."

"I told you, I'm not that interesting. But I do enjoy poetry too. What little I know if it."

"Really?" He tossed money on the counter before she could pay. She frowned and, without thinking, he brushed his thumb over her bottom lip. "You're far more beautiful without the frown. It's my round anyway."

Her expression was a cross between consternation, anger and appreciation. There was a story there, he could tell. Question was, should he pursue it now, or wait?

"I like to pay my own way."

"Next round you can."

She lost some of the tension in her face and nodded. "Thank you."

He grabbed the beers, and she got Erin's water. Again he sort of shielded her with his body as he muscled through the crowd. It was . . . delicious to feel protected by a man as big as Cope was. He was so much, just took up so much space. He seemed more serious with her of late, and it drove her mad. Sometimes she allowed herself the opportunity to obsess over whether he was actually showing romantic interest in her, especially after the things Elise and Erin had said earlier. Mainly she just told herself he was flirting like he did with everyone else. Nothing more.

When they got back, he followed her into the booth, his body pressed against hers until she felt faint with his nearness. God, what a fabulous night this was!

"Which poets do you like?"

"Mary Oliver. 'Wild Geese' is a poem that breaks my heart each time I read it. It's so beautiful, achingly so. Marge Piercy, love her fiction too. Edith Wharton." She hadn't had much time to explore things like poetry, but Mick would e-mail her poems, song lyrics, he'd write her letters with photographs and dried flowers tucked between the pages. She smiled, thinking about how her brother had always known when she needed those little check-ins from him the most.

Cope slid a fingertip down the tender skin of the inside of her forearm, snagging her attention. "I like that smile. What are you thinking about?"

"My brother Mick. He's the one who introduced me to Mary Oliver. He's one of those people you love getting letters from."

Cope's smile warmed her in a way not at all connected to sex. It was understanding, open and interested in what she was saying.

In order to be heard over the music and dull roar of people shouting to speak to each other, he had to lean in close, his breath against her neck and ear. "Oh, like with ticket stubs and funny newspaper articles tucked inside? Sometimes just a photograph of a beach or a tree?"

"Exactly! He can go months without a word, and then one of those. Usually just when I need it most. Who's your letter sender?"

"My dad's brother, my uncle Ted. My mom always jokes that he's an old bum, but he sails all over the world. Or he did. He worked on crews on every boat imaginable. He'd send the family these letters. Once every six months or so a packet of them would arrive filled with sand or shells, these small-town news stories, drawings and sketches. It was like Christmas when that packet arrived."

They talked, shared and laughed for some time. Long enough that Ella forgot anyone else was around but for the moments they'd been jostled by their friends getting in and out of the booth. He'd stayed so close, reaching out to touch her often, leaning in to speak quietly in her ear as he explained something.

Cripes, she was going to combust at this rate.

On one of those rare moments when she took the time to look around at their friends gathered, she caught sight of Erin. Ella wanted to stay and talk with him more, but Erin was looking tired. She tried to hide it, but Ella saw through it. Ben and Todd would soon enough too.

"Erin looks tired. Back me up when I suggest we go back to Brody and Elise's," she murmured, and Cope squeezed her hand quickly in answer.

"Why don't we go back to Brody and Elise's? Getting loud and warm in here. We forgot the cupcakes over there anyway. They're in my car, and it would be a sin to let them go to waste." Her car was back at the house because they'd taken a limo to dinner and then to the club.

Elise turned to look at Erin and then back to Ella, nodding. She stood, and Brody with her. They were so beautiful together, Ella thought, right, in synch. "You know my opinion on cupcakes."

"I want pizza." Brody joined with the others of his tribe—the tribe of giant men—and they eased the way out of the club onto the sidewalk outside. She breathed deep, letting the relative silence and the freedom from the crush of people slide through her, calming her.

"Wait." Cope touched her to stay her movement. "Now I want to look at your ink. I wanted to do so at the house, but you got rushed off." She bit back a moan when he circled her, tracing the blossom on her shoulder. "It's so beautiful against your skin. I can't wait to see the whole thing."

She blushed, gripping her coat tight against her belly. Taking the shiver of pleasure as a sign she was cold, he chuckled and helped her shrug into her coat. Something like that from another man might have bothered her. It might have felt like manhandling. With Cope, from Cope, it was nurturing without feeling coercive or paternalistic.

"Limo is going to be pretty full," Cope said casually as they walked toward the lot next door. "I drove. You want to catch a ride back with me? I haven't had a drink in hours, so I'm fine to drive."

Had they been talking for hours? It seemed like ten minutes. And did she want a ride from him? Really? Was that a trick question?

"Ella, get out of the cold!" Elise called to her, waving at the limo. "The boys will meet us back there."

Damn.

The men moved to Cope's SUV and began to pile in, so she smiled at him. "Thanks anyway, I guess they have it handled."

He walked her to the limo door and helped her in. "I'll see you back at the house. Save me a cupcake."

She waved as he shut the door, and the limo pulled away.

"Oh my god, I'm so sorry," Elise said. "I thought after I spoke that you might want to be alone with him in the car. You two seemed to really be, um, wow, *with* each other tonight."

"He was just being polite."

"He's never that polite to me," Elise said, one of her eyebrows sliding up.

"That's different. He'd never flirt like that with a friend's girlfriend." She was insulted on his behalf. He'd never do anything like that!

"Exactly! You're a single woman in his eyes, and I can only say it's about time." Erin leaned back with a smirk. "And don't think I don't know you called it an early night because of me."

"Are you kidding me? I'm too old for all that noise. I have presents in my trunk too."

Erin's face lit, making Ella laugh. "Presents! Wheee!"

"You're a present whore." Elise grinned.

"Totally."

"We should have taken over Adrian's house tonight," Elise said as they got out once they arrived home. "Had a slumber party."

"He would have loved that." Erin snickered. "He has a movie theater and soda on tap. I would live in his house if I could. I also know Brody would be a grumpy butthead if he had to be separated from you tonight." Erin looked up and caught sight of Todd as he waited on the porch. "I sleep better at home anyway," she said, her voice fading at the end as her man caught her attention fully.

They were all going to have hot sex that night, and Ella was not. She frowned a moment until she caught sight of Cope, but he was on his phone, looking serious.

When he hung up and turned to face her, she knew he was going to tell her something she didn't want to hear.

He caught up to her in the front hall where she'd removed her coat and pulled her boots off. In her bare feet, he nearly towered over her. She wondered idly if she'd have been nervous if it were anyone but him.

"Hi, there." She smiled up at him, still slightly tipsy.

He grabbed one of her hands and squeezed. "Hey. I'm sorry, I can't stay. We'll talk more tomorrow, okay? We're having a problem with one of our systems. I'm on call tonight, so I have to go."

"Sorry to hear that." She shouldn't be disappointed, for heaven's sake. He had a job to do. He owned his own business, so of course he had to do stuff like this. At least he wasn't a cop anymore. She knew she'd have worried way more in that case. As a friend, of course.

"Listen, how about we carpool tomorrow? It can be our little nod to being green and stuff. Also, we live close enough to each other so it makes sense." He cocked his head, and she probably would have agreed to just about anything he'd proposed; the way he looked at her was irresistible.

"I have to be at Adrian's a few hours early to help out."

He grinned, and everything in her body did the wave.

"What a coincidence, me too. Works out even better." That damned grin again, and she was totally lost.

"All right. If you're sure you don't mind. I'll be out front at two, okay?"

He frowned and still was beautiful.

"How about no? What do you think I am? I'll park and come get you. You're not going to wait in the cold for me at the curb. Go on in and have a good time. I'll see you tomorrow. I may even be back here later on, depending on how complicated this call is."

She watched him hug Elise and Brody, kiss Erin's cheek and wave good-bye at the room full of people before he moved back to where she stood.

"See you tomorrow, Ella."

It was the way he looked at her, she decided, that was different. He looked into her face, into her eyes and held her gaze.

"Yeah, see you then." She waved like a doofus and didn't even pretend she wasn't looking at his ass as he walked down the front walk to his car.

"Whoo," she muttered before turning back and going into the main room.

Cope slumped through his front door some hours later, exhausted and annoyed that he'd missed his chance to get closer to Ella. The elderly lady he'd spent the last several hours with had reminded him of his grandmother. So he'd stayed with her, had some tea and talked her through the system for the dozenth time until she felt comfortable enough for him to leave. It would have felt insulting to everyone if he'd just reset the system and left, knowing Mrs. Morgan was spooked and lonely.

So now here he was, alone in his half-empty condo, still aching for Ella.

He didn't bother turning on the lights. He knew the way, around the coffee table and across the rug. And the moon was setting, casting a silvery light on the walls.

She'd been vivacious earlier that evening. Aglow with joy and sensuality. He smiled as he leaned into the shower to turn the faucet on. He stripped off, tossing the clothes in the direction of the laundry basket, another task he needed to finish up soon or he'd be wearing parachute pants and a long-sleeved tie-dyed shirt to work.

The heat of the water against his muscles felt good, rippling through him, relaxing. He breathed in deep, remembering the way she'd felt, her body backed up to his as they'd danced.

He'd kissed her. Impulsively. But he couldn't find it anywhere within himself to be sorry. They'd been together, dancing. There'd been a sort of magic about it. Just the two of them in a sea of undulating bodies.

And when she turned, her mouth curved into a beautiful smile, so totally open and engaged with him there'd been nothing else to do but kiss her. Just a quick slide of his mouth against hers. He'd swallowed the gust of her surprised sound.

He'd done it on impulse, yes, but he'd done it in public, marking her in some sense, wanting everyone to know she was his.

What he'd really wanted, as she'd looked up at him back at Brody's place, was to push her back against the wall, his hands sliding down her sides, his mouth on hers, swallowing her needy little sighs.

He soaped up, his eyes closed, head tipped back as the water rushed over his body. Kissing her wouldn't be enough. He'd invite her back to his place. Not the condo, but his house.

Her skin would glow in firelight, he decided. He'd build a fire to keep her warm. A woman like Ella needed some TLC, some cosseting and adoration.

That first time, he'd start at her toes and work his way up. He knew she spent a great deal of time on her feet. He could scent the warm almond oil he'd use, massaging her heels and instep.

The feel of her, after wanting it for so long, would be intoxicating. As intoxicating as the permission to slide his hands up her calves and thighs, kissing in their wake. He knew she was sensitive about her scarring, but he didn't see a single part of her as anything but beautiful.

He'd take a long, closeup look at the tattoo on her back as he left a trail of kisses up her ribs and then across her belly, avoiding her pussy and breasts for the moment, rolling her over, moving up her spine to her neck.

Slick with soap, Cope fisted his cock, imagining her taste when he made his way back down the sweet belly and to her pussy. He grew impossibly hard just thinking about it, thinking about how she'd feel against his mouth.

He fucked his fist over and over as he imagined licking her until she came, imagined how her kiss would taste as he moved up her body, notching his cock against her, slowly pushing into her body.

He'd have to pause to push orgasm back. She'd be hot and tight, and just being in her would have pushed him to the brink.

Tugging on his nipple ring, he picked up the speed, the friction pushing him close to the edge. He imagined fucking her senseless. Slow and deep until he'd roll her, bringing her astride him.

She'd rise above him, her hair playing peek-a-boo with her face, riding him all while his hands roved over her body.

His fingertips would pause at her clit, fingering her until she exploded around his cock. Her eyes would widen and blur, would drift nearly closed as he came deep within her body.

He came hard, leaning against the shower enclosure when his knees went to rubber.

And still sleep didn't come for some time after he'd cleaned up and gotten into bed. His attention was taken up with Ella Tipton, and he decided he liked that a great deal.

4

"All I'm saying is, be careful with her."

"Brody, dude, really? You think I'm going to use her and dump her in the middle of nowhere when I'm done?" Cope rolled his eyes as he locked his front door. "It's not even like I'm going to ride while you're gone, which I remind you is *just a few days* anyway. I have my own bike for that if I actually got a few hours free and a clear day. Pussy."

Brody laughed. "Fine, you'll take good care of my bike while we're at the coast. Sheesh, I'm just being responsible."

"Yeah, you're the very picture of responsible. Why are you bugging me anyway? Don't you have, like say, an engagement party to attend?" Cope checked to be sure the champagne he picked up earlier that day was still safely in place in the back of his truck so nothing rolled around and got broken.

"Everyone is gone. Adrian came over a few minutes ago to pick Elise up. The house is so quiet without Rennie here." Brody chuckled. "Funny how used to her constant singing and talking I've become. It's like having Erin living here. Come over and hang for a bit. Todd is ferrying Erin around, so Ben is going to stop by here on his

way over to Adrian's and before I run to pick up Rennie and Elise's
parents."

"I'm on my way to Adrian's too. I have the champagne. You're the
one who had to have some special-order type champagne. Plus, I'm
picking Ella up and giving her a ride. Believe me when I tell you, she's
way nicer to smell than you are. And she has breasts. Automatic win."

"Ella, huh? Yeah, I saw the beginnings of this brewing a while ago.
You be careful with her too."

Cope frowned. "What, you think I'm going to use her and dump
her in the middle of the wilderness too?"

"Shut the fuck up. You know I'm not insulting you."

"I beg to differ. I gotta go. I'll see you in a few hours." He hung up
and put the phone in his pocket before backing out of the driveway
and heading to Ella's. It burned through him, the anger that he'd be
judged like that. And the unease that he'd had the other day when
he'd first thought about how his past might come up in a negative way.

His pocket buzzed, most likely Brody calling back. He'd probably
surprised his friend, but there was only so much a man should have to
take. Sure, he flirted; sure, he had lots of women; and sure, he didn't
take most of his romantic relationships seriously. But he never lied to
anyone; he never treated women with disrespect or unkindness. Most
important, Ella was special. She wasn't like any other woman, and he
should be trusted to know that.

It stung that anyone who should know better would think
otherwise.

Not that he should be surprised; his own family often did that.
He was the handsome one, the rogue. No one expected him to do
well in school. That was Ben's area. Those labels had stuck, his father
still trying to high-five him at the idea he was pulling pussy every ten
minutes.

He was more than that, damn it. Ella saw it, responded to him in a
totally different way than other women did. That got to him.

His funk disappeared when he pulled up outside Ella's building. In fact, he was invigorated just knowing she'd be with him in a few short minutes.

She didn't have her full name on the outside buzzer. A point in her favor. Just her last name. Smiling, he hit the button, and within moments she answered.

"Yes?"

"Hey there, it's Cope. You ready?"

"Can you help me with a box? I'm sorry, you're probably dressed up and stuff, but it's got some of the—"

He grinned at her voice. "Red, just buzz me up, and I'll help."

"Oh, yeah. I'm three B."

He whistled as he rode the ancient, creaking elevator and got off at her floor. He remembered the apartment number, of course, but it didn't seem necessary to tell her that right then.

Her door opened, and she peeked a head out, smiling when she saw him.

"Hi there. Come on in."

He went inside, breathing her in as he passed her. She always smelled warm and sexy.

"Have you eaten today? I have leftovers. We're a little early and I thought you might be hungry and . . . and stuff." She blushed.

She wore snug yoga pants, those weird boots women wore with the sheepskin lining, and a form-fitting long-sleeved shirt. "Not that I'm complaining about how you look now, but shouldn't you be dressed up?"

"I'm so bad with getting messy; I'd stain the dress before I got three steps out the door. Elise knows this, and my dress is at Adrian's. I'll get dressed there. Apparently Raven has volunteered to do makeup and Elise's hair."

He raised his brows, and she laughed. "I know, I know. But Elise is trying very hard to make room for Raven in this shindig, and it appears Raven is trying hard not to be a cow. Elise wants to make Brody happy. It's nice that Raven seems to want that too."

"Raven isn't all bad. I know she has her moments, but she loves Brody and Erin. I like her, and not in that way, so don't frown."

"It's none of my business either way. Raven's a popular woman. She's beautiful, and there's something about her that people are drawn to."

He stepped close, putting his hands on her shoulders very gently. *"Not in that way."* How could she even think for one second that he'd prefer Raven over her?

She nodded, her gaze still locked with his. He wanted to follow up with the fact that there were no other women when it came to her, but he thought it was best to slowly seduce her to keep from spooking her.

"Good." Without thinking, he kissed her quickly and stepped back.

Eyes wide, a pink blush on her cheeks, she held up a bag of bread, and he nodded. "Yes, thanks, I'd love a sandwich."

"Sit, please." Her voice was hoarse, her movements less graceful than normal. *Good.* He got to her as much as she got to him.

Sitting back, he took in the parts of her place he could see, which was most of it. The place wasn't big, not even a full one bedroom. Her bed was just off to his right in an alcove of sorts with a desk and a window complete with window seat. Pillows and thick, fluffy blankets told him she liked comfort, though he imagined the place would get chilly too, given the age of the building.

The table he sat at would fit two people at most, which was fine with him. It meant he would have her close. It also gave him the opportunity to watch her move, that quiet efficiency he so admired, back in place.

She turned and caught him looking at her ass. She rolled her eyes. "Is ham all right? I have avocados too. They came in my produce box, and they're very good."

"Awesome. Yes, please."

She grinned, and he couldn't help but respond and grin back. "I like your place. The last time I saw it, you just had a lot of boxes. You've made it a home."

"Thank you. It feels that way. I can work and work and at the end of the day, it's here with all my stuff." She put a sandwich in front of him, perching on the chair next to his. They didn't touch, but the energy between them was a delicious weight, humming against his skin.

He ate rather than touch her. God, he wanted to touch her.

"You look very handsome," she said, looking at her hands. The way her head was bent, he caught the whole milky pale column of her neck, from nape down her back, the hollow just beneath her ear.

Freckles lived all over her skin, which turned him on so much right at that moment. He wasn't even sure he liked them before, or even thought about them one way or the other. But her freckles begged to be touched and kissed, to be licked.

"Are you all right?"

He nearly choked on his sandwich. "Fine. Fine. Um, thanks. For the compliment and for the sandwich. I don't get dressed up very often. I suppose I'll do this again, only dressier for the actual wedding. What about the bridesmaid's dresses? Something you can wear again?"

She laughed again. "Well, people like to say that, you know— about bridesmaid dresses. It's a myth. Have you ever seen a woman in a bridesmaid dress when you go to the Met?" She stole a pickle from his plate. "I'm joking. Partially. These are pretty, and the color is flattering. You have no idea the stuff the bride can put a redhead in. But Elise has a lovely sense of style, and wow, you could not possibly care less." She stood and took his plate. "I forgot how much you eat. Hang on, I'll make you another."

"Hey, I'll have you know I work a lot with my body. I need the calories." He patted his belly, and she watched his hand a moment, catching her bottom lip between her teeth as she blushed yet more.

His breath caught at the sight of her square, white teeth pressing into the fleshy curve of her lip. She put another sandwich in front of him, which he ate rather than give in to what he really wanted. Instead, he allowed himself a vision of leaning in to press his lips against her pulse.

He found himself surprised by how much he enjoyed that they were taking it slow. Liked watching her gentle to him. Each time she did something that showed him how much she trusted him, pride flushed through him. She deserved all his attention on her as he got to know her on this entirely new level. It was achingly sexy, this dance they moved through. Delicious with anticipation. He let himself luxuriate in the slow woo, the seduction of it rather than a quick fuck with someone he didn't plan to see in a week. He'd never used his sexuality like this, hadn't turned it up full blast to enchant a woman this way. But by God he wanted her, and why not show her just exactly what she did to him?

She sat, looking to him with one raised brow. "You don't have an extra bit of fat on your body. So I think you're safe. What's your father like?"

He cocked his head, trying to figure her out. Sometimes she said the most seemingly random things. Asked him questions that at first glance were out of the blue, but in fact, she had some big giant web of ideas, and usually within a few minutes, he'd realize why she asked. It kept him on his toes, that quirky way she thought and acted. And he had to admit he liked knowing she really listened to him enough to ask him the questions to start with.

Before he could reply, her cell began to ring, and she frowned, looking at the screen. "It's Elise. Hang on."

He tried not to be too obvious as he trailed his gaze down, over the curves of her breasts. Her nipples stood against the fabric of her shirt. He'd thought, so many times, of how they'd feel in his hands, what the weight would be.

"Yes, of course. Not a big deal. Love you too. See you in a bit." She ended the call and turned her attention to him again.

"Everything all right?"

"Elise just wanted to borrow a piece of luggage. Would it be too much to ask that we drop it by their house before we go to Adrian's?"

"Ella"—he hesitated—"you can ask me anything, and I'd do it if it was in my power."

She stopped what she'd been doing and straightened, her hand on her heart, big green eyes blinking. "Thank you, Andrew. I believe you would."

And with those words, he was lost in her. She meant it. Saw him as a man who kept his word and one who could be counted on. It wasn't a calculated statement; she just said it because she believed it. He would have ripped an organ out and given it to her if she'd asked.

The moment between them grew heated until she sighed and took a step back. "I'll just go grab it then, while you finish your sandwich." She hurried from the room, and he ate, smiling. Ella Tipton was going to be his. Not just in his head, not just to flirt with. No, he wanted her in a way he'd never wanted anything before, and as it happened, Andrew Copeland was a man who didn't give up until he got what he wanted.

She grabbed the little bag when they pulled up outside Brody's. "I'll be out in just a moment."

He snorted. "Why don't I take it for you? It's a little chilly out there, and it's pretty warm in the truck."

She handed it to him, touched. "Are you sure? It's not a big deal at all."

"Be right back." He eased from the car and jogged to the front door, where Brody met him. Brody waved and then blew her a kiss. Laughing at him, she waved back, blushing furiously.

"All right then." Cope got back in the driver's seat, and they pulled away from the curb. "I've got the champagne, so let's get on over there. You owe me a dance or three tonight, just sayin'."

"You're a great dancer. I, um, noticed last night. A lot of men don't seem to like dancing."

God, the way his mouth looked when he smiled totally made her weak in the knees. He wasn't even looking at her, and the force of his attraction still made her all tingly.

"Ben told me when I was in middle school that girls loved boys who liked to dance. I can't lie. I totally started dancing at the dances to get girls."

She laughed again, totally charmed. "It seems to work for you."

He took her hand and kissed it. Hot and slightly openmouthed, his lips touching the tender skin between her knuckles, and she felt it from toes to nipples.

"Does it? 'Cause I'm working it, beautiful Ella, I'm working it."

Ella found herself flustered around Cope when he treated her like a woman instead of a friend. Or when she thought he did, because—hello—why on earth would he when he had women homing in on him like some sort of freaking cupcake or something. But he'd certainly never kissed her before last night, much less done that hot hand thing. Lord above, it was hot and all distracting and totally yummy.

She did notice a difference in how he acted with her. Not just the kissing and the way he got so very close to her when they were together. He was more intense, focused. He looked at her mouth a lot. Oh, and her boobs. Which wasn't unusual in a man after all. But still.

As they drove to Adrian's place, Ella simply enjoyed being with him. There was this fluttery feeling in her belly that she realized was the birth of far more intense things between her and Cope. Like it was seconds before the first kiss with someone new. She hadn't felt that in years. But the memory of it paled in comparison to the reality of what

Cope did to her system. Even if it never went anywhere, Ella planned to grab every bit of it she could.

When they arrived, Adrian ambled out, all long, lean and sexy. He did that tip of the chin thing men do with each other, in Cope's direction. "Thanks for bringing this." He turned to Ella. "Hey there, Ella. Erin and Elise are in my guest room getting dressed, I said I'd send you when you arrived."

She blushed. Adrian Brown was something else and then some. Always totally sweet to her and every other person in his life from what she'd seen in the years she'd known him. He was so regular and down-to-earth in his behavior—though not his looks—if she hadn't seen him on stage, she wouldn't have pegged him as a celebrity.

"Okay. Thanks, Adrian. Let me know if I can help at all."

Cope took her hand, staying her. He stepped close, so close he brushed against her when he breathed. His gaze locked with hers and ensnared her. Her heart thundered and she was sure her hands would be fluttering all around if he wasn't holding them. She prayed they weren't sweaty. "I'll take care of the stuff you've brought. And don't forget my dances."

Even breathless and turned-on, she did manage to engage her brain enough to speak, thank God. "Thank you. And thanks for the ride." For long moments they stayed there in Adrian's drive, just looking at each other. A noise behind them shook her free, and she ducked her head. "See you later."

It was a miracle she didn't fall over her own feet, she was so hormone-addled, but she got her legs working and moved past Todd, who'd come out to help unload stuff.

She managed to get into the guest room where Erin sat propped up on the bed, no shoes on, munching on an apple.

"Hiya, cupcake."

Ella moved to kiss her friend's cheek. "How are you feeling?"

"Swollen. Pregnant. The usual. You? I hear you rode in with one

Andrew Copeland. How did that go? Did he try to touch you in any no-no places?"

Ella burst out laughing. "You're really horrible, you know that? He did not. Not that I'd have stopped him, of course. He . . ." She paused, not knowing how to put what he did to her into words.

Erin leaned forward, interest on her face. "He what? This sounds very promising."

"He's helping Adrian bring in a bunch of stuff. Where's Elise?"

"Right here. Just grabbing a bottle of wine for the two of us." She tipped the bottle in Ella's direction. She turned back to Erin and handed her a glass. "You get lemon slices and sparkling water. Todd said he'd bring you a salami sandwich in a few minutes."

"I swear, I can't get normal pregnancy cravings, oh no. I have to eat salami like it's my last meal, every meal."

"Ew." Ella took her glass of wine from Elise. "Thanks."

"Before we do anything else, Ella needs to finish her sentence about Cope, because you were *not* going to tell me that he was helping Adrian move stuff. He what? Did he kiss you?"

"Yes."

Both women gasped and moved closer. "When? Oh my god, why didn't you tell me!" Elise demanded.

"It wasn't just now. Last night and it was just a peck. Today was a hand kiss. He just, he stirs me up. He's just so, gah, he's overwhelming and sexy and I love the way he makes me feel when he turns all that attention my way. That's all I meant."

Erin smiled, a secret smile that made Ella just a tad nervous.

"He's sweet on you. Enjoy it. God knows you deserve some excitement and attention from a man as flat-out hot as Andrew Copeland."

"A-men. Also, if anything else happens, I expect to know about it. Well, I'll give you time to shower and stuff, and then you have to call me." Elise laughed. "Your dress is in the bathroom. It's really cute, and I plan to borrow it very soon."

"Yeah, yeah. I figured that was the case when you helped me pick it out." She sipped her wine but left it on the bedside table before going in to change. "Glad you chose white wine. That way when I spill, it won't show," she called out as she got dressed.

It was the right length; the cut at the hem didn't show her scars at all. The color was rich against her skin, a deep plum, setting off her hair and her eyes. The material hugged her body, emphasizing her breasts and making her butt look pretty darned sexy too. The heels were low but feminine. She wasn't very graceful; higher heels, and she'd have been on her ass. She even had a little sweater thingy Elise called a shrug, which she could wear to cover her arms in case she got cold. Or embarrassed. Quite a bit of her tattoo showed through the cutouts in the back of the dress.

The dress had been a bit of a bone of contention between her and Elise. Elise had wanted to buy the engagement party dresses for everyone, and Erin announced her wedding present was to pay for the wedding, including the clothing for everyone.

Ella had been very uncomfortable with anyone else paying for her clothing and had argued with both of them about it. Finally, she'd burst into tears, and Elise let her pay for it, though naturally the dress was some expensive number so there'd been more struggling because then Elise didn't want to choose a dress that would stretch Ella's budget.

In the end, they'd chosen the more expensive dress that Elise wanted for them originally, and she'd agreed to let it be a gift while also putting a lot more energy into the planning of the party and wedding as her way of saying thank you.

"You look so pretty. The dress fits you perfectly and makes you look all hubba hubba and stuff." Elise sidled up to Ella and put her arm around her shoulders.

"I don't know how I let you talk me into this dress." She looked at her reflection and then back to Elise. "And speaking of pretty, good lord, Elise, you look amazing."

"*Pffft.* I look fine. Brody's gonna love this dress because my boobs are on display. You know how he feels about boobs."

Ella snorted. "I'm pretty sure it's a basic male preference. Most of the time anyway."

Raven came into the room, the scratchy velvet of her voice filled with concern as she spoke to Erin.

Elise and Ella's eyes met in the mirror. "She's really good to Erin, you know. And she loves Brody," Elise murmured.

"Not in that way," Ella said, then remembered that moment with Cope earlier when he'd said the same thing.

Elise laughed. "Doesn't matter if she does. She can't have him."

"You make him happy when you make an effort with her."

"Don't tell her this, but she's not half bad once she stops being such a bitch. It's just that for her, apparently it takes like two years to warm up to a new person. She and I actually had a fifteen-minute conversation wherein not a single bit of sarcasm or biting commentary was used. I don't think we'll ever be as close as you and I. And there's only one you, so there's good reason for that. But I think we're beginning to achieve some genuine like for each other."

Elise put her head on Ella's shoulder a moment; the tenderness of the gesture made Ella reach up to squeeze Elise's hand. "Thank you for being my friend. Truly, Elise, I don't know what I'd do without you."

Elise sniffled. "You're going to make me cry. Stop it. Rennie will be here shortly and then Brody and there'll be more tears."

"Time to face the makeup music," Raven called from the other room.

"Onward and upward." Elise dabbed her eyes with a tissue and headed out into the room where Raven was.

Raven had a huge train case opened up and set on a table near the large wall of windows. "Elise, you first. Adrian just poked his head in to say Brody was on his way to pick up Rennie and your parents, so let's get you set so you're ready when they arrive. There's a photographer milling around down there too."

Elise sat in the chair, and Raven began to work on her.

"I think you should put hot rollers in your hair, Ella. So it's all sleek and poofy without looking like you're rushing a sorority. There are some on the counter in the bathroom already heated up. You know, just in case you decided you needed them. I like to be prepared like a Boy Scout." Erin smiled sweetly.

"You're bossy."

"I know. But I'm pregnant, and no one is going to stop me. This here's what's called taking advantage. You'll look pretty either way, but why not knock Cope off his feet?"

With a snort, Ella opened the door for Todd who, true to his word, brought a sandwich in for Erin.

"It smells way better in here than any other place in the house. Can I stay?" He looked to Erin, trying to appear pitiful, and Ella laughed, heading into the bathroom to deal with those curlers.

She watched them in the mirror, laughing when Ben strolled in, tossed a bakery bag to Erin and then got on the bed on her other side. "If he gets to stay, I do too."

Some time later, Raven did her makeup, even doing something to Ella's hair to keep it smooth and in place.

"You're good at this." Ella looked at the other woman. "Thank you."

"My aunt ran a beauty shop out of her kitchen. I learned a few things about hair and makeup from her."

"Really? Where at? Here in Seattle?"

"Happy Bend, Arkansas. Not much happy, though there was a bend in the road here and there." Raven shrugged. "Don't know why you're worried about wearing dresses; your legs are nearly as nice as Elise's, and your rack is very impressive for such a lean woman. Men like that. So what's the deal with Cope?"

"I knew you were putting on your company manners," Ella said, raising a brow in Raven's direction.

"I'm trying!" Raven threw her hands up.

Ella laughed. "Tell you what, I know you are. And I appreciate that. You can be who you are with me. I'm no threat to you, and for what it's worth, even though you can be a total bitch, I like you. You're a survivor. I don't know your story, but I know you have one."

Raven's mouth curled into a smile. "Yeah, don't we all. A bitch, huh?" They began to walk out of the room. Elise and Brody stood in an alcove near the head of the stairs, his arms around her, her face tipped up toward him.

"A *total* bitch. But you're okay as long as you're not wreaking havoc with them." She jerked her head toward the couple. "You seem to have gotten over it."

"If she'd given me an inch, I'd have taken it. Brody and Erin are my family. I don't have a lot of people I can count on in the world; they're two of a very small group. Turns out Elise is good enough for him. She not only loves him, but she gets him, lets him be who he is and trusts him to do the right thing. Which is good, since he's the right-thing sort of guy. God knows he thinks the sun rises and sets with her and their daughter. They suit him. I can't deny it."

Rennie's laugh floated up the stairs as they went down. "Ella!" Rennie clapped her hands and zoomed over, giving her a big hug. She looked around Ella's body. "Hi, Raven."

Rennie was fascinated by Raven. Like she was fascinated with bugs and butterflies and whether or not fairies existed. This wide-eyed interest in everything she did or said seemed to surprise and stump Raven, leaving her flustered and unsure how to react. Admittedly, it was all kinds of fun to watch.

"Hey, kid. How's tricks?"

Rennie's eyes widened. "I've been meaning to tell my momma that I need a magic set. Then I could do tricks. That would be awesome."

"Your dad might be better for that pitch," Cope said as he sidled up to where they stood.

Rennie nodded, tapping her chin with a fingertip in a very fine imitation of the way Brody did the exact same thing. "Hmm. I'm going to have to think on it. Be stratesick. No, strategic, that's it."

"Very good idea." Ella smoothed a hand over Rennie's hair. "You look pretty today." Her dress was similar to Elise's, with a little sweater to match.

"Rennie, honey, are you in here?" Adrian called as he came into the house from the backyard.

"Uncle Adrian! Over here." Rennie waved, and Adrian started over.

"Baby, we're doing some pictures outside; you don't want to miss out." Adrian held a hand out, and Rennie took it. "Ella, wow, you look fabulous." He shot her a grin.

Raven had melted away, and Ella knew it was because she and Adrian were like oil and water. He saw her as a potentially destructive influence on his family and asserted a very protective stance around Elise and Rennie. For that alone, Ella would have adored him absent all his other fine personality traits.

"Help yourself to some food and drink. Dinner will start in half an hour or so." Adrian waved as he and Rennie headed outside.

Once they'd gone, it was just her and Cope. The sounds of the party began to rise—nothing too loud, it was pretty intimate, less than thirty people. But there was a lot of joy in the air, and she felt it too.

5

"Andy, hold up a sec," Brody called as Cope left the table to get Ella another glass of wine. He'd managed to hog her all to himself for the last forty-five minutes at their little table near the dance floor. Eventually he'd have to share her, but he'd enjoy what he had for the time he had it.

"Nice party, Brody. Congratulations." Cope smiled. It was good to see his friend so happy. Startling to see the way Brody couldn't seem to tear himself away from Elise and Rennie for very long. They were his anchor, but not in a negative way. He and Ben had shown Cope just how that sort of connection was unique and special instead of a burden.

"I said something earlier that bugged you. I'm sorry about that. You've been my friend a really long time. I've never doubted you, or that you were a good guy. I was being protective of Ella, but I went about it wrong."

"It's fine. No harm done." But he appreciated the apology nonetheless.

"Always harm done when you hurt a friend. You're changing. Not that you were an ass with women in the past, so get that look out of your eyes. You look at *her* differently. Different than the way you looked at the women you've been with before. I know what that is. Elise changed *everything* for me. It's hard and sort of scary sometimes. Hard to let go of who you were to make room for who you can be. And I didn't make that any easier with the way I acted."

It was a sore spot, Cope knew, but it did make it better to hear someone he respected say that. To know he was changed by Ella and that it showed.

Adrian approached. "What's going on? And man, since I've had three glasses of champagne and I can claim tipsiness, I have to tell you both that Elise and Ella look amazing tonight. Damn, Brody, your fiancée is freaking beautiful. Don't know how you rated someone like her. Must be payback for all the nice shit you've done for me and Erin since forever."

"Just making amends." Brody tipped his head in Cope's direction. Because he was never really angry to begin with and because he knew his friend cared about him and Ella both, he made a joke to ease the mood. "He's making sure I'm not mad because I'm keeping an eye on his bike for the few days he's taking Elise out to the coast."

"Speaking of romance and stuff, this thing with you and Ella, it's pretty wow. I believe there was eye-fucking last night." Adrian sent him a raised brow.

"That was the only kind. I'm taking my time with her."

Adrian laughed. "Well, you turned it up full blast. She deserves that."

Cope nodded. "She does."

"I need to get popcorn because this will be amusing. Maybe I'll swoop in and snag her. Take her to some swank resort on a private island. Spoil her mercilessly and have sex with her a few thousand times."

"Ha. If you could walk again after I broke your legs." It was a good thing Cope knew Adrian wouldn't do anything like that. Jealousy was an odd sort of feeling. Not entirely unpleasant, but pretty unusual. He couldn't remember the last time he'd felt jealousy over a woman.

Adrian's brows rose. "Wow. You *are* gone for her. About damned time you took yourself seriously and stopped fucking every woman who crossed your path." Adrian's smile was rueful then. "We're getting too old for that shit."

"I don't regret what I was before. I didn't have an epiphany or a checklist as to when I'd fall for a woman in a big way. She's always been special. Always been different. Maybe it's that she was my friend first. I don't know."

"Nothing to regret." Adrian shrugged, diffusing Cope's defensiveness. "You and I like women a lot, and unlike my ugly brother here, we have an unusual amount of talent with the fairer sex."

Brody rolled his eyes. "It's that she sees you. All of you down to the bone."

That was exactly it.

"Humbling, that. Scary, because underneath is where you put all the shit you don't want others to see and judge. So she'll make you a better man because you want her to see you that way." Brody shrugged.

Adrian stood there quietly for long moments, along with Cope.

"Yeah. That's it, I guess. You're pretty smart for an old guy."

"Oh, go on then, cover your emotions with humor."

Cope realized for the millionth time just how fortunate he was with his family. The one he'd been born to and the one he'd made with his friends.

"And now I'm off in search of a drink for that gorgeous redhead I'm wooing." He paused and looked at the Brown brothers. "Thanks."

"Meh. Just don't fuck up my bike."

Just across the yard, Ella stood with Elise. "You just, god, you glow with love for that man, and he's mad for you." Elise's smile in response to her comments made Ella give in and hug her friend. "I'm so happy for you. What you have together is so special. You and Rennie have your prince charming."

Elise's laugh had some tears in it. "I know. I have to keep pinching myself because he always seems too good to be true. But he's mine. Damn, Ella, that hunk of thousand-watt hot over there is all mine."

Both women looked to Brody, where he stood with Adrian, their heads close, laughing about something. Trouble most likely, but the best kind. Brody wore a pinstripe suit. He cleaned up very well. He even had a pocket square, red with white silk. He'd told her earlier that the red was for Elise and the white for Rennie. The man really was a dream. Adrian looked ridiculously handsome in his paler pinstripe suit, his hair longer than his brother's. Even in the years she'd known him and Erin too, there were times when she had to pause when she remembered they were both so famous.

"Don't take this the wrong way or anything, but holy crapweasels, he's so hot."

Elise tipped her head back and laughed. "He is. He totally is." She linked her arm through Ella's. "And speaking of hot, it's *not* my imagination that Cope has been looking at you all day like he wanted to take a big bite of you. I'm thrilled for you."

They walked through the crowd. Not so much a crowd, just a group of their closest friends. Laughter and conversation littered the air, falling into the place between the notes of the music the DJ was playing.

"This is all so lovely."

Elise nodded. "It's amazing to me that I have all these people who love me, love my kid, love the man I love so much." Elise motioned at the guests. "I'm glad you're here. Now, you were about to tell me what's going on with you and Cope."

"I don't know. I don't!" she said quickly when Elise turned to her and raised a single brow. "He seems different. But I'm different too. Or I'm trying to be. Anyway, I'm not Raven." She tipped her head to where Raven and one of her friends had set up camp near Cope and flirted with him madly.

"Let's be thankful for that," Elise mumbled. "I assume you mean more sexually bold?"

Blushing like crazy, Ella nodded and then shrugged. "She's bold all around. Goes after what she wants. Annoying or not, it's a great personality trait."

Elise shook her head. "Ella, you're the boldest person I know, and I'm not just saying that. You've come back from some pretty dark stuff. You're about to get your master's degree, for heaven's sake. You've put your life back together, and now you've found room for a man in it, and look at who you've ended up with? You didn't even go for training wheels dating; you headed straight for the expert course."

Ella laughed. "He sure isn't the bunny slopes."

"Listen, if he wanted that, wanted Raven, he could have it. But he doesn't. He's not hitting anything any of these women are pitching his way. I know you've noticed that, since you've been watching him all day as he's been watching you. Just, you know, jump on him already."

Ella hesitated, chewing her lip a moment, wondering if she even knew how to be in a normal romance with someone. It'd been a long time since she'd been in one.

She was scared of fucking it up with her baggage and issues. Scared she couldn't measure up to these other women who were not her.

Elise turned to her, taking her hands in her own. Understanding played over her features. "You're scared."

Ella grinned briefly, thinking about how Elise had barged into her life and hadn't put up with any excuses from Ella to keep her out. The friendship had happened suddenly, in the midst of Elise's growing relationship with Brody. Elise had been in the café at closing, and the two women had gone out to dinner. Talking with Elise had felt so natural and easy, so it hadn't entirely been a shock when the attack came up in the conversation. Ella didn't talk about it very much, about the time before when she'd slowly begun to unravel as her own person. Of the day he'd forced his way into her apartment and tried to kill her. In Elise's eyes Ella saw pity, but more empathy, far more understanding and most of all, acceptance.

Elise waited, letting Ella spool up the words however she needed to.

She let out a long breath. "Scared. Confused. Giddy. Off balance totally. I haven't jumped on anyone in a very, very long time. He's so . . . God, Elise he's totally out of my league. He's like, an expert at being a man. Not that I should be an expert or anything; that came out wrong."

Elise's shoulders began to shake until she let out her laugh and threw her arms around Ella. "I'm sorry, I am! You just do that thing when you're all flustered and excited. Your voice gets higher and higher, and you sound like a cartoon. It's adorable and makes me want to hug you."

"That's the second wonderful compliment I've received of that sort lately." Ella knew she had a funny voice. She'd hated it until the eighth grade when, over the summer, she'd decided it was cool to have a voice like no one else's. Most people still thought it was odd, but being complimented about it or having people appreciate it pleased her.

"Anyway, I don't know what the heck to do with it. I don't even know if it's anything to be thinking about. He flirts with everyone. Now I'm part of that group, but what it means beyond that? Who knows? I like that it makes my belly fluttery, though. I haven't had this sort of reaction to a man, well, in a very long time." She shrugged, still smiling because it did make her happy, just being a silly, normal woman who was crushing on some totally unattainable guy.

"Well, yes, he is the kind of man who, you know, owns it. Brody is like that. Ben and Todd. Adrian. All in their own way, but it works. Makes them supersexy and sometimes sort of overwhelming for that woman they've decided to focus on so completely." Elise smiled as her gaze snagged on Brody. "I'm not trying to rush you into anything you're not ready for. But I definitely think what he's got is more than just a realization you're a girl. He's got a realization that you're you. He wants it."

"No matter what, I feel excited about it. As long as I don't mess things up and ruin our friendship. I like Andrew a lot."

Even though she'd been people watching as they'd walked around, her gaze had always returned to him. She stared this time, greedily taking in the way he leaned against one of the tables in Adrian's sweeping backyard. The water lay at his back, a stretch of blue as deep as his eyes. He looked handsome there, ocean and sky at his back, the fairy lights strung through the trees looking almost like stars.

Portable outdoor heaters had been set up, so despite the evening chill, the area was warm enough to enjoy being outside. Adrian had done a lot of work. She'd helped some, but the bulk of the planning had been done by him. The yard was so lovely, it was clear he'd had it all done with Rennie and Elise in mind. The beds overflowed with early fall flowers, and large vases and containers of cut flowers filled the air with their scent. The Brown siblings were tight that way, all pleased and loving with each other.

"Changing the subject now before I throw up from nervousness. This is the best engagement party I've ever attended. The food is ridiculously good. And the view, wow, I'd sleep out here every night if I lived in this house."

"I know. This has been a very perfect day. My life is so very wonderful. Never thought I'd have two rock stars singing a song my soon-to-be-husband wrote for me." Elise laughed. "Been a wild ride, falling in love with Brody."

Elise squeezed her hand and then waved as Rennie squealed and ran toward them.

"I'm so glad to see you, Ella!" Rennie threw her arms around Ella's neck when she bent to hug the little girl.

"Hi there, Irene." She kissed the top of Rennie's head. "You sure do look pretty in that dress. I can't wait to see you rock the maid of honor job."

Rennie grinned. "Thanks. Remember you promised to help me practice. Since you'll be in the wedding too, I can help you practice when you help me."

"That's a really good idea. Deal." She held her hand out, pinky finger extended. "Pinky swear."

Rennie lit up, and they clasped pinkies for a moment. "Pinky swear."

"Look at all my favorite beautiful women in one spot." Brody approached, sweeping Rennie up in one arm and hugging Elise with the other. "And each one of you is absolutely gorgeous." He looked to Ella. "I can't say it has nothing to do with the way you can see my work, just a peek of it, when you don't wear the matching jacket, Ella." He grinned.

"That won't be happening any time soon. It's too cold outside for that tonight."

"I'm telling her she should do a grand unveiling when it warms up and you finish the whole thing." Elise leaned her head against his shoulder, and a twinge of envy soured Ella's belly for a brief moment. What would it feel like to be able to lean on someone like that? To know they'd catch you if you fell, that they'd be there for you without fists and cutting words?

"There you are." Cope approached and handed Ella a glass of champagne. "Have you been hiding?"

"More like you've been blinded by a sea of barely concealed womanflesh." Elise smirked.

"Can't blame that on me! I was just scoping out what new tray of goodies was coming out of the kitchen, and I was beset." He turned his attention back to Ella. "And here was the woman I was looking for the whole time."

Ella sipped her champagne, liking the way his attention worked with the bubbles to make her feel light and silly. "So what you're saying is breasts just happen?"

"If the day is very good, yes." He grinned, and she laughed. "Come walk with me, Ella. Protect my honor."

Ella rolled her eyes at him but linked her arm through his. "Where are you taking me?"

He drew her away, weaving them through the tables and around the people until they'd ended up on an overlook with a pretty wooden bench. "How about here?"

She sat and looked out over the water, glittering with the light of reflected stars. "So pretty tonight." Shivering, she didn't relay the next part, which was that it was cold.

"Here." He took his suit coat off and put it over her shoulders. Instantly she sighed as his warmth surrounded her.

"God, thank you. That's so much better."

"Glad to be of service," he murmured, his body very close to hers. "I haven't told you in about an hour or so, but you look gorgeous. Purple is really your color."

"Thank you. I was afraid I was too pale or that the freckles would overwhelm the color."

"You have the most beautiful skin, seeing more of it only helps. Speaking of seeing more, I caught a glimpse of the tattoo. I forgot to ask you last night, but when will it be totally finished?"

"Brody will put on the final touches when I finish at the end of this quarter."

"He's adding a piece with each milestone?"

She nodded. "Yeah. I know some might think it's silly to place so much importance on finishing a paper or whatever. But considering where my life has been, they're huge steps."

"They are. I agree. So how are you? I mean really?"

She looked at him in the quiet dark and thought about the million ways she could answer that question. "Depends on what you're asking."

He took her hand and she let him, liking that he held her without crushing her, but also with some pressure. The scent rising from the inside of his suit coat made her feel drunk. He smelled really good, making it hard to think clearly without just sniffing him.

"I'm asking whatever you want to answer." He paused for a while, and she let him. "I figure it this way, you're surrounded by people who care about you, and they are afraid to stir up bad feelings. So they don't talk about it, the attack and your recovery. Now, it could be you don't want to talk about it ever again, and I respect that. But I figure it could also be that you'd like to talk about it every once in a while with someone who has watched you triumph over a series of events that would have driven a lesser person to insanity."

She swallowed past the lump in her throat.

"I'm good. With everything." She shrugged and continued to look out over the water. "Two years ago I didn't even know if I'd be able to walk again. Hell, five years ago I had to ask for permission to wear a certain sweater or even answer the phone." She hadn't meant to reveal that last bit.

He held her hand and said nothing.

"I'm nearly done with all this school. I may have a job when the new year starts. I have friends and family who care about me." She sipped her champagne, draining it.

"I'll be back in a moment. Don't move!" He got up and jogged around the bend. While he was out of sight, she gave in and let herself bounce her knee to free some of her nervous energy. Damn, he got to her. Maybe it was the way he was so steadfast and strong. Or his voice. Or the way he focused so totally on her, listening to what she said. Or the way he looked. Whatever it was, he left her scatterbrained and blurty.

He came back into view with an armful of things.

"First." He put the things down on the bench before unfurling a blanket. "Here, this should help. Adrian told me to let you know he has more if you need them." He sat again, getting tucked in beneath it with her. He then handed her another glass, this one warm. "Mulled wine. Erin says it's her best recipe and to drink an extra mug for her."

Ella laughed. "Done." She sipped, the warmth trailing down her throat and into her belly. "She wasn't lying."

"Last, I'm so hungry I thought a plate of a few somethings might help."

"Thank you." She ducked her head with a smile.

"You're welcome." He tucked some of her hair behind her ear and got lost in the feel of his fingertip brushing over the skin just behind her earlobe. He swallowed and moved his hand away.

"For everything. I mean, you're a great listener."

"You're my friend, Ella. I hope you know you can tell me anything."

She turned to face him, tucking one of her legs beneath her. "I know that. You're an honorable person. I respect that. It's just hard sometimes, hard to say what's inside because it sounds so bad." She blinked back tears. "I'm mostly past it, but there's still shame. I'm still afraid, even though I have no reason to be. I hate that."

6

"Scared how?" He'd deal with the shame part later. An engagement party probably wasn't the place for that. But he could help her with the fear; it's what he did for a living, after all.

"Putting my work hat on for a bit, I looked your place over, just quickly, when I was there earlier. You have good locks. The building is old, but it's well lit. I checked some crime stats, and the neighborhood you're in has a really low crime rate, especially violent crimes. You're three floors up, which makes the fact that you have all those windows much less of a problem."

"It's not that. It's not a fear like that. It's . . ." She chewed her lip for a moment. "I know all those things. I appreciate that you looked. I feel safe in the building. I feel safe at work. I don't go around worried all the time. Even when I'm at work and a client goes crazy, I can handle it."

"Because you're an eminently capable person. Hello."

"Ha. Not so much, not all the time anyway."

"So what do you mean then?"

"This is embarrassing."

"Then don't go on if you don't want to. I don't want to put you on the spot. I just wanted you to know I was around to hear whatever you wanted to say. Or not."

She chewed her lip for long moments, and then she blurted, "Sometimes, totally out of the blue, I go to the grocery store in the middle of the day, and I get so freaked out I can't get out of the car. I don't like that . . . that uncertainty in my life."

Ah, there it was. *Control,* or lack of it. That's what drove her now, and he got it. He could help her take control.

He exhaled softly, taking her hand again, sliding his thumb back and forth over her knuckles. Funny how fragile she felt and what a contrast it made with how strong she really was. "Give yourself a break. First and foremost, Ella, beautiful and strong, let yourself be fucked up. A little. It's okay."

She blinked several times and took a shuddering breath.

As much as he loved his friends and celebrated their upcoming wedding, he wished quite fervently that he and Ella were in a more private place better suited to such a conversation. The last thing he wanted was to set her off balance so she'd have to explain it to anyone or feel embarrassed over it.

She'd opened up to him in a way he was totally certain she had not to very many others. He fought back a tide of emotion. Pride in her, that she'd opened up to him, that she was so amazing. Awe at how strong she was and that she didn't seem to get it. Anger at her ex. Fear that he'd never be able to get her past this place. Fear that he'd never have her.

Suddenly the idea of not having her was simply unbearable.

"I can help you. If you let me. If you want me to. I can help you with part of the fear."

Her breath caught. "How?"

"A place can be safe, but this isn't about a place, is it? Sometimes it's just you, and then what? Is that it?"

Tears glistened in her eyes. He nearly shut up, not wanting her to hurt more.

"How about you let me give you some self-defense training? One-on-one. I can give you the tools to open that fucking car door and go shopping. Or at least another reason to try."

When she answered, her voice was small but lined with steel. "I am so very tired of being afraid and debilitated."

He wanted to kiss her so badly he had to swallow it back. When he'd first seen her come out, the lush plum-colored dress hugging every inch of her body, her breasts showcased pretty damned spectacularly, he'd choked on the sparkling water he'd been drinking. She wasn't one to dress up very often or to wear more than a hint of lip gloss. But there she was, her hair shiny and smooth, her eyes and lips done up, wearing a dress that snatched the breath from him. She was breathtakingly beautiful. What he'd been the most touched by, though, was the way she'd been. More carefree than he'd seen her in years. Enjoying herself, being with her friends and, if he wasn't wrong, aware that she looked pretty and enjoying that.

She was blossoming, and it looked just right on her. "All right then. I know you're busy, but how about we try for three times a week? Do you exercise regularly?" He was pretty sure she did. Her body was toned. He knew this because sneaking looks at her body was one of his favorite pastimes.

"Not like you do." She frowned, her nose wrinkling. "I do okay though. I work out in the mornings before I go to the café. Forty minutes every day. You, well you're always biking and hiking and camping and stuff. And liking it. You're going to run circles around me." Her frown lightened, and she snorted.

"Well, of course I am, gorgeous. I want to see you admire me when I'm all manly and stuff."

She laughed this time, hugging him quickly. "Thank you."

"No problem. We can work out in the gym space at Erin's building. That's where we do most of our workouts. That okay?"

"Yes. Thank you, Andrew. Really."

"You can bring me lattes or sandwiches, and we can kick fear's ass." He grinned, and she relaxed as he'd hoped she would.

"Deal. Earlier we got interrupted. You were going to tell me about your father." She settled back, side to side with him again.

"I was going to ask you why you were asking."

"Well, at first it was because of genetics. I think I was going to ask if he ate a lot like you. And now because of the way you answered my question with a question. I know there's trouble because of Ben and Erin. And Todd. Is he mad at you because you took Ben's side? Were you close?"

That was a question and a half. Interestingly enough, one most people didn't ask. But she did. And he liked it. There was something about sharing intimacy that wasn't simply about sex that made him want to grab her and run away with her, keeping her all to himself. He'd never had that before with a woman. Hell, he didn't really have that with anyone most of the time.

It was a reminder that they'd been friends for a long time before this new twist in what they were to each other.

"I don't know really. Stupid, huh? We had a close family growing up. My parents hung out with Todd's parents so much it was like we were all related. Todd may as well be my blood relation, we're that tight. Hell, our fathers have been as close as brothers until, well, you know that part of the story. I grew up fishing and boating, woodworking and carpentry. My dad and I used to do carpentry together. He isn't mad at me for taking Ben's side. I think he's just mad at the world for changing. He doesn't understand it, and instead of dealing, like everyone else, he's just throwing a tantrum. My mother had a hard time, but she worked it through. Ben is the favorite, so it was easy for her, I think. But my dad, he's sort of stuck there. He loves

Ben, Ben loves him and he's still the favorite, even when they don't speak."

She looked at him through her lashes. "You're my favorite. Just so you know."

Her words settled in and made him warmer than he'd let himself think he could handle. It was a tossed-off sentence, but it was precisely what he wanted to hear. And on some level she knew it. *Knew him.*

He grinned, resting his head on her shoulder a moment before going on. "Things are not the same, I guess. I feel bad for Ben, because he and my dad were tight. I feel bad for my dad because he's lost Ben, and he's not brave enough to make a step toward him."

"And here you are, so fabulously you, and your dad doesn't notice," she said quietly. "He sucks."

Cope laughed, the knot his father made in his gut easing a bit. "He's old and set in his ways. That's what my mom says. He loves us all. I just don't think he knows how to relate to us when it comes to personal lifestyle choices."

"I'm sorry. I wish I could help. I've got my own struggles with my parents over my choices, so I don't have much advice. Though, through all the tension, I've never doubted their love or support for me." She sighed. "What's your favorite thing to do on a Saturday morning?" she asked suddenly.

He wanted to follow up on the comment about her family, but he'd wait. Things were heavy enough just then, so it would do to lighten up. "I'm restoring my house. I like to get up early and work on it. Silly, I know."

She turned and looked at him, not through her lashes this time, but those brilliant green eyes of hers locked on his. "That's not silly at all. It's wonderful. I had no idea. I thought you lived in a condo in Eastlake."

"I'm still there until I can move into the house. The condo is on the market though. I bought a house in Ballard. It's what the Realtor called a fixer-upper. Ha! It was a total mess. But that's sort of what I wanted. I wanted to take on a project where I could make exactly what I needed. Obviously I can't afford to build from scratch, especially here in the city, so I'm doing the next best thing and restoring."

He wasn't sure why he'd just told her all that. He rarely spoke about his love of carpentry. His friends and family knew about the house and the project, but not the extent of what he was doing.

People tended to think about him in certain ways. It didn't make him bitter or angry; he tended to be the most laid back of the men he knew. But it was close to his heart.

"That's awesome, Cope. I'd love to see it sometime. I can't do a whole lot of construction stuff; I don't really know how. But I can paint and plant things. If you ever need help, I hope you'll call me."

He grinned. "Really? I can always use an extra pair of hands."

"Yes, of course. I'm a pretty quick learner if there's something I don't understand." She said the last, her chin jutting out almost defiantly.

Some things went deeper than a physical scar. "He told you you couldn't do anything?"

She hesitated so he stayed quiet, waiting for her to decide to share.

"Sort of. He was good at it. He didn't"—she ducked her head—"he didn't hit me all the time. Just to underline a point here and there. But he was an expert at making me feel small and dim. I played my part, and now that's over. Even with my family and friends though . . ." She sighed. "It's just that sometimes people have this idea of you. They know you in certain ways, and it's like they're incapable of seeing other facets. It's not done out of meanness, but it limits nonetheless. A person is more than just who they were growing up, or one horrible period in their life."

He didn't say a word. Just squeezed her hand and looked out over the water and glittering lights. He knew what she meant. More than he could express to her just then.

The stuff she'd shared was major and deep, personal, and he was hungry for more. It was a chore not to push her to share. But he got the feeling she needed to tell it at her own pace, so he reined it in.

"I used to be a cheerleader."

Well now.

"You should know I have a thing about cheerleaders. Can you still do the splits? Do you still have the uniform? Um, when I say that, I mean cheerleaders of age and all. I'm a pervert, not a deviant."

She laughed. "Glad to hear you're on the right side of that divide." She was quiet for a while before she added very quietly, "I used to be someone else."

"No. You used to have a different sort of life. And now things have happened to change you."

"No. I used to have no fear. None." She shrugged. "Everything was an adventure, a challenge to be taken."

"I'm not the same person I was when I was twenty-two either. Who could be? And who'd want that?"

They sat, quiet with the noise all around them.

"As for the splits? I haven't tried in a very long time." She was amused, but sadness edged her voice too.

"If you ever decide you'd like to give it a try, you know where I am. I'm always happy to spot you. Now, about that uniform?"

She turned to him with rolled eyes, playfully batting at his shoulder. "If I did, I doubt I'd be able to squeeze into it."

A comfortable silence settled in as they picked at all the munchies on the plate he'd brought back with him. Both seemed to understand the depth of what had been shared, the intimacy they'd built. He couldn't regret it at all.

"Would you like to dance?" he asked sometime later, after they'd demolished the food and drink. "Seems a shame to waste that dress." He paused. "Though, I could be perfectly content to sit here with you and imagine you in that cheerleading skirt."

She laughed softly. "All right then. Though I must tell you how utterly relaxed I am right now under this blanket with you. In addition to your other fine qualities, you put out a great deal of body heat. It's a dream of mine."

"What? All my body heat at your disposal? I'm always pleased to be your dream. I'm just as happy to stay right here." Plus, right there they were totally alone. He had her all to himself, and he selfishly wanted to keep it that way. Damn, he shouldn't have even suggested moving.

"I picked up some Pablo Neruda," she said in her seemingly random way, standing and holding a hand out. "Come on, you know you want to. It'll keep us warm."

He took her hand, considering pulling her back to his lap to show her what he *really* wanted to do. He hardened at the vision of her on his lap, riding his cock as the moon lit her skin. But he stood, thinking about the root canal he'd had the month before to quell the raging hard-on. He took her hand in his own, and led her toward the dance floor. "You did? How do you like him?"

"I got a collection written in Spanish. I like it better that way. Of course I'm rusty, but what I can understand still is sensual, sexy, beautiful. I like it."

She'd looked it up for him. Had read it because he'd mentioned it. He didn't know why that floored him the way it did, but wow.

He twirled her, loving that she still wore his suit coat, pulling her to him. The song was slow enough he had the excuse to sway, her body pressed to him. Her scent surrounded him, and everything was right.

" 'You've moon-lines, apple pathways . . .' " he murmured.

She turned her head, looking up to him, a pleased smile on her lips. "That's lovely."

"Pablo Neruda. One of his love sonnets called 'Morning.' " One of his favorites.

"I'll have to see if it's in the volume I picked up."

He would read them to her as they lay in his bed, limbs entwined. Yeah. He closed his eyes and breathed her in.

"What's *your* favorite thing to do on a Sunday morning?" he asked, and she looked surprised and then pleased. Her face was always so incredibly animated, everything she felt was obvious in her features. She was a horrible poker player, but it was one of his favorite things about her.

"What? You asked me." He grinned, and she burst out laughing.

"I like you, Andrew. You always make me smile. Um, let's see. I love sleep, like with an unholy level of obsession. I don't get enough probably. So I'll sleep late, until after noon at the very least. I'll get out of bed only long enough to make coffee and grab a fresh chocolate croissant and get right back under the covers where I'll read the paper and maybe journal awhile. Total, utter laziness."

The perfect Sunday if she added him to that bed. He'd be sure to bring extra croissants. "Very nice. A lazy day is one of life's greatest pleasures."

The song wound down, and Adrian's voice sounded. "Rennie and Ella, can you two come up here please?"

"Whoops." Ella stood back and let go of his body. "Be back in a bit."

He ignored her good-bye and walked toward the stage with her, waiting to the side with Brody and Todd.

Rennie spoke excitedly in a stage whisper to Adrian and Ella. Ella nodded and took her hand, drawing her into the lights more.

"Rennie would like to say her good-byes." Ella handed the mic to Rennie, who continued to hold Ella's hand.

"My momma said I could do this instead of the toast thingy." She grinned, and Cope found himself joining her.

"I have the best mom in the world. She's pretty and smart and she's a great dancer and makes my favorite tacos all the time. She tucks me in every night and don't even, oops, *doesn't* even complain when I brush her hair and catch a tangle."

Elise had joined Brody, who wrapped his arm around her as they watched their daughter.

"Mom and I had a good life before Brody came. But it's way better now. Brody reads me ten princess books when I ask, and he lets me paint my toenails if it's only very light pink or crazy colors like green. He even plays Barbie with me. We got a good family, and I just wanted to say thank you to Brody and Aunt Erin and Uncle Todd and Uncle Ben and Uncle Cope and Uncle Adrian and Gran and Pops. And Ella, who made me a peanut butter marshmallow sandwich to eat tomorrow morning because she loves me and knows they're my favorite."

Brody went up and swooped Rennie high into his arms and kissed her cheek. He spoke to her softly, and she giggled, hugging him tight. Ella dabbed her eyes with a handkerchief Adrian handed her.

Elise took the microphone, and Ella stepped back. "Thank you everyone for coming. You're all incredibly special to us, and having you here to share tonight with us makes it all the more special. I expect to see each and every one of you in two months in this very backyard for the wedding, you hear me? Thank you to the Browns and Copelands, who've extended their family and affection to me and Rennie. Thank you to Ella, who does more for people than she'd ever admit. Any girl who'd put on deodorant for her bestie because her bestie had forgotten and the dress was too awkward for me to do it myself is aces. And she makes peanut butter and marshmallow sandwiches for my kid. What's not to love?"

She turned to Brody. "And thank you to Brody, who made room in his heart and life for not only me but our daughter. I never expected you, Brody, but every day I thank God that I found you. I love you. Thank you for making my dreams come true."

Brody waved it off, moving to Elise to kiss her while still holding Rennie. "I'm the lucky one. Elise, you fill all my empty spaces. You and Rennie are the reason I wake up smiling every day."

"Enough! You guys stop it, or I'm going to cry." Adrian took the microphone back, hugging Elise quickly. "Let's get the music started again."

Ella hugged Rennie and handed her off to her grandparents, who delivered hugs, kisses and good-byes before leaving.

Cope moved in to swoop on Ella, but Raven and her friend stepped into his path. He sighed inwardly. Unlike his brother, he saw the good in Raven. She was an odd duck, but beneath her blunt, socially maladjusted manner, she cared about her friends. Didn't mean he always liked her or wanted to be around her for more than a few minutes here and there, but he understood why Brody still cared about her.

She'd come on to him a number of times over the years, but he'd turned her down, not wanting to get anywhere near the nexus of the drama she often created. Didn't mean he hadn't flirted with her; she was a beautiful woman after all. But he wasn't interested in what she was offering.

The one he wanted to look at most wasn't there, though; she was just past them, holding Elise's hands and talking, both women smiling. Erin joined them with Mary, another friend, and he couldn't help but notice he wasn't the only man staring at the four of them.

"Hey, ladies, nice to see you." He kept it casual as he skirted Raven and her friend to get to Ella, only taking his gaze from her to keep from walking into someone.

"Where you off to? We're going to head back to Raven's place after this. You want to join us?" Raven's friend grinned his way.

"Not tonight, ladies, though thank you for the invitation. I'm here with Ella." He'd never really felt the need to make such a thing clear. But he did now.

"Good." Raven shrugged at his confused look. "She's a nice person. I like her."

Raven kept surprising him, even after all the years he'd known her. "Yeah, she is. You two have a good night." He nodded and moved on his way.

Damn. He caught her staring. Ella knew she blushed furiously, but the slow, sexy smile he sent her took the edge off her embarrassment, warming it into pleasure. She was emotional enough after Rennie's speech, and she'd not-so-casually looked for him, only to find him with Raven and her friend again.

She watched, her insides warming up as he shook his head to whatever they offered and looked to her, at first with surprise and then, when he'd caught her looking, sly pleasure.

"I say this because I love you. You need to bang that drum, Ella. Bang it like there's no tomorrow," Elise whispered into her ear.

"So romantic," she murmured back, trying not to laugh.

"Don't judge, El. Don't judge. I'm gonna play rock band on my soon-to-be-husband's body all night long."

At this, she lost her battle and giggled, right as Cope reached her, taking her hand.

"What's this all about?" He kissed her knuckles again, casually but sparking heat.

"Elise is giving me her secret recipe for biscuits." She smiled widely, and he raised his brows at her.

"Must be some kind of biscuits then, by the look on your face."

"Biscuits are serious business, Andrew. They're irresistible, and you can never have only one."

He drew her away from the crowd, back toward the house where it was quieter. "I really must try these biscuits. You're clearly eating different ones than me, and while I've enjoyed them, I'm apparently missing out on something."

Oh, how she wanted to be bold and say something suggestive just then. She didn't really know how. It wasn't that she was ashamed or anything, but she didn't have much experience with this stuff.

"I have to tell you, the blush you're working right now really makes me curious."

She nearly choked; instead, she tried to smile serenely, but she probably ended up looking like she was drunk.

"What made you want to be a social worker?" he asked.

"I thought about being a doctor like my brother. But I totally suck at math and science. It's sort of a requirement and all, so that was out by the time I needed to choose my classes for second quarter of my freshman year at the UW. I volunteered on a crisis line, and that's sort of how it started. I thought it was a great direction. I just got . . . sidetracked for a while."

"Would you like to go for some coffee?" Cope asked suddenly. "Looks like things are winding down here."

Oh, *that* feeling was one she hadn't felt in years. She gave herself a long moment to simply luxuriate in it, that giddy joy at being asked to coffee by a handsome man. Didn't matter if he only meant it as a friend; it still felt awesome.

"I really would, yes. But I promised to help wrap things up here. There are little gift boxes, and I need to check those, actually right now." She looked toward the table they were meant to be on and motioned, beginning to hurry over.

"I can help. Just point me, and I'll do your bidding."

"All right then." God, he made her fluttery. "Um, come with me." She waved at Adrian and pointed to the empty table, indicating she was going to put the little gift boxes out. He nodded.

"They're in Adrian's bedroom. Through here."

"I know where it is." He laughed. "How do you?"

She turned as she opened Adrian's door. "How do *you*? Is there something you haven't told me?"

"I don't like that type of dude."

Nearly choking, she turned to him. "What type of dude do you like?" He could *not* be gay! She'd seen him making out with women and he had been sort of romantic with her and, oh man, what if she'd misunderstood the whole thing?

He slid his thumb over her bottom lip, sending shivers through her. "I'm just teasing you. I like women. One in particular."

She blushed and damned her skin for showing it so easily. "Oh. Well, all right, because I was wondering if all those women hanging all over you every two feet you move were overcompensation or what."

He chuckled. "It's not that bad."

She turned and motioned toward the bed. "Ha! In any case, I see the platters are here." She put the pretty boxes she and the rest of their friends had tied countless ribbons and bows to, on two large platters. "This way when people leave they can take one with a cake box."

"Cake box?" He helped her stack and then made sure it wasn't too heavy before taking his platter out first to clear a path. "You okay with that?"

"They're not heavy. And cake boxes are self-explanatory. They have little slices of cake in them. The caterer will be bringing them out soon. These other boxes have a picture frame in it with a save-the-date card for the wedding. You know those cameras at all the tables? We'll have the pictures developed and available at the wedding for people to grab and put in these frames."

They put the platters out, and Ella watched carefully as the caterers added their boxes.

"Wow. That's amazing and thoughtful."

"Oh, it's nothing. I just read about it in a magazine and thought it would be fun. I may have talked Elise into having a photo booth at the wedding. Everyone loves pictures."

"Ella, you rocked with this whole thing." Adrian came over and hugged her tight. "If the social work gig falls through, you should look into event planning."

"*Pfft.*" Ella arranged several tea light candles on the centerpiece towers. "I didn't do very much. Heck, you did more than I did."

"Yeah, yeah, I had *people* do that." Adrian caught a glimpse of Cope, and Ella didn't miss the raised brow.

"I think your brother is trying to get your attention," Cope said to Adrian as he moved closer to Ella.

Adrian just laughed and kissed Ella's cheek one last time before strolling off again.

What the heck was that all about?

"There's going to be a rush over here." Ella handed him two cake boxes and a gift box. "That should be a nice snack for tomorrow morning."

He put his arm around her waist, keeping her at his side as they stepped away from the table. She wouldn't have moved for anything.

7

It had been another week after the engagement party before they could both adjust their schedules to begin the lessons. She'd received word just an hour prior that she'd gotten the job at the nonprofit dealing with family violence. She'd start full time in January, but begin shifting her schedule that following week, slashing her job at the café in half and spending the extra hours at her new job. Being the kind of person she was, she'd prepared for this eventuality. She'd prepped the new manager who'd taken over for her, doing a very good job in her stead. The new part-timers would be trained well enough to be totally up to speed by the time she left the café behind totally in late December. A new year, a new job, a new step in her life.

She hadn't been this silly and nervous over a man in years. She'd met Bill in her sophomore year of college. He'd taken over her life slowly. She hadn't noticed until it was too late and he'd entrenched himself into her life so deeply she hadn't quite known how to get him out.

The past was past. And this was her life now. Andrew Copeland was not even from the same universe Bill vomited out of. Cope had called her several times and had come into the café nearly every day. Their first training session had been thick with romantic tension. He hadn't even tried to kiss her. He'd remained all business, despite all the chemistry zinging around. But afterward, he'd touched her cheek, just lightly, and it had felt as intimate as a tongue kiss.

Still, she'd finally allowed herself to accept Cope just might be sending romantic signals her way. On the elevator up she made herself focus and tried to calm the fluttery bits.

He'd be up there waiting for her, Andrew Copeland of the sexy blue eyes and the just-too-long black hair. Working out with him was a big test, she told herself. A test of will, because, boy, did she want to touch his belly, slide herself against him. And she could under the guise of this class. She learned a lot too, even from just one class. Felt more confident as she'd practiced the moves he'd shown her the lesson before.

As she got off the elevator, he pushed from the wall where he'd been standing and moved to her, his gaze lazily sliding up her body until it reached her face. His smile was easy and no small amount of sexy. "Hey there."

She let the attraction wash through her like a drug. He made her all tingly, just from a hello and a look. All that pseudo calm she'd talked herself into believing she had, washed away.

"Hey yourself." She had rushed over, getting dressed in the bathroom at work to save time. Of course, that meant she didn't have a damned bit of makeup on. Still, he'd seen her without it more than he had with it, and he still flirted with her, so maybe he had a freckle fetish. Ha.

The practice mats were in a side room, which made her rest a bit easier, as no one could see her in there. She wasn't graceful or muscular. She could barely walk without tripping or looking generally dorky.

"Tonight let's work on some basic defensive moves. Okay?"

He took it slow with her, building trust, helping her overcome any residual nervousness or fear she may have had. She appreciated that he did it but didn't make a big deal of it. He just kept a pace that worked for her.

"What are you thinking about?" he asked when she managed to block his blows three times in a row. "You get this fierce look on your face. Good job."

"No, it's too embarrassing. You'll laugh."

"Well, of course I will. But you should tell me anyway."

Gah! He was so . . . He just said everything right and they had this rhythm and she'd never had rhythm before and it set her all off kilter.

"I just think of a song."

"You know I'm only going to pester you until you answer the question all the way."

He showed her in slow movements how to break a grip on her wrist. He'd introduced it a few days before at their first lesson, and she'd practiced every day. He nodded proudly, and she wanted to flutter her lashes at him.

"Tell meeeee," he sang.

"Metallica. 'Master of Puppets.' It gets me in the mood." She'd pinned her hair back with a headband, so she couldn't drop her head and hide behind her hair. Instead she jutted her chin out and frowned. "Don't judge me!" she teased.

He laughed. "No judgment from me. I listened to '. . . And Justice For All' so many times I had to buy a replacement, twice. Ah, no, like this." He ran through the angle of her move again, and she tried once more, getting a feel for it.

"Did you make out in your parents' basement to it? Mick, my brother, got caught down there, and my mom still gives him the stink eye when we're down there watching movies or whatever."

He moved quickly, circling around her until he stopped, very close to her, his nose just inches from hers. "Did *you* ever make out down there?"

He might have taken it slow with the lessons so far, but he didn't seem to find any trouble knocking her ass to the mat when she wasn't paying attention.

She grunted as he helped her to her feet. "Again, let me make you laugh. I lived in fear of getting pregnant. I was in the room when my aunt gave birth. It was, well, I won't go into detail, but that kept my virginity intact for three more years. Plus, by the time I was old enough, my parents were on to the basement as a make-out spot. We used to drive down to the street behind the high school where it was quiet at night. It was a third base and holding sort of place."

He licked his lips, and she nearly let out a groan at how good he looked just then.

"Ella, you and me." He paused, and right before her eyes, he took on that sexy attitude of his and it made her all breathless in a way that had nothing to do with the workout. "We should go out. On a date, all official like. Pizza and pool with the rest of the crew?"

She swallowed hard, her heart fluttering in her chest.

"Really? Me?" Oh god, she actually said it out loud like a dork.

Cope saw her surprise and wanted to laugh at how clueless she was to her own appeal. He did like it that pleasure shone in her eyes. "Oh yes, you. How can you not have known?" He gave in and laughed. "You're *delicious*, Ella. I want to take a big bite."

Her hands flew up nervously as she blushed. "I . . . oh. Wow. Well, jeez! You flirted with me and all. But how was I to know it was different than any other day? Andrew, you flirt with everyone. I had a feeling you"—she shrugged—"changed the way you saw me. Or something. You started acting different about six weeks ago."

God, she was so beautiful, especially when she got flustered. Her skin gleamed, so pale. The slice he seemed totally fascinated with the most, the nape of her neck, called to his mouth. She wasn't even wearing makeup, but she didn't need it. She was clean and fresh and utterly

Ella. And he wasn't lying when he said he wanted to take a big bite. Or a lot of long, slow licks.

"My manner is flirtatious and friendly. I'm a flirty guy. People like to be flirted with; it makes them happy. But you're different." How different he continued to realize each time he was with her. "What you failed to notice all along is that I've *always* wanted to ask you out. I've *always* been attracted to you, so I decided after a long while of wanting you, that it was time to make my move at last. I come into the café every day. I kissed you at Elise's bachelorette party, on the dance floor. Remember?"

She pressed her fingers to her lips, and he had to close his eyes for a moment.

"Yes. I remember it."

Good.

They sparred for several minutes more, neither saying much.

Finally, as she toweled off and they'd finished, she turned to him again. "I just, well, I didn't think it was real. The kiss I mean. I thought it was just a fun, happy kiss to a friend."

He needed to fix that right then. His gaze locked with hers, he walked her backward until she bumped the wall next to the door. "Does it make me *happy* to kiss you?" Leaning in, he brushed his mouth over hers, taking in the soft sigh she gave in response.

She opened slowly to him as he deepened the kiss, settling his mouth on hers, tasting, teasing, drawing her taste into his mouth.

Her nipples were hard against his chest. He wondered if he should wish he couldn't feel the points of her need against him, or if he should keep on reveling in how good it felt. Being a hedonist at heart, he went with the latter.

She settled in as he pulled her into him, her arms twining around his neck. Heat flashed through him and he didn't resist the urge to break the kiss and lick up her neck. Sick bastard that he was, the taste of her skin only drove him more crazy. If he didn't step back now, he'd be taking her to the floor and fucking her right then.

Licking his lips, he stepped back, grabbing the strap of her bag. He needed to rein in his need for her, to savor the little nips he'd taken from that delicious mouth.

Internally he battled with himself. He knew he was pretty fucking smooth with women. He knew they liked him, wanted more of him than he usually was willing or able to give. But this was not the same. She was not just any woman, and while he had no problems using his skills and wiles to woo her, he desperately hoped she saw him as more. Felt as if she did, especially after the engagement party, which had left him with the feeling that she understood him to the bone.

He'd never been so . . . unsure and off balance with a woman before. He wanted to do everything right. Wanted to take it slow, but not too slow. Wanted to ravish and worship every inch of her. It was disconcerting and frustrating. And part of that filled him with the surety that she was worth every little twinge of doubt.

That and the way she looked at him just then as they approached the elevator. She touched her lips with her fingertips and his cock stirred to life again, just when he'd wrangled it into submission.

"The kiss was real then and it was real just a minute ago. Despite what you might think, I don't just lay my lips on any old woman." He could still taste her. "Just ones I find myself unable to stop thinking about."

She turned, and in two steps he had her backed against a nearby wall. She swallowed hard, blinking up at him. Not afraid. What he saw in her eyes cheered him. Desire.

"I should seek treatment for the need to get you against walls and doors so I can get up on you." He said it as a tease, but it wasn't far from the truth.

The need to kiss her coursed through him. But he didn't give in, instead enjoying the sexual tension.

"Can you drop me at my condo? I bused in today."

Clearly she hadn't expected him to say that. Her grin was wry. "Yes, of course."

And *then* he dipped his head to take her lips, just a brief breath of a touch. She sighed into it, dizzying him with her response.

His phone rang, and he groaned at the ring tone. Ben's home number, so he grabbed it and answered.

"If you two even think of leaving this building without coming up here to say hello, I'm going to pout."

"Hey, Erin." He looked to Ella. "Erin says she'll pout if we don't go up to say hello."

Ella rolled her eyes. "All right. She's such a baby."

Overhearing the jest, Erin laughed and hung up as the car arrived on their floor. As they went inside, she tossed "Yes" back over her shoulder.

"Yes, you'll go out with me?" Inside the elevator she was so close, so warm. He had sweats on, and in a short period of time, she'd know just how much he liked her being so close and warm.

"Yes, I'd like to go out with you for pizza and beer. It's my last full day of school and my last day as manager at the café on Friday too, so that's something else to celebrate."

"I'll pick you up at your apartment at seven." He had to call on years of nonchalance to not sound like a stalker.

Luckily, she smiled. "All right then."

Erin was in the hall with Todd when they got out. She waved. "Come on in. I just made cookies."

He hung back, after seeing the look in Todd's eye. The women went inside.

"What's up?" he asked Todd quietly.

"Your dad called Ben a few minutes ago. He went to take the call outside, but he hasn't come back in yet. If I go out, well, Erin will know there's a problem."

"On my way. Near the greenhouse?"

Todd nodded, and he headed to his left when everyone else had moved to the open kitchen on the right. He caught sight of his brother standing next to the hot tub enclosure.

"Got a cigarette?" Ben asked when Cope walked outside.

"No. Hang on." He went back inside, quickly locating the French cigarettes his brother smoked occasionally.

"Here." He handed over the sleek black case and a lighter. He braced himself, knowing it must have been very bad indeed to drive Ben to smoke.

Ben lit one, looking out over the city. "Dad called."

"Todd said. What happened?"

"He wanted me to know he'd be happy to start a college fund for the baby."

Knowing there was more to it than that, Cope leaned against a nearby bench. "That so?"

"Yeah. As long as I get a DNA test to ensure the baby is mine, everything will be just fine."

Cope blew out his breath. "Jesus. What the fuck? Why would he do that?"

"Mom and I had lunch a few days ago. She wanted to be sure Erin had what she needed. She came to look at the nursery, all that jazz. She must have talked to him about it." Ben shrugged, but Cope knew his brother's eyes, and there was pain there, far more than the DNA comment would have caused.

"Ben, what is it really? Not that the comments about the DNA test don't suck, but you're upset, like really upset. What else did he say?"

"He said if I was thinking like my old self, I'd be finding myself my own woman or not watching so carefully when Erin went up and down stairs." Ben's voice thinned at the very end as Cope's head nearly blew off.

Cope didn't really know what to say. What *could* he say in response to that? He grabbed his brother's arm. "You know this is not right. And frankly, it's not about you at all."

"I know my father intimated I'd be better off if the love of my life fell and lost the baby. I never . . . I don't even know how to process that."

Cope's head reeled at what had been said, at the damage his father had done. "I don't either, to be honest. But I do know he's out of order, Ben. He is wrong, and you need to step back before this goes any further. This is not healthy for you. I love you, Mom loves you, Todd, Erin, all our family, blood and not, you have people who wish you only the best. At some point, you're going to have to let it go. Let him go if he can't find a way to not be a snarling fool."

"I know."

"Still hurts though." He hugged Ben then, and his brother hugged him back.

"Yes. It does, Andy."

Ben hadn't called him Andy in years. His brother was ripped open inside, and who wouldn't be? Thank God he'd come up to check in. To be there when Ben had needed him.

"You can't tell Erin. I don't want her to know. Her blood pressure has been elevated lately. I don't want any more stress on her. It's poisonous to imagine anyone wishing that on you. She doesn't need it."

"Of course. But she's going to find out eventually. She'll be able to tell you're upset. How are you getting around that?"

Ben heaved a shaky sigh. "She'll know I'm upset with the situation in general. She can't imagine—who could?—that he would say such a thing. I just can't bring this into our life, our family. That child is mine, no matter whose DNA it carries."

"Of course. No one who knows you would ever think differently." What outsiders would think was another thing, but none of that mattered just then anyway. "What can I do? Whatever it is, you know if I can do it, I will."

"You did it, man. You did it." Ben stubbed the cigarette out and grabbed his glass. "Thanks for listening. I know you've tried to help make him see reason."

"You're my brother and he . . . Well, I know he loves you, but this is . . . He's gone round the bend. I'm sorry."

"Yeah." Ben shook his head and stood up straight. "Let's go inside. Erin will be worried. By the way, how are things with our lovely Ella?"

"They are good, Ben. God, she's . . . I'm having a really great time getting to know her on this other level. She's here, now, with Erin. I just asked her out, and she accepted."

"And then you had to come up here to deal with family crazy. Sorry." Ben paused before opening the doors. "I like her. She's different than your usual type."

"What does that mean? And don't apologize for needing some fucking support. That's what brothers do."

"Why are you so bitchy?"

Good question. "What do you mean my usual type?"

"The one-night-stand type, Andy. Do you deny that?"

"No. But it's not like they were all bad or terrible." Or that he was.

"Of course not. Nothing wrong with fucking. But Ella is not that. She's different. She's not itinerant. She's the kind you bring home. Well, maybe to us instead of Mom and Dad. What's up your ass, anyway? I clearly touched a nerve, but I can't fix it unless you tell me what I did."

"You have enough shit to shovel right now. I'm fine."

His brother just looked at him in the way big brothers did, arms crossed over his chest, one brow up.

"Fine! I just hate that you see me as some asshole who only wants women for fucking."

"Is that what you think? You think I don't see you as worthy of something way more than a string of women you like, but don't like enough to share more than your cock with? You're not an asshole at all. But those women you blew through were not worthy of you, and you weren't being very worthy of yourself. I'm not judging the sex part. I'm judging the part where I stand here on my balcony with my pregnant wife inside being taken care of by the man I love. I know what it means to fit after feeling like I never did my entire life. You deserve that."

Oh. "Sorry I snapped at you."

Ben snorted and opened the doors, herding Cope back inside. "Comes with the territory. I snap, you snap, it's what you do with people you love. Just don't fuck this up."

"No pressure or anything."

Ella figured something was up when Cope went out to see his brother, but she wanted to check in on Erin anyway.

She loved this place. Beyond the initial *Oh my god this place is huge* impression, it was a home. A home Erin had built with not just one man, but two. It had been an unusual situation, but the longer Ella had known the three, the more sure she was that it was quite simply perfect for them. She'd rarely seen such love and commitment between two people, much less three.

"I can't believe you were here in the building and weren't going to come say hello to me. Todd, baby, can you please get Ella some tea?" Erin looked back to Ella. "Just made a pot of some calming blend crap I have to drink instead of coffee."

"We were just finishing up when you called. I figured you'd be resting or busy."

"*Pfft.* All I do lately is rest. Sit, sit. How are you?"

Ella sat, and Todd put a mug of tea at her elbow, squeezing her shoulder before he moved back to Erin's side. "Thanks. I'm good. Just had a workout with Cope. Started Christmas shopping yesterday. Thinking about a trip to see Mick this summer for a week. You?"

"Christmas shopping in mid-October? Show-off!" Erin winked.

"It's all good. I miss you at the café already, and you're not even totally gone yet. Things are fine, so get that worried look off your face. You are meant for other things, and it's not like we won't see each other since you'll be able to have a social life now that the balance is in favor of your other job."

Ella worried about leaving the café as Erin's pregnancy neared its end. But the guy taking over was good, had worked at the café nearly as long as Ella had and he cared about the place and their customers.

Erin was right. It was time. Even if taking that step did scare her. She smiled at Erin, noting how her friend's face had rounded as she passed into her eighth month. Ella thought it looked good on her but also that she looked tired.

"Of course we'll still see each other. My new office isn't even three miles from here. It's not like I'm going to disappear. You're stuck with me."

They chatted for several more minutes, Erin showing pictures from the most recent ultrasound, talking about the baby's room and other gloriously mundane things.

"It feels like forever since we've just hung out like this. Only this time we get the hot guy to bring us tea and baked goods." Erin smiled up at Todd, who kissed her quickly.

"We've all been so busy. It'll be better soon. I hope. We just need to carve out the time."

"Starting Friday." Cope strolled into the room and sat at the table, sneaking a cookie from the plate. "Ella's coming to pizza, pool and beer with me."

Erin's eyes lit, and a smile of a different type marked her lips. Ella wanted to laugh. Truth was, she still felt pretty giddy about it herself. Ella had to admit she loved the way he'd verbally underscored the *with me* part.

"Hey, Ben." Ella knew something was up with him. He usually

had a smile on, an easygoing walk. Just then she could see the stress around his eyes.

But he smiled at her, genuinely, dropping to kiss her cheek before settling on the nearby counter. "Hey, Ella. I was just telling Cope I was glad we'd get to see you more often outside the café."

Not that she'd comment, but he was talking about her to his brother? Part of her way deep inside fluttered and warmed. Fuck that. It was already fluttery and hot from the way Cope had kissed her. Twice. He'd been all manly and in charge. The way he backed her up against stuff, god, it pushed all her buttons in the best kind of way. Still, she needed to focus on that moment with her friends instead of the way she would be totally giving her vibrator a workout when she got home.

Ben was bothered by something. She wanted to follow up and ask him about the sadness in his eyes but worried that it might upset Erin, so she kept it to herself. She'd ask Cope about it when they left.

They stayed another half hour or so until Cope pleaded having to get up early the next day. She hugged Erin tight, urging her to rest, and said she'd see them all at the end of the week if not before.

"You okay?" Cope asked as they walked to her car in the building's garage.

"Just tired, I guess. Was Ben all right? He looked upset."

Cope watched her carefully as she peeked into the backseat before unlocking.

"Good. I like seeing that." He stood at his door until she got in and then followed.

"What?"

"You're being safe. It's second nature. You have no idea how many people I work with who don't even lock their front door, much less check the backseat."

She stared at him, wondering just when everything between them had deepened. She felt raw and exposed, but she wouldn't turn back time to what they'd been before, either. This time in her life was diz-zyingly confusing in a rather unexpectedly delicious way.

Ducking into the car and starting it gave her a chance to compose herself. "Thanks. I suppose there are things in life you learn the hard way. I'd have preferred to learn this lesson from the hot young stud teaching me self-defense."

"Hot young stud, huh? Hope we're both talking about me, or I'll be all embarrassed."

She laughed. "Yeah, I'll wait for that moment."

"Ha. I wish you could have skipped that hard lesson too. To answer your question, it's the usual stuff. My dad called. Ben's upset." He shrugged.

"Do you want to talk about it?"

He paused, and she didn't push. God knew she understood what it meant to have to stay silent on things. But that came at a price, and she hated to think about Cope having to pay it.

"I do. But I can't. Not now."

Her heart ached at the sadness in his tone.

"All right. But if you change your mind, you know where I am."

"I do. It means something to me that you care. That I know you do." He shrugged, and she felt the emotion behind the words blanket her.

They drove on for a while in comfortable silence until they got to his condo. Once she turned the engine off, the silence drew around them. Just Andrew and Ella. Alone. Butterflies in her belly, nervous and excited all at once. He did something to her, and she liked it.

He smelled incredibly good. Manly and sexy, and how is it that she'd never really noticed how good a man could smell? She hoped he couldn't see her sniffing at him and think she was a weirdo.

He looked out the window for the longest time, and she unabash-edly stared at him, taking that opportunity to do so without him noticing. Truly Andrew Copeland was simply ridiculously handsome. Outrageously so. Strong features, his cheekbones were perfect, his lush lips surrounded by a closely cropped goatee and mustache. His lashes, dark and long, only highlighted the intense blue of his eyes. Add the body, tall, broad, muscled and tattooed and the slow, sexy drawl and you had an irresistible picture. And that didn't take into account what a fabulous person he was in addition to the way he looked.

Each time she was with him, she learned more; he let her in a bit, and that trust, being a woman who found it hard to give trust herself, meant a lot.

Andrew Copeland was so much more than she'd known before. Complicated. Sensitive. Talented.

He sighed, not in a beleaguered way, but as if he'd come to some sort of internal decision. She fisted the fingers itching to touch his skin. To comfort and to inflame.

"Andrew, thanks for all your help tonight. With the lessons and all. I appreciate it."

He turned to her, and the breath gusted from her lips at the raw intensity he wore on his features. She swallowed and tried not to gawk. He was so utterly gorgeous he stole her words. And he didn't look grateful just then. He looked hungry. *For her.*

He took her hand, turning it upward, and pressed a kiss to the heart of her palm, sending a shiver through her.

"You move me, Ella. It's my pleasure. It's win-win for me. Keeping you safe and being with you."

She struggled to keep her composure, leaving her hand in his. "I can't believe you're saying all this after all these years."

"At first you were with someone else. And then you were hurting and had other priorities. I had to wait it out. Wait you out."

She wanted to cry, wanted to jump on him, wanted to throw her arms around him for understanding and for wanting her anyway. He said things to her, things that burrowed beneath the self-doubt and pain, warming her, making her believe in more than just getting through each day.

All she could do was look at him there, so very close to her, smelling all sexy and stuff, rumpling up her thoughts.

"Damn it, Ella," he stopped, running his free hand through his hair. He leaned toward her, and she stilled inside, knowing he meant to kiss her. Again.

She closed those few last inches, moving her body to his, the center console keeping her from jumping into his lap. The last thing she saw was the curve of his lips right before he made contact. Her eyes slid closed as the warmth of him blanketed her.

He took it slow, his hands grasping hers instead of holding her body close. Her system lit up like a pinball machine. She'd never been so ridiculously turned on by a kiss. How long had she waited for this? How long had this moment played itself in her fantasies?

Reality was far better than a fantasy.

Cope thought he'd die when he finally touched his mouth to hers, but then she made a soft squeak, moving closer to him, letting go of one of his hands to slide the other up the wall of his chest and up his neck into his . . . she tugged his hair, just enough to let him know she wanted more and wanted him closer. Waves of warmth, of pleasure and desire, rippled outward from his scalp down to his toes, making a long visit to his cock. He was pretty sure his cock was even more excited than the rest of him. It was different because she'd made the first move this time. She'd closed the gap between them in that shy/bold way she had.

He groaned into her mouth as she opened to him. Her tongue was tentative at first, nearly shy. Her taste, bright and seductive, drove him, along with the curve of her bottom lip, so juicy it called out to be nipped.

So he did, and the sound she made tore at his self-control. So much so that he laved away the sting and began to pull back before things got any hotter. He wanted to take her long and slow, not in a car on a street outside his house.

At the loss of contact, her lids flew up, and the stormy green haze cleared, leaving her expression distressed. He laughed, feeling much the same way.

"I know. But if I don't stop right now, the police will be called, and I'll have to explain to an old workmate of mine why I'm necking with a beautiful woman in public." He rubbed the back of his neck and gave in, leaning toward her to take her lips again.

This time *she* nipped his bottom lip, sucking it into the heat of her mouth, and his cock wanted to burst through the front of his sweats. He'd be masturbating about three seconds after he got through his front door at this rate. Again. His cock would fall off at this rate.

Breath heaving, he pulled back, pressing his body to the seat to keep from lunging at her again. Damn, she tasted so fucking good, like nothing he'd ever imagined before but would be damned without now.

Still, he didn't want her to think he didn't want more of her. But he'd not scare her with the realization that he wanted all of her. Not just then. "Tonight has been a very big win in the fantasy-gone-reality column. I've wondered what you would kiss like for years. That peck from the dance club wasn't nearly enough."

She smiled as she sat back into her seat, the worried look in her eyes fading. "Really? *Me?*"

"Yeah, you."

"And?"

"Better than I imagined. I'm planning to do more of that on Friday. Just sayin'." He opened his door and got out before he did anything else. The last place he wanted to feel the glory of her nipple against his palm was in a car after all the drama of the conversation between Ben and their father. And *damn* did he want to feel that.

He bent and looked inside at her and smiled. She returned the gesture, nearly felling him with the look on her face. "Night, Cope. I'll see you on Friday."

"Night, Red."

Her laugh topped his day, wore away some of the sadness about his dad, and he straightened, closing her door and waving.

He strolled away, looking back at her, watching her pull out into traffic and drive toward her place.

8

Ella wiped down the stainless-steel counters in the small kitchen in the café for what would be the very last time. She smiled as she did it.

"I'm going to miss this," she said to Erin, who sat nearby drinking tea and eating almond cookies Elise's mother Martine had brought by sometime earlier. Her OB had told her she needed to spend more time off her feet and resting. "Well, not the cleaning up part. I'm just fine to hand that off to one of the others. But I suppose, feeling a part of this place, like it was mine too."

"If you make me cry, I'm going to pinch you." Erin winked, her eyes already shining with tears. "This is an awesome time in your life, Ella. Celebrate it. All the best parts of your past will still be here without the crappy pay and having to wipe stuff down."

That was true. "Pay wasn't so crappy because my boss was a soft-hearted wench. This café was my safe place for several years. It'll be hard to lose that."

"*We're* your safe place, El. Me and Elise. The guys. We're your family. You don't need to pull lattes. You have your degree, you have a great job and you'll take the crappy part of your past and use that to help people get to the good part of their future."

"Now you're going to make *me* cry, and I can't pinch you because you're pregnant." Ella sighed and hopped up to sit on the counter. "I feel like it's graduation day in a sense, you know? I'm scared. Not that I can't handle my new job. I love that job, and I think I'm a good fit for it. But you know, the other things in my life that are all changing all at once. It's exciting and scary."

"The dating stuff?"

"That and having a social life. I feel . . . exposed maybe? I didn't do so well the last time I tried this. What if . . ."

"What if it's you? What if you're just a horrible judge of character, and you'll attract some guy who'll do to you what Bill did?" Her tone told Ella that Erin thought it was all bunk.

Damn. Well, she supposed that's what you got when you had real friends who understood you, warts and all.

"Yeah, I guess so. Am I so obvious?"

"Here's how I know. I rolled out of a self-induced haze of self-loathing and fear to see Todd. Could I actually have something with this man who had gone from my life years before? Could I, totally messed up and broken, risk opening up to anyone new? And then there was Ben." Erin laughed. "Just when I'd figured out how to be with Todd, here comes another man into our life. I took chances, and yeah, I was afraid."

Ella grabbed a cookie. "But look at you now."

Erin rubbed her hands over her belly. "Yeah, look at me. Happy. In love. Loved like I'd never imagined before. It's not easy. It hasn't been easy. I hate that Ben and his father have this huge gulf between them. I hate that two of Todd's siblings won't even speak to him. I brought that into their lives, and I regret it."

"That's not your fault."

"It's totally my fault, El. But that's all right. Because in the end, all that's anyone else's business is that everyone in our relationship is treated with dignity, respect and trust. We have that. It's not traditional. It's not what anyone's mom and dad would have planned for, but other than the basics, it's none of their fucking business. I'm not giving in because some jerk can't deal with something that isn't his to be worried over. What's it to Billy Copeland that Ben is in love with two people? How is that any of his business? It makes Ben so sad, and that's what bothers me."

"I'm sorry about all that. And you're right, it's not their business, and it's not their choice."

"And there's not some flaw inside you to blame for Bill. *You* broke up with him. *You* got a protection order. *You did everything right*, Ella. *He's* the one who was wrong. He's the one who hurt you. Andrew Copeland is a lot of things, but he's no thug. He's *gone* over you. I've never seen that before. And you are blossoming at this new stage in your life. Your eyes are clear, there's a bounce in your step and you will make this work. Because you're you."

"I invited Bill in." She hopped down from the counter and began to put things away. Hanging the spoons, tucking clean linens back into drawers. "I brought him into my life. I chose him. I loved him at one time."

"It's not as if you didn't pay for that. An awfully big price for such a stupid mistake. So you liked the wrong dude. You had kicked him out and had moved on nearly a year before the attack. You made the right choice, Ella."

Ella didn't know about that. Sure, she wore scars that reminded her every day of the cost she'd taken on for knowing Bill. He'd hurt her. But she'd allowed him to. What did that say about her? She heard the bells above the door chime. "Duty calls."

"Go home early to get ready." Erin came out right behind her. "You've done your job here." Erin took her hands. "You helped me through some rough times. Just your staying here through school while I got my life in order and through the pregnancy this far has been so important. Thank you."

Tears sprang up, and she couldn't stop them. She hugged her friend. "You saved me, Erin. You went to court for me, with me, you stood up for me when I couldn't be there, even though you had bad memories. You gave me more responsibilities and a decent paycheck here so I could be independent and finish school. You have always been my friend. I'd never in a million years be able to repay you for your myriad kindnesses."

"Aw man, you two."

They broke off the weepy hug to face Adrian, who stood at the counter, grinning.

"No tears. This is a happy day." He winked at Ella, reaching out to thumb away a tear on her cheek.

Ella liked looking at Adrian Brown. His was a face that called out to be looked at. But it was his voice that always made her pay attention. He had a very specific sort of cadence to his voice. Not an accent, but he held on to the words as if he tasted them. Listening to him speak was like lying in a hammock, rocking slowly, the breeze caressing your skin. He had this way about him, honey-slow and sweet.

He had a stunning amount of charisma, the sort of man who could make just about anyone feel special just by being near. It was all part of a whole package that was only enhanced by the fact that he was an extremely nice man.

"It is. I know it is, thanks to you both." She mopped at her eyes like a doofus and sniffled her tears away.

Erin looked back toward the kitchen and then to Ella again. "I forgot to grab my schedule book. Ella, hon, can you go and get it for me? It's on the desk in the back."

Ella nodded. "Lock up, will you, Adrian? It's officially after closing," she called over her shoulder as she went into the back to grab Erin's book.

She should have expected it, but it was still a surprise when she came back out and saw all her friends had gathered with food, smiles and even balloons.

"Surprise!" Elise bounded up and hurtled Ella into a hug. "You're now living your new life. How totally awesome is that?"

Tears gone, Ella just grinned at the assembled group. Brody, Elise, Todd, Ben, Erin, Adrian, Rennie. *Cope.* He looked at her then, and there wouldn't have been a way to tear herself from that gaze, even if she had wanted to.

Truly, what a gorgeous sight he made in nothing more complicated than jeans and a sweater. The toes of the boots peeking from the jeans and the way he stood telegraphed that he was way more than just a pretty face. Mmm, he totally pushed every button she had.

Talking went on all around her, but her attention was snagged on Cope. He walked toward her until he was right in front of her, stealing the air from her lungs. He leaned down and kissed her, right on the mouth, right in front of everyone else.

At first she was startled, but then she sank into it, letting him take, giving back in full measure, and Lord above, she liked it. Just two or three months before, even the thought of kissing someone would have given her some serious sweats. Any reaction other than pleasure seemed silly just then; the glory of the way he tasted sang through her system.

It was him, Cope, the way he was with her, the fact that she knew him and trusted him. That made her open, comfortable to be titillated and seduced.

It wasn't a long, sloppy kiss, but it wasn't the way you'd kiss your friend either. She resisted the urge to slide her fingers over lips that still tingled when he pulled away slowly, his body heat still against her, his scent wrapping about her senses.

"Congratulations, Ella Tipton."

She swallowed hard and looked up into his face, loving the details

of him. "Thank you, Andrew Copeland. I can't believe you're all here."
She should have looked around at the assembled crowd who laughed and
talked, filling the space with their own brand of boisterous noise. Should
have, but made no move to do so and look away from that mouth.

"Christ, Ella, when you look at my mouth like that, it's all I can do
not to snatch you up and get us both out of here and behind a locked
door." His voice was low. Intimate. Tense with desire, and she felt it
to her toes.

She made a man like Cope feel that way? Just by looking at his
mouth? Power unfurled in her belly, warm and pleasant. Who knew?

"I kind of like that, Andrew. I must say." She knew she blushed,
but it felt too good to hold back.

Startled, he laughed and kissed her again, keeping an arm around
her waist as he broke from their embrace and they turned to talk to
their friends.

"You guys are all so awesome. Thank you. Really." It had been a
few years since anyone had thrown her a party of any kind. The last
one had been a subdued one when she'd been released from physical
therapy. This was way better.

Elise hugged her again. "Did you think we'd let your last day go
by without cake? Hello, we're an *any celebration is good enough for cake*
crowd, after all."

"I figured we'd have cake tonight."

"Um, duh. But that's pineapple upside-down cake." Erin shrugged
and then handed Ella a giant slice of double chocolate mocha cake.
"This is chocolate death. Two very different, albeit necessary, flavors
when it's a party for Ella."

Ella had been notorious for her love of cake, and over the years,
it had become their little social thing. Her way of being part of the
group, even when she didn't do much socially with them. They'd celebrate things large and small over cake and have an excuse to just hang
out and enjoy each other.

She took a bite and had to close her eyes to have a private moment with her taste buds. "This is a whole lot of yum on one fork, I gotta say."

"You like? Karen said to let her know what you thought. She was thinking of calling it the Ella." Adrian put a second slice on his plate.

"Karen, huh? You still seeing her?" Karen was the owner of a bakery in West Seattle. Adrian had met her when they were planning Elise and Brody's wedding, and they'd gone out here and there.

As he'd spoken, Cope had moved so that he rested behind her, her body leaning against his, his arm wrapped around her waist.

"I like her. She likes me. She's not looking for more than dinner now and again, and I'm too busy to be looking for anything else right now." Adrian shrugged.

"She makes a mean chocolate cake." Elise refilled Rennie's milk as she spoke, and Ella found herself charmed by the routine of mother and daughter.

"She totally does." Adrian agreed quite cheerfully and went back to his.

Ella snorted a laugh and absently began to straighten things up until the café's new manager sent her the stink eye. "Nope. Not your job anymore. Sit and eat cake. I can wipe a counter down."

So she sat eating cake, drinking coffee and just hanging out, feeling freer than she had in a very long time.

"So I have a question."

Ella looked back to Cope and wanted to sigh wistfully at how pretty he was. "What's that?"

"Clearly you're Irish. If the red hair and freckles hadn't been a clue, you having a brother named Mick would do it. But Tipton?"

She laughed and turned up her Irish. "Ah, 'tis a complicated tale, that. Mick's given name is Michael, but everyone calls him Mick. For my uncle on my dad's side and my great-grandfather on my mother's side. *His* father came from Ireland. He was a laborer when he arrived and eventually settled in New York. Then my grandfather was out here when he was in the navy, and he came back after the war and got a job at Boeing. His daughter, my mom, Moira, met James Tipton while they were juniors in high school. James comes from a family where his grandmother came from Ireland to work at her uncle's clothing shop in Rhode Island. Now, here's the great shame." Ella shook her head mock-sadly. "The man who won the lovely Rose Byrne's heart and who became James's grandfather was himself an immigrant from England. William Tipton. We forgive him, though, because he let his children be raised up as they should be: Irish and Catholic."

Cope studied her a moment before deciding it was all right to laugh. "I can't believe I never heard that story before."

"My grandmother used to say that my grandfather was just as Irish as his children and wife were. My family sort of takes their Irish seriously, but not so much it's not a laugh."

"All right then. Now I know what not to bring up when I see them next."

"Just keep an eye on the nearest exit. They do like to talk about it. A lot. You should see holidays when we're all together, generations of us. It's loads of gingers with freckles. We do have some goth ones in the generation just younger than mine. Take a moment to imagine Hot Topic black hair dye on someone with my complexion."

Cope choked on his cake, and she patted his back. "I can't believe you just called yourself a ginger. I mean, you totally are."

"I wasn't aware it was a secret."

He looked up, his mirth gone, the intensity back again. "Some people get offended by the term. God, do I love red hair."

Oh, the stuff he said! She took a deep breath, simply enjoying the back-and-forth with him. "Well, it's a good thing for me, huh?"

"I plan to make it so, yes."

"Whooo. You're really good with all this. I feel like a total amateur by comparison."

He kissed her fingertips. "You do just fine."

Before she could make an idiot out of herself, Rennie bounded over and pulled up a chair. "I have a school fund-raiser coming up. Can I put you down for a box of these fine chocolate treats?" She thrust a paper at them.

"I most definitely would. How about I take five boxes? That way I can give some to my mom. She likes fine chocolate treats too." Cope pulled money from his wallet as Rennie flirted with him. The little girl was as bold as Erin but graceful like her mother.

"I'll take three. I'll give some to my mother too. I'll be sure to tell her it's from you." Ella grinned.

Rennie neatly printed Ella's and Cope's names before getting down to the business of some good school gossip. Ella was not only charmed by Rennie but by the way Cope was with her. So gentle and silly. It was funny how all the men she saw on a regular basis were scary on the outside, big and braw, but gentle, truly kind and careful with the people they loved. It was disarming, Andrew Copeland's sweetness made her gooey and witless in a most delicious way.

"Do you need a ride home?" Cope asked her later as they left the café, full of cake and coffee.

Her smile was pretty much the same one she'd had on her face all afternoon. "No, but thanks. I've got my car here. I had to run some stuff by my parents' house for Mick. My mother is doing a big care package for him. And you don't care." She laughed.

"If it concerns you, I care."

They paused at her car once she'd unlocked the door. "He's in Central America, out in a lot of really far-flung and rural places, so he'll be thrilled to get magazines, his favorite cookies, that sort of thing." She snorted. "Do *you* need a ride?"

"I'm tempted to lie just to get some more time with you, but no, I'm just up the block too." He slid a knuckle up her throat. "I'll see you in a few hours then."

She nodded and fell into the soft kiss he gave her before stepping back to let her into the car.

"Bye."

Holy smokes. Ella licked her lips as she drove away, not allowing herself a look into the mirror to see him again. She'd get into an accident if she caught sight of those legs, those thick, hard thighs, that butt, oh that butt.

She sighed happily and settled into the seat. She had a date. With Andrew Copeland.

It was that happy thought that guided her to Café Diva to grab some beans. She was dangerously close to being out of coffee. In the old days, as in until that moment, she'd have grabbed some from the back of the café and buy them wholesale.

Erin used to get pissy when she tried to pay, but she'd understood the whys of it and respected Ella's need to do things that kept her independent and in control of her life.

But it wasn't the old days. And today would be the day she bought her coffee from the same place the café did. Like an adult. She might have told Cope about it, had thought of it, but maybe she just wasn't ready to say it out loud yet and own how lame it was.

So she parked her car, only a lucky four blocks down. The area was thick with businesses, and parking was at a premium. Having lived in Seattle her entire life, she thanked her parallel parking skills after only two tries.

The sidewalks were crowded with people out for the afternoon. Cafés were full as the shoppers went from the metaphysical bookstore to one of the last indie record stores in town. Fabric from the clothing shops brightened a day mostly made gray by the lack of leaves and the cloud cover.

Diva loomed just ahead, fairy lights strung in the window. The scent of freshly made donuts reminded her to grab some of the spice ones her father liked so much. She smiled, thinking of how pleased

he'd be when she dropped them off when she delivered the other stuff
for Mick.

At the crosswalk, traffic had bottled up, jostling everyone waiting.
Someone bumped into her. She lost her footing on the slick sidewalk,
and a hand caught her upper arm, hauling her upright.

Panic began to boil up, and she began to argue with herself furiously to calm down and handle it. There was talking. To her as they
asked her things. She managed to respond as she nearly gagged on the
fear and then the shame.

She got across the street, sweating despite the cold. Pushing it
back, pushing it back even as her muscles jumped and her head hurt.

Each step got her closer to the doors. Luckily for her, the woman
behind the counter recognized Ella and waved, beckoning her deeper
into the dimly lit coffeehouse. Normally, Ella loved the feeling of
the place. Big comfortable chairs and couches littered the room. The
newsstand just out front provided plenty of material to while away a
few hours drinking coffee and munching on their ridiculously good
donut holes.

Right then it felt claustrophobic and overstuffed.

She managed to get a bag of coffee and to get back to her car. Once
the door closed and locked behind her, she gave in and let the tears
come.

9

Ella stood in front of the mirror. For a time she'd debated even going out that night, but in the end, it had felt like she'd have given up if she had canceled. Besides, why not look on this night with her friends as some sort of treat or bonus after that fucked-up foray to get coffee.

She took a sip of the strong brew, softened with lots of milk and sugar. Before she got into the shower she'd put on a pot to brew, and when she'd gotten out, Elise had put it on the bathroom counter to wait for her. Each drink was a little victory lap in her head. She owed part of that success to Andrew and the classes he'd given her. He'd planted the seed within her, the confidence in her inner and physical strength.

Elise had come over early to help her turn her normally flat-ironed, smooth, chin-length bob into a tousled mass of big curls. She was Ella still, but with sparkles, and who didn't like sparkles?

"You look so pretty." Elise stood just behind her in the doorway.

Ella looked back at her eyes and the job her friend had done. Some brushes and what seemed like two dozen little pots of color, and suddenly Ella's eyes were mysterious and sexy. Combined with the hair, she didn't feel so very bad in comparison to the other women she'd seen Cope with in the past.

She took a last measuring look and realized something. "I don't look startled."

"Startled?"

She hadn't told anyone of her experiences some hours before. "Sometimes it feels like that's my go-to expression. Startled. Frightened. Like a high-strung teacup-sized dog."

Elise leaned against the doorjamb. "Hmm. I've never thought of it that way."

Ella of the mysterious eyes looked at her friend's reflection in the mirror. "What do you think of it as?"

"Well first of all, you're long and lean with a big rack. That's not in a teacup dog neighborhood, dumb ass. And then, I have to say, startled is never a word I associate with you. You're eminently capable of most any task. Keeps my life in perspective, that's for sure. I envy your focus."

Ella turned, raising her brows in surprise. "My focus?"

"You know, El, you're so much more than the time you were with Bill and the attack. You took something shitty and you made a new future. Most people don't do that. They hang on forever. It's easy to stay in that pit of despair. Or let it be your excuse for not moving on."

She understood the tendency. "So my focus is bad?"

Elise laughed. "No, goofy! What I mean is you're good at things. You handle things. You make up your mind to do something, and you will stop at nothing until it's done. *That's* focus. You let yourself forget that. The thing with Bill was fleeting. You were Ella before, and you're Ella now. You are tenacious. Your eyes, your facial expression more often than not is determined, focused. Startled is what happens to deer when you surprise them. You are a lot of things, but that's not one of them."

Elise tossed a scarf her way, and Ella tried it with the slim, deep blue scoop-necked sweater she wore.

When the fear and shame choked her enough to gag just from being jostled by some random person on a street in full daylight, it seemed to her the thing with Bill was more than simply fleeting.

It had claimed parts of her psyche, and she hated that. That's why she wrapped the scarf just so and put on pretty earrings. She would not cede to him one more inch of herself than he'd stolen. "I've been one thing for so long I sometimes forget I wasn't always that person."

When she was growing up, she was good at everything. She was on the honor roll all through school. She was a cheerleader, on the debate team. In the winters the Tipton clan went sledding and skiing, though ice camping was still the kookiest idea she'd ever heard. She'd been vivacious and outgoing. There'd been boys including her high school sweetheart, the sweet boy who'd fumbled around with her in his parents' basement on the fold-out couch.

Sometimes *that* past was hard to bear. Hard to bear because in the middle of the night when she was alone and couldn't sleep, she drowned in the memories of who she was and then of the fall she'd taken into who she'd been with Bill.

Elise nodded, listening.

"I hate that person. She's weak and a victim."

"And you have no idea how she could have ended up in that place where she made choices she never imagined she'd make. Enduring things she knew were bad." Elise understood that.

"Yeah."

"Let me say this. You're making the right steps in the right order. You got your life together first. You got yourself in shape physically, you took care of school and now have a way to not only support yourself in the future, but you're helping people who also made dumb choices and ended up hurt. And now you can have the room to explore being a woman again, in the romantic sense."

She pulled her boots on as she thought about it. "Yeah, I think so. But Elise, Cope is so, gah, he's just like, a jump to expert level. Maybe I should date with training wheels men first. When he kisses me, oh my god, it's like all my body lights up. I've never been so hormonal! He touches me, slides his thumb over my knuckles, and it makes me quivery."

Elise smiled knowingly. "That's the best, isn't it? He's been hungry for you for a very long time. But, wow, the way he is right now? It's intense. He wants you in a way he's never wanted a woman before. At least not in the time I've known him. He wears what he feels about you on his skin. Aside from being sexy, it's beautiful to see."

"Do you think? Oh never mind! It doesn't matter. Here's what I think. I like Andrew Copeland a lot. I've known him for years. I *trust* him. I also know I've never felt so fluttery and discombobulated over a man, and I'm digging it. I've decided to let myself be happy about being giddy. I've decided to let myself go with it, wherever it goes, without second-guessing."

"I'm on your team for all that." Elise grabbed her coat. "Brody made me promise to leave before Cope got here. I'm going to run back home. I'll meet you at the pub."

Ella laughed. "He did?"

"He did. I'm guessing there was some guy meeting or something. Erin and I have been taunting them that five beefy dudes have to unite to stand against us three. *Pfft.* I think they just want to give you both some space. They're already sure of Cope's intentions toward you. Brody said he couldn't think of a better man for you."

"Aww! So sweet, these boys. All right. He's supposed to be here in fifteen minutes, so go on home. I'll see you all in a bit."

Elise hugged her. "I'm so excited for you! I felt like such a rock star each time Brody looked at me when we were falling in love. I still do. Cope looks at you that way. It makes me giddy just watching you two."

"Stop planning our wedding already!" She gave her friend a playful swat. "It's our first date. Let's not rush this. I'm having this lovely time with a man I've crushed on for years. I know he's a nice guy, but he comes in bad boy wrapping paper. This is all a lot of wonderful stuff. Enough wonderful without all the forever I see in your eyes."

Elise, still laughing, left with promises to see her again shortly.

Cope stood on her doorstep and took a deep breath. Damn, it felt good to finally be in this place. Years he'd wanted her. At first he told himself it was stupid and to ignore it. Then he knew she wasn't ready, but he never let go of his attraction to her. And then she began to blossom and open herself up to more. And led him to be standing on her doorstep ready to take her on their first official date.

He wasn't outwardly spiritual or woo woo in any way, but he did believe, quite strongly, in fate. He knew he was right where he was supposed to be. Taking the first step in what he hoped would be many into a relationship with Ella.

He knew exactly what he wanted, and it was right on the other side of the door.

He heard music, her scratchy, cartoon-voiced humming and her steps as she moved around. He smiled as he knocked.

When she opened the door, her gaze slid up his body and to his face, her lips curved into a smile he knew was just for him as she caught sight of the armful of flowers he carried. All as he stood there stunned. Her hair was tousled, like she'd just woken up and rolled from bed. Her eyes, normally gorgeous and often doe-wide, looked mysterious and smoky. The sweater molded to her breasts and down her waist to well-worn jeans.

She looked good enough to taste. He'd developed some sort of physical addiction to her, to touching her now that he could after so many years of yearning.

"Hello, Andrew. You look very handsome." She managed to be sweet and come-hither all at once as he handed her the flowers.

"Honey, whatever I am, it pales next to you." He reached up, caressing the side of her neck, up the smooth silk of her skin into her hair. Many men had a thing for long hair, but he loved the sight of a woman's neck, and hers was the ultimate aphrodisiac.

"You look beautiful. Sexy." He moved closer to her; she held her ground, looking up into his face. Without breaking his gaze away, he closed the door at his back. They stood alone in the quiet, small entry. She wore perfume, earthy and spicy. Interesting, he hadn't noticed any perfume before. How could he have missed it?

"I've never experienced anyone like you before," she whispered.

"How so, Red?" He kissed the tip of her nose because he could and because those freckles called to him.

"No one has . . ." She licked her lips. "You look at me, and I feel like I've had a glass of champagne or something. You make me drunk with, *gah*, I don't know, your sexuality maybe, your presence. Whatever it is, you have it on at ten, and I can't seem to get enough."

Her skin, so pale, sprinkled with ginger freckles; the curve of her cheeks, the lush pillow of her bottom lip, that red hair he was so in love with, that and her voice, the voice no one else on earth had, everything about Ella Tipton called to him. No one was like her. He wanted to laugh, but she'd just exposed herself in some sense, and he didn't want her to hesitate to do so again.

"I think that may have been the best compliment I've ever been given." He dipped his head and kissed those lips, the wrapping on the flowers she held crinkled, their heady scent mixing with whatever perfume she wore and the heat rising from her skin.

He groaned, the flowers stopping him from hauling her against his body. Frustrated by the reality that they would be expected at the pub by their friends. When all he wanted was to take her to her bed, undress her slowly and kiss every single inch of her body.

She sucked his tongue, bringing his hips forward into the softness of her body. The fingers of her right hand dug into his left biceps, holding him in place as he plundered her mouth. Damn it, she tasted so good he never wanted to stop kissing her.

Still, he did bring her the flowers, and he hadn't gotten three steps into her place before he started smooching on her. He broke the kiss, resting his forehead against hers as he tried to get his breath—and his control—back.

"I missed you yesterday. I tried to stop by the café, but my schedule was crazy all day long." He followed her into the tiny kitchen, where she put the flowers, none the worse for wear, into a vase.

"Well, I did see you today."

He liked the amusement in her voice.

"Well sure. But not yesterday."

"As much as I like seeing you, I figured you were busy. Ben came in to give Erin a ride home, and he said you were taking your mom to a doctor's appointment in the afternoon. Is she well?"

"She's fine, normal, pretty healthy. But the stress of this rift over Ben is hard on her. She's having trouble sleeping and all that sort of thing."

Her smile softened, and she reached out slowly to cup his cheek. "I'm so sorry. I wish I could help."

She was helping, and she had no idea. Just the way she listened, the way she calmed him down and made him warm and happy was helping.

"I really wish I could have you all to myself tonight." He hadn't been prone to blurting in a very long time, probably since he was a teenage boy.

She grinned, ducking her head, the delicate pink of her blush rising up her neck and making his mouth water with the desire to kiss her just there, at the base of her hairline where he was sure she'd be very sensitive.

He sighed. "But we have a date. They're going to be in our business enough as it is. Imagine if we were late."

"Enough for what?"

He exhaled slow, looking for his self-control. "Long enough to make it count."

The moments between them thickened, the energy between them heating. It felt good to be with her, good to have this back-and-forth, and the sexual tension made him as antsy as he'd been at sixteen. Just bursts of desire as he thought about her all day long. When they finally landed in bed—and he knew without a doubt they would—it would be something major.

He held his arm out. "Come on, before I decide to take that invitation in your eyes." They walked to his car, his arm around her shoulders.

The drive to the pub wasn't very long. Long enough for his car to smell of her, just lightly, almost as if he dreamed it up. By the time he parked the car near the pub, it had wended its way through him, exciting every part of him, body and mind.

"Did you get a new perfume?" Again with the blurting. She smiled at him, amusement in her eyes.

"No. Well, sort of. One of my new coworkers gave it to me. Her sister is some essential oils whiz. It's got frangipani in it and something else, I can't remember what just now. I thought it was lovely. Is it too much?"

"Not at all. I love the way it smells. Warm. Sexy. Provocative." He smiled slowly. "Did you put it on *all* your pressure points?"

Her eyes went half-lidded. The long silence inflamed him and then made him nervous and the blurting thing seemed to need to return.

"I'm so glad I can finally say all the stuff I've been thinking. You're so sexy, and it's driven me nuts. I just, god, I just don't want to scare you or freak you out. Will you just, you know, give me the sign if I push a button or go too far? I'm torn every time I'm with you." Now that he'd said it, he hoped like hell she took it the way he thought she would. He had this need to tell her what she did to him. He wasn't used to that. Wasn't used to being unsure about a woman. Brody had laughed when he confessed this to the guys. Had laughed and laughed and then said, "Welcome to being in love."

Cope was pretty sure that's what it was. Love.

She turned to face him better. Even in the dim of the car, through the gap in her coat, he saw the shadow of her nipple on her right breast as it pressed against the sweater.

He licked his lips, imagining her nipple there, what she'd respond like. His cock ached, hardening against the zip of his jeans.

"Torn how?"

"I'm caught between this intense desire I have for you and wanting to protect you and take it slow."

"Oh." She smiled, cocking her head. "Sometimes I don't know what to say to you, Andrew."

God, she undid him.

"I vote for honesty. I'm not going to judge you. I like all of you, Ella."

She swallowed, licking her lips and driving him even more crazy. "That's a very nice thing to say. I . . . God!" She hit her thigh with her fist, and he took it, unfurling her fingers and laying a kiss on the heart of her palm.

She gasped softly but didn't take her hand away.

"You don't have to say anything. I don't want you to feel like you're being tested." He looked up at her. "It's just me."

"Okay, so don't laugh. I don't know if I'm doing this right! But since you voted, I will too. I vote, if it matters, for the former. Go with desire. I like the way you make me feel when you get up in my space and flirt. No, not flirt, you"—she licked her lips—"you turn your sex up so high it makes me sweat. But in a good way. No one has ever wanted me like that. It's ridiculously awesome."

He groaned, really wanting her to himself at that point. "Babe, you have no idea how much desire I've got pent up for you. I don't want to scare you. I know it's been a while, and you've only recently begun to have a more active social life and date."

"Andrew, you don't scare me. Not in that way." She paused, cocking her head to look him directly in the eyes. "Never in that way. But . . . you disturb me. You're big and bold, and I've just never truly imagined anyone like you saying this stuff to me." She laughed, lightning quick, catching her bottom lip between her teeth a moment. "Okay, well, I may have *imagined* it, but I never thought it would happen in real life. I don't know how to say this right, but I really dig that you want me. No one has ever regarded me with this"—she waved her hand at him—"level of sexual intensity before. It's . . ." She lowered her voice. "It's the most thrilling thing I've ever felt. It's dirty but only in, like, the best sort of way. I've never felt dirty like that before."

Relieved and admittedly pleased, he leaned back, relaxing a bit. "Well, I can do dirty as long as you understand it's the good kind."

Her laugh seemed to surprise her as much as it did him. She clapped a hand over her mouth, but he took it, laughing as well. Looking down, her hands in his, her fingers entwined with his, something inside him burst and filled him in a totally different way. She may not have felt that wanted before, but neither had he. He wasn't just Cope with her; he was Andrew.

What an odd moment; steeped with a lot of sexual energy, so much his cock ached, his balls crawled close to his body and every inch of his skin was hypersensitive to her. At the same time, it was sweet, old-fashioned in some sense, and he believed it was about Ella's spirit more than anything.

"I still want you to tell me if you're bothered." And he had to admit to himself, the idea that he could touch her more, talk to her more on a physical/sexual level greatly appealed to him.

"You're my friend, and I trust you. That you'd even worry about any of my past issues making me feel scared by your incredibly flattering attention only underlines how amazing you are. I promise you I'm not afraid of you. I may have some button pushed at some point—goodness knows I have a few of them—but if that happens, it won't be your fault, and wow, I sound so creepy."

He started to speak, but she pressed her fingers against his lips.

"What I'm trying to say is, I'm more than all right with the way you're being. I like all the sexy stuff, and back to your original question, maybe you'll find out later on. About the pressure points, I mean."

The top of his head nearly blew off at the idea of it. Of sliding his mouth along her neck, down in between the mounds of her breasts, the curve of her belly, south, past the desired valley of her pussy, to the backs of her knees perhaps.

"It will be my pleasure to await that moment."

Quickly, he leaned in, kissed her hard and pulled back, getting out to open her car door to recover from a hard-on the size of Wisconsin.

Cope opened her car door, and she took the hand he'd offered. He tried not to stare, it wasn't that she looked so very different than she normally did, but he wasn't normally her date either.

It made a difference, he realized as he leaned down to kiss her again. His to touch at long last. Her arms wrapped around his neck, and she fit perfectly against his body. "Ella, I gotta tell you I like the way you feel on me."

She hesitated and then snuggled closer. He smiled against her skin. "I like it too."

He kissed her again, just a quick one, before spinning and escorting her through the front doors of the pub, her hand in his.

10

Ella was pretty sure her smile might have looked scary or maybe just goofy. Either way, she was so freaking happy, she didn't care. He held her hand like she was his. While she'd been down *that* road, it was different with Cope. He didn't own her the way Bill had. That she knew it, felt it and wasn't freaked by this different version made her feel all well-adjusted and stuff.

Or something like it.

And she needed that feeling after her experience earlier in the day, needed to know she was capable of getting past the fragments of her past left inside her gut like jagged glass.

Their friends had already gathered in their normal spot near the pool tables in the back where the booths were gargantuan. Elise grinned and waved, the sparkle of the diamond Brody had given her at their engagement party catching the light.

Cope took her coat and hung it on the nearby rack with everyone else's before sliding into the booth beside her.

"Pizzas ordered. Beer should arrive momentarily." Brody leaned back, his arm around Elise.

"We were just ready to draw lots to see who'd play the first game. Erin is making some janky argument that since she's pregnant she should automatically play first. I, of course, call bullshit on that." Adrian rolled his eyes.

"I *am* pregnant, mister! I'll have you know my feet swell when I stand too long. The doctor even said so, smarty-pants." The impact of this statement was undermined by Erin's inability to deliver it without a snicker.

"Then you'll have sausage feet whether you play now or the next round. I'll even haul a stool over for you so you can sit and watch between rounds. When it's your turn, that is."

The server arrived with the beer, so the argument went away until everyone had filled their glasses.

Except Erin, who was drinking water with a twist of lemon. She lazily poked at Adrian again. "Shouldn't you be out cashing in on your rock star cred to pull some chicks?"

"Plenty of time for that after I play pool. Great thing is, my rock star cred won't evaporate by morning or anything."

"Children, please." Brody sighed and grabbed the straws. "Longest is in first game. Winner keeps playing, other three drop out. And so on."

Ella shook her head when he gestured her way. "Oh no. I'll just watch."

Cope nuzzled her temple. "Why?"

"I totally suck at pool. But I don't suck at eating pizza and drinking beer. So I'll watch from here."

"How you gonna get better if you don't play?" Adrian asked with a grin.

"Who's to say I want to get better at pool? Hmm? What if I just want to watch all you guys bend over so I can ogle your butts?"

Elise laughed. "Put that way, I can truly see the appeal."

Ella was just content to just sit and chat, taking one long look at Andrew Copeland's ass and then back to their group at the table.

"So how have you been?" Adrian asked, sliding a huge slice of fully loaded pie onto his plate.

"Since you saw me last this afternoon?" she teased.

"Yeah, but Cope came in, and I didn't get much of a chance to talk with you. He's an Ella hog." He took a measuring look at her. "How's life?"

"Um. I don't know. Mainly the same as it was last week, or even last year. But totally different. Which makes no sense, but that's the only way I can describe it."

"No, I get it. And good. I imagine if it wasn't a good thing, you wouldn't look so happy. When you first started at the café you were like this. And then it faded. Slowly so that I didn't really see it until I'd come back from a tour and you were not the same."

"Something like that."

"No, I mean it. But you've been coming into focus over the last year especially. You're blooming, and it's beautiful."

She blinked back tears. "Thank you for that. It feels like each day I have that's just normal is a win. And then I add in the other stuff. Good friends. Family. A good job." She looked over to the pool table where Cope had just bent to take his shot. A lock of hair had fallen over his forehead, his biceps gloriously bulgy against the wool of his sweater. She smiled at him as he noticed her. He blew her a kiss and took the shot, making it.

"That's part of the way you glow." Adrian spoke softly. "The two of you light up when you're together."

"As I told Elise as she eagerly planned the wedding earlier tonight, it's our first date. I like him. He likes me. I don't know what else it is past that."

"Little liar." Adrian smirked as he took a big bite of pizza. "You and Cope have been having foreplay for years now. More for him than you, at first anyway."

"Ew. Well, okay not ew, but what the heck did I miss?" Elise slid into the booth. "Foreplay for years?"

Adrian laughed. "I was disagreeing with Ella that this was her first date with Cope."

"Oh that. Yes, I agree that they've been dancing around each other for years. Though Ella didn't know it for some reason."

"Okay, hello, I am right here." She took a bite of her pizza and looked back at Andrew, catching his gaze immediately because he'd been looking at her too.

Cope moved to her, dropping a kiss on her forehead. "What's that smile for?"

"Just looking at you makes a girl happy, Andrew."

He grinned, a dimple showing just to the right of his mouth. "I'm at your service."

"Stop flirting and take your turn," Ben called to his brother.

"Hush, you. I've got something more important to do first." He kissed her again, this time on the lips, and went back to the game.

"Anyway," she said, blushing madly as she returned her attention to Adrian, "it's different. We know each other, yes, and there's a level of trust between us that I don't share with too many people. I haven't dated someone in years. *Years.* Believe me when I say this is new."

"But good, right? 'Cause, honey, you're giving off loopy happy like mad. There's something major between you and Cope." Adrian filled her glass as he spoke.

"I don't really know what it is beyond good, but yes, it feels major. Maybe just to me. But really good in any case."

Elise raised her glass, Adrian and Ella doing the same. "To really good. Also, dude, we've gone over this; it's not just you."

That was something Ella could wholeheartedly endorse.

Todd won, and Elise went over to take Ben's place. Erin managed to con Adrian into letting her play another round in his place.

Todd only rolled his eyes, standing behind Erin, his hands on her belly.

Cope slid in beside her, closer than he had to, not that she was complaining.

"Hey there."

"Hi. Sorry you didn't win."

"Not a chance with Todd playing. He's good. The only person nearly as good is Erin. Anyway, I'd rather be right here."

She poured him a beer, sliding it and a plate his way. "Plenty of pizza left. I saved you three slices of the everything."

"You're pretty perfect. Thanks." He dug in, totally satisfied with his life at that moment.

"You're welcome." She wore her joy on her skin, in her features, making the smile she gave him utterly infectious. Fuck, he was happy to be there with her. It did something to him, to watch her there with his friends, with those people he loved, and to know she felt the same about them. To a guy like him, a guy who put a lot of importance on connection to family and community, that she did too was simply a sign of how perfect she was for him.

"Are you free next weekend?" He needed to get that established right off. She wasn't just some woman he dated, they had more, and he wanted everyone to understand that. Especially Ella. The challenge would be to let her see his intentions without making her feel hemmed in or controlled.

"Sure. Wait." She eyed him carefully. "For what? My answer depends on yours. Ice camping? I'm busy. Other things that won't get me killed or give me frostbite? I'm available."

He laughed. "I was thinking of going to the ocean. No hiking or anything. One of my friends owns a house out there and offered it to me for the weekend. If it wasn't so damned cold already, I'd suggest a trip out on the bike. But we can save that until the spring since we know how you feel about ice camping."

She looked at him seriously without speaking, and he got nervous. "I mean, obviously he's got more than one bedroom. It's not . . . that's up to you. God, I'm fucking this up." He actually fumbled; he never fumbled. Good god.

Laughing, she hugged him briefly. "Yes, I'm free." She leaned a little closer. "It sounds like fun."

Her voice rose in a delightfully squeaky way at the end.

"All right. We can leave Friday night and get back Sunday after breakfast? Does that work?"

She nodded slowly, and he went back to his pizza.

The group hung on for another two hours until Cope was just about ready to text his brother to get the hell out of there so he could leave with Ella. Finally Erin stood and stretched her back.

"I gotta call it a night, boys and girls."

Everyone got up and tossed money down, put coats and hats on and headed toward the sidewalk just out front.

"You ready to go?" Cope said it quietly, his lips close to her ear. "Care to come back to my house for a while? I've got some ice cream to go with the cake you have left over."

"Mmm, cake." She actually giggled, and his cock hardened. What the hell else was she going to do that would turn him on so unintentionally? "Your house? Or the condo? I mean, yes to either. But I'd love to see the house."

He smiled at how easily flustered she got. "My house. I've finished enough that I've decided to live there. At least on the weekends. It's got a well-stocked fridge, my couch and electronics in the bedroom." And a bed. He shivered a moment at the thought of her in it, at the very real tension between them that could lead them there. But he didn't want to rush her.

"Are you cold?" She angled her head to see his face.

"Nope. I'm . . ." He broke off to return Brody and Elise's goodbyes.

"I expect to hear every last filthy detail," Elise whispered to Ella, though not quietly enough.

Ella's laugh resurrected the shiver.

"Have her home by midnight, son," Ben called to him.

"Ha. Take care of your pregnant wife. Ella is in good hands."

There was much hooting and laughter at that. Ella waved at them all with both hands. "Moving right along. Jeez. See you all later. Don't forget about me now that I'm not going to be pulling your coffee every day."

"Oh my silly, sweet Ella." Erin hugged her. "*This* is what we do. Every Friday night we come here, eat pizza, drink some beer or water, and we play pool while we catch up. Every. Friday. You are one of us, and you will have more time to do such things now that you have no more school and only one job. So there. There's no forgetting, dumb ass."

"We're like the Mafia. Once you're in, you're in for life." Cope hugged her to him. As if he had any intention of not seeing her every chance he got. *Pfft.*

"See you all next week. Erin, get some sleep!" Ella let him open her door before she turned to him, her breath white in the air. "Take me wherever you want me to go."

His heart stuttered as they stood there in the cold; snow fell but melted before it hit the ground.

"All right. Do you trust me?"

Again that slow, measured nod.

"Good."

11

Her heart beat so fast it would have been easy to blame her breathless state on that. But she knew that was a lie. It was him. One hundred percent the way Andrew Copeland waltzed his way right into her body and played her like an instrument.

Other than those few delicious kisses, he hadn't even touched her yet, but she found herself so turned on that even shifting in her seat was enough to send a ripple of pleasure through her from her pussy outward. They drove toward Ballard with an easy silence. Tom Waits whispered and howled quietly over the speakers.

"I had a good time tonight."

She winced inwardly at how lame that must have sounded. Instead, he reached and took her hand, squeezing it gently. "Me too, Red." He took a right onto a cul-de-sac. "Ah, here we are."

She looked down the street and knew without having to be told which house was his. He pulled into the narrow driveway, and she tried not to gape.

He must have spent a lot of time on this house. The others on the street were of like architecture, but his had been lovingly restored to its faux Northwest Tudor–type beauty. "I love the brick. You did some major restoration out there, didn't you?"

He turned and smiled. "Yeah. I do too. I worked out a barter, partially anyway, with a friend who knew how to be sure the brick met code and all that stuff." He hopped out and ran to her side to get her door. He seemed to like doing it and it didn't bother her one way or the other so why not?

"Come on in. It's going to be cold. At least the part I'm not living in yet. Have faith, Ella Tipton. I will build a fire and get us nice and cozy."

She smiled and let him help her out.

"I have a great deal of faith in you, Andrew. Show me the outside too. I can't see it all really well now, but I still want to see."

His smile was altogether new, something she hadn't seen from him yet. Pride, yes, but something more. She knew she liked it and wanted to see it again, knew without a doubt it was something he showed few.

The backyard was partially done from what she could see by muted moonlight and the back porch light.

"I'd like to put a water feature out there. Some benches. The trees provide great shade, and it's really a nice place to sit in the evenings. Brody and I put a small pond and rock waterfall in at Elise's parents' place a few months ago. It kicked my ass, but now I know how to do it."

"I like it out here. Lots of trees. A water feature would be lovely out there, especially if you had comfortable benches or a glider swing or something. Are you going to do some outdoor lighting too?" Her teeth chattered, and he laughed, putting an arm around her and sweeping her up to the back door.

He had two locks and, as she discovered when they got inside, a good security system. It didn't surprise her; the man did this for a living and all. But she relaxed more.

"Do you want some tea? I have some good whiskey to go in it. That'll warm you up." He grinned.

"I'll make us hot chocolate if you have the fixings. But only after I get the tour of the inside."

"You don't have to." He lost his confident stance, just for a moment, recovering quickly, but not so fast a girl with the same problem couldn't catch it.

She took his hand. "I know I don't. But I want to. You created this with your hands and labor. It's special. I want to see it."

He blushed. That touched her enough to tip more than halfway into love with Andrew Copeland. The man, she suspected, didn't show all of himself to many. So when he opened that part of himself to her, it shook her to her core. Cocky was charming and sexy, but it wasn't devastating. Humble, pleased by compliments on his work, the kind of man who read poetry and created the beauty she stood in right then, well, that was another thing entirely, and she had no defenses against that.

He led her through the parts of the house he'd finished, avoiding the bedroom for the moment. She asked questions that showed him she was truly interested and not just entertaining him.

That she found something he'd loved doing so much so beautiful turned him inside out. Exposed.

"I love it. The attention to the detail and design really takes it to a whole different level." She walked around, looking closely. "Did you study design at school?"

"Thank you" seemed sort of small for the way her praise made him feel. So he smiled at her and nodded. "Thank you. I think so, and I'm pretty glad you do too. No, I didn't study it, but I'm wildly flattered you'd think so. I just love carpentry and building. I like working with my hands."

"You're very gifted." She bent and peered closely, sliding her fingertips over the curve at the base. "Did you do this banister yourself?"

He had to swallow hard at the sight, at the graceful way she caressed something he'd made, the way it was so obvious she appreciated the beauty of it.

"Yeah. Though I'm still working on the other side. You like?"

She turned to him, her attention focused on his face as intently as she'd focused on his work. "I'm astonished, Andrew. This is"—she shook her head—"this is incredible. I can't believe you did all this. I had no idea how talented you are."

Warmth hung in his belly, in his chest.

"Thanks." He ducked his head again, the heat of a blush on his cheeks. "How about that hot chocolate?"

"Coming right up."

She made it, seemingly at ease in his kitchen, which only made him want her more.

"I like this house a lot." She stood, stirring the saucepan of hot chocolate as he rustled up plates and mugs.

"I do too. It's been a long time, but I feel really good about where I'm going with it."

"I can't believe I had no idea you were doing this." She filled the mugs, and he hummed his pleasure at the rising scent of cinnamon.

"Well, it's just a little project." He shrugged. "The living room is still sort of a mess. I'm mainly in the bedroom, where I've got a couch and the television. And a fireplace. Interested?"

She nodded, and they carried their loot upstairs, and he led her through the big French doors.

"Holy crap." She halted, looking around the space. "This is, well, wow, Cope, this is magnificent. I keep saying 'wow,' which is more about me just being totally overwhelmed by how much you've done and how beautiful this all is. I'm very impressed."

He indicated she put the mugs down on the table near the couch before he turned and bent to build the fire. It felt strange, her seeing such an intimate part of him and appreciating it. Good. He realized he'd half expected her to not get it or to wave away how much work he'd done. Shyness, something he hadn't felt in a very long time, settled into his system as he built the fire.

He came back and settled with her on the overstuffed couch. The fire began to crackle and pop. He'd gone with natural gas fireplaces downstairs, but he wanted the real thing in his bedroom. Seeing the way the color of the flames lit her skin, he knew he'd made the right choice.

He'd never had anyone up in his room. Not since he had the furniture moved in. It seemed fitting it would be her, then, to be the one sitting there with him, filling his senses with a thousand different zings of chemistry.

"Thank you, again. Really."

She sipped her cocoa and looked at him over the rim of the mug. "You should be really proud of yourself. This is a major undertaking. Lots of skill here. And time, I imagine. How do you get it all done around your day job and training friends how to fight off attackers and flirting with women at the pub?" The smile she quirked up allayed any ideas of her jealousy.

"I like to work here on weekends and at nights. At first it was a big job, so all I could see was how I had to do X, Y, Z before I could move on. After a time I realized part of living here was making the physical changes to make this house truly my home. I do what I can when I can, and I don't resent it when I have other things to finish up." He shrugged.

"That's a very good way to look at it. It's quite an accomplishment to have done all this. What does your family think?"

"Oh well, they don't really; we don't talk about it much."

She leaned forward, putting her mug down and turned to him more fully. He liked the way she firmly gave him her full attention. It was rare to see in most people who generally only half listened while they texted or thought about television or whatever.

"Why is that? I'd imagine Ben would be over here helping you with stuff all the time."

"He's got a baby on the way. They've all got stuff going on. It's just a house. Erin, Ben and Todd did a huge remodel not so long ago."

She wore a sour look for a moment. "Erin hired people to do the renovation. Which is great, but not what you're doing at all." She motioned around the room. "This is all you."

She pushed every single button he had. Disoriented, he shoved a hand through his hair, moving it back from his face. He was Cope, the easygoing lady-killer, and here he was, sniffing after a woman who already had immense power to pull emotions from him in the most unexpected ways. Mainly because she saw he was more than Cope, the easygoing lady-killer.

"I need a haircut," he mumbled, feeling suddenly totally out of his depth. Did he even have any depth? Was he just a fraud?

She put a hand over his, sifting through his hair herself, her fingers sure and firm against his scalp, bringing a groan of pleasure from him.

"No. I like it." The statement was shy, but she meant it. He tipped his chin to see her face, as always, struck by how it appealed to him so deeply. "I mean," she said, licking her lips, "if you don't have to cut it for work or anything. It's just, it suits you."

"You do something to me, Ella," he said, moving toward her slowly, not wanting to spook her but needing to kiss her.

"Glad to know I'm not alone," she said, her lips moving against his just as he made contact.

Her taste wended through him, opening doors he'd welded shut, some he hadn't even known existed. Like a key.

Forcing himself to take his time, he moved enough to slowly unwind the scarf she wore around her neck loosely so he could put his lips there. When he did, when he finally pressed his mouth, slightly open, to the pale expanse of skin just behind her jaw, she took in air, letting it out as a soft sigh.

She was warm there, and, as he'd hoped, sensitive. She tilted her head back to give him more access, her fingers gripped in the material of his sweater.

Slowly, drunk with her taste, his lips slid over the hollow of her throat, and she stuttered a breath. It wasn't until he licked over the freckles just below her collarbone that she uttered his name, softly, raggedly.

It was enough to challenge his control, enough to rip his defenses to shreds. Not enough; everything.

She arched, changing their balance, and he went with it, landing on top of her, the long, wiry length of her body beneath him, her breasts pressed to his chest.

Her eyes, which had been closed, slowly opened and focused. With her watching, he bent to lick over the exposed curve of her left breast and then the right. He'd meant to tease her, but got caught in his own trap because he could do nothing but bow his head over her and breathe in before sliding his hands up her sides. In another breath, her breasts were in his palms, and they both groaned.

Cope had to lever up a bit, nipping her bottom lip before turning his attention back to her breasts. "You have no idea how long I've wanted to touch your breasts."

"Glad you finally got to it," she said, her voice squeaking. Her grip tightened as he slid his thumbs back and forth over her nipples.

"How are we doing?" he asked.

She yanked at his sweater. "Huh? Shirt off. Please, Andrew, I want to see you."

Well then, that was a good answer. He moved to kneel above her, her eyes roving over his body as he pulled the sweater over his head and tossed it somewhere behind them.

"Oh." She sat, taking in the upper body she'd remembered from some backyard party two summers ago. It was better than she'd remembered. Forgetting her hesitation, she had to touch. Hard, acres of muscles, olive-toned skin, tattoos and . . . "You got a new piercing."

Until she came to work at the café and saw Brody and his crowd of friends, she'd never considered piercings or tattoos to be sexy. But over time she'd changed her mind. She'd met and looked at a lot of really hot bad boys with ink, and by that point, she found it incredibly sexy.

Something about the barbell in each of his nipples made her mouth water. It was hot. Hot, hot, hot, and he wore them with such confidence it only made him more attractive.

"About six months back." Absently, he flicked a fingertip over his left nipple, leaving her dry-mouthed as well as achy.

Because he seemed to enjoy it and certainly because she did, she continued to touch him. Unable to help herself, she leaned in and kissed his side, her lips against his rib cage. He made a ragged sound, pushing against her.

Inside she warred with herself, because she needed him, trusted him, but she hadn't been so unsure of any situation so important for a long time. But his skin, his hands and mouth, the sound of his voice, they lured her into him, into wanting more than she'd ever imagined.

Control slipped from her fingers, and it was delicious and scary all at the same time.

"Ah god, Red, you feel so good," he rasped as she ran her hands up and down his torso, over the intricate lines of dragon scales of the huge Chinese horned dragon on his back and sides. Swallowing hard, she touched each nipple ring with her fingertips and had to close her eyes a moment.

When she tipped her head to look at that handsome face again, he was looking down at her. "You like what you see?" he asked with that quirk of the mouth that showed the dents of his dimples.

Her eyes widened as she remembered her fantasy of a few months ago, when she'd imagined nearly this same thing, though she was bolder in her imagination.

"What is it, baby?" He arched into her touch. "God, I love it when you touch me. So long, so long I've wanted this."

When he said that, it always stunned her. How could he have felt this way for years, and she never noticed? She'd wanted him forever it seemed, and now he was there and her hands were on him. How funny life was sometimes.

If her imaginary Ella could be bold, why not the real Ella too? At least a little?

"I had this fantasy about you. Well, okay, so I've had *way*, way more than one, but a few months back I was imagining you. You and me together, and you asked me if I liked what I saw. Just a little déjà vu, I guess."

"You had fantasies about me?" He took her hand gently, bringing it back to his nipple. "I like it when you twist, like—fuck yes—like that."

She twisted, not too hard or too far, but her pussy muscles clenched as he hissed with pleasure. That's when the inner Ella took over and licked from his belly button up to his chest.

It felt awesome.

He was so handsome, so big and male and confident. She loved it. Loved how ridiculously sexy he was. And damn, he was beautiful. She'd never known a person who wore their skin so well, who exuded all the things sexy seemed to embody. Being with him the way she was just then was like hitting the lotto.

She laughed at the thought, and he pounced, pulling her sweater up and over her head. Then he quickly looked at her face, panicked, until he saw she was okay.

Hmm.

"I'm fine." Reaching back, she divested herself of her bra.

"Wow." He whistled with wolfish appreciation. "Those are fucking magnificent. You have no idea how many times I jerked off thinking of them."

Her breath caught as shivers went through her.

"Too crude? Sorry."

She stood and moved to the bed. "Not too crude." Just totally not something she was used to. There'd never been dirty talk with Bill or the only other boy she'd slept with. Plenty of sex with the first boy-friend. Not a lot with Bill.

"Hot." And it was. So much so that it sent her reeling. She stood on shaky ground, mainly with herself and her confidence. Being with him, while totally right in so many ways, made her unaccountably nervous.

Which she knew was stupid. So. Perhaps they could work out something that would help. If he could trust her enough. If she could trust *herself* enough.

He grinned and stalked to her. "Yeah?"

She nodded and put her hand out, touching his chest, but holding him off. "I really, *like beyond really* want to have sex with you right now. A lot of sex. For a long time."

"Why you stoppin' me then, Red?" His hands slid over her belly. "Before I give attention to these." He thumbed over one of her nipples. "I want to see your back. Please?"

He must have some sort of pact with the devil. It was really the only way to explain how he always just seemed to know exactly what she needed to hear and when she needed to hear it.

Because it also gave her a way to hide her face, she turned quickly.

He moved close, so close she felt him, even though he wasn't touch-ing her yet. So close she could smell his skin and whatever shampoo he used. Thank god she had on her cute underpants.

"Brody is the king. Jesus, this is amazing. You've kept this whole design to yourself. We've only seen bits and pieces."

"He is. Brody being the king, I mean. I haven't shown it because, well, I'm not like Erin or Raven. They're so bold! It feels private to me, I suppose, something I've done for myself. Also, my back isn't nearly like theirs."

He leaned in and nipped at her shoulder. "Isn't nearly like theirs how? And does it have to be like theirs? It's better. If you could see yourself like I see you, you'd have nothing at all to say about others being bold. You are beautiful. Your back is beautiful, and Brody worked the ink to fit you and your skin tone perfectly. It's you. What made you think of this?" His fingertips made an alluring trip along her spine.

She smiled, flattered and pleased. "All I had at the beginning was this card my brother sent me. It came with one of his letters. It was a picture of a cherry tree next to this beautiful, rough-hewn water pond. The tree was perched at this precarious angle on the slope, but it had grown deep and strong. It didn't stand tall, because it had to adapt and grow strong from another angle." She shrugged. "You gotta have the sun. Anyway, he designed this sketch after I told him I wanted to do something large and why. There's one more part left to go, but really, it's pretty done. Just three floating petals from the tree left to add."

He kissed her shoulder, over the place he'd just nipped, his bare skin making full contact with hers.

"Amazing and beautiful. I admit I like it when ink means something to the person who wears it. It fits, strong and adaptable, like you."

She took a deep breath, leaning back into him fully, just enjoying him.

He leaned down to murmur in her ear, "It's going to be a miracle if we don't pull this house down around us when I finally get inside you. We got us some fireworks, Ella. Strong and hot." He slid an arm around her waist, his palm flat against her belly. "Now, why did you stop me? Because you say you want to have sex, and believe me, I do too. But you hesitated before I looked at your tat. I don't want you to hesitate around me. Especially here when we do this. Here, between you and me, when we're fucking, having sex, making love, whatever and all the above, I want there to be no hesitation and no fear."

12

He was right, and she agreed with him.

"I completely agree. But you may not, once you hear my proposition."

He turned her in his arms, brushing her nipples against his chest until she squeezed her thighs together to try to ease the weight of desire, even just a bit.

"Ella, woman, I *have* wanted you. Admired you. Been attracted to you. Liked you. Pretty much crushed on you like a lovesick boy for years now. I'm not leaving this bedroom with you until I've made you come at least three times. I need to be in you."

She blushed and decided to just machine-gun it all out so she couldn't overthink. "Okay, so the deal is, we've established that I want you inside me. We've established I'm not afraid of you. You're teaching me how to tackle the last few things, teaching me to gain more control over my life."

He nodded, solemn, his focus on her completely.

"So, um, I have a control problem. I mean, gah! I don't know how to explain it."

"Red, just tell me, and I'll do it. Even if the most beautiful tits on earth weren't brushing up against me this very moment, I'd still move mountains for you."

"God, you're so unexpected! I need to be in charge this first time," she blurted.

A slow, sly smile crept over his mouth. "Is that all? You can tie me up, spank my ass, blindfold me, well, that would suck because those freckles, that skin, those fucking breasts are so hot I'd hate not to be looking at them. But do what you will. I am yours to command."

"Really?"

He laughed. "Ella, yes. I want you. We're halfway to naked, and what do I care if you want to hold the reins? Tell me what to do, whatever."

Cope had been so worried she would put a halt to the entire thing, and this is all she needed? He'd go buy her bitch boots and a whip if she wanted it. He got it; she'd been controlled, and she wanted some control now. Fine. What did he have to lose by letting her have it?

"It's not like you think. Not really. I don't need to hold the reins. I don't think I'm cut out for being a dominant. Dominatrix? Whatever. I just need to be in control this first time. I know I'm not making sense. I'm sorry."

He looked at her, into her eyes, and he understood. She didn't want to top him, she just wanted to be on top, so to speak. Maybe to manage all the newness and doing something she hadn't in years. Maybe to wrestle back the past. He didn't know for sure. But he'd set the pace, and she'd stop him if he went too far. That's how he interpreted it anyway.

"You make sense just fine." He kissed her then, felt her relax against him, her arms encircling his neck and hauling him closer. "Guide me. Tell me what you want."

He loved the way she had to close her eyes for a moment to get herself together. Her nipples were hard, swollen, and made his mouth water. She wasn't afraid of him, thank God. She was horny. He could deal with that quite easily.

"I want you to touch me. Be with me."

"There's so much of you, I don't even know where to start," he murmured before humming his pleasure and licking over the freckles on her shoulder. "Damn, you taste fine."

She reached between their bodies, yanking at his belt, getting the jeans open, and she laughed.

"Didn't anyone tell you laughing at a guy when his dick is in your hand is bad form?" he teased.

"You know I'm not laughing at this." She squeezed him. "Though I must admit I'm a bit scared of it. I've looked more than a few times, and I knew you were, um, talented in this area. But this is, well, you're gifted."

It was his turn to laugh.

"I laughed because of course you don't wear underwear. Though I might have sprained my wrist if I'd have known."

He bent his knees to take her breasts in his hands and put them together to swipe his tongue over them again and again.

"Wait." He stood up, his pants open, cock out. "Your wrist? Holy shit, you mean from masturbating?"

She nodded.

"You should tell me about it." He grinned, and to his surprise, she turned off the overhead light, leaving the room lit by the fireplace. The surprise part was when she pushed him back on his bed and pulled off his jeans and socks.

"Wow." She looked him up and down. "You . . . your body is . . . Whew, I don't think I've seen anything so amazingly masculine ever."

He liked that. He stretched, putting his arms above his head, and she laughed, pouncing on him. "Tease!"

He kissed her, gently rolling her over. "Nope. I always deliver."

She smiled. "I want to look at *your* back now. I've seen it from a distance, but now I can look close. And touch."

He was probably going to die by the end of the night with her talking this way, but he managed to push himself to stand, and she—God help him—totally braless, those breasts swaying, taunting him, followed.

"Brody does such amazing work." She ran her hands all over the Chinese horned dragon on his back, trailing her fingertips over the place on his biceps where the tail wrapped.

He closed his eyes as she touched him. Gentle, hesitant at first, but then bolder, which he liked. Liked that she trusted him. Loved that she wanted him.

"Chinese horned dragons have protective qualities. They're very strong. Can't this one produce rain?" She pressed a kiss to his spine.

"Yes. The horned dragon." He turned, needing to touch her more. "Your pants are still on."

"You're pretty bossy for someone who just agreed to let me be in control." She said it, brow furrowed, trying to look serious. But the wide green eyes taking in his chest and his nipple rings said differently.

"I want to see you. I'm naked here." And so hard his cock tapped his belly. "You should be naked too. It's only fair."

"You're very full of it." But her hands went to her zipper, and he could have sworn he felt each click of the teeth separating deep in his gut.

"Holy shit."

He stared, openmouthed, as she stepped from her jeans, leaving her in thigh-high socks and a pair of boy-short panties with little kisses all over them.

She held her hands clenched in front of what he couldn't wait to touch. And taste. "Why do you look so stressed?" He kept his voice gentle, even as he took her hands, untangling them and kissing her palms. "You still with me? What's next? Definitely the panties and the socks. And then the bed, I hope. Though I can do standing up, sitting down, on the floor, over the couch arm, whatever you desire."

She blushed and in one quick movement slid her panties down her

legs and stepped out of them. He hoped she ordered him to do something really soon. Like before he embarrassed himself.

"Bed, I think. For this first time." She cleared her throat and stood
a bit taller. "Yes, that's what I think. Um, by the way, I don't need to
control *every* move you make. I'd wager you have way more moves than
I could even imagine."

He laughed as she moved to the bed. Quickly, he joined her, sliding
his hands up her legs, from her ankles to her mid-thigh where the socks
ended. An intriguing trio of freckles peeked from beneath the top.

"It's all been practice for this moment." He wasn't going to tell her
that right then he couldn't even recall another woman he'd been with.
She took up every bit of his attention and memory.

He began to roll down the left sock, leaning down to kiss the skin
he exposed. But she stopped him.

"I'd feel better with them on."

He licked up her thigh, over the crease where thigh met leg, and
delighted in her swallowed gasp. "Are you cold?"

"N-no." A sound came from her, low and ragged, as he breathed
over her mound, the sticky-sweet scent of her pussy greeting his senses
and laying him low. He rubbed the side of his face up her belly, kissing and licking to her breasts, where he planned to spend some quality
time.

"Then what is it?"

"I'd just feel better with them on." She squirmed, making an adorable squeal when he licked over a nipple.

"Is this about your scars?"

She stiffened, and he regretted bringing it up. Still, now that he'd
said it, he had to tread carefully.

"I just want them on. I feel more comfortable with them on. Do
you want to have sex or not?"

He rolled to the side and moved up so they could face each other.
"I don't want to have sex when we're like this."

She tried to get up, but he put an arm around her waist to stay her. "Let me go."

He sighed, letting her go. It took every bit of his control to stay there, watching her spring from his bed. "Are you really just going to leave? Now? After all this? We're building something here, Ella. Don't be a coward. Not when I know for a fact just how brave you are."

She stared at him for a long time without speaking and then plopped into a nearby chair. "You don't know shit about me, Andrew."

"Bull. I know you, Ella. I know you are strong and smart and steadfast. I know you have scars on your leg and you're afraid I'm going to see them and judge you. Fuck that. The only person I judge is the man who gave you those scars. And what are scars to me anyway? Huh? Jesus, what do you think I am? What have I done to ever make you think I'd reject you because you had some scars on your leg?"

"They're not *just scars*!" Angrily, she shoved the sock down to expose her leg. Tears brightened her eyes, and he shook his head, moving to her, even as she held her hand out to stop him.

He didn't want to blow off her concerns and the way she felt about herself, but at the same time, he looked closely and then pressed a kiss to her calf where the scarring was worst. He ruthlessly held back any pity at the sight of the scars, though he knew what sort of pain she must have experienced healing and in physical therapy. Pity would only make her withdraw from him further.

"They take nothing away from your beauty. *Nothing*. I don't care about this. Don't you get it? You're not diminished by this. It's just another part of you."

She pushed at his head, but he didn't move back until he'd kissed her knee. "It's ugly."

He laughed. "Ella, nothing about you is ugly. The scarring isn't severe. You're beautiful. Long and lithe. Your legs, even with the scars, are strong and shapely."

"I left. I did what I was supposed to do." Her jaw squared, she

looked pissed off. He realized it was the first time she'd ever said anything like that to him.

"I know. You did." He paused, still naked, cock still at full alert as
he knelt at her feet. "I want to see every part of you. From your head
to your toes, Ella. I want all of you." Deliberately, he caressed her calf
without breaking his gaze. "Don't hide this from me."

He got to her, and that made her nervous. She'd built a wall around
herself, protecting her emotions from anything dire. Even her family
was outside it to a certain extent. It wasn't so much that he was pushy,
but he refused to be put off. She couldn't hide from him because he
demanded that sort of honesty.

Could she give it?

"What do you say, Red?"

Before she could answer, he turned and pressed a hot, openmouthed
kiss just behind her knee where the scarring was the worst. Something
ripped from her as she looked down at him, his eyes closed, his mouth
pressed to her leg, the hand holding her firm but gentle. His hair so
dark against her pale skin.

Emotion flooded her as he touched the daily reminder of her shame
and stupidity. He didn't see them that way.

He opened his eyes, those deep blue eyes, and kept his gaze on
hers as he kissed a little higher. Using his body to open her thighs up,
exposing her pussy to him right at face level. She swallowed past her
fear and discomfort and reached out slowly, her fingers tunneling into
that thick, soft hair.

"Higher," she whispered, not knowing how the words she'd been
thinking had escaped.

Up he went, dropping kisses against the hypersensitive skin of her
inner thighs. Every once in a while he'd stop and lave his tongue over
a patch of freckles, which melted her insides for more than one reason.
How something so sweet could also be so ridiculously hot, she didn't
know.

But it was.

He slowed just an inch away from her pussy, and she couldn't stop her annoyed sigh.

"What now?" he asked, his grin so wicked she nearly came just looking at it.

Was he going to make her say it? She debated just letting it go. It wasn't like she'd been given oral sex in a really long time, so she couldn't really miss it. She could easily ask him to be inside her.

"If you can't say it out loud yet, just nod or shake your head when I say it. Okay?" He added that last bit, she realized, holding back a smile.

She nodded her head.

"Would you like me to lick this beautiful pussy until you come?"

Hearing the words come from his mouth, knowing they were about her, made her weak in the knees. Left her dizzy and titillated. Outside a porno flick, she'd never actually heard a man say it in that voice, much less to her.

When she nodded, she hoped she didn't look as eager as she felt.

"Scoot to the edge of the chair," he said, pulling her hips gently, helping her get into place. "There." He spread her labia open and looked at the heart of her. The intimacy of it, the depth of connection and trust she felt for him made it hard to breathe.

Then he licked her, and she lost her mind. She wanted to watch, but as his tongue made long, slow sweeps through her pussy, up and around her clit with just the perfect amount of pressure, she forgot, letting her head rest against the back of the chair, her eyes sliding shut.

His shoulders, the smooth, hard contour of his muscles, played against her inner thighs. He slid his hands, bigger than she'd imagined now that they lay against her skin, up her belly.

"God, you're talented," she whispered when his fingers found her nipples.

She hadn't been expecting it. Usually it took her longer to reach climax, but it hit her hard as he sucked her clit into his mouth. Her back bowed, mouth opened on a sigh of his name, as orgasm took hold from toes to scalp in a long, seemingly endless flood of pleasure so intense she saw stars.

"Sorry about that. I meant to drag it out."

When she opened her eyes, she found him resting, his head on her thigh, looking up at her with a smug, satisfied grin.

Ella couldn't help but laugh. He was irresistibly unrepentant. "Don't apologize. Hey, wow, listen to me." Her voice had roughened, toning down the squeak and higher pitch.

"Sex voice." Standing, he extended a hand to her, which she gratefully took, not knowing if her knees were ready to support her just then.

"What?" She shook her head. "While you tell me, on your back on the bed. Do you have condoms?"

Cope nearly choked as he moved to obey, getting on his back and really liking the way she looked crawling onto the mattress at his feet. "Yes. I have condoms." If he could keep from coming before he even got inside her.

It had been close enough as he'd been surrounded by her. Scent, taste, the feel of her all soft and wet against his mouth and lips. She lived inside him now, filling him in ways he wasn't sure how to process.

"I meant, you know, the way your voice changes after a really good orgasm. I can't wait to hear it again and again." He reached for her, and she obliged, scrambling atop his body.

"I've never had this happen." She slid her pussy against his cock; her breath caught as the head brushed over her clit. And then she did it again.

"You've never had sex voice?" he managed to say through a clenched jaw. Christ, he was the first to ever give her a mind-blowing climax? That was fucked up. Nice, he couldn't deny, being the first one to deliver it to her, but no one should be their age and have not experienced being a little fuck-drunk.

"No."

He reached for the condom he'd put on his nightstand a few days before. He'd tucked five more in the top drawer because he'd been a Boy Scout, after all, and being prepared would be a far better fate than not.

"So fast? I thought I'd reciprocate." When she licked her lips, she ground herself against him again. Only his eyes had been glued to her breasts as they'd swayed.

"If you put your mouth anywhere near my cock, I will blow. And it'll be over for a few minutes until I can recover. Have you ever thought about piercing one of these?" He pinched a nipple.

"Will I turn into a pumpkin at midnight?" She leaned to the side to see the clock, and her angle changed until the tip of his cock fit against her gate. "Oh." She stilled before circling her hips just a tiny bit. Enough so that the scalding heat of her slicked over him.

"Jesus. You're going to kill me. Order me to put this condom on and fuck you. I'm begging you."

"Go on then."

He wasted no time rolling it on, tossing the wrapper in the general direction of his wastebasket. And then she was over him, reaching back and guiding him into her with excruciating slowness. Sweat broke on his brow as she began to sink down on and around him.

Tight. Tight, hot and wet. So much so that she brought him to the brink by the time she'd fully taken him into her pussy.

Looking up at her, he was struck by the moment, by the long, pale beauty above him, that hair tousled around her face so sexily. Every inch of her skin exposed to his gaze, his hands and his mouth. "Never in my life have I seen anything so beautiful."

"I was thinking the same thing. I feel like I've won that big sweepstakes with the giant check and the balloons and camera crew."

Normally when women went on about his body or his looks, he became warier because they most often were just into him for that reason. But when Ella complimented his looks and his body, it was different, truly flattering.

She mattered, and part of that was that he mattered to her.

Then she leaned down, kissed him softly and began to ride.

Her hands braced on his hips, she rose and fell on him as he tried to hold back enough of his attention not to come, thinking of algebra and how he needed to get varnish . . . *fuck*. "Holy crap," he muttered as she swiveled on him. Well, *that* wasn't going to keep him from coming.

"What? Am I doing it wrong?" she asked, her words slow and thick. Damn. If he could hear that voice at least once a day, his life would be so much better.

"Just the opposite, Red. You're so right I just may come so fast you'll never want to do this again with me."

Her sleepy look vanished, replaced by surprise. "That's not going to happen." She wore a smirk as she said it, which only made him laugh. It'd been years since he'd laughed and talked so much during sex.

"Good to know."

Even through the condom, the heat of her drove him mad, made him yearn to be inside her, skin to skin. The pleasure of it was nearly painfully sharp, so tight. He wanted to break her fast—and clearly she'd been on one for some time, given the way her body surrounded him so snugly—with flat-out awesome sex. But she'd brought him to his metaphorical knees with the way she'd given herself to him, to this between them.

And so here he was, the experienced guy, self-assured and sexually confident, totally at the mercy of this redheaded siren rising and falling over him.

She stilled, her body pressed down as far as she could go against his, his cock deep inside her pussy.

"Everything okay?"

"This is so good." She stretched each word out, still not moving. "I can feel your . . . I can feel you move around inside me."

Her blush turned her skin an alluring shade of pink.

"My cock? It's twitching in there because I'm trying not to come."

"I'm not very good at this. I want it to be good for you."

Man, did he want to punch the ex in the face about eleven thousand times a day. "Ella, I was ready to come even before I got all the way inside you. That's one of the definitions of good for me. Not so good for you." He laughed. "*I'm* supposed to make it last. Also? I like being inside you. More than just about anything else I can think of at this moment. I can't imagine where you'd get the idea you weren't good at this." He could, obviously, but he wasn't going to go in that direction.

Ella didn't say what she was thinking right then, which was that he'd been with women who knew how to use their bodies better.

Instead, she concentrated on her body, on his as he fit inside her so well. Experimenting, she circled her hips, still seated against his. From the gasped snarl he gave in response, she figured it was something to keep in mind for next time.

Next time.

She laughed out loud, just for the joy of it all.

"Whatcha laughing about?"

She liked this position because she got to look down at the most beautiful man she'd ever seen. He wore a smile on that mouth of his. Mmm, that mouth.

"Just enjoying myself."

"Happy to oblige. By the way, it's my turn next. We'll see how I can torture you then."

She gave him another swivel and leaned forward to begin a slow, torturous up-and-down pace.

"If that's supposed to be a threat, you're doing it all wrong." His turn, huh? Having control this time was nice, something she needed to get over the fear. But she wasn't sure she'd need it again. Still, the idea of a little back-and-forth excited her. What would he do with his turn?

"Gonna kill me first," he gasped out as she changed the pace, speeding up, adding that circle as she took his cock into her body fully once more. It felt so unbelievably good. Sex had *never* felt like this before.

And then he reached between them, touching her clit and sending a ripple of pleasure through her system. "Oh!"

One of his eyebrows rose, and his mouth quirked up, but he didn't move his fingers away. He kept them there, sliding back and forth over her clit, building another climax. One she hadn't thought possible.

It filled her, a rush of pleasure flowing through her body, bringing her pace faster, harder against him as the need to come grew. At last she could hold it back no longer as it sucked her under, her inner walls contracting around his cock as he thrust up when she came down.

Her nails scored his sides, and he gave a long groan and came, his fingers digging into the muscle of her upper hips, holding her in place.

Limp, she rolled to the side, trying to get her breath back. He pulled her close, and she nuzzled his neck, loving the way he smelled and the security of his arms around her.

"Yep. Totally going to kill me. But I'll die a happy man," he murmured against her hair, making her laugh again.

"Yeah. I was right."

She managed to flop onto her back. "About what?"

"Chemistry, darlin'. We have it."

She smiled.

13

Cope had been smiling pretty much nonstop since, well, since he'd first gotten up the nerve to ask Ella out, but most definitely since they'd finally gotten naked and sweaty at his place.

Four days. It had been four days since he'd held her, kissed her, touched her skin.

Friday night had been the finest sexual experience of his life. Sharing with someone he connected to like he did Ella had been mind-blowing. The reality of her, of being inside her, her taste on his lips, her skin under his hands, had been far better than even his wildest fantasies about her.

She'd unleashed something deep inside him. Had held up a mirror, and the man she saw—the Andrew she believed him to be—was so much more than the Cope he'd allowed himself to coast into. He'd alternated between shame that he'd been so lazy and pride that she saw far more than the surface. Unerringly, Ella Tipton had stripped away all the artifice and struck deep, to the heart of him. That was humbling.

He needed to hold that to his heart just then. "Dad, wait."

His father turned around and, seeing it was Cope, slowed down. Cope knew if he'd run his father to ground at home his dad would have just used his shop to hide behind. Instead, he knew his dad and Todd's went to the Renton Fish and Game Club three times a week to shoot guns and the shit with all the other old retired cops.

Cope put his hands in his pockets and leaned against his dad's driver's side door.

"I didn't expect to see you today. I just finished up in there." Billy motioned back toward the building he'd come from. "But I can always stand some more."

Another area Ben had excelled in, marksmanship, was something he and their father had shared. Or they used to. Cope was good enough for the job, better than most in fact, but he wasn't Ben. His scores didn't still remain on the wall of fame like Ben's did. But Ben and their father didn't go shooting together anymore.

"Nah. I'm good. I was just at the range on Friday. Listen, Dad, I need to talk to you about Ben and the baby."

His father's smile slipped away, his mouth hardening into an implacable line. "Subject's closed, boy. Your brother has his head in the wrong place. More like he's using the wrong one. You have nothing to add."

And that was really the heart of it, wasn't it? His father truly believed that. "Bull. Dad, you can't call him and hint around that he'd be better off if Erin lost that baby. She's been having problems lately with her blood pressure. Did you know that? Can you imagine what you made him feel like when you brought up the chance of her losing the pregnancy? What the hell were you thinking? You can't possibly wish this. It's like you're a total stranger."

The narrowing of eyes and crossing of arms had kept Ben and Cope in line as boys, even into their teen years and beyond. Right then, though, Cope was more afraid his father had damaged the family past all ability to fix.

"This is none of your business, Andrew. If you and your mother would stay out of it, I'd have talked some sense into your bother long before now. He's not in his right mind. I won't pretend otherwise."

"It's going on four years now, Dad, that Ben's been with Todd and Erin. *It's not a passing phase.* This isn't about Ben's cock. Do you think so little of him that he would just make disastrous choices to get laid? Come on. As far as business goes? This is *my* business. My family is my business. You made a comment about your grandchild dying. How is that sense? That's crazy and hateful. Even if Erin was bewitching Ben in some way, what's it to you? This is nonsense, and you're ripping the family apart."

His father leaned close, but Cope stood his ground. "He's my son. He's meant for so much more than this. He's not even gay. I could deal with that. But he's got one of each and neither of them is worthy of Ben."

"Are you even listening to yourself? He's happier than I have ever seen him. Is he in a relationship you can talk about in the annual Copeland Christmas letter? Probably not. But so what? I'm with them all the time; I have zero doubt that he's not just loved by Erin and Todd but adored by them. They're making a family together. He doesn't need your approval of where he puts his johnson."

"Watch your mouth, Andrew."

He rolled his eyes at his father. "He loves them right back, you know. They're good together. They're having a baby, and it's *theirs.* Not Todd's, not Ben's, but *theirs.* I'm not asking you to think this is all great. I'm telling you, you have to find a way to deal with this. Mom is sick all the time. Holidays are the pits since you refuse to allow them in the house. We're all in the middle, and you're pushing everyone away."

"Why are you here? This is between me and Ben. Your mother has nothing to do with it either."

"Does she know you made that little crack about Erin falling down some stairs?"

Cope dodged his father's fist as Mr. Keenan came charging toward them, hauling Cope's dad back. "Billy Copeland! Stand down, man. This is your boy!"

"You're tearing us apart, Dad. I hope you realize this before it's too late. Some things you say can't be taken back."

"I should have said more a long time ago. Look at you! Can't be bothered to do anything but hit on rich women and charge them too much for security services. Your whole life is about getting ass, Andrew. Your brother is wasting all his promise in this stupid whatever the hell he's in. I failed the both of you."

Cope felt it like the slap it was. He took a step back. "Yeah, you did fail." He looked to Mr. Keenan. "I apologize that you had to get in the middle of this." He turned and walked away, his good mood disappeared.

For a moment after he'd walked into the café, Cope watched the table where his mother was sitting and knitting. She'd aged a lot over the last several years. The estrangement between father and son had torn her apart. And it hadn't just been their father who'd reacted so strongly against Ben's choosing to be with Erin and Todd. Their older sister had taken their father's side along with Todd's oldest brother and his wife. Holidays, once boisterous and filled with Keenans and Copelands, were now a more subdued and careful event. He knew it had taken a toll on everyone. Even his father's rock-solid friendship with Todd's father had taken a huge hit. After that morning, Cope feared there'd be permanent cracks between them.

"Hey, Mom." Cope kissed his mother's cheek before sitting down with her at the table. They regularly met at the café for lunch or coffee. It made Erin feel better to see her there, and it helped his mother feel more connected to Ben and the baby to come.

Cope walked it like the minefield it was, just relieved one of his parents wasn't acting like an idiot.

"You look good. I swear if I didn't know it was impossible, I'd ask if you grew an inch or two. Tell me what's putting that sparkle in your eye."

"As it happens, I'm, um, I don't know what to call it. Courting? Seeing someone in the early stages and trying to convince her she should take a chance on me. Whatever you call that, that's what I'm doing. It feels really good."

Ella came out from the back, her laugh catching his attention, yanking his gaze from his mom's face to where she stood in jeans and a long-sleeved shirt. She wore that smile of hers, the one he saw too rarely but yearned for. Open, joyful, it made her even more beautiful.

What an unexpected pleasure it was to see her, to hear her after not seeing her for a few days.

His mom laughed in the background. "I see. This lady you're courting, is it Ella?"

He turned back to her. "Yeah. I'm pretty smitten."

"She's a nice girl. Troubled past though." His mother searched his features, and he wasn't sure whether to be insulted or amused. Not clear on whether her comments were negative toward him or Ella, or whether he was taking it wrong. After his father's comments earlier, he knew he was oversensitive, so he tried to blow it off.

"Who doesn't have a troubled past these days? She's a good person."

His mother merely smiled mysteriously and then waved to Ella before turning back to him. "I know she is."

The *she* in question walked over with a carafe of coffee and a bowl, which she placed in front of Cope. "Nice to see you today, Andrew." She indicated the bowl. "Soup. Chicken wild rice." She topped off his mother's cup of coffee. "Any more coffee cake, Mrs. Copeland?"

"That would hit the spot nicely, honey."

"How about you, Andrew? Want a latte? I set aside one of those cinnamon scones you like for your dessert."

She knew he was a total whore for those cinnamon scones.

"I thought you were only in for mornings a few days a week."

"I'm here for lunch with Erin and Elise. I arrived first, though I heard banging around in the back, so I bet Erin is here now too and just came in through Brody's shop. I figured I'd bring you some food and coffee while I was here." She cocked her head.

"Well, since you're offering and all." He took her hand, kissing the knuckles. "Don't tell anyone, but you're my favorite barista. Any bread to go with? Or a sandwich?"

"I'm toasting the panini right now. Turkey and roasted red pepper. Latte?"

Man he wanted to lick her. Instead, he'd take what he could get. "You're good to me. And yes on the latte, please."

"You got it." She smiled and headed back to the coffee bar where the new manager laughingly got out of the way so Ella could get back there and make Cope's latte.

"A lovely girl."

Cope tore his gaze from Ella. "Yeah. Inside and out."

Erin came out from the back, and her face lit when she saw them both. "I had no idea you were here! I'm sorry." She sat with them, and Annalee gave her a big hug, followed by Cope's kiss on the cheek.

"How are you?" Cope's mother looked Erin over. "Nearly done with this blanket." She held it up, and Erin smiled happily.

"Wow. It's so beautiful! I can't wait until you're done. It's going to go in the nursery, on the rocker in there. Keep the baby warm while I'm nursing or rocking him . . . or her to sleep." She winked.

Elise came in, and Cope realized, not for the first time, just how beautiful and special the women in their circle were. She saw them and headed over with hugs for everyone.

And speaking of beautiful, Ella came back to put a latte and his sandwich on the table. "Here you go."

Erin snorted. "You're off duty. Sheesh, I can't get rid of you."

"I'm hard to shake off. Like the flu." Ella fluttered her lashes. "Why don't you have lunch with Andrew and Mrs. Copeland? Elise and I will just be over there." She pointed to a table in the corner where they all usually sat.

Cope liked Ella even more just then. It had taken a lot of time, but his mother and Erin were truly trying to be close, especially for Ben's sake. It made him happy to see Ella get that and try to help foster it.

"I'll be over in a bit. I'm sure Cope and his mom have a lot to talk about. But I'll grab both of them for some visiting while I can." Erin grinned and settled back into her seat.

"Hang on. I'll bring you some soup."

With that, Ella swayed off.

"She's a nice girl, that Ella." His mother sent him a raised brow, and he laughed.

"You don't have to put on a show, Mom. I totally agree with you."

"Not a show. But she's going to be work."

Ella came back and put some soup and bread in front of Erin. "Eat," she said, before going over to where Elise had settled in.

Cope watched her, hungrily taking in the way she moved.

"Jeez. Hello! Mother and pregnant sister-in-law here. Remember the other women in your life."

When he turned back, Erin was grinning at his mother.

"Anything worth having takes work," he quoted to his mother.

His mother reached out, squeezing his hand. "That's very true, Andrew. It makes me glad to hear you say that about a woman. A woman who's worthy of you for a change."

"Amen. All these floozies you've chosen, not a one has been good enough. Ella though, well, she's got guts. Style. Courage." Erin spooned up some soup.

"The women I've been with in the past were not bad people!" No, they weren't Ella, but no way was he going to have a conversation about sexual prowess and loving women who were in charge of their sexuality with his mother sitting there. "Anyway, I've already said it

several times; I totally agree with all the compliments about Ella. I'm
the one who's probably not worthy of her."

"Andrew, now you're talking crazy." His mother tsked his way,
shaking her head. "When you finally realize a woman of substance is
worth the work, you're taking yourself seriously too. Lord knows I've
been waiting for that. You're worthy. I promise. I'm your mother, who
else would know better than me?"

Erin laughed and nodded.

Had he been the only one not to see it?

Elise took a bite of her sandwich and leaned forward after shooting a
look toward Cope. "You'd best tell me every last dirty detail. I know
it had to be dirty, because he's a dirty, dirty boy."

They had seen each other over the weekend, but Rennie had been
along, so it wasn't the time to share any sex details. They'd spoken on
the phone, but again either Rennie or Brody had been around.

Ella looked over her shoulder, and they both laughed, catching
Cope's attention. He sent her a raised brow and then blew her a kiss.

"My god, he's like, lethal," Elise whispered.

"You should see him naked."

The laughing started again.

"So? Like, hotter than the sun?"

"His body is so spectacular I think I forgot my address just because
my brain stopped thinking of anything else but the way his abs look.
He's all muscular and tight. Golden brown. Both nipples pierced." She
fanned herself with her napkin. "I feel bad for talking about him when
his mother is just over there."

Elise rolled her eyes. "*Pffft.* It's not like she can hear us. Keep it
going. What else? Obviously you two did the deed."

"Twice."

"Nice! Brody has excellent recovery time too. He clearly knows what he's about. No man walks the way he does without being the shit in the sack."

"Such a way with words, Elise. Yes, yes, he knows what he's about. He's so, god, overwhelming. He's got such a sweet side to him. Did you know he was restoring a house in Ballard? It's magnificent. He's done all this work on it, and it shows. I had no idea."

Andrew Copeland was a far more complicated man than most would have suspected, though she often felt he liked it that way.

They'd sat in his bed, naked, eating cupcakes and drinking hot chocolate as he'd quoted Neruda. In Spanish. He'd reduced her to a pile of goo after that. More goo. Gooey-er? Whatever, that bad boy exterior had melted away, and she'd realized he had a soft, creamy center. More than that, he was so much smarter and accomplished than she'd ever given him credit for.

"He's something else, Elise. I felt all weird because, let's be honest, he's got way more experience with sex than I do, and he's so confident and stuff. But he, I don't know, he made me feel good, confident, like no matter what I did or how I did it, it was awesome. No one has ever made me feel like that." And she didn't quite know what to do with it all.

"When Brody and I hit that place where we both had fallen for each other in a big way, I think we sort of reeled with it. How can you process something so intense after not having that connection to anyone before? You and Cope have known each other for years. You're friends first, and that's lethal because he knows you. Knows you in ways some new guy you met and dated wouldn't. That's something good."

"Maybe. I mean, I do love that we're friends. I trust him. He makes me laugh. I don't feel like I always have to explain or entertain, whatever. Cope's just easy to be with, exciting, hot. All the best things about a man."

Elise took a peek at Cope again before asking, "So, um, did he go downtown?"

"I could totally pretend I don't understand your vulgar implication." Ella gave a mock-stern face. "But yes. Yes. Oh. My. God. Yes."

"What are you two hussies talking about?" Erin brought her food over, grabbing the empty chair they'd saved for her. "You're getting Cope all worked up 'cause he knows you're talking about him."

"I'd wager groups of women talk about Cope all day every day all across this fine nation of ours," Ella murmured and sipped her coffee.

"Spill the sex details." Erin didn't bother with any niceties.

"She already did. You're too late. Ha." Elise winked at Erin, who snorted.

"I'm totally convinced the details bear repeating. Plus, I'll pester you nonstop until you spill, so just don't waste my time. I'm gestating here."

Laughing, Ella leaned in and repeated some of the stuff she'd just told Elise.

Erin nodded. "This is all very good. He's all off-balance in the best sort of way. Like Brody was when Elise came around. It's fun to watch."

"I don't know about that. He's very self-assured." Whereas she was not.

"Trust me on this. I watched Brody fall and fall hard. I watched Arvin and Maggie fall in love. Hell, I watched Todd fall in love with Ben. All these hypermasculine men love to pull as much pussy as they can, but once *the one* comes along, they're charmingly befuddled and single-minded." Erin leaned back with a sigh. "That was very good. Thanks for bringing it to me, Ella."

They chatted for a while, but Ella had to get back to work, and Elise had afternoon classes, so their group disbanded. Ella had been surprised to see Cope still there with his mother. Annalee waved at her, wearing a big smile. Cope spoke to her for a moment and then got up, moving to the door to intercept Ella.

"You leaving? I'm sorry we didn't get a chance to talk." He traced a fingertip along her bottom lip, making her achy and tingly. He must have known this because he got the look. Oh that look of his. Turned her to putty every time.

"Gotta get back to work. I have a client intake in half an hour. I'll see you tonight?"

"I'll pick you up on the way and drop you home."

She knew better than to argue. He seemed to like ferrying her all around, so who was she to disagree when she liked being with him?

"Six thirty then?"

"Yep." He leaned in and kissed her quickly but thoroughly. "See you then, Red."

Blushing, she was sure she was every bit the red he loved to call her. She rolled her eyes and hurried out, not grinning until she'd pulled away and had turned the corner so no one could see her reaction.

14

He'd been preoccupied the whole time they worked out. Even as he went over various ways to break out of someone's hold, as he patted her butt or snuck kisses at the back of her neck, his voice held sadness.

She hated to hear it.

"I'd prefer to sneak out tonight," she said as they packed up. "I just saw Erin earlier today, and I think she's stressed and not feeling especially well. I don't want to bother them. Can you just drop me home?"

He took her bag and then her hand. "I can do anything you like, Red. Come on, I think I'd like to just get out of here too. I'm tired today."

They rode down the elevator in silence, but he stood close, and she was content to simply be with him.

"You're upset." She waited until they'd gotten about a mile from Erin's before speaking.

"I'm relieved to be with you. You do something to me, help me find that calm, quiet place inside where I can hear myself think. Hell, see? I didn't even mean to say that, but I did. You draw things out that I don't mean to share. But when I finish, I'm relieved, not sorry."

Wow. That was some commentary. It made her happy. But *he* wasn't happy just then. Not totally.

"Can I buy you a slice of pie?" In for a penny and she did have pie at her house. Pie made everything better. "Well, not buy. I have pie at my apartment. I can guarantee that my mom's pie is a million times better than store-bought anyway. She had me convinced when I was little that love was the secret ingredient. I nearly got into a fistfight with some other neighborhood kid who denied it. Oh, and I have decaf coffee. Or we can stop at B&O if you'd rather. If you want to talk to me about it, you can."

He was quiet for a long time as he drove, and self-consciousness crept in.

"You don't have to. I know you're tired. We can have a rain check and do it another day."

He laughed, taking her hand and kissing it quickly before letting go. "I'd love a slice of pie. I just don't want you to go to any trouble."

Despite her renewed state of fluster after his casual hand kiss, she managed to keep going. "It's pie. I can handle it."

"Of this, I have no doubt. You're an eminently capable person. I'm always impressed by you. And I want to be with you."

"Oh. Well, good." He found street parking a few blocks from her building, and before she could, he reached back to grab her gym bag, carrying it to the doors and then up to her apartment.

"Have a seat at the table, and I'll get the coffee started." She motioned and bustled about her kitchen, trying to find her calm again. "Pumpkin or apple spice? My mom makes the best crumble topping for the apple pie, if that's something you like." She'd made an effort, going over to her parents' house to drop things by for Mick and, while she was at it, delivering some of the donuts her father loved. Her mother had then stopped by her office that morning, delivering two pies.

It had been a while since she'd felt so much hope.

She turned and caught him watching her.

"I like the way you move, Ella Tipton. Just so you know."

Ella had no idea what to do with the things he said to her some-times. He seemed so casually sure of himself. But she liked it most of the time.

He grinned at how flustered she was. "Apple then."

She gave him a big slice. Having seen him eat, she knew he had a big appetite, and of course her mind wandered to how that translated to sex with him.

Sex had always been something she wished she was better at. Bill had been good at first. Kind. Saw to her needs in all sorts of ways, but he'd started to say things about how she was too eager for it, or too carnal, and how she was in danger of whorish ways. So she'd shut down. There'd been no girl on top. No oral. Missionary with the lights off. She'd kept totally silent because once when she made a sound, he'd told her she was wanton.

Now she had let the total opposite into her life and her bed, a man who seemed to love it when she was wanton. At times she struggled with what the heck to do with all the hormones running riot in her system all because of one Andrew Copeland who currently stared at her like he planned to do naughty things to her.

Which, she thought, wasn't a bad way to end her day. At all.

First things first, though. She put the plate down in front of him and joined him with her own slice of pumpkin. "Coffee will be done shortly. Do you want to talk about your dad and Ben? Is that why you're upset?"

"I do, but I can't, not right now. God, I wish I could." He sighed. "It has nothing to do with you, though, please understand." He looked so miserable she wanted to kiss his forehead. Instead, she leaned for-ward and took his hand.

"I understand far more than you think I do." She paused, licking her lips. They were on the verge of something, and she wanted to move carefully because they both deserved a deeper level of honesty. And because she cared about him and saw he was hurting.

"Sometimes things fall apart, Andrew. Sometimes you have to watch people you love be in terrible pain. And you're afraid that you can't fix it. And there are all these allegiances you have and you're trying to protect everyone and it's not possible to do that, of course, and so you feel terrible guilt because damn it why can't you just fix it? And then you can't speak about it for one reason or another. And silence when you're being torn up inside is pretty painful."

Her lip trembled, and Cope's heart ached. Her eyes held unshed tears, and he had to keep looking up at the ceiling to stop his sympathy tears in reaction.

"I respect your silence if that's what you need to do. But I'm here to listen to whatever parts of the story you can tell me. Or not. I'm here either way."

Then there was quiet as she met his eyes and smiled, and Christ, he just sort of fell all the way into balls-out love for Ella Tipton.

"Now, coffee is ready." She stood after a several long moments. "I'm going to make it and we'll have pie and talk about other things for a while at least."

The coffee was warm and good, what he needed along with the pie and her company. Even with the seriousness of the discussion, his attraction to her was undeniable. After being happily single for so very long, the utter certainty of how he felt about her fit him like a second skin. Each time they had these moments, he got to know her better, understood her more.

Something about her made him want to share. Christ, he found himself drawn to the way she just listened. He felt so quiet with her. Quiet so that he could enjoy the way she made him feel, the bloom of this new facet between them. Their chemistry was incredible, sensual, the tension between them growing in a way he'd never experienced before. So. Fucking. Good.

At the same time, it was all wrapped up with his need for her to know he was more than just that guy who'd flirted with her for years. With his concern that he'd rush her or hurt her unintentionally by pushing a button or acting like her ex for some reason.

"Thank you."

Surprised, she smiled. "What for? Pie? I can't take credit, it's my mom. And I'd eat every last bit of it if I didn't share it."

"I'm always thankful for pie. You're a good listener. Most people are good talkers. You're a good listener."

"Thank you for that. I figure if you can't be there for your friends, who can you? I don't want you to feel like you have to say anything to me at all about it. The last thing you need is more pressure. You're here for pie and coffee. That's all."

"You're not even going to try to kiss me good night?" He put his hand over his heart and pouted.

She blushed and then laughed so hard he had to lean forward and pat her back. More as an excuse to touch her than from alarm.

"Sometimes I don't know how to respond to the stuff you say." She rolled her eyes and sat back.

"That a good or bad thing?"

"It's an entirely Cope experience." She turned, pink. "It's good. Mostly." She tried to look severe but failed.

"I do like that for some reason." He relaxed, letting go of his hesitation. "I just feel this need to fix this, and I can't. It's miserable and there's so much anger and I worry things have been said and done that can't be taken back. My life seems very full of it at times. Sometimes, Ella, I wonder what's wrong with people. I get so down about the things people do and say to each other."

She tipped her head, and he reached out, sliding the edge of his thumb along her jawline. Her skin was so soft, pliant, and her lips parted in pleasured surprise as he stroked over the space just below her ear.

"And then you." He smiled. "You and my family and friends. You all remind me that there's so much more to life than the stupid shit people say and do. Thank you."

She blushed so prettily all he could do was smile at her like a total moron. She made this night better, made knowing his father had said those horrible things to Ben sting a bit less.

"There have been times when I was sure I would break. And then someone reached out, just checked in on me, sent me a card, stopped by the café to see me, whatever, and I made it through another day. That's all we have."

His everything was turned inside out because she was this thing he'd never considered he'd ever deserve, and it bloomed before him.

"I need you, Ella. Can I have you?"

She put her coffee mug down and nodded, a serious look on her face. "It's your turn."

Now it was his turn to be surprised by something she said. "That so?"

"If I recall. Though the second time on Friday was sort of mutual, I'll give you credit. Because it was a really lovely second time."

" 'Let me, then, be what I am, wherever, and in whatever weather . . .' "

She stood, holding her hand out. "That's lovely. What is it?"

He took it and let her draw him toward the bed.

"Neruda's 'It Means Shadows.' You let me be Andrew. Not very many people see the difference."

"I like Cope too, you know. But you can always be Andrew with me. And quote me lines of poetry. That's a bonus. Don't hide who you are with me. You don't need to. Here and now, it's just me and you."

He drew in a shaky breath.

"I know. Thank you for that."

She pulled her shirt up and over her head, surprising him with her boldness, pleasing him with the sight of her breasts and with the knowledge that she wanted him as much as he wanted her.

"Don't thank me, Andrew. I like who you are. I like *how* you are."

His control was gone, sifted through his fingers like sand. In two steps he was against her body, his mouth seeking hers, his arms encircling her, holding her close while he plundered her mouth with his own.

Her taste, always Ella, tonight a bit of nutmeg and the creamy coffee she'd been sipping, sang through his system, smoothing the jagged parts, exciting his senses.

They tumbled to the bed, a tangle of arms and legs, clothes flying everywhere. He fell into her every time he touched her, but just then it was fast and hard, submerging himself, letting the shock of homecoming rush through him.

He groaned as her bare breasts slid against his chest, the heated silk of her skin, the hard points of her nipples. And again when her nails dug into his biceps as she urged him closer. Some primal thing deep inside roared to life. She wanted him as desperately as he did her. He'd pleasured her enough that she wanted more, trusted him to give it to her.

That was big.

So big he tucked it away to think on later.

He ducked out of her way when she reached for his zipper, wanting to put her first and knowing if his pants came off, he couldn't resist being inside her. He had other plans just then.

Ella watched as he shimmied down her body, pulling her workout pants and underwear off. He paused at the socks, but then as he turned to look into her face, he drew them down her legs, first one, then the other.

He didn't then pay any attention to the spot with the scars, instead lowering his head to kiss up her inner thighs and across her belly. He'd been wearing his beard scruffy over the last few weeks, and she loved the way it felt against her skin. Not scratchy at all.

Erin had told her that all the guys with beards used conditioner to keep them soft. She shivered at the mental image of Cope standing in a shower stall, head tipped back as water sluiced down his body, his arms raised to wash his hair so his biceps would be all bulgy.

She sighed, always sort of awed at how much power he had over her libido. The intensity was marvelous but a lot to process.

He chuckled against her skin, but when he spoke, his tone was rough and jagged. "I love that sound you make. Makes me all hard and needy for you."

She made it again at his words and then he spread her wide and began to lick though the folds of her pussy, slow and torturous.

This Cope was more intense than the one she'd had sex with before. This was Andrew, mysterious and sensitive and pretty damned alpha male. She may not be at a place where she could admit it out loud, but it blew her socks off when he got like this.

Each time his tongue made it to her clit, he used a bit more pressure, building her pleasure relentlessly. Up and up he drove her as she clutched at the blankets. He held her hips, keeping her exactly where he wanted her. Her back bowed as he drew her clit into his mouth with just the right pressure, and she came so hard the neighbors would probably avoid her eyes at the mailboxes for a while.

Her body still humming with all that energy, she got to her knees and pushed him on his back. When she scrambled atop him, he smiled and put his arms above his head until she could barely tear her eyes from those damned biceps.

When she did, she wasn't sorry as the warmth of his neck blanketed her face when she nuzzled at the place where it met his shoulder.

She took her time, exploring his neck, over the blade of his collarbone, across the hollow of his throat and the rise of his pecs. Exploring him slowly, she sampled his skin with kisses and licks. Learned just how much he not only loved it when she played with the nipple rings, but that he made that guttural growl when she licked and nibbled his nipples.

"These are so sexy."

His sleepy eyes lost their haze and focused on hers. "You're what's sexy, Ella. God, look at you up here, driving me mad with kisses and caresses."

She scooted farther down, unbuttoning and unzipping his jeans, pulling them from his body. "Boxer briefs today?"

He laughed. "I had on denim and I was going to be working out, so I didn't want to, um, chafe."

In one movement she'd taken his shorts, and two more yanks and his socks were gone.

"I can't even believe this moment. You naked in my bed. My bed. Who knew?" Giddy, she kissed up his legs like he'd done with her. His thighs were as rock-hard as the rest of him.

The power of it warmed her insides. Confidence, yeah, that was the word she was looking for. It fit like she never left, but she pulled it tight around her, not willing to let it go.

The muscles in his abdomen jumped as she licked down over them.

"I don't want this to go to your head or anything"—she looked up from where she'd just situated herself, right above his dick—"but your body is hot. I've never, ever seen a man who looked better." And he was hers. At least for the next little while, because she knew as well as he did that they had some major chemistry.

"Too late," he said, strain in his voice. "It's already happened." He rolled his hips, bringing the head of his cock to her lips, so she kissed it.

She prayed he didn't notice what an utter novice she was but hoped she made up for her lack of prowess at blow jobs with enthusiasm. Something she had in great quantities when it came to him.

It wasn't as if she had *never* done it before. Just not in six years.

Closing her eyes, she took him into her mouth slowly, listening to the sounds he made in response, listening to his body language as he arched into her or trembled. His taste was something she'd never forget for as long as she lived. It mixed with the salt of his skin, the scent of his body, into a potent cocktail that seemed to drive her mad with want for him.

He guided one of her hands to his balls, so she experimented, making a few mistakes, but it wasn't brain surgery, after all, so it wasn't too long before she found a rhythm and a few moves that seemed to really work for him.

Finally, he took her shoulders and pushed her back. "Wait. Red, wait. I want to fuck you. I need to be inside you."

"Oh cripes, well, I hope you have a condom, because I just realized I don't have any at all." Wow was she a total dork. How could she forget?

Instead of anger, he just grinned at her, melting her spine until she collapsed onto the mattress beside him.

"I was an Eagle Scout, you know. I'm prepared for anything when I know I'm going to see you." He hopped from the bed and walked over to his pants, digging through his pockets. While his back was to her, she admired the hell out of his ass.

His body was a delight to say the least. His inky black hair, just a tad too long, wide shoulders, strong, muscular back covered in a massive tattoo of his Chinese horned dragon. Narrow waist, spectacular ass, powerful thighs and calves. She wasn't above being totally wowed by how gorgeous he was. He worked hard to keep himself fit; she knew that. But she also detected some wariness on his part when his looks came up. Oh sure, he flirted, but when a woman had been all about his looks, she'd noticed that he tended to keep them more at arm's length.

Not that she'd watched him snag a million women, wishing she was one of them. Not her. Nuh-uh.

As if he'd sensed her mental lying, he turned, holding up the shiny packet. "Got it." He had it open and rolled over his cock by the time he'd reached her again.

"Wow, that's some skill."

"All practice for you. I'm a very quick study when there's something I want."

He crawled over her, kissing all her best parts until he reached her mouth and settled in. She traced her fingers up his back, digging into that solid muscle to urge him closer, to urge him inside.

"You got a place to be?" he asked, teasing around her entrance with the head of his cock until she whimpered. "What's your hurry?" At that, he slowly pressed inside her as if he had all the time in the world and wasn't ready to explode like she was.

"My hurry? I'm going to die if you don't just get in there and start moving. It's really rather unfair of you to break my sex fast and introduce this diet of you and stuff, and then expect me to be patient about getting more." She furrowed her brow, and he laughed, pushing all the way in at long last.

"Better?"

She squirmed and caught the strain on his face.

"Ha! You want it too."

"Darlin', of course I want it. It's pretty much all I think about all day long, every day. Being in you, hearing your squeaks and squeals and the occasional sex sigh. I like those too. Now, let me do my work here."

He began a slow, deep rhythm, his gaze locked on her face, her eyes.

"You feel so good. So hot and tight. Makes being in you like this totally torture, but the best kind. It feels so amazing it's almost too much."

It wasn't enough. Just not quite enough. She wrapped her legs around his waist, and it adjusted her angle, getting him in deeper. *That* was enough.

It was even better when she noted the sweat on his forehead and the strain in his muscles. He was getting closer. She tightened herself around him, making him gasp, and she did it again a few more times for good measure.

He whispered in her ear. "Make yourself come around me."

Now *that* was wanton.

She slid her hand between them, her gaze still locked with his. She'd never in her whole life done this in front of anyone else! But she wasn't embarrassed, especially when he groaned once her fingers found her clit and began to circle it.

He hissed. "So good, so good . . ."

She wasn't long this way and when she hit her peak, he groaned her name, following her into climax.

Cope came back to her bed after cleaning up and smiled when he noted she'd crawled under her blankets. He'd never had such desire for anyone or anything in his whole life. He wanted her. Wanted her right then, tomorrow and the day after.

He burrowed under the bedding, sliding his body along hers and sighing contentedly when she snuggled into him.

"That was pretty awesome, Ella Tipton."

"Thank you. The feeling is totally mutual, Andrew Copeland." She yawned, and he toyed with her hair. "Will you stay?"

Nothing and no one could tear him away. Warmth that had nothing to do with the blankets stole through his insides at the shy yet offhand way she'd asked. How far they'd come in the time since he'd decided to finally make his move on her. "Perfect. Now I don't have to move for hours and hours. I don't have a damned thing to do until about nine."

She snorted. "Lucky you. You may change your mind about staying when I tell you I have to be up at six thirty so I can be out of here by seven thirty at the latest. I have an appointment at just after eight."

"Sounds like I'm on coffee duty tomorrow then."

She smiled, her eyes drifting closed. "Sounds like heaven."

15

When she checked her mailbox on Friday afternoon, it was stuffed with a fat manila envelope. Brow furrowed, she worried until she saw the return address and last name in the upper left corner. Cope.

Once inside her apartment, she opened the envelope and treasure after treasure slid from it.

Leaves pressed between wax paper.

An antique postcard from the Seattle World's Fair. To someone's Aunt Rose, from Josie. The handwriting was that of a young girl, enamored of the city, of the press and flow of traffic and people.

Three packets of tea, all described in some other language, the furls and pitch of which she was unfamiliar with. One was perfectly square and covered with a sort of parchment. The ink was deep purple. One deep sniff, and smoke met her nose. Spice and smoke. She'd have this one first.

He'd torn a page from a magazine. A feature on best breakfast places to go in Seattle. He'd written in Sharpie at the bottom: "We need to have waffles after a long walk in the morning mist. Then I can take you back to bed."

Wow.

And then a small square of paper. Turning it over revealed a pen-and-ink drawing of a woman's neck, collarbone and the upper curve of her breasts. From the freckles so accurately placed, he'd drawn her body.

She couldn't tear her eyes away for the longest time. It was stunning. Simple. Elegant and sensual. All things she never considered herself. But there it was. Through his eyes, she was all those things.

The sketch was most likely the finest compliment she'd ever received.

At last the folded sheaf of paper. She held it, drawing out the unexpected pleasure he'd given her. The weight of the paper was substantial. It pleased her to think he'd chosen it specially for her. He may have kept a sheaf of writing paper for general reasons, but she preferred to think he'd done it for her.

Unfolding it, she realized what beautiful handwriting he had. Each new thing she discovered about him only made her like him more. She had no idea he was such a talented artist with pen and ink as well as wood. Who knew he'd have a fountain pen with ink the shade of a bright summer sky? Andrew Copeland was one complicated man. Something confirmed as she read his words.

The tea is to take you away from your desk, from your dreary day and off, far away. Warm breezes, time to simply drink and enjoy the sights, sounds and scents of the world. When you come to me here at my house, we can share a pot as we laze about on a cold and rainy evening.

The sketch isn't nearly as good as it could be, as strong as my memory of that part of you I love so much. The long line of your neck, your skin so pale and perfect. And like a surprise, freckles spattered here and there with artful chaos.

I saw the postcard in a bin at an antique store in Marysville. I've been saving it, not knowing you needed it until after I slid the leaves into the envelope.

Upon night's breast, I fly to you each time I close my eyes . . .

Andrew

Whoo. She fanned herself a moment, trying to keep her bearings, when in reality, he'd shaken her. Her defenses against him crumbled. No one got to her the way he did.

She sat, the sky outside darkening, and realized her feelings for Andrew Copeland were beyond her ability to control.

"Where's Ella?" Adrian looked up when Cope came in through his front door.

"Hi, Cope. How's it going? I'm great, Adrian, and how are you?"

"She's pretty and has a great body. You're a pain in my ass."

"Just remember, she's *my* girlfriend, dickhead. As it happens, I'm picking her up in an hour and taking her to the coast. We'll be back Sunday afternoon."

Laughing, Adrian led him back down to his home office, which included his recording studio.

Cope tossed a file folder on the tabletop. "I wanted to drop this by on my way out of town. These are all the plans for your tour security. The label people have finally accepted we're doing it each time, so the process was far easier. I briefed Jeremy on the phone earlier today. He'll hold off faxing the info to the label until you approve it. Want a rundown?"

"I really want to postpone all this, is what I want." Adrian shoved his hands through his hair.

"Worried about Erin? Your first show isn't until mid-January."

"I want to be around for my niece or nephew, you know? Don't pretend you don't feel the same way. She's my sister, and I've been around for all the big moments in her life. It's going to be hard for her sometimes. You know, thinking about Adele and all." Pain shadowed Adrian's features for a few brief moments. "She'll need me. Need everyone in her life to help."

"She will, Adrian. She's got Todd and Ben. My mom and Todd's mom. She's got me, Brody, Elise, Raven, Ella. And you're fucking loaded, if you recall. Just fly back as much as you can. You and I both know she'd hate it if she knew you postponed a tour for her."

"It's more than that. I don't want to miss this. I want to be around for the baby. Adele was such a joyous part of my life. This baby should be too."

Cope sat back and gave Adrian a close look. "Do you want me to talk you into it or out of it?"

Adrian looked up, startled, and then he laughed. "That's the question. Too bad I don't know the answer. I don't want to miss this stuff. The first smiles, rolling over, sitting up. These are things that happen in those early months, and I'll be on a stage in some other state."

"True. You can video call and conference. She can get it all on video for you. Ben and Todd have both purchased swanky new cameras, and Erin's office has some great tech, so you can webcam each other. It's not perfect, but even if you don't trust Todd and Ben all the way, you have to know Brody will watch her like a hawk. She's got plenty of people who'll protect her and the baby."

"Sure. Of course Brody will, because that's what he does. So what does that make me?" Yeah, yeah, he was a bit morose. So what? He was in indie rocker; it came with the territory, right? But damn, Brody was a hard act to follow, and Cope understood that better than Adrian might think.

"The baby brother of a man like Brody. Course, it doesn't hurt that you're a rock star and stuff. I don't have a music career. Just Ben for a big brother. The man who is good at everything. I know what it's like to have a big brother who everyone looks up to."

"I feel ungrateful. I love Brody. He's more my dad than my brother, and he deserves all the accolades he receives. I wouldn't be where I am today without him."

"Sure. Doesn't make being in someone's shadow totally easy to bear, though. And it doesn't make you ungrateful. Can you cut the tour down? Do fewer cities?"

"No." He sighed. "This shit has been in place for months now. The dates are set, the venues are booked and publicity is already in place. There's all this stuff in my contract holding me to tour dates, and I get why."

"It's three months. Twelve weeks. You can do it. The more records you sell, the better it is for your career."

"After this, I'm not touring for a while. Everything I want and need is here at home. If I sell well now, I can take off a year or so. I've wanted to for a while now. It's only a matter of time before Elise gets pregnant, and I want to be here for that too."

"You've got TBC Security protecting you, no matter what you decide." Cope indicated the file folder. "And you've got me and the rest of your friends behind you."

"Thanks, man. It means a lot to me. So, back to your *girlfriend*. How are things?"

"Good. She's good. We're good. It's early days. A week now, since that first date. I'm taking her to the coast. One of my friends has a house right on the sand, terrific view, fully stocked kitchen. Two days, just us. I think it should be good. I like her. She likes me." Cope shrugged, but his grin canceled out any nonchalance he'd been going for.

"Tell me what it is about her." Adrian leaned back to grab a bottle of juice, tossing it to Cope.

"The very first time I went into the café, years and years ago, she made me a latte. It was her eyes that day. And then the freckles. She was different then. I don't know if you remember or not. But she was more upbeat, vibrant, outgoing. And slowly over the years it dimmed until she kicked him out. Then I thought maybe it was possible to ask her out. And then there was the attack, and she had to have the time and space to get her shit together. To get her life back."

"I've seen how you look at her. Watched you watching her for years now. To be totally honest with you, it's one of the reasons I haven't made a move myself. How long have you crushed on her?" Cope's gaze sharpened, and Adrian snorted a laugh. "Surprise, dude, your girl is hot. Ella is something special. Do you think no one but you noticed?"

"As long as you know she's taken now, I got no problems admitting that my girl is hella hot. As for crushing on her? God, years. Since before the assault. Since she started at the café and I didn't know anything about her. I watched her fade into her relationship with that piece of shit, and then she got up the courage to leave, and I thought, hey, now's the time! And then he nearly killed her, and she needed the space to rebuild her life." He shrugged.

"You weren't ready for her last year. Or the year before that either." Adrian sipped his juice. "You are now, and so is she. I'm glad to see it."

Cope shrugged. "Just promise me we won't have to bang a drum or anything if we talk about our feelings."

Adrian rolled his eyes, shooting him the middle finger.

"Just making sure. Anyway, it's probably true about me not being ready before. Neither of us would have been. It seems like this is a huge transition in her life, and I hate to think I'm a rebound. But I have to believe what I feel when I'm with her. I believe our connection is real."

"Don't blow it."

"Trying not to. What about you then? You're the last single guy in the group now. You interested in forever and that stuff or still happy with lots of starlets in your bed?" Cope laughed for a second. "Okay put that way, how can you not be happy with starlets in your bed? What I mean is, are you looking for a relationship or happy playing the field?"

"God, listen to us talking about our feelings and shit. *If* I found the right woman, yeah, I'd like a relationship. But it's hard, being on the road. Trust is always an issue. Then again, I'm not on the road like we were at the start. Karen the baker is a nice woman. I like her. But I don't think she's the one. And I begin to wonder if it's worth the effort unless I feel that connection. Hell, I'm not sure I'd know that connection if it hit me in the face. There's so much to dig through sometimes."

"How do you know they're with you for you instead of for the fame and money?" .

"Fucking Andrew Copeland and his ability to ask questions most people just never say out loud." Adrian groaned. "I don't. Which is why I don't have a hot redhead in my bed like you do."

"Isn't whatserface? The one from that doctor show, a ginger like my girl?"

"Sophia Green? Yeah, she was a redhead. And she was amusing for a while. But she liked the cameras a lot. I don't. I don't want to have my personal life being discussed ad nauseam on the Internet. I want to eat dinner without fifteen dudes with cameras just three feet away. I fucking hate being in L.A."

"You do have a lot more freedom up here than you'd have in L.A. The bodyguard is working out then?"

Cope's company had hooked Adrian up with a low-key bodyguard for when he was in Los Angeles and on tour. It was a stupid pain in his ass, but given what happened to Erin and Adele, it was necessary, and Adrian had appreciated it. "He's good, thanks."

"Nice. We'll be sure to get him to cover the tour then. I can work some of the dates, just FYI. We did an analysis of each venue so the security plan was specific to each event as well as an overall plan. Just let me know what you think after you read it. If you have any questions, I can walk you through it now, or you can call me and I can go over it later. It's up to you."

"Jeremy will call in a few hours and tell me what to think." Adrian shrugged with a grin. "Hey, don't give me that look. I have plenty of details to worry about and obsess over. Jeremy's my manager; he can handle this sort of thing so I don't have to. If I do have questions, I'll give you a call." Adrian paused. "Listen, next Friday night. You and

Ella come out. Brody and Elise have the night free, and we're doing a *Godfather* One and Two screening. Takeout too. Of course, if Erin goes into labor, we'll all be at the hospital."

"Sounds good. I'll let Ella know."

"Hell yeah. I hope she wears a turtleneck." He waggled his brows, and Cope shot him the evil eye.

"I'll see what she's up to and hopefully make it."

"Cool. You two have a good time this weekend."

They walked out together after he showed Cope the new editing bay they'd just completed.

"I'll see you soon. I'll have my cell with me if you read over that stuff and you want to talk about it."

Cope backed out and was gone, leaving Adrian standing outside, looking over the front garden. Peaceful. Even in the middle of the city it was peaceful here. Aside from the occasional fan who camped at the gates at the bottom of the drive, he lived a normal life in the city. No paparazzi to speak of, people left him alone in the grocery store and he was near all his favorite people.

He was unsettled. Erin was part of it. He wasn't used to seeing her need to rest so much. Her blood pressure had been slightly elevated, so she'd been taking it easy, and thank heavens she'd been cleared to go back to work here and there. She'd been going stir-crazy and Adrian knew how much she worried and felt the need to simply go about her life with some level of normalcy.

Maybe it was the changes in their circle with Ella and Cope coming together the way they had. It wasn't that he'd ever really crushed on Ella; not like Cope had. But he supposed he'd finally hit the age where he realized he wanted someone to come home to. A hand to hold on a morning walk. Someone to pick up the phone and sound thrilled when they heard his voice.

The big house was awesome. He'd worked hard to earn it. So had Erin. He took a side path through the gate into the expansive backyard overlooking the Sound. A flash of color caught his gaze and he smiled, seeing the flutter of the tassels on Rennie's pogo stick where she'd left it, propped up against the side of his deck. Being an uncle was one of his favorite things. He dug kids a lot. Which was good, because he knew Erin's baby would fill the place with bright toys that squeaked or made music when they got stepped on.

Home was important. His brother had found it, his sister had found it and one of his best friends may have found it too. Life was very good indeed. He'd do this tour and use the webcam idea to be there in some way for the new baby and, more important, his sister.

16

Cope stopped at the grocery store near Ella's building to grab a few extras for their weekend. Wine. Cheese and crackers. Chocolate. And a few boxes of condoms.

"My goodness, is this just a party for two, or can a guest join in?"

He looked up from the acres of boutique chocolate and found . . . Sandy? Cindy? Candy? Whatever, a woman he saw on and off for a stretch the year before. Talk about inventive. Whatshername there was like a sexual encyclopedia. And a yoga teacher, so she was extra bendy too.

Without thinking, he crooked a smile her way. "Not that the invitation isn't enticing and all, but no. I'm not partying with anyone else but my girlfriend these days." That also came out without thinking. He liked that last bit better.

"Girlfriend? You?" She laughed, making sure he saw all her parts jiggling. Not a lot of subtle, but she wasn't hiding what she was either.

"Yep. Even us old dogs can learn new tricks." He grabbed several of the dark chocolate truffle bars she liked so much. "Nice seeing you."

"Cope, you're not boyfriend material. You have to know that. You're a great fuck and all, but you're going to be cheating on this poor naive girl before she knows it."

"I don't cheat on anyone, thank you very much." This offended him deeply. He might have liked to fuck a lot of women, back when he was with Candy—yeah that's right, Candy—but he didn't lie about it, and he wasn't a cheater. He had principles, damn it.

"You're not a one-woman man, Cope. You like women. You like sex. One woman can't satisfy you. Is she a freak? Does she let you bring home friends? Maybe I'd like her. We had some good times with a few of my friends, remember?"

It was like some scene from his past playing through the middle of the grocery store. Like Scrooge being visited by women of years before.

"Look, we had some fun and all. But that's in the past, and I've moved on."

"Don't kid yourself. You and me are alike. We don't do relation-ships. We do each other. You'll fuck up and prove me right."

Still laughing, she moved past him with a little wave, leaving him pissed off in her wake. He wasn't like her anymore. He had changed, and it was all about Ella, damn it. He could do it. He was boyfriend material, partner material even. It wasn't even a matter of changing; he'd just been waiting for the right person, and he had her.

Ella smiled as the scenery whizzed by. "The trees are so pretty. I'm glad I brought my camera."

"Camera, huh? We gonna do anything to be recorded for posterity?"

She snorted a laugh. "Um. No." Not that she didn't have a detailed memory of just how he looked naked. One she called up frequently because, well, hell, because he was *fine*!

"Party pooper. I made reservations at a little Italian place near my friend's house. It'll be a late dinner. That okay? I can stop now if you're hungry."

"No, I'm good. I eat at nine and ten a lot. But I'm sleeping late tomorrow."

"Red, we're sleeping until at least eleven. Then I'm going to ravish you, and we can nap until we decide if we want food or not."

She felt her grin all the way to her toes. All the happy he brought to her life made her giddy. "It's been a very long time since I've smiled this much," she murmured, watching the sky purple, deepen into night. "Thank you."

"No. Thank you. Thank you for the package. I had the perfect frame to put the drawing in. I'm . . . well to say I'm touched and flattered doesn't really do justice to how it made me feel. And you've been hiding another talent from me. Are you good at everything?"

He took her hand casually. "Now *I'm* touched and flattered. Which talent are you referring to?"

"The drawing. And what poem did you quote?"

"That's mine, the poem that is. Just a little something. The drawing's just a scribble. Nothing major."

Was he kidding? "Nothing major? Get out of town. It's beautiful. So you're a poet, and artist and you do amazing woodwork? Damn, Andrew Copeland, you're hiding your light under a bushel."

"*You're* beautiful, Ella. I just let the pen put a small part of you on paper."

Do you just not know? How can you not see how wonderful you truly are? She thought about this a lot as they finished the drive west. How could he not know? Did his parents just not ever tell him how wonderful he was? Despite his father's asinine behavior of late, Annalee seemed to adore her children.

"Here we are," he said, pulling down a quiet street that fronted the sandy dunes and the water just feet away.

"Wow." She got out once he'd parked. The sharp scent of sand and salt water painted the evening air. It was cold enough she needed to clutch the front of her sweater together to ward off a chill.

And he was there, beside her, putting his arms around her. "Mmm. You feel good. Come on inside. We'll drop off the bags and head to the restaurant."

The place was lovely, romantic and intimate. The meal had been pleasant as Andrew held her hand while they talked about everything under the sun.

Until the bill came.

She reached for her bag, and his eyes goggled. "What are you doing?"

"Helping pay."

He shook his head. "No you're not. I invited you away for the weekend. I invited you for dinner. I've got this."

She narrowed her eyes at him. "I want to help."

"You tried this the other day at Top Pot too. I've got my own company; I make more money than you do. It's silly to try to pace me like I have a mental tally in my head. I don't."

He studied her as she tried to figure out how to let it go or else make him see her perspective.

"Remember when I told you you were transparent, and everything you felt showed on your face?" He kissed her knuckles. "Tell me. This is clearly more than you feeling generous or like you ordered lobster or something."

"I like to pay my own way. Paying my own way means I own everything in my life, all my decisions, good and bad. No one can take it away from me because it's mine."

He got it then.

"Ella, I get it. But I'm not him."

She put her fist on the table, and he took that one too, kissing it, unfurling her fingers and wrapping them with his own. "I'm not keeping a tally, nor do I want to. I have no desire to control your life or your destiny. It's dinner, and I'll be taking you out a lot; it's what couples do. You can't pay every time, nor do I want you to. Why don't we meet in the middle? You can pay the tip?"

"The middle is twenty percent of this meal? I told you I didn't become a doctor because I hated math, but that doesn't mean I don't get math at all."

He sighed. "Since you're being so honest, let me be too. I hate this. I hate that, even though I know this isn't about me, that it's about me anyway. I don't want to tell you what to wear or who to be friends with. I want you to be in my life because you like it. I get this, I do, but I don't want it to be part of what we have."

She blinked several times, peeked at the bill and tossed down a tip closer to 30 percent than 20 percent. "What? The service was very good, and they did those substitutions for us."

He grinned, kissing her hard and fast. "All right then."

Bundled up, they'd walked along the beach, not needing words. He kept an arm around her, loving how they fit together so well. And when they got back to the house, they'd paused on the deck, looking out over the water, listening to roaring white noise of the sea.

Funny how quickly he'd gotten used to how she looked as his woman. Having her there to put an arm around, to hold her hand. But it was his ability to touch her, touch every part of her, that he loved most. She was his to caress, to kiss and nuzzle, his to breathe in at the hollow of her throat.

He turned her to face him, the deck railing at her back. "Hi there." He kissed her.

"Mmm. Hi yourself. I'm stuffed, warm, wrapped in your arms. Dude, this is pretty damned good as life moments go."

He skimmed his hands up, over her hips, beneath the hem of her sweater until they found her breasts. "Love these."

She smiled, head tipping back, body arching into his touch.

"I knew she was in there," he murmured, nuzzling her neck as he moved the cups of her bra down to get to her nipples.

"Who?"

"The woman who arches her back to get more from me. Sensual. Beautiful. The woman who glories in her sexuality and allure."

She snorted a laugh, and he pulled her inside.

Not bothering to stop pulling her clothes off as they made it to the pillow-strewn floor in front of the fireplace, he rolled her onto her back. "You laugh?"

"I'm so not those things. *You* are those things."

"I have an aching cock that says different." He looked at her as he eased her panties off, leaving her totally naked to his gaze. He loved that she no longer hid her scars from him. Dropping a kiss on the hollow of her hip, he licked his way to her belly button.

"It's my turn," she gasped out.

"I'm trying," he said before finding her clit and giving it a lick.

"Oh. Well, that's not what I meant, but"—she made that sex sigh he loved so much, and he wanted to laugh at how easily swayed she'd been—"I'm so easy."

He did laugh at that while he situated himself between her thighs. "Thank God for it."

Two orgasms later, he slid into her body just as she opened her eyes and met his. The shock of recognition made him freeze a moment at the raw intimacy of it. He was exposed. Turned upside down by the way she *saw* him.

She used that moment to change her position and roll him over. "I like it this way. I like looking down at the most beautiful man in creation. Naked and spread out for me."

"You give good compliment, darlin'." What else could he say? That he was ass over teakettle in love with her? He wanted to, but he didn't want to scare her or move too fast.

Still, as she undulated her hips, rising and falling over his cock, she burned herself into his heart, into his soul, and there was nothing else inside but what she did to him.

He came as he looked up her body, over the curves of her breasts, the points of her nipples, puffy from desire, the line of her collarbone and the elegant neck. "Beautiful."

He was addicted to Ella Tipton's presence in his life. Needed her in ways that scared him, even as they thrilled him.

Ella smiled up at Cope as he put a mug of tea at her left hand. She'd been working on a paper, the last major assignment she had. She finished her practicum already, had done her fieldwork. Essentially, she was done once the paper was turned in.

But she was neglecting him, and he'd taken the time to be with her. He was probably mad about that.

"I'm sorry. Let me put this away, and we can hang out," she said, finishing up the sentence she'd been typing into her notebook computer.

He leaned in, touching her arm. "Hey, no stress at all. It's important, and I'm not going anywhere. Just reading the paper and watching you. Take your time, Red."

Oh. The shame of it washed through her as she realized she'd been reacting like she had with Bill. Stupid and totally unwarranted.

She got up on not quite strong legs, and he jumped forward to steady her. "Babe, you okay?" He peered into her face, and to her great mortification, she burst into tears. He drew her into his arms, running his hands up and down her back. "Shhh. What is it? Ella, what's wrong?"

"I'm sorry."

He picked her up then, like it was easy, and bought them both to the couch before sitting, keeping her snuggled in his lap.

"Sorry for what? Did I do something wrong?"

Which only made it worse that he'd think it was him instead of her being all stupid and bound up inside over something that happened to her years before.

She shook her head. "No. Not you at all. It's me. Just something stupid."

"Your ex?"

"I'm dumb, Andrew. To be affected by something that happened so long ago. You've never done anything to merit a reaction like this. I'm"—she clapped her hands over her eyes—"humiliated. I'm so sorry. We can go back to Seattle. I've ruined everything."

He tightened his hold, kissing her cheeks, kissing her eyelids and her temple. "Shhh. You're not dumb. You're one of the smartest people I know. Tell me. Tell me and let it go."

She didn't want to taint the weekend with that. "It's not a pretty story. It's not nice, and I don't want to bring it here between us."

He tipped her chin up, kissing her lips softly. "Baby, it's already between us. You're apologizing for something I don't even understand over something that seems like nothing you'd need to apologize for."

She tried to duck her head, but he wouldn't let her. Finally she shook her head and moved his hand. "I can't. I can't look at you when I say it. I can't. Please."

He paused, blinking a few times. "Christ. Ella, I don't know what to do here. I don't want you to be ashamed. It's not your fault. I don't want you to think I agree that whatever you say is something you can't say to my face. Because you can trust me not to judge you."

"I can't. It's too humiliating. Please. I want to try to tell you, but I can't deal with looking at you when I do. You're something beautiful, and I don't even know how I ever ended up with you like this. You're something right. But what was before wasn't right."

"All right. Tell me how you need to tell me. But I want you to understand something, Ella Tipton. You can tell me anything. I admire you. I like you, and though it's probably the way wrong time to say it, I love you. Look away if you need to, but you need to know that."

She blew out a breath, her eyes widening and her heart thudding in her chest. Maybe he meant it like he loved her in the same way Elise loved her.

"You're totally transparent, did you know that?" He grinned, kissing her hard and fast. "We can talk about the love thing after you tell me the other stuff. It can be a palate cleanser."

She frowned at him, but he kept wearing that damned sexy grin. She took a deep breath and ducked her head. But left her hand wrapped in his. "It's just that he had to be in the center of my focus at all times. I couldn't read at home or do homework. He would be insulted if I paid attention to other stuff. It was just second nature, I guess. To see you there and feel guilty. And then ashamed."

"It wasn't the act of me bringing you tea that brought this on. Ella, please look at me."

She did, raising her eyes to meet his, hanging on for dear life.

"You smiled at me. You finished your sentence and then said you'd be right with me. I told you it wasn't a big deal. It was after that when it hit. What was it that pushed your buttons?"

"It hits sometimes. Well, no, these days it always hits in some totally random and unexpected way." She licked her lips. "I knew you didn't mean it that way. I knew you weren't upset because I brought along my work to begin with. I wouldn't have before. I gave up pretty much everything for him, so he could always be number one. You're not like that. I know it. But some part of me deep down reacted that way. Like an animal. It's not about you at all. I dragged you into it."

Cope wanted to protect her from anything and everything that could harm her. He wanted to wrap her up and keep her safe. Holding her there as she couldn't even look him in the eye over something she was not at fault for was torture. Because he wanted to fix it for her, and he couldn't.

"Part of you will probably always react that way. It's meant to be there, Ella. It's the survival instinct."

"When I first left, for months after that, I didn't have panic attacks.

I didn't freeze up at random. He didn't hit me every day. Not even every month. He terrorized me and made me small. That was his control. So when I left, I had it back. And then it slipped away."

"I imagine someone breaking into your apartment with the intention of killing you would kick that animal part of a person into high gear."

"I'd like very much to be normal all the time. Or at least crazy in good ways."

"Everyone's a little crazy. Life makes a person crazy. You've endured a lot, and yet you're surviving. Thriving. Graduating with your master's degree! You have a new job. You have friends who love you. You have parents who love you. And me."

Once he said it, he couldn't not say it again. He now had a powerful need to make sure she understood just exactly what he meant.

"I know. I'd planned to wait to tell you for at least a few more weeks. But I've known you for years. I've known you and been falling in love with you every minute of the last six years. You're going to say it's sudden. You're going to say I don't know what I'm feeling. And so I'm going to stop you before you do and tell you I know my own heart. I know the difference between how it feels to hold you, between what it means to know when you pick up one of my phone calls, I'll hear the smile in your voice, and how it has ever been before. I love you, Ella."

She gaped, starting to speak and breaking off several times. He satisfied himself by kissing each one of her fingertips and thinking up ways to make her come as she reeled through ways to deny what he was saying and couldn't.

Finally she slumped, snuggling into him and whispered, "I'm glad I'm not alone."

"No arguments?"

"I'm leaving a door open for you to exit through gracefully if I finally reveal something horrifying to you. I wouldn't blame you."

"Now you're insulting me and my taste."

She snorted, but stayed cuddled on his lap. "Well, you fell off the gorgeous blond woman wagon and into me. Jeez, Andrew, I can see the difference between me and the women you're usually with."

He pinched her side, but not hard enough to really hurt. "Hey. You know what else? Who am I with right now? You. Yes, you are different and that is why I love you and can't even remember any of them. Hell, Red, I can barely remember my own name when you come into a room."

"You've befuddled me on a regular basis for years now," she muttered. "And you're still doing it."

It was his turn to snort. "Good. It'll keep us both on our toes. Gonna be a bit of a bumpy ride, I imagine. At least you're female and there's only one of you. Maybe my dad will finally be satisfied. But it's doubtful you'll be spending any time with him anyway."

She sat upright and swung her leg around to straddle his lap and face him. All thoughts other than shoving his cock deep inside her as she rode him just like this flittered away. His hands moved to the curve of her waist, and she cocked her head, giving him a good look.

"Tell me. I'm not going to say a word to anyone. Don't carry it around with you."

She'd opened up to him, and he yearned to share, so he did. "He tried to punch me." He said it fast, in one burst of air and sound. "He called Ben and said horrible things. I can't repeat it because it's vile and because I promised Ben. But it was enough that I went to see him to urge him to get his act together and mend fences because it was nearly too late. He didn't react well. I haven't been over to their house or spoken with him since that day. I'm worried about my mom. I haven't told her about it, but she knows something worse than usual happened."

She kissed his cheeks before sliding her arms around him and hugging him. "I wish I could help you."

"You do. That's what you're not hearing. You make me better just by being around."

"Ditto," she said with a sniffle. She moved a bit and then giggled. God, he loved making her giggle. "Um, it feels like I'm making a few things better," she said, grinding herself over his cock.

He leaned her back to the couch. "Oh, sweet Ella, you always make that part better." He unbuttoned her sweater, sighing happily when he'd exposed her bra and then her breasts. "Even betterer-er than before."

She laughed again, her voice lowering the way it did when she wanted him.

"I think you're supposed to kiss it to make it better." She reached between them and down the waist of his jeans, grasping his cock. "Should I do that?"

17

It wasn't more than a few days after he'd returned from the coast when Cope opened up his mail to find a bright red envelope. He smiled once he saw the lettering and recognized Ella's address.

Wanting to read it but hearing the honk of Ben's arrival—his neighbors would love the honking at seven in the damned morning—he tucked it into his messenger bag and rushed out to where Ben sat in his truck, idling at the curb.

" 'Bout time," his brother said by way of greeting when he'd gotten inside and buckled up.

"If you were even halfway punctual I'd be offended. As it is, what was I supposed to do? Run out and jump in through the window like we're Bo and Luke Duke?"

"Don't test me, asshole. I need caffeine."

"Good thing your wife owns a café then, huh? Not as fun to go there now that my Red works elsewhere three days a week now."

"*Your* Red, huh? That's nice to hear. Christ, I feel like such a shitty brother for ignoring you. I'm sorry I haven't been around much for you to talk to about this."

"You've got a lot to deal with at the moment. I told her I love her this weekend. We had amazing sex. She gets me. It's just . . . I don't know, man, magical, I guess. She's the one. I *know* it right to my toes."

Ben smiled. "I'd say, *so fast?* But I know you. If you say it's the real deal, I believe you. And it's not fast when you've known a woman six years. Not really."

He was so glad his brother got that. Cope hadn't spoken to anyone about telling Ella he loved her, but he knew it would come up that he told her after only dating her a short time.

"This is what I told her. Mom wants me to bring her to dinner. I'm running out of excuses."

"Why try to get out of it? Mom's a great cook, and you know, if this thing with Ella is going to be serious, you'll need to get her around the Copelands anyway."

"I'm not speaking to Dad, and I'm sure as hell not taking Ella around with all this tension. Mom likes her, she likes Mom. Maybe we should go out to dinner or have her to the house here. The kitchen is working, and I'm nearly done with the dining room." Ella had convinced him to let go of the condo and move into the house full time. He'd come home Sunday, and she'd even helped him pack the rest of his stuff and take it over.

"Anyway, I want Ella and Mom to get to know each other better and on a different level, without all that baggage. It's going to be enough pressure as it is."

"You don't have to estrange yourself from them for me." Ben's voice had gone from lighthearted to sad.

"I'm not estranged from both of them. He needed to hear a few things, and he didn't want to when I confronted him." Best not to share the part about the near miss with the punch.

Ben pulled up in front of the café. "You didn't tell me you confronted him. What happened?"

Cope opened his door. "Nothing worth writing home about. Come on, let's get some coffee, and I'll sulk that there are no women working the morning shift now that Erin is at home."

Ben caught up with him at the door. "You know I don't expect you to do this. I don't want you having problems with your own damned parents because of the fucking life I lead."

"There should *be* no problems with your own damned parents because of the life you lead, Ben. That's the problem. *Not* the way you live, but how he's reacting." Cope went inside, his brother right behind.

"Don't think you can just avoid telling me the story," Ben said under his breath as they waited for their drinks. This time of day the café was packed with people from the neighborhood on their way to work.

"I don't need to clear it with you." He grabbed his latte, tucking a buck into the tip jar.

"You're being stubborn."

Raven waltzed in and waved when she saw them.

"How's Erin?"

The woman was many things, some positive, some negative, but one thing Cope never found fault with was her loyalty to Erin and, with some glaring exceptions, Brody. He knew his brother did not trust her fully, but though they couldn't understand just what it was between Erin and Raven that made them close, everyone in the group honored it.

"You should go over to the house today. She's going stir crazy and would love the company. She's not supposed to be on her feet for more than a few hours a day. Todd is on Erin duty, so I'm sure he'd like the break too. They tend to get on each other's nerves when it comes to her health." Ben snorted.

"That's because they're nearly exactly alike." Raven's smile softened. "I'll stop over in a few. I'm just doing a quick coffee run for the boys next door." She jerked her head toward the tattoo shop. "Hey, speaking of following up on people, I haven't seen Ella around in a few days. How's her new job?"

Cope smiled, thinking of the envelope in his bag. "She's good. We'll be at pool on Friday, so if you're around, you can see for yourself."

"That sounds good. I hadn't realized how much I'd miss her until she was gone and I didn't see all that red hair or hear that squeaky voice. Tell her I said hey."

She was off, leaving them alone. They managed to play nice until they got to Ben's place, where they took their argument up again on the way through the side door to their home office.

"There's no reason for you to get caught up in this mess. Who knows, maybe Ella will soften him. She could soften just about anyone, your lady."

Cripes, he got giddy thinking about her sometimes. "She's special that way. But while this involves you in some ways, this is about family. My family as well as yours. He's wrong. He's hateful, and I'm not having it. I don't want to be around it, and I sure as hell don't want Ella around it. Anyway, that's enough for now. Go and check on Erin; I know you want to. I'll take the conference call."

"What did he do, Andy?" Ben stopped him just inside their office door. "I need to know."

"Go see your wife. You don't need to know."

"Fuck you. I've told you stuff. Pay up."

He slumped into a chair. "I went out to the range to talk to him. It was ugly. So ugly he tried to punch me. Todd's dad came out and pulled him back. I don't know what happened after that, because I left and I haven't spoken to him since."

Ben blinked and leaned back against the doorjamb. "What the fuck? He tried to *hit* you?"

"I have to do this call. They're expecting it. Go. Kiss your wife. He's not worth it." He began to dial, and his brother sighed.

"We'll talk more about this later." Ben left right as his conference call began.

"I'm leaving," Cope called out later that afternoon. "I have shit to do, and you're all fine here." He bent and kissed Erin's cheek. "How go things?"

"My blood pressure is better. Good enough that I can come out to pool on Friday if I sit the whole time."

"Maybe." Todd didn't even look up from where he was working on tightening a washer on a leaky sink.

"You're not the boss of me," Erin tossed back without heat.

"I beg to differ."

"That you have to beg to differ proves my point." Erin beamed at Cope, who wisely hid a smile.

"My cue to leave. See you tomorrow," he called to Todd. Ben had left to go deal with a client, so Cope had been able to avoid any further discussion of their father.

It was a warm day, so he decided to skive off and work on the house. Being late afternoon, he wouldn't be worried overmuch about any noise from the saw or any of his equipment, and he needed to work for a while to get his head together.

First though, he sat on his bed and slit open the top of the shiny red envelope. She'd written the address in metallic ink. Her writing was all loops and swirls. He'd expected it to be precise, but it wasn't. It was feminine and sexy.

A card came first. On the front, a photograph of a circular stairwell taken from the bottom. Light shafted against the gleam of the wood and the strength of the wrought-iron railing. He sat looking at it for a long while, felled that she got him in a way no one else did. Those curves and lines were beautiful and appealing to him in a way few would understand.

But she did.

Inside was a note.

Andrew,

I made you this playlist. Enter your e-mail address and it'll load directly to your computer or iPod. It's sort of a mixtape. Which makes me feel uncomfortably teenaged. And yet, they're songs I have in my mental Andrew Copeland playlist.

I don't have poetry like you do. I only know that I love how my sheets smell after you've been in my bed.

Ella

He held that card for the longest time, wishing she understood that she *was* poetry to him. Smiling because she made him a mixtape and because he loved it that his scent marked her sheets. He closed his eyes, imagining her rolling into the spot he'd been in, breathing in against his pillow. The way he did when she had been in his bed.

Inside the envelope he found a bird's feather nestled in a folded sheet of brightly colored tissue paper.

He'd sent her a letter a week ago. She'd shyly told him how much she'd loved it, and it had made his day. It wasn't that he expected her to reciprocate, but he was very glad she had. The paper smelled like her.

She was there, in his life. A constant in a wholly new way. A better way, because now he got to kiss her and touch her and see her naked. Her body was hot enough with clothes, but it was her insides he found so totally appealing. She wasn't totally normal—who could be after what she'd endured? For that matter, he wasn't either. But she was Ella, and she lived with an honesty he found awe-inspiring, so what was normality compared to that, anyway?

He grabbed his phone to call her but got her voice mail instead.

"It's me. Wanna have dinner tonight? Thai takeout? Burgers? You decide. I'm at the house now. You can bring a bag if you'd like to stay over."

He disconnected and changed from work clothes into ratty jeans and a T-shirt to work in, heading downstairs, whistling the whole time.

Ella parked in his driveway, and balancing the bag of takeout, she headed to his back door. She figured the least she could do, since she was not an ace at any of this carpentry stuff, was to bring fuel for him to continue his work.

Also, he invited her there. Invited her to stay the night like real couples did from time to time. This made her smile. Something about him going out of his way to be with her, to touch her or kiss her, drove her crazy. It had been a very long time since it had felt like someone wanted to make a relationship with her.

His door was unlocked as he said it would be when she'd checked in earlier. She headed into the kitchen to put the food down and hang up her coat and bag. He'd been working on the pocket doors fronting his home office. She could smell the oil he used and then stilled, standing in the hallway, on her way to seek him out. She knew that scent, which meant she'd been there enough to know it.

A giddy little thrill riding her spine, she turned the corner and saw him. The giddy went away as a hard shock of lust slammed into her.

He stood, slightly dusty, slightly sweaty and a whole lot work-rumpled as he ran his hands over the wood like a lover. A high casement window shafted pale sunlight over him, tinted just orange because the winter sun was setting. Dust motes danced around him, his hair gleaming.

But that wasn't all.

He wore a pair of pale denim jeans, worn thin in the right places, nearly snow white against his thighs and at the bottom of his zipper.

The hole on his thigh showed hard, olive skin, as the muscles moved while he did. His arms and chest were showcased to their advantage in the faded, thin cotton of the T-shirt.

He was a carpenter fantasy wet dream straight out of a dirty letter to a skin mag.

She simply watched him there, letting the desire in her build up, warming her until she needed to move, to speak or make a sound, because the ache of not really having him became too much.

"Hey," she said, walking again, moving to him because there was no other place she could be.

His face lit when he saw her. His smile sexy-sweet.

"Hey, Red. I didn't hear you come in. Don't get too close, I'm a sweaty, dusty mess."

"God, but I know." All she could think about was getting him naked, so she did.

He lit up the moment she touched him, taking her in his arms and hauling her to his body roughly. His mouth met hers, her lips opening to him as he took over, his tongue sliding along hers.

She drowned in him and went willingly when he spun her, pressing her against the wall behind her. She moaned, and he paused for a moment. She realized he probably worried he'd hurt her or scared her. To underline just how her moan was the good kind, she pressed her hips forward, grinding into his cock.

"Christ, you're so beautiful," he managed to say after breaking the kiss. His nimble fingers had her sweater unbuttoned and had popped the catch on her bra before she could gather enough brain cells to speak. "These. I. Love. Your. Tits."

She laughed, tipping her head back as he kissed his way down her neck, unerringly to her nipples. He was very good at that. If she could speak again, she'd tell him.

"Bedroom." Pulling away from her, he began to tug her in the right direction. She stopped him, and he turned back to look at her.

"I'd fuck you right here, right now, but I don't want you to get hurt on any of the stuff I have out."

"It's my turn, and if you don't fuck me right here and now, I might die."

He stopped and took a deep breath, the blue of his eyes deepening. "Let me shower," he said after backing her against the wall again. "I'll be right back."

She grabbed his belt buckle. "No way. Now." In moments she had his pants open and down.

"I'm sweaty." He meant it as a protest, but he just said it automatically. He clearly didn't mean it, since he thrust into her grasp.

She smiled up at him as she got to her knees, having totally changed her mind about needing to be fucked that instant. He groaned when she pulled his cock free. "I know. You're so hot. You're sweaty and dusty and just all sexy and I"—she stopped, licking the head of his cock—"wanted you the instant I saw you, your hands on the wood, caressing it like you caress me."

He paused, the intensity in his features changing to something else. His shirt was off in moments, and he moved around her, yanking his jeans down and then trying to get her sweater off.

"I was doing something!"

"I heartily approve of what you're doing. But don't kneel there on the hardwood. Let me get you into the other room on a pillow."

She pushed his hands away and licked over the head of his cock, sucking it into her mouth slightly. "Sometimes a girl likes it a bit uncomfortable and dirty." Which was true, but she'd surprised herself by saying it out loud.

Awesomely enough, she'd surprised him too, and it gave her an advantage as she went back to what she was doing. Something about making him feel good by going down on him really turned her on. Made her feel powerful in a totally new way.

The need he'd awakened inside had bloomed, sometimes overwhelming her. Usually when she was with him it hit her in a wave of heat and craving. She'd been emboldened just by being with him. What an odd and fantastic experience that had been.

The floor against her knees was just uncomfortable enough to keep her hyperalert; the scent of wood dust hung in the air around clean man sweat from a job well done. She breathed in deeply, loving it.

His groans made her wet, made her feel empty, achy. His taste wended through her, and she wanted more.

"Red, god, please, stop, stop, stop. I want to fuck you right here and now." He pulled her to her feet. "Don't move." In two seconds he was back, rolling a condom on, and she'd managed to get a leg out of her jeans.

"Look at you. Mussed, lips swollen from my cock in your mouth," he murmured as he came back to her and in one totally rock star move, had eased her weight up and then down onto his cock in one thrust.

Not knowing how it escaped, she couldn't regret the half shout of pleasure at the shock of the invasion, of her body settling around his so easily, the way made slick already.

"Hot and wet. My favorite things on you."

"Mmm." She put her hands on his shoulders and levered herself up and then down again, rolling her hips as he began to thrust so hard her boobs bounced. Pleasure flooded her system as he fucked into her body.

Where she gripped his shoulders she could feel the tremble of his muscles. "Don't hold back. I'm, oh god, I'm fine, and I want this. I want it all."

He groaned, ragged, needy, and pressed deep and hard, his grip on her hips tightening, sending a wave of delicious sensation through her.

"I want every bit of you, Ella," he ground out though a clenched jaw.

"I'm right here. Take me." Each time he was with her, he showed her just how beautiful sex could be. He was the reason she'd been able to walk through that door and act on her desire in the first place.

He thrust harder and harder, driving her mad with sensation, but not quite enough. She hung on the edge of climax.

"Shh, lean toward me. Change your angle. Let me help you."

She dragged her eyes open to find him looking at her, hunger stamped on his features. When she leaned forward, she knew immediately why he'd suggested it. The length of his cock brushed against her clit at this angle, providing the perfect amount of friction to shove her into climax with a surprised gasp.

"Christ," he hissed as he held her, thrusting harder and harder until one last press deep, and he went to his knees, her legs still wrapped around his body.

Before she could disentangle herself, he stood again and took her into the bathroom connected to the master bedroom.

"You're very strong." She waggled her brows at him, and he laughed.

"You're good for my workout. This is far more fun than lunges or running a few miles."

"Your back might appreciate it if you put me down."

He let go, and she slid off, kissing his neck, taking one last breath of him.

"You're not heavy." He kissed her as he pulled her jeans and panties all the way off. "Shower with me."

"Okay." *What the heck? Why not?*

He drew her into the huge, double-headed shower stall with him.

"Since you're so dirty, let me soap you off." She smirked and ran her hands all over his body, slick with soap.

He stood there, water sluicing over his muscles, over his tattoos and piercings, and never took his gaze from her. What surprised her so much was that his attentions never made her nervous. The way he looked at her made her warm inside. Made her feel confident and sexy.

"Best greeting ever." He grinned and began to soap her up too. "You totally objectified me. It was awesome."

She laughed, caught off guard. "I did. But never fear, I like you for your mind too."

No one made him feel so fucking secure in himself. No one saw him the way she did. She tiptoed up to get his hair, and he ducked a little to help. Her fingers were strong and firm against his scalp, feeling so good he had to groan.

"I was a shampoo girl when I was in high school. For gas money."

He laughed. "Feel free to practice on me anytime."

Later, as they perched on his bed eating takeout, he leaned in and kissed her. "Thank you for the letter. I haven't had anyone make me a mixtape in a very long time. What came over you, by the way?"

She expertly wielded her chopsticks, spearing a mushroom and popping it into her mouth. "You mean the letter or the way you looked like a dirty, dirty carpenter wet dream when I came in and then had to have you?"

"You're a wonder to me. You know that?" He stole a spring roll from her plate, and she sent him an arched brow.

"I can't be the first woman to see you all sweaty and work-mussed and have her hormones shoot into overdrive at the very sight."

"The first woman who mattered. Yes."

She smiled and ducked her head in the way he'd come to love seeing when it was sweet, not so much when it was from her embarrassment or shame over something from her past though.

"I missed you. You were there and you looked . . . God, I don't know. Just all über manly and stuff. You touched the wood like you touch me. I love to watch you working."

"I like it when you don't hold back with me. Makes me feel like superman."

She blushed. "You feel that way to me too."

She knew just what to say.

"Did you bring a bag? Because I'm beginning to crave you in the middle of the night."

"I did. Didn't bother with pajamas as you only get annoyed when you have to wade through any clothing at all to get to me."

"It's your fault for being so irresistible."

His cell phone rang. "Sorry, Red, it's Ben's ring. I need to get it."

18

"Oh my god, if you people don't leave me alone, I'm going to . . . I don't know, but it'll be bad."

Ella looked at Erin, saw the annoyance first and then the worry just beneath it. Elise turned, worry on her face too.

"Hey, why don't you go call your mom?" Ella touched Cope's hand. He'd been tight and stressed-out since the call came in from Ben that Erin was in the hospital. "I'll come get you if anything happens. You know she'd want to know."

He let out a long breath. "I don't want to leave just in case they need me."

"You want me to call for you?"

"No. Fuck. She can wait. It can wait."

"Okay then." She took a step back, knowing being hurt was silly. He was worried about the baby. They all were.

"Ella, make them all go." Erin reached a hand out, and Ella stepped forward to take it.

"Baby, you need to stay still and let them fuss." Ella squeezed the hand not hooked up to the BP cuff.

"Elise. Come on, tell them it's okay."

Elise stepped closer, putting her chin on Ella's shoulder. "They know. But they love you and the baby, and they worry."

"There are too many people in here." A nurse bustled in and glared. "All but the mom and her two men. Y'all need to go. There's a waiting room if you wish. But she's going to drink this and then rest for a while before we release her tomorrow. Best thing is to go home and wait."

Ben's shoulders slumped, and Ella turned, hugging him. Just needing him to know she cared. He sniffled and hugged her back. "Can I get you guys anything? How about some blankets and pillows? I know you'll both be staying here with her overnight."

"Could you?" Ben looked down at her, so much worry on his face that her heart ached for him.

"Of course. I'll run to your place right now." She turned to Erin. "Do you want me to bring anything specific?"

She got a list and directions to where everything was and kissed Erin's cheek. "I'll be back as soon as I can. I'll bring you back some Red Mill too. For you, O Pregnant One, I'll make you something healthy instead."

"*Pffft.* Healthy. Healthy sucks." Erin pouted, and Todd kissed the top of her head.

"I know, doll. But once the wee one is out, you can go back to your normal diet." Ella patted her hand. "I'll be back as soon as I can. I'll have my phone if you think of anything else you need." She kissed Erin's cheek, followed by big hugs from Todd and Ben.

"Thank you for this," Todd murmured.

She touched his cheek. "Of course. That's what friends are for, right?"

He nodded, and she grabbed her bag, moving toward the door. Adrian looked lost, so she stopped for a moment. "Hey, she's going to be fine. The doctor said she just needed to be off her feet. She's here being watched by the best."

"I'm scared," he said softly, his voice nearly breaking.

"I know. She is too. Ben and Todd are too. Brody is. Cope is. I am. Elise is. We all are. Thing is, this is reversible with rest. That's what the doctor told us, remember? Just blood pressure and water retention. It's not full blown preeclampsia yet. And if they need to, they can deliver the baby immediately. This is the floor where they deliver babies, remember. These are all health professionals trained specifically for this situation. Now, listen." She paused. "Hear that?"

The little patter of the heart monitor they'd put on Erin's belly sounded clearly in the room. "He or she is so much like her. Can you hear it? That's a bold heartbeat. Bold and strong. Just like his or her momma."

He hugged her again. "Thank you, Ella."

"You know where I am if you need anything, okay? I'll bring back food for you guys too."

Adrian looked to Cope. "You're a lucky man."

"Let me run you over." Elise smiled and then laughed. "You know what I mean."

"I do. Thanks. I rode in with Cope, and I know he wants to stay here."

Andrew had been looking at her as she'd been comforting Adrian. She could see the worry all over him. "I brought you; I can take you back."

She sighed at his tone, feeling horrible in general. For her friends and for Andrew more specifically. She knew more than most that he wanted to fix things, and this was something he could not fix.

Ella took his hands, drawing them to her mouth. His expression softened, and he pulled her into a hug, kissing her temple. "I'm sorry I snapped at you."

"You're worried. You get a free pass today. Shall I bring you back anything?"

"I'm going to take you. I know where everything is anyway. And then I can be sure you get home safely before I come back." He looked toward Elise. "I got this. Be here for Brody."

"Hey, do you have a place for Rennie to be tonight? Would you like me to take her back to my house? I can get her to school in the morning."

Elise walked her out into the hallway as everyone said their good-byes to Erin under the stink eye the nurse sent.

"My dad took her to their place tonight. Thank you for offering, sweetie. I'll go home to get her later. Brody won't want to leave Erin, but I can't do much for either of them. I'll get her to school in the morning and then come here to check on everyone."

"I'll take the morning shift at the café tomorrow, so I'll be around if you need me to grab her after school or whatever. Call me." She hugged Elise, who hugged her back tightly.

"Thanks."

Cope worried the whole drive over to Ben's place. He knew it was silly, knew Erin was in good hands. But it scared him shitless to think about what his brother would go through should they lose the baby or Erin.

Ella left him to his thoughts. Another thing he appreciated about her, she seemed to understand when he needed to think and be left alone. She didn't try to guilt him into paying attention to her or pout like so many other women he knew did.

She took his hand as they got out and made their way to the elevator.

"I'm sorry I was short with you earlier. I'm an asshole."

"You're not an asshole. You're worried about your brother and Erin and the baby. It's okay you know, to be human. Also, I'm not made of glass."

She forged ahead when the elevator arrived on Erin's floor. He unlocked the door and turned off the entry alarm.

"I didn't say you were made of glass," he said as he led the way to the master bedroom.

"Erin says she's got a bag there already. Her labor bag. We'll need an overnight bag of some sort with a change of clothing for Ben and Todd. If you know where one is, I'll get some bedding from the linen closet in the hall."

She moved efficiently, gathering things and putting them in a central place. He didn't know why he worried about her; she didn't seem upset or angry or even hurt.

"All right." He hefted the bag he'd tossed clothes into for Ben and Todd along with toothbrushes and some deodorant.

"Ben just called my cell and said to not bother with pillows or blankets. The hospital brought them stuff for that. I got the book he's reading and Todd's e-book reader." She held up a tote. "Tossed in some magazines and a notepad and pen for Erin. I called in the order for Red Mill too. I ordered some for you as well. I'm going to cab back to your house to grab my car once we get back to the hospital. That way you don't have to worry about getting me home, and you can focus on Erin."

"Like I'm going to be all right with that? We'll drop everything off, and I'll take you back." He grabbed the tote she'd been carrying and kissed her quickly. "Don't argue. There's no reason for you to take a cab when I love being with you and can take you."

She looked at him sideways with a smile. "Whatever you say, Andrew."

"If only it was that easy," he muttered, and she laughed.

"You had easy, Andrew. You profess some sort of dislike for that in a woman now." She smirked.

"I like it in *you*. A lot. Just for future reference and all."

"You should call your mother. Or I can. But she should know."

"Why you gotta ruin all that sexy back-and-forth by bringing my mother into it? Anyway, I'm driving; I can't call anyone."

She heaved a sigh. "You're very difficult when you don't want to do something. You know that? Though the way you stick out your bottom lip, daring me to reach over and give it a nip, is quite adorable." She dug around in her bag and pulled the phone out. "Number? I'll call."

"Just don't, Ella. Seriously, I don't want you to be in the middle of this mess. You don't deserve that."

She touched his arm. "Andrew, that's her grandchild. She's making the baby a blanket. I've spoken with her about the nursery and the baby dozens of times. No matter what your dad has done, Annalee loves that baby already. She's going to want to be there for Ben too. Let me make the call. Then your father isn't even part of it. Todd already called his mom, she and Annalee are friends. Can you imagine how she'll feel if you don't call? Plus, if I may be so bold, she's your mom, and it's totally her job to comfort you, and you need it."

"Damn, you have that guilt thing down." He gave her the number as he was lucky enough to find a space in the tiny lot adjacent to Red Mill.

"I'll call, you go get the food. It's under your name."

He gave her a dirty look as she went for her wallet. "Please don't insult me by trying to pay."

"You're easily insulted if that's what gets you all het up." She primly said this and then began to dial the phone before he could reply. Knowing he had it better if he left, he did, grinning at her as he did.

Thank heavens Annalee answered and not Billy. Ella didn't want to deal with that jerk right then.

"Mrs. Copeland? It's Ella Tipton. From the café?"

"Of course, honey. Is everything all right?"

"It should be. I wanted to let you know that Erin's spending the night in the hospital. They're observing her because her blood pressure is very high and she's retaining water. They'll watch her carefully, but they think she'll be fine to go home tomorrow and be on bed rest for the remainder of her pregnancy."

"Oh no!"

Ella gave her the information and Erin's room number, reassuring her that Erin would be all right and her sons wanted her to know. In truth, Ella thought Cope and Ben would be comforted by her presence, but she left that unsaid. It was scary territory, getting to know Andrew's mother in an entirely new way.

Cope came back shortly, arms laden with bags of food. The smell of it made her mouth water, even though they'd eaten some hours before.

"I added rings for you."

She smiled. "You're good to me." Meaning it.

He turned to her. "I love you, Ella. I want to make you happy. I want to make you half as happy as you make me. Thank you. Thank you for being here for me today. It means a lot."

She swallowed hard, trying very much not to cry. "I wouldn't be anywhere else."

"I know. Thank God for it."

19

"We've missed you around here, honey. How's things?" her mother asked, feigning nonchalance. She hadn't been around for dinner in a while, mainly because she'd been working at her job and dashing back to the café to be sure all was well there too. With Erin on modified bed rest, she spent more time at her house or with Cope at his place.

But she'd missed her parents, even with all the drama. Things had gotten better, and she thought maybe she could invite Cope to dinner here and there. But first, she had to tell them more about him to make them feel better about the situation.

"I'm dating."

Her father whipped his head around, his gaze on her narrowing suspiciously. "That so?"

She girded herself against what she knew was her own past coming back to scare her parents even more. "His name is Andrew Copeland. You've met Cope at the café a time or two, remember, Mom? He's tall, dark and ridiculously gorgeous. Co-owns a security consulting business with his brother and Todd Keenan." Her mother did not understand the two men one woman thing, but she had said if that was

Erin's choice and they all knew the boundaries, it was none of her beeswax. If only some of Ben and Todd's family members could feel the same.

"How old is he?" Her father had relaxed a little when she'd mentioned Cope owning his own business, but the age thing might be a big deal.

"He's thirty-six."

Her father scowled. "He's like a decade older than you are? What's he need with a woman so much younger?"

Her mother shook her head. "So exactly how long have you been dating this man?"

"I've known him for six years now, but we started dating a little over a month ago. I see him about four times a week when I can. He's giving me self-defense training, so we do that three times a week."

Her father's anger melted a bit. "How do you feel about that?"

She shrugged. "I feel like I have some more control. Like if I was going to be attacked again, I could at least handle it better. Or something. I know it gives me some control over the fear." It was the most she'd said about the attack and the fear she was left with in a long time.

"Handle it better? You were attacked in your own home by a man who kicked a door in and tried to beat you to death. You fended him off even with the burns. You handled him, Ella. You never quit. I'd say you handled it damned well."

Her heart kicked in her chest at the way his voice broke at the end. "Do you really see it that way?" She sent him a watery smile.

Her father cocked his head at her. "Baby girl, do you think we'd see it any other way?"

"It's just that, well, I know you're disappointed in the choices I make."

"We'd like you to be safer. And yes, I think you'd be safer here with us. But that doesn't mean we don't see you as the fighter you are.

Daddy and I didn't raise quitters." Her mother's matter-of-fact delivery made her feel better.

"Don't you think we get it? We love you, Ella. You came into this world and we guided you up, watched you grow into an amazing woman. You needed to go out and live in a way that you spit in the eye of what happened to you. Every day, even when you'd sweat and try not to cry." He shook his head at her. "You think we didn't notice?"

"Just because we knew you had to pull away from us to prove to yourself you could do it, doesn't mean we weren't scared for you. Doesn't mean we couldn't see the toll on you. You're my baby. It tore me up every single time I'd watch your hands shake when we got into a crowd. To see the dark circles under your eyes because you worked so hard at school and your job. Of course we wanted you here. Here is safe. We could protect you. So we wanted that. And I still want that. I can't play cheerleader to some of the stuff you do, because I just can't. But that doesn't mean I don't support *you* and respect the way you have risen above and found your way back to the Ella you were before he came along."

She sighed, feeling better than she had in a long time for a host of reasons.

"I'm not going to be able to get back that far." She shrugged. "That person is part of me, but so is who I was with Bill. No, no, he's not Voldemort; we can say his name." She paused, trying not to smile at how they had no freaking idea who Voldemort was. "The bad guy in the Harry Potter books. Anyway. I don't want to forget it. I won't be that cheerful, carefree person again, not totally. I can't. What he did to me. What I allowed myself to become has changed me in ways I can't get past. So I've learned to deal with them. To accept that I will always have a darkness inside, maybe a kernel of fear in my belly that will explode for no reason, hurtling me back years to a place when that fear was normal." She realized this as she spoke. "I think I've finally realized and accepted that triumph. It means I react strongly when it happens because it is not a normal occurrence in my life anymore. I do not live in fear. I have my moments. I am not totally over it, and I don't know that I can be."

She sipped her tea, accepting totally the truth of what she'd just said. "Being with Andrew has helped me realize many things. I do have good judgment. I was worried I'd just have to give up on men forever as I had such terrible taste or what have you. But he is good and kind, and he gives me the space to be not quite whole and not quite normal. I don't feel broken when I'm with him. Because those jagged edges are part of who I am. He sees them and accepts that they're part of me." She'd been pulling herself away to protect that part of her she needed to survive and get past the fear. It had been right there, though she'd never seen it. Apparently her mother saw it too.

Ella took her mother's hands and squeezed. "I feel like if he can accept them, I can too." As she said it, a knot, the low-lying knot in her gut that Andrew would wise up and leave her, was gone. He told her he loved her, and while she fiercely wanted to believe him, the doubt had remained, knotted with the fear. Until she'd spoken aloud the things she supposed her brain had been mulling over as the frenzy of the last few days with Erin out of the hospital had taken top priority. Once she'd said it aloud, the power of it had freed her from the fear.

"Those of us who love you never felt otherwise." Her father patted her hand before grabbing a roll.

"Are you serious about him?" her mother asked, steering the conversation back. "What does he do at this security firm?"

"Yes, yes, I'm serious about him. I like him. I trust him. He values the things I do like family and friends. He owns this business with his brother and Todd, and they do all sorts of stuff from setting up security systems to bodyguards and personal security."

"All right then, when do we get to meet him? All official and everything?" her mother asked.

"Can I invite him to dinner next week? I was thinking it would be a good time if you don't have any other guests invited."

"Yes. I'll make a pot roast. He's not a vegetarian?"

"Yum. He'll love it."

Her mother grinned. "Well, isn't that nice? I'll do a coconut cake too."

"You're the best mom I've ever had." Coconut cake was her absolute favorite dessert ever, and her mother's offer to make it meant she was pleased with the news about Ella dating. It felt *good* to have this rhythm with her parents again. She'd needed this connection. Had missed it desperately.

When she left, it was with a lightness of heart and a certainty she hadn't had in a long time.

It was there, waiting in his mailbox. The envelope was deep blue this time, the ink metallic silver. A fountain pen? He smiled as he took it into the house.

Inside, she'd tucked three origami cranes. He held one in his palm, looking this way and that. The sharp, precise lines belied the whimsy and artistry.

He called her, knowing she'd be arriving home from work.

"I had no idea you knew origami. You're a surprise to me sometimes, beautiful Ella."

Her laughter was his reward. "I made them when I was in an interminable meeting day before yesterday. I hadn't remembered I knew how until my hands remembered for me."

"You busy tonight?" He needed to be with her. Loved the way it felt to hear her voice, to smell her on his hands, in his house, loved to walk around a corner and see her there, perched at the center island in his kitchen, sipping tea and reading through a client file.

"I will be for about an hour or so. I'm actually walking to Erin's front door as we talk. I'm having tea and cookies with your mom, Elise and Erin. But since I don't want to tax Erin too much, I'm only staying for an hour or less. This was our agreement, and you know how she can be."

"You're having tea with my mom?"

She paused and lowered her voice. "Is that a problem?"

"No." He said it, and it was true. "I wanted you to spend more time with her. Get to know her better now that you're my girlfriend." He said it, and that was true too. He liked saying it out loud. "I just didn't know. Caught me by surprise."

"All right. How about I cook you dinner? You can come by in say, an hour and a half? You can stay over if you like."

"I'll see you then, and how about I bring something by so you can relax?" He knew Thursdays were a hellish day for her. She'd have done the morning shift at the café and then headed to her other job, broke for an hour with her advisor and then back to work.

He heard Ben in the background and smiled at Ella's response to his brother. Light and teasing.

"I'm sorry. Ben came out to see if everything was all right. I'll see you in a while then. And thank you."

He said his good-bye and went off to shower and get ready to meet her at her place.

"That was your brother. He says hello and that you owe him a call." Ella went inside as she spoke to Ben. She knew she had a goofy grin on; hell, who wouldn't?

"How are things going between you two?" Ben leaned back against a side table, crossing his arms, and wow, a girl would have to be dead not to notice the way his biceps got all bulgy when he did that. And while she had nothing but love and admiration for what the three of them shared, Ella was not above checking out Todd's butt or Ben's biceps. She was human, after all.

"Good." She blushed.

"That's what he says. You two are good for each other. Come on through; Erin and my mom are in the living room with Elise."

She grabbed his hand quickly. "How are you? Can I help with anything?"

He hugged her, kissing the top of her head. "We're all fine. Erin is going stir crazy, but between you and the new manager, she doesn't have to worry about the café at all. Everyone visits and calls. She's writing songs again, so Adrian has been here a lot. The two of them bicker regularly, which keeps her sharp and entertained. Though, poor Adrian, he takes the brunt of her pissy moods when they work together."

Ella laughed. "They have an old rhythm. It works for them. Plus he's no pushover. I'm sure he appreciates the time with her anyway. You know where I am if you need me for anything, all right?"

"Yes. Thank you. I do know that. *We* know that." His smile was crooked and reminded her a lot of his brother.

When they got to the living room, she dipped to kiss Erin's cheeks. "Hiya. I brought a pie. My mom wanted me to tell you it's low-fat and low-sugar. She says the blueberries are good for you."

"Gimme." Erin's face lit up as she took the pie. "Please tell her I said thank you."

"Hello, sweetheart." Annalee smiled at her as she came into the room holding a tray with tea on it. Elise followed with another tray of cookies. "You know, I think it's high time I got to meet your mother, don't you?"

"Hello, Mrs. Copeland. It's lovely to see you." Ella knew she blushed, but it was still weird. She wanted Andrew's mother to like her and think she was good enough for her son. "I'm sure my mom would love that. I'll speak with her and get some dates and get back to you on it."

"Oh that would be just fine. And I'm Annalee, please."

Rennie bounded into the room and into Ella's arms for a hug. "You're here! Ella's here, Momma!"

"I know, noodle. I told you she'd get here soon." Elise winked at her daughter and then leaned in to kiss Ella's cheek.

They sat and had tea. Rennie had some juice as she painted Erin's toenails a pretty shade of red.

"I think Andrew will have the wainscoting ready in time for Thanksgiving. I truly don't know where all his endless talent comes from. You must be so proud of how creative he is."

The others looked to her, surprised. "Wainscoting?"

"In his house. Speaking of that, I know he was hoping on having the night before Thanksgiving dinner there, but since Erin's going to need to stay closer to home, perhaps we can have a birthday party for him there? We can set Erin up on the chaise so she's not up and around. It can be quieter than Thanksgiving, but I know he really wants to show all his work off. Now that he's living there, it's like he's gone into overdrive. So much is getting done. It blows me away."

"He's living in the house in Ballard? Full-time?"

Ella looked at them and saw they did not know much about what Cope had been doing in his house. At first she'd been horrified, as if she'd told a secret, no matter how unintentionally. But as she sat there, the embarrassment faded into mild agitation that not a single one of these people knew a damned thing about Cope's inner life.

"None of you knew? Really? He's been living in the house full-time for weeks now. He's an artist. Did you know that? He does these amazing sketches. The woodwork he does is beautiful but strong, like he is. He's put his heart and soul into that house. He's been doing it for two years." She didn't mention poetry. That felt intimate, a sensual secret she carried in her heart, a side of him no one else saw.

Ben sat down heavily. "I've picked him up there a few times in the last few weeks when we've had some consults first thing. I never went inside. I feel like an asshole."

"No. Please don't." She swallowed hard; this was really far out of her comfort zone. But he was worth it, damn it. "I mentioned it because I thought you all knew. He knows you're busy and preoccupied with Erin and the baby." And other stuff, but she wasn't going to bring that into the conversation. "He's so talented with his hands." She blushed furiously, nearly choking on the cookie she'd bitten nervously. "I didn't mean it that way."

Annalee patted her knee. "Ella, I do like you. Of all the girls Andrew has been around, not a one has seen that other side of him. Remind me to show you all the scrollwork he did for me in my sewing room. Put in chair railing and all sorts of things. He's a sweet boy."

Oh. She smiled at the other woman. The woman who understood that hidden part of Andrew too. Warmth flooded her. It meant more than she could really think about just then. Knowing that this woman appreciated the whole of Andrew Copeland.

"It's been lonely for him." Annalee stirred her tea absently. "He's a very complicated boy. Wrote me poetry when he was growing up. Always a sunny day when you're with Andrew. I suppose you saw right through that. The two of you are a lot alike. Which cheers me." She looked back to Ben, who listened to the talk of his brother with avid interest. "I worry, you see. I assumed things all my life, all my life as a wife and mother. I assumed my family was strong enough to weather even the fiercest of storms."

Annalee sighed, and Ella recognized the sound, the weight of duty, responsibility, pain and fear so very clearly.

"I definitely think a birthday party is a great idea," Ben said.

"Good. I think it should be fun, though if he hates it, I'm blaming it all on Erin." Ella grinned at her friend, who rolled her eyes.

"By the way, Ella. Our new part-timer has been working out great. I upped her hours. Which means you can now work more at your other job. Or maybe sleep more."

Spend time with Andrew.

"Spend time with Cope." Elise smiled serenely.

"He's so handsome, Ella." Rennie sipped her juice. "I never seen no boy looking cuter than he does. He gots that dimple that comes out when he smiles. His hair is so pretty."

Elise sighed. "Lazy grammar girl. You *haven't* seen *any* boy and he *has* a dimple. In other words, I totally agree that our Cope is cute."

"You told Dad that Cope and Ella would make adorable babies. Are you making one now?" Rennie looked to Ella, who was quite sure she was beet red by that point.

"Nope." She cleared her throat and caught sight of Annalee struggling not to laugh. "Making babies is serious business. I've known Andrew for many years now, but we haven't been dating long enough for us to get that far in our thinking."

"He looks at you like Dad looks at Mom." Rennie said it like it was fact, and something inside her yearned for that to be true. "Also, just so you know, Irene is a great name for a baby. If Aunt Erin doesn't use it on her baby, you and Cope can have it."

Elise groaned in the background.

She nodded her head seriously at Rennie. "Thank you for that."

When it was time to leave, Ben walked her to her car. Naturally she'd protested, but he just gave her the exact same look Cope did when she tried to argue with him.

"Don't fuss. You're family, Ella. And we take care of each other. You're Andy's girlfriend, and above that, you're our friend."

"Thank you."

"No. Thank you, Ella. I guess I'd gotten so used to the laid-back thing my brother does that I just forget he's deeper than most people assume. I feel like shit for that. He and I used to hang out a lot more, but since the pregnancy and with Erin being on bed rest, we've not been around each other as much as we should. Or I should say I haven't been as connected to his life as I should. He's been here for me at every turn. I can't believe I didn't know about the house. I mean, I've been inside it here and there. But I haven't seen it since before Erin got pregnant."

"I'm so out of my depth here, Ben. I don't know what's okay to share and not okay to share. I never had this with anyone before. I do think he'd like to hang out with you more often. But he understands your focus is on Erin right now. And that's where it should be."

Ben opened her door after he looked to be sure her backseat was clear. "Ella, you're doing just fine. I hope I haven't made you feel as if you're caught in the middle. You genuinely care about Andy, and he obviously cares about you to expose a side of himself he so rarely shows anyone. Also, in case you haven't noticed it yet, we're a big, nosy bunch who have horrible boundaries with each other." He grinned, and she saw so much of Andrew in him it was impossible not to smile back.

"I care about your brother a great deal. He's very important to me. I want to sing his praises all the time, of course." She snorted. "But I don't want him to think I'm going around him."

"My brother knows Erin and my mother. He knows you can't stand against either of them. They have witchy ways when it comes to finding stuff out you never meant to reveal. "Anyway, please tell Andy I'll see him at work tomorrow and that I asked about the house. I mean, I'll ask about it tomorrow too, it's stupid that I haven't before. Just tell him I said hey. I'll get back with you about the birthday party stuff."

"Good. Call me if you guys need anything. Even if Erin just needs the company."

Ben hugged her tight. "I'm so glad Andy finally got up the nerve to ask you out." He grinned. "Go on now. Be safe and good night."

20

Cope looked at her, always ensorcelled by how effortlessly beautiful she was. Hair tucked behind an ear, her face nearly devoid of makeup. Her eyes lit up at his attention.

"How was the tea and cookies?" He snagged a corn muffin, thinking of Ella naked.

"It was good. Erin looks much better this week, don't you think?"

"She's not as swollen. Todd and Ben seem calmer too."

"Ben says he'll see you tomorrow. He asked about the house. I told them about the wainscoting. They're all excited to see it."

"You all talked about me?" He sounded surprised.

She looked up and laughed. "Of course we did. We're women; that's what we do. You've certainly been around women long enough to know this, Andrew Copeland. By the by, Rennie informed me Irene was a great name for a baby girl just in case we were trying to make one. She says if Erin doesn't use it for her baby, we're welcome to it. Your mother seemed pleased by this information."

"Wow. Rennie's on her game today." He tried not to laugh but failed.

"She also told me you're the cutest boy she knows and that you have great hair. Naturally, we all agreed with this because, hello, you're very pretty, and your hair is one of your finest attributes. Other than your ass. We did not speak about that, however. Your mother seemed relieved by that part."

He cringed. "Great." And then he realized what else she'd said. "Ben asked about the house? Out of the blue?"

"I brought it up. I admit I bragged on you a bit." She ducked her head, blushing. "But he followed up with questions. They all did. I think everyone is excited to see what you've done with the place."

"You all talked about me?"

"Duh. We established this what, three minutes ago? I really do like your mother. She said you used to write her poetry when you were growing up."

"You told them about the poetry?"

Her eyes widened, and she shook her head. "No. I wouldn't do that. Not that it's anything to be embarrassed about," she added quickly. "It's something that's ours. Intimate. I wouldn't do that."

Of course she wouldn't. Christ. "I'm sorry, Red. I didn't mean to accuse you like that."

"I'm feeling my way along here, Andrew. I don't . . . this isn't something I do. I'm sorry if I broke some rule about not talking about you to your family. In the future, if there's something you don't want me to bring up, you should say so."

She got up and went into the kitchen.

What the hell was he doing? He *liked* that she'd spent time with his mother. Liked that she was already close with his sister-in-law and brother too. They all seemed to like her as much as he did. Though right then they might have been preferable to her than the dumb-ass way he was acting.

He followed, pulling her into his arms from behind. "I'm sorry. Really. I don't know why I reacted that way."

She turned to him, and the look in her eyes sliced through him. Was this how the ex had been?

"Shall I tell you why I think you acted that way?"

"After I kiss you." He slid a thumb over her bottom lip. "If that's okay with you?"

She nodded, and he took her mouth, her taste settling in, calming, soothing, clearing up all the static. She was home.

"That's so much better. Now, do enlighten me on why you think I reacted like a cock."

She smirked, and they both felt better. "You're afraid of showing the best part of yourself and having them reject it. You're Cope, the pretty boy. Cope, the easygoing brother who always shows up to help someone move, the guy who flirts with everything with a vagina and breasts. That's easy. Who can hate that guy? So you fucked around with women you didn't really even like. It was easier that way to walk away and keep it all about sex. And who can say anything about it? You're charmingly up-front, and these women can't seem to get enough of it.

"But you're so much more than that. You're a man who can make art from wood. A man who can take pen and paper and draw the heart of a woman." She sifted her fingers through his hair. "It's easy to be Cope. But it's intimate to be Andrew. You're exposing yourself in a way that could be terribly painful if people don't react the way they should."

"What do you know about that?" He didn't say it to be hostile, but it rankled that she saw him so clearly, even as it brought him to his knees to be known so well.

"I know that I lived on autopilot for years. I got up; I survived the day. I slept and got up to start over. I know that it's the people closest to you who can do the most damage. I know that love and trust go hand in hand. I also know that your brother, your mother, your sister-in-law and your friends love you. I know I'd never do anything on purpose that would bring you pain. Not ever."

He hugged her. "Are you saying my heart is safe with you?"

"Yes."

"I like it that you hang out with my family. I like that we're all part of the same group of friends. Obviously I don't want that stuff I told you about my dad to get shared with my mother, but Ben already knows. I ended up telling him after he pestered me relentlessly about it."

She sent him a raised brow. "You can't avoid it forever."

"I can start with not wanting to talk about it now."

She snorted. "You're lucky you have such nice hair," she muttered.

"I am?" He kissed her neck, and she didn't push him away. "Even when I'm a total asshole?"

She laughed. "Andrew Copeland, you're a pissy butthead sometimes, yes. But you're not an asshole. Believe me."

"Even if I say I'd really love to have sex with you right now? And it's my turn."

She laughed again. "You *always* say it's your turn." She tipped her head back, allowing him access to her neck.

"Do I? I should be disciplined, don't you think?"

"Sure. No sex for you. That'll teach you."

"*Hmpf.* I vote no."

He danced her toward the bed, pulling at her sweater and T-shirt as he did.

"You're still my favorite Copeland. Just in case you were wondering."

He straddled her body after he'd peeled her clothes off. "This is good to know. Because I'm the only Copeland who gets to look at these every day." He dipped down to swipe his tongue over first the right nipple and then the left.

"Erin would probably frown on me showing my breasts to Ben, yes. Though I haven't consulted with her on this point. However, hers are so gargantuan right now, I'm not sure it's much of a fair comparison."

God, she was pretty. Running his hands all over her body, he marveled in her, the shape and feel of her body—curves, sharp lines and muscle—against him, beneath him. She looked up at him the whole time, those sexy green eyes half-lidded, burning for him. That secret self only he saw, opened up like a flower.

The change when she let her sensual self take over was incredible. Her movements slowed down, her voice lowered, she even smelled warm, like honey, sticky-sweet. She was only this way with him. She didn't need to hold back, and she knew it.

That she knew he was different and opened up made him feel like a rock star. Made him feel worthy in ways he'd never imagined before.

He moved, sitting and helping her onto his lap. Laughing, she helped get pillows behind his back, and before he knew it, she had him suited up and was sliding herself down over his cock, her body settling around him, driving him mad with the heat, the tight caress of her flesh against his.

"I'm pretty sure it's actually my turn," she murmured as she rose and fell over him.

"Whichever. Whatever. You're on me, I'm in you, that's what matters."

She managed to open her eyes to meet his gaze, that connection clicking into place all the way down to her toes.

She was helpless against him in a way that left her far more vulnerable than she'd ever been with Bill. Andrew Copeland was her heart. Just how this had come to be, even when it had happened, she wasn't sure. But it was there. He lived inside her, past all those walls she'd erected to keep herself safe.

"Waltzed right in and made yourself at home." She smirked.

He felt so good inside her she simply let herself feel what he did. Filling her up more than physically.

She arched, offering as much of herself to him as she could. He touched her like she was fine and precious, like he couldn't *not* touch her. No one had ever made her feel so cherished and sexually irresistible.

"I did? I'm a scoundrel that way." He nuzzled her neck, licking up to her earlobe, which he took between his teeth until she squeaked with pleasure, and he chuckled.

"I'm so easy when you touch me." She laughed as he took two handfuls of breasts and hauled her closer.

"Thank God for it. I like you being easy for me."

Climax slammed into her as he slipped his hand down to her pussy, finding her clit ready and slick, needing to be touched. She held on tight, trying to breathe, falling in deep as he played the rhythm of her body.

"Hope you realize I'm one of those guests who just won't leave," he mumbled sometime later, their bodies tangled in the mess of sheets, underwear and blankets.

"Thank God."

"I'm sorry we fought."

She rested her head on his shoulder, idly playing with one of his nipple rings. "Do you never have fights with your other women?"

"That part about the women before. About how I didn't like them." He took a deep breath. "Cut pretty close to the bone."

"I didn't want to hurt you, but I see you, Andrew. I know you. I can't lie about how exceptional I think you are, and I can't lie about what I see in you."

He shook his head. "None of them were what you are. This is new for me. Not how I feel about you, I've wanted you a very long time. But dealing with your feelings and remembering I want you to be around tomorrow." He snorted. "Takes getting used to. Though I want to, which is also new."

What girl didn't want to hear that from a man like Andrew Copeland? She knew part of why it thrilled her so much was, hello, he was hot and had been the freewheeling sexy boy with a thousand women fawning over him. But she believed him when he told her how he felt about her. However improbable it was, she *had* been different. What they had was different than what he'd been before with those other women.

Another part of her realized it was actually true. She'd seen him with various women over the years, and she'd lay odds that none of them had seen the inside of his house much less gotten an "I love you" from his lips.

"I don't want to hurt you. I'm not good at this. What if I fuck it up?"

"You're going to hurt me." She licked over the hard muscle of his pecs. "This is inevitable, because no one can hurt you like someone who's close to you. We'll fight. You're a pushy, bossy man, though you like to play laid-back. I know you, Andrew; you're not laid-back about important things. And that's where we're going to tangle. Because I don't know how to be a girlfriend, and you don't know how to have one."

He snorted as he stroked over the hollow just below her ear, sending shivers through her. "Least you've finally been able to call yourself my girlfriend. This is progress."

"But we're not what I was with Bill. Don't think I don't understand this."

She shifted to look at his face better. "Hot damn, you're pretty." She kissed that mouth of his, meaning to be quick, but with him, she never knew if it would be a sweet pause or a fast-moving wildfire.

He groaned, opening his mouth, sliding his arms around her, holding her body to his as he took over, devouring her with such self-assured sexuality she nearly melted on the spot. Parts of her were significantly wetter than before, so maybe that's where she was melting.

"What's making you smile?"

"I made up a horrible joke in my head. But I can totally laugh at it that way. Saves embarrassment of saying it out loud."

"Come on, I promise to laugh at all your jokes. It's part of the boyfriend job. Though you can't tell anyone this, I'm new at it too."

"Never say," she murmured as she sat up. "Andrew, I simply must tell you that you have the most beautifully male body I've ever seen. You're, god, you make my mouth water."

He blushed and she smiled down at him, surprised and touched by how sweet and shy he actually was when it came to the big, important stuff.

"Flattery will get you just about anywhere with me, Red. Then again, all you have to do is ask, and it's yours. I'm putty in your hands."

Reaching down between them, she grasped his cock, giving it a friendly squeeze. "I promise to be gentle."

And she was. Mostly.

21

"Are you getting enough sleep?" Elise looked over Ella warily. "You have dark circles under your eyes. Is Cope pestering you to have sex instead of letting you sleep?" She then laughed, making Ella groan and roll her eyes.

She'd stopped over at Elise's to drop off a book she'd borrowed and to visit for a few minutes in the midst of a really insanely chaotic period of time where she'd been running from place to place, trying to stay afloat in a sea of to-do list items.

"I'm fine. Just had to catch up on some client work. I did it after Cope was done *pestering* me and he'd gone to sleep. This week has been rushed, and I've had a lot to do. It's just until Erin is better and I finish these last credits. It's not that much longer."

"You're going to get sick if you don't get more sleep."

She grinned at her friend. "Thanks, Mom. But really, I'm fine, I promise. We got into a bit of a tiff and then, well, you know the making-up part. That part took a few hours. Believe me when I tell you I'd trade what that man can do with his hands and mouth for a few hours' more sleep any day."

"You slapper!" Elise dissolved into laughter. "Makeup sex is the best. What'd you fight about?"

She sighed. "Do you know it's been something like five years or so since I've shared any details about an argument with someone I'm dating? God, no, more like six, since I didn't really share much about Bill. I'm out of practice."

"And it's hard to share when you took all that weight on yourself for so long." Elise smiled at her. "He's not Bill."

Ella laughed. And then she laughed some more at the very thought. "No. God, no, he's not Bill. Andrew is kind. He's sweet and loving, and he listens to me. He even gets pissy with me."

"This is good? That he gets pissy?"

"Yeah. Because pissy can be survived. Pissy is what you get when you're dealing with someone you trust. See, I'm not even sure if he gets it, but we fought twice, not even fought. He's worried about Erin and stuff, and he snapped at me. But I batted it away and kept on. It never occurred to me, not even for a moment, to be afraid or unsure. I just let it roll off and gave him shit right back."

"And that's huge."

Of course Elise got it. Ella nodded. "Yeah. Like beyond huge. What's funny is I never expected it to be any other way. I suppose I've just known he was different from go."

"That must knock him for a loop. Those boys are very confident and stuff. But, wow, are they protective of the women they love. And don't look at me that way; he loves you. He wears it on his skin like a neon jumpsuit."

Ella blushed. She hadn't told Elise of Andrew's declaration of love. Hadn't told anyone. She believed it, accepted it and carried it around like a touchstone. It felt like magic, as if she'd break the spell if she said it out loud. "Like the crazy inmates at the county jail? Great."

"Oh yes, totally like that." Elise jerked her head toward the interior of the house. "Come in? Have a glass of wine? Rennie is sleeping, and

Brody should be home soon. He stopped by Erin's on his way home from the shop."

"I wish I could, but I have to run."

"All right. Oh and hey, the seamstress called today. Your brides-maid dress arrived, and you'll need to go in for a fitting. She suggested we wait until after Thanksgiving. Erin, well, let's just get through the pregnancy and delivery, and then we can think about that part." Elise hugged herself.

"She's going to be all right. How could she not be?"

Elise sighed. "It happens every day. She's strong, and it's looking like the modified bed rest is controlling the blood pressure. But she has to be careful. They've put her on a special diet, which she hates. But Ben and Todd won't let her get away with any nonsense, even if she tried it."

"She's scared. She'll behave because she's a good mom already. Though I'm sure that's enough pressure right there. Knowing what it means to have a child, but also what it means to lose that."

"It makes me nauseated to even think about what it would be like for her right now. But she's got a group of people who love her to help with everything. And she knows it. Rennie and I lucked out to end up here with these people in our lives. To be loved the way they all love. It's a gift."

Ella nodded. "Yeah, it is. Listen, I really do have to run. I'll see you soon though, right?"

"You free this weekend? Brody and Adrian are taking Rennie to the movies on Saturday, so I have a free afternoon if you want to grab lunch."

"That sounds great. Why don't we find out what Erin can eat on this new diet, and we can make it and take it to her place? Free Todd and Ben up for a while and give her some new faces to look at."

"Great idea. I'll call her and make the arrangements and get back to you with details." Elise hugged her. "Talk to you soon."

Ella waved and headed back down the sidewalk to her car just as Adrian and Brody pulled up.

"Why, if it isn't the loveliest redhead I know," Brody said, grinning as he pulled her into a hug. "You here to get my lovely wife-to-be in trouble?"

"If so, can I watch?" Adrian winked at her.

"Mmm-hmm. If there's trouble anywhere around here, I doubt it's coming from me. This is a whole lot of Brown maleness right up on this driveway. How's Erin?"

"She was actually getting tucked up into bed when we left. She's doing all right. Her BP is much better today, but she's still pretty swollen in her feet and ankles. They're monitoring her and the baby, and everything looks good, so they're going to go ahead and let her stay home on bed rest and not push labor unless it gets worse."

"I'm stopping by tomorrow after I get off work to check on her. You guys please let me know if you need my help."

"You're leaving? Come on inside and have a glass of wine with us." Brody touched her hand.

"Thanks. No, Elise already asked, but I do have to go. I have a really full schedule tomorrow, so I need to get home to rest."

They both escorted her to her car. And it was then Andrew pulled up. Her heart skipped a beat as she took him in, saw the surprised pleasure on his face at the sight of her.

"That's our cue to beat it." Adrian knocked once on her car's roof. "Have a good night, Ella. See you soon." He and Brody waved at Cope and headed inside, while Cope headed straight to her.

"Hey, Red, fancy seeing you here." He leaned in her window and kissed her soundly. "That's better. Takes the edge off."

She just let that soak in, smiling at him. "I was just on my way out. Glad I didn't miss you."

"Are you free tonight? I know I slept over last night too, but I've come to notice something peculiar, Ella. I sleep much better with you next to me." He leaned closer. "I promise to make you breakfast in the morning."

She groaned. "I'm mightily tempted."

He brushed his thumb against her cheek. "I didn't notice these dark smudges until just now. Here's what I'm going to do. Come to my house. I'll run you a bath, complete with Epsom salts. Fix you a cup of tea and tuck you into bed relatively unmolested. I'd say totally, but we both know I can't resist just a little bit of kissing and touching."

"I have to get up at five. You don't have to be up until seven. That's a lot to ask when sex isn't on the table."

"We haven't done it on a table yet. I'll put it on the list for next time." He touched her again, just a butterfly against her cheek. "It's up to you, but I don't care if I only have you until five, I just want to be with you. Though, how about we switch locations since you're so tired and you have to be up really early. Your house?"

She smiled. "All right. But I can't guarantee I'll be awake if you aren't there in half an hour or so." Yawning hugely, she turned the car on, and he stepped back.

"Be right there. I was just stopping off to check in with Brody about something. That can wait, though. I'll call him about it."

Before she could protest, he'd jogged his very fine ass back to his truck, making her all swoony and lightheaded.

He knocked on her door, excited to see her, to be able to touch her. Silly how quickly seeing her every day had become necessary.

She opened, and he realized just how tired she must have been. Even her normally very straight posture was slumped a bit. He stepped inside, waiting for her to close and lock the door before he took her into his arms.

"Baby, you're knackered. I'm sorry I pushed to come over. I'll go home." The last thing he wanted was to make her more tired.

She smiled up at him. "Plate on the table for you. I need to shower. Cookies in the jar."

Okay then. He considered following her into the bathroom to help with relaxation and stress relief. He sure knew a bunch of ways to work out the kinks. But that's what most likely kept her awake the night before.

He looked at her table, where she'd prepared not just one sandwich, but three. *Meatloaf? Awesome.*

"The woman is a goddess," he mumbled as he put on a pot of tea for her.

He loved the way she looked all fresh from the shower. Her hair pulled away from her face only emphasized the beauty of her features, the size of her eyes.

"Thank you," she said, taking the mug of tea. The apartment was cold, he knew, due to an aging radiator. But she had on her sweats and a long-sleeved shirt. He made a mental note to bring her some wool socks and to look into radiant heat for the floors in his bathrooms.

Wow. He stilled a moment, startling himself with the idea of living with her. And then being stupefied that he'd startled as he was ass over teakettle in love.

Living together was a huge step. Natural with the course they'd set. His place was bigger and safer for her. He thought of his house with her stamp on it, that simple femininity she had, the bold sense of colors and style.

He thought of his brother and the melding of three very distinct styles and personalities in their apartment. They worked as a unit. He admired their effort and commitment to each other, their energy put into maintaining such a complicated but totally loving relationship, which was not only intact but thriving.

For a time, Cope had worried that Ben would fall away from Erin and Todd, that in the end, Ben would end up alone and broken. Now he knew that wouldn't happen, but there was still the worry of loss.

He'd spoken with Ben earlier that day, and his brother had been scared shitless and trying to hold it together when he was around Erin.

It hurt, seeing his brother so worried and not being able to help. He worried about Erin too, but she wasn't his wife. What would it be like to have that threatened? It made his anger at his father even worse.

Still, he was there with Ella, and for that moment, everything was right. He watched her as she laid out her clothes for the following morning, content to simply be with her.

She yawned, and he turned to the bed, pulling the blankets back. "Get in, babe. Snuggle down, and let's go to sleep."

"Mmm, that sounds very good." She drained the tea, and he took the mug and the plate his sandwiches had been on and put them in her dishwasher.

"Be right back," he said, stepping into the bathroom to clean up. By the time he'd come back, she was facedown on the bed, totally asleep. She was also topless. "Lucky me." He grinned and slid into bed, loving how she moved toward him, even in sleep seeking his body.

He turned the lights off, but there was plenty coming in from the streetlights outside. Enough to see the beauty of her. Moonlight and stardust, Ella was all that and more.

She already had achieved that depth of sleep where she'd transformed into a soft, warm, substantial weight against him. As much as he loved how she felt, totally relaxed and unafraid, sexy and feminine, he felt bad that he hadn't seen how exhausted she was before that evening. Especially when he'd been the one who kept her up the night before. Twice.

Thinking back, he realized he'd noticed she was tired here and there, but it passed quickly, and there'd been something else to worry about.

The woman was a caregiver down to her toes, and that's exactly what she'd been doing. Erin had tattled on her earlier, telling Cope what Ella had been doing at the café, organizing the employees to take up any and all slack, checking by a few times a day to be sure all was well. She'd also taken to stopping in to visit Erin whenever she could break away from work. On top of that, she worked her other job, which he knew took a lot of paperwork and time, and spent time with him. No wonder she was paler than usual; distracted even.

It was his turn to take care of her for a change. Ella Tipton needed to be cherished and taken care of, and Andrew Copeland was just the man to see that it happened.

He thought of getting up to crack a beer and do some sketching, but he didn't want to wake her. Instead, he grabbed a nearby scrap of paper and one of her pretty pens and began with the trunk of the tree that marked her spine.

Like the line of her back, the trunk was sturdy but inherently feminine. He'd seen it multiple times now, and each time he loved it more. And was convinced Brody understood Ella better than most, maybe almost as much as Cope did.

22

"Come now."

Ella recognized Ben's voice on the phone when she picked up. Dread filled her. "Erin? Is she all right? Is the baby all right? Where are you?"

"We're back at the hospital. In the L and D unit. A floor below where we were before. Everyone's okay, but—" He broke off with a curse.

"I'm on my way right now," she assured him as she stood, grabbing her things and heading to the doors to the parking lot. "Family emergency," she called out to the receptionist as she rushed by. Fear chilled her. It had only been a few weeks since the last scare. She'd hoped that Erin would be fine.

In the car she ruthlessly tamped down the panic and fear, focusing on her friends, knowing they'd need her to be clearheaded and in control so they didn't have to be. Still, she was thankful the hospital wasn't that far away and it was early enough in the afternoon she didn't have to battle her way through the unholy mess of Seattle traffic to get there.

Once inside, she rushed to the labor and delivery unit. There was a waiting room just outside, where Brody stood in front of closed glass doors. She went straight to him, hugging him.

"Tell me."

He kept her hand in his, the worry etched into the skin next to his eyes. "The swelling is back; her blood pressure is bad. They're running tests to see how her kidneys are doing. She's freaked out." His eyes shone with unshed tears.

"How is the baby?"

"He's kicking like a champ," Ben said as he entered the room. She rose to hug him and noted the blond ponytail whip past, toward Brody, as Elise entered. The noise level rose as Rennie plopped herself down next to Brody and began talking.

"He?" Brody asked and they all turned.

"Surprise. I think I'd have preferred to find out another way, but we're having a boy." Ben's smile was sweet, genuine and totally worried.

She stood straighter. "I'm here to help. Tell me what you need, and I'll make it happen."

Todd came in. "You're a good friend." He smiled at her before turning to everyone else. That's when Cope flew in the door.

"What's going on?"

"They're checking her out to see if the cervix is thinning. She's at thirty-five weeks, so they'd like to wait even just a week or two if they can, just to give him some more time to bake in there. But if her other tests come back and the numbers indicate danger, they'll need to induce and get him out of there for both their sakes. She made me leave for this part." He snorted. "It's not like I haven't seen the goods before."

"No one wants their cervix probed with their husband in the room. Um, well not like this." Elise reddened, and it lightened the mood a little.

"Hey, Red." Cope put his arms around her, kissing her soundly. "I was gonna call you once I'd gotten the scoop. Glad you're here."

They settled in on the uncomfortable couches to wait. Rennie didn't want to leave to go to her grandparents' house. She was so very worried and upset about Erin and the baby that Brody and Elise had allowed her to stay. But Ella knew Elise must have wanted to focus on Brody to get him centered.

"Rennie, you want to come with me to grab some coffee for everyone? Hot chocolate for you, my treat."

Rennie nodded seriously, but it was impossible to miss the calculated gleam in her eyes. Ella just waited for it.

"I sure am hungry. Do you think they have slices of punkin bread like you guys have at the café?"

Brody laughed, leaning over to kiss the top of Rennie's head. "Work it, kid."

"I promise to bring some back for you too. But not punkin, 'cause I know you don't like it as much as the lemon."

"Always thinking of others," Elise murmured with a smile.

Ella stood. "Got your walking shoes on? Zip your coat up, and we'll walk. Just a few blocks away. Near a bakery too, you know, just in case they don't have any punkin bread left at the coffee shop."

"Want some company?" Cope offered, but she saw his worry and knew he needed to be there for Ben.

"We're good. Thanks." She touched his cheek, and he leaned into her hand. "Stay here where you're needed. Rennie and I will be back shortly."

Cope watched them leave, torn.

"Go on. It's not like we're going anywhere. Erin is stable, the baby is fine, his heartbeat is strong and he's active. You have a phone, so if anything happens, I'll call you right away." Ben looked at his brother.

He wanted to, but he also wanted to be there for Ben. "She's getting coffee, it's okay. She'll be fine. What can I do here for you guys?"

"I called Mom. She's on her way. She made a comment about him, but I warned her not to bring him into this mess." Ben meant their father, and anger washed through him anew.

"All right. Is the café covered? I'm on the pager, Kylie said she'd stay on to cover the phones just in case." Kylie was the office manager who they'd hired a few months back to run their main office. They'd been working out of Ben's house, but with the baby coming, they'd wanted to shift back to their main digs and keep family separate from work.

"Café is good. I called over there after Ben called Ella. They're closing early today but will work out a schedule to be open as much as they can the rest of the week. They run fine without Erin; just don't tell her." Brody smiled briefly, and Elise put her head on his shoulder.

"Well then, let's sit and wait."

Ella thanked the man who held the door for her when she and Rennie returned with full arms. Coffee, tea, snacks and a bunch of magazines in her tote. If Erin had to stay, she could at least have some reading material.

Rennie bounced along, keeping Ella's attention on her rather than panic about Erin, and for that she was grateful. Until she turned in the elevator to face the doors and caught sight of Billy and Annalee waiting to get their ticket to get into the parking garage.

"Hey guys," she said when they got back to the waiting room. Ben had gone off with Todd to check on Erin. She handed the two trays of drinks off, dropping her bag at the corner of Cope's chair.

"Thank you, Red." He handed out the proffered drinks and passed around the snacks while Rennie settled in with the coloring book Ella grabbed at the little newsstand where she got the magazines.

"I left something in my car. I'll be right back."

Cope put a hand on her arm. "That's okay, I can get it for you." He waggled his brows at her. "Or I can escort you."

"Why don't you do that?" Perhaps he could deal with his father and keep things low-key.

They went out, and she opted for the stairs rather than the elevator for speed's sake.

"Am I that irresistible? You're running to your car? I'm talented, but I'm not sure my talents extend to getting nasty with you in a parking lot of the hospital."

She turned to him as they reached the parking level. "Your father is here. I saw them waiting to get a ticket to park. I'm trying to head them off."

He paused, his hand on the door. She blushed. "I'm sorry. I know it's presumptuous of me. For all I know you've all made up, but when I had coffee with your mother last week, it didn't seem like it."

"You had coffee with my mother? You didn't say."

Right then she felt accused, and when she was only trying to help, it pushed her buttons. "I wasn't aware I had to clear it with you."

"I didn't say you did. It's just that I, fuck, fuck."

She turned and saw them come into the elevator lobby. Annalee looked upset, and Ella couldn't blame her. Billy, well, she was sure the man loved his kids, but he was acting like a total ass. *Hmpf*, a lot like his youngest son, who scowled at her and then at his dad like she'd arranged it instead of trying to help.

"Hi, Annalee. How are you?" She moved past Andrew and hugged his mother. "Come on up. Ben said you were on the way, so I know he's waiting for you." The elevator dinged, and she shot a look at Andrew, who did have the good sense to look at least slightly abashed.

"You'll stay here and speak with your son," Annalee said to her husband as she got on the elevator with Ella. "Thank you, honey. I tried to tell him not to come."

"Maybe this can be a good moment for them to get past all this nonsense." She hoped so.

"I hope. He's a stubborn man. Prone to saying things before he thinks. Stupid." Annalee shook her head.

They entered the waiting room. Brody saw her and stood to give

Annalee a hug. "We're all just waiting to hear back. They've been monitoring Erin's protein levels and, um, a kick count? Yeah, that's it, a kick count on the baby. Ben went back to see what was going on."

"Sit, here, would you like a coffee?" Ella held out the one she'd gotten for herself. Annalee most likely needed it more than she did.

"And some lemon cake." Rennie handed the little bakery box Annalee's way, giving the right kind of distraction. Ella looked over Rennie's head to Elise and smiled.

"Where's Cope?" Rennie asked. "I was saving this brownie for him. Ella says these ones are his favorite."

Annalee looked up at Ella and smiled, before answering. "He's trying to talk sense into someone."

Ella just hoped it didn't involve fists this time.

Mrs. Keenan came in moments later and headed straight for them. "Dean is down with Billy and Andy. Hopefully he won't have to break up a fistfight this time."

Ella put her head in her hands as the room fell totally silent. "I know Andrew would prefer that Erin not hear about that part," she mumbled.

"It's not my boy who should be ashamed; it's his father. Stupid, stupid man."

"This isn't the time or place for any of this nonsense." Ben came into the room and hugged his mother and then Lorie Keenan. "Rennie, Erin is going to have to stay here at the hospital for a few days; she's going to need pretty pictures for the walls in her room. Can you do that for me?"

Rennie nodded solemnly. The kid was a really talented artist, and silly coloring books aside, she'd probably do a few masterpieces for Erin. "I don't have any of my papers here, but I do at home."

"Why are we talking about my father being an ass, and where is Andy?" Ben murmured to Ella. He held back a curse when she explained it.

"He wants to fix things for you. He's a fixer, you know."

Ben looked confused for a moment, and she wanted to sock him in the belly for not knowing what was right in front of him. "I'm giving you a pass because you're under a tremendous amount of stress. But you need to give your brother some credit. He's an incredible person who truly cares about the people he loves."

His smile then was amused and affectionate. "I do. And it makes me happy you see it too."

She waved it away. "We'll talk about it later. How's Erin?" she asked, this time louder.

"Sneaky," he muttered. "Her protein levels are higher than they like to see. But Alexander is doing really well according to the doctors, and Erin is really reluctant to induce until another week or two has passed if we don't have to." He shoved a hand through his hair right as Andrew came in with Dean Keenan and Billy Copeland.

Ella took Ben's hand, squeezing it.

"So they're going to keep her here for another few days to monitor the situation more closely. They've got on-call surgeons and OB/GYNs if she has to deliver quickly. Total bed rest is apparently not the best thing for her, so she'll be up and around a bit, but at least between me and Todd, we can make sure she doesn't overdo."

"Can we see her?" Brody stood.

"You can, but no one other than immediate family. This is the L and D wing, so all access must be cleared by the nurse's desk on the other side of those secure doors. No children other than siblings, sorry Ren, I know she wants to see you."

Rennie nodded solemnly, looking very much like her mother just then. "I just want her to get better. His name is Alexander? The baby's a boy?"

"He is, and yes, Alexander Copeland Keenan is his name."

Her eyes lit up. "That's a cool name. Do I get to babysit him? I mean if Momma's around and stuff? I won't break him."

Ben smiled genuinely. "I can't imagine Alexander would pass up time with you. You're his cousin, so he's going to love being with you." He looked to Brody. "I can't wait to have a family like yours."

"I'm a lucky man."

"Alexander is a great name, honey." Ella knew that Annalee's father had been named Alexander; it was a good, strong name. Annalee moved to her son and hugged him. Ella stepped out of the way but not before catching the snort of derision from Billy Copeland, who still stood near the elevators.

Ella cut her eyes to him. She caught his gaze and narrowed hers, warning him to shut the fuck up. This was not the time or place for any nonsense, and she had had enough tiptoeing around his behavior.

He continued to look at her until she cocked her head and crossed her arms over her chest.

"Go on back, Brody. I told them to expect you."

Elise told him to send Erin their love, and the big man left the room, looking ten kinds of worried. Rennie was a good kid, better than most she knew, but there was no way Rennie would be able to hang out in a hospital waiting room all night long

Ella interrupted. "Elise, it's Friday night, and I don't have to be anywhere tomorrow morning. Why don't Rennie and I grab some pizza and DVDs and crash at my place for the night? You can call me in the morning, and I can bring her home or to your parents' house." She made sure to say it quietly enough that Rennie, who squealed with delight and ran to Adrian as he got off the elevators, couldn't hear.

Cope moved around his father and over to Adrian, clearly explaining the situation.

Ben looked down at Elise. "Elise, they're not going to allow anyone else in to visit with her at this point. There are restrictions to keep everyone safer from the flu, she's in the high-risk pregnancy rooms and only immediate family is allowed. Hell, they tried to stop me the first time we came by."

Annalee's brows flew up, clearly outraged on her son's behalf. "They did?"

"Mom, people treat us like that all the time. Heck, it took you about six months to come around."

To her credit, his mother smiled up at him and patted his cheek. "I was a fool. But my grandbaby is going to be here soon, and that's what matters. You happy is what matters. Erin makes you happy. Todd makes you happy. It's not what I imagined for you"—she laughed— "but it's yours, and because it's yours, it's mine too."

"Could have made better choices with the right head."

Ella marched up to Billy Copeland and took his arm, drawing him into an elevator that had opened up. She punched the down button and turned to face him, just as she caught sight of everyone's shocked expression before the doors slid closed.

"Okay, you, I'm not related to you, nor am I married to someone related to you, so I'm just going to say what everyone else has *nicely* tried to tell you for years now. Shut up. You're an asshole, and that's your prerogative. This is America after all."

They arrived on the bottom floor, and she led him, still shocked, out and into the parking area foyer.

"Oh no." She shook her head, putting her fingertips over his mouth. "You've said enough. And then some. It's my turn now. You're a cancer in your family. Why, I don't know. Oh what? You think you're the first guy on the planet who didn't like who his son or daughter ended up with? You think you're special? What you are is a coldhearted prick who seems to get off on abusing his family for kicks. Maybe you didn't get enough hugs as a child, maybe your pea brain is too small to see how ridiculously and totally in love your son is with the people he's made his life with. Maybe you're one of those ignoramuses who thinks his opinions are facts. Frankly, at this stage, I don't care."

"Just who do you think you are?" His stance shifted, got more aggressive, but she was filled with so much righteous indignation and anger for her friends and for the man she loved, she held her ground despite the tiny frisson of fear deep in her belly.

"I think I've been friends with Erin Brown for longer than you've known her. I think I'm a person who watched her fall in love with your son every day. A person who watched your son fall for her and then for Todd. Oh, get that look off your face. It's not like anyone is asking you to watch them have sex. Anyway, why is it you're so fascinated with how your kid has sex and with whom? Seems to me that's *your* issue, not his."

"You're dating Andy, aren't you?"

"Yes. So now you can be unhappy with his choices too. I'm sure that will be a comfort to you at holiday dinners. Or when that baby says his first word, starts crawling for the first time, takes his first step. Your wife will be there for it. Are you so angry, so bitter and hateful that you'd willingly check out?"

"Ella, that's enough." Andrew stepped out into the area from the stairwell. "It's not worth it."

"Andrew Copeland, if this isn't worth it, you please tell me what is." She turned to him. "This man showed up here and has not done a thing to support his son who has to be terrified of losing his child. *Why are you here*, Mr. Copeland?"

"This is family business. You're not family, and I don't have to make excuses to you."

"Fine, though I can't be disappointed that you're not family. What I can do is say what I'm thinking, because you're not man enough to stop me. No one will stop me from speaking my mind ever again." She said the latter to both of them.

"And what's on your mind then? That I should throw a party for my half-gay son who is maybe having a baby, maybe not? That I should celebrate this baby who should not have ever been conceived to start with? What kind of life will that child have? You think all the other kids are going to be so hip and with it that they'll accept two dads and a mom who looks like a pen exploded on her?"

"Is that what you think people want from you? Really? Your level of hubris is unbelievable. This isn't about you. Don't you get that?"

"Ella, honey, just let it go." Cope touched her arm.

"Let it go? Are you kidding me? He comes here, stirs trouble, and no one wants to say boo to him. Why? It's a serious question." She knew they had a complicated relationship. What father and son didn't? But this man didn't deserve two sons as wonderful as Andrew and Ben.

"You are not family. You're the problem!"

"You are, and you're acting like a thug. And for whatever reason, you're getting a pass. Not from me. The fact is, I *am* family. I'm more family to Erin than you will ever be, and I don't need your permission to tell you I think you should go if you can't at least be halfway supportive. My friend is in the hospital, scared about losing her child."

"Get this woman out of my face, Andy."

Andrew put his arm around her shoulders. "Dad, I think you need to take a breath and calm down. This isn't helpful, and you promised to behave if you came upstairs."

"I'm not taking any direction from this woman or from anyone else. This is none of her business."

She started to speak, but Cope squeezed her shoulders. Which frustrated her, but it wasn't the time for that. She knew he was most likely embarrassed by his father's behavior and perhaps even hers. But she'd deal with that later. This man should not be allowed to make Erin, Ben or Todd feel bad here and now. If he wanted to hate at his own home, that was his choice. But not here. Not now.

He relaxed a little when she kept quiet. "Dad, we've discussed this, and you had options. You came here, so I'd imagine somewhere inside, you want to be helpful and loving. But on the outside? Not so much."

"I'm not having this conversation with her here."

Ella sighed but said nothing else to him. She turned to Cope. "I'm going back up." She wanted to warn him again not to bring his attitude back up in there, but it felt like overkill, so she let it be.

Halfway back up the stairwell it hit her, and she had to pause, holding her belly. She'd done it. She'd stood up for her friends in the face of exactly the sort of aggression Bill used on her to keep her compliant.

She'd wanted to turn and run a few times, but she'd stood her ground.

She pumped her fist into the air once and smiling, began to climb again.

23

"Everything all right?" Elise sidled up to her once she got back. The room was emptier than it had been; Todd's parents sat near the windows, Lorie's head on her husband's shoulder while she worked on her knitting. Todd sat with them, talking quietly with his father. Now there was a man who had problems and sincerely worked to get past them.

"Where's Ms. Irene?"

"She's with Adrian, cheering him up. She told him he needed to look at the fish on the floor below us. That's where her pediatrician is. They have big tanks but also play sets, which I wager Adrian has now figured out. Good thing he's smitten with her."

"It *is* a good thing. It's a good thing she's surrounded by people who love her and appreciate her for who she is."

Elise's brows rose for a moment as she drew Ella farther from the others. "What the hell happened down there? Do I need to hunt that asshat down and kick him for you?"

"Where's Annalee?"

"She hit the bathrooms. Probably needed some time alone after her dumb ass of a husband humiliated her the way he did. Ben went back to yank Brody out so Adrian could get in."

"Has anyone called Raven? I know she'll want to be here."

"You're totally avoiding the subject. I called her. She's in Portland and on her way back now. What the fuck happened? And do not ask me another question having nothing to do with that dingus Billy Copeland."

"Testy. The cute blond ponytail prevents you from truly taking the rank of head bitch in charge, though."

Elise fought a smile. "Hurry up. Brody will be back soon, and he'll frown on gossip."

"I just told him to be supportive or get out. I don't think anyone needs that negative energy."

"I imagine he was very receptive to that."

"Whatever. In my opinion, if he comes back up here and he can't be civil, they should have security remove him. I don't care if it hurts anyone's feelings or not; Erin is the important one here, and I've had it with all this tiptoeing around what a big giant cockhead that man is. Trying all that aggressive stuff on me like I was one of his minions."

Elise's expression softened. "He threatened you?"

"Not outwardly. He's one of those men who uses his body to make the threat. You know, *Grrr, I'm big and mighty. Watch me stick my chest out and fear me.* I've met that one before. Done with it. My impression is that he loves his sons. I believe that, honestly. But he is so wrapped up in the kind of relationship Ben has with Todd and Erin that he's got a disconnect the size of Texas about it."

"Cope's down there with him?"

"Yes. So hey, you want me to sweep Rennie out of here and keep her for the night? I'd love to, you know. I love your kid."

Elise hugged her. "I know, and that makes me so happy. You know Rennie adores you. Brody and I are going home. He wanted to sleep out here tonight, but we're ten minutes away, and they've promised to call if there's any problems. Apparently Erin just flat-out insisted he go home as there was nothing he could do. He can't say no to her."

"She's right. But that doesn't make it any easier to deal with when someone you love is in trouble."

"I feel like you're going through all this stuff and I'm only seeing part of it. I want to hear all about how things are with Cope and all this stuff with his family and how that's affecting you. I'm being a shitty friend. I'm sorry. We need to catch up so you can fill me in."

"Don't apologize! You're planning a wedding, raising a child, and dealing with all this stuff with Erin and the baby. We talk all the time anyway. It's just that I'm trying to process it still. But when I get it figured out, you'll be the first to know." Or maybe the second. A lot of it had to do with Cope, so she'd probably talk to him first. "I got through it, though. That much I can process now. I was scared when he was so angry. Not that he'd hurt me; I don't think he'd go that far."

"The man tried to punch his son!"

"Yeah, he's a dingus. But that's part of their macho dude thing. I've seen Ben and Andrew shove each other and get in each other's faces before too. I can't even imagine punching my child, even if he were an adult. I'm not excusing that. He was wrong and he's being a dick, but I don't think he'd strike a woman. But my stomach hurt, you know? It pushed buttons I keep forgetting I have. I stood my ground, Elise. I stood it for Erin and for myself. Maybe even for Andrew too."

Elise smiled. "Yeah. You're stronger than you give yourself credit for."

"Sometimes."

They settled back onto the couches to wait. Adrian and Rennie came back from their sojourn just as Brody came out.

Brody turned to his brother as they all walked to where everyone sat. "She's good. Tired. Scared. They've got a heart monitor on her belly, and she's counting kicks every two hours. Kid's strong, doing just fine at this point. Visiting time is up in an hour, so she made me promise to take you and Rennie to a movie and dinner. I counteroffered with a DVD and dinner at home."

"More evidence that she's on the mend." Ella grinned.

"Don't know where that stubborn streak comes from at all," Adrian muttered as he came through. "My turn to run in and see her. Don't leave though; I've promised your daughter that I would hang out with you all tonight."

"So he doesn't get sad all by himself." Rennie squeezed his hand before reaching for Brody's.

"I think that is a very fine idea. I also think Ella needs to come too." Elise grinned. "We'll even let you have black olives on the pizza."

Ella rolled her eyes.

"Oh please, please? That would be so fun!" Rennie hopped on one foot a moment before she remembered where she was. "Sorry, Dad."

Brody's entire demeanor softened whenever he dealt with Rennie. It made Ella all smooshy inside to see it happen. He turned and knelt so they'd be eye to eye. "Muffin, you don't have to apologize for being you. It's a fine quality, you know, to be happy and excited about the world. Erin's going to be okay, and so is the baby. So you can dance and hop and be Irene all you want."

Elise looked to Ella over the two of them, her lower lip trembling just a little bit.

"You drive a hard bargain, but how can I say no to hanging out with all my favorite people?" She had planned to spend the evening with Andrew, but she was unsure that would be happening with all this upheaval.

"Bring a bag and stay over. That way we can stay up after and chat over a bottle of wine," Elise said quietly. "Oh, unless you were planning on staying over at Cope's place. He can stay at ours too. Goodness knows he has before."

"I honestly don't know what his plans are. I'll leave him a voice mail though, to tell him where I'm going and to invite him. I wish I could help more here."

Annalee came into the room. "Are you all right?" she asked Ella quietly. "Was he horrible?"

"I'm fine. Really. I hope I didn't upset you, but I feel quite strongly that what Erin, Todd and Ben need right now is not to be mocked or treated with anything less than support. She's my friend, and she's been there for me when most everyone else wasn't. I will carry that in my heart until the day I die. There is no excuse for this hateful tantrum. I know you're in the middle, and I've been there too." Though Annalee didn't seem like she was controlled, her husband was a total asshole, and Ella would not allow him to harm Erin.

"I had been hoping he'd come around. I don't expect you to understand; you shouldn't have to. He isn't normally like this. I've been praying it was a lapse in judgment and he'd finally see his way through. Dean has; most of the others have. That's his boy." She shrugged, and Ella gave in, hugging the other woman.

"I don't need to understand, and I don't judge you for trying to."

"I wish I could." Annalee shook her head.

Adrian came out with Ben, and both men headed their way.

Ben hugged his mother again. "Why don't you head home? I'll keep you in the loop about everything. Todd and I will be allowed to stay in her room tonight, even though she's insisting we don't need to." He rolled his eyes. "It means a lot to me, to us, that you're here."

"Oh baby, where else would I be?"

Ella needed to give them all some space, probably needed a little herself too. "I'll see you all in a few hours. You call me if anything changes or you need anything at all. Do you guys have a change of clothes and toothbrushes? Stuff like that?"

"After the last time, Erin made us put bags in the trunk just in case. We're good." Ben leaned down to kiss her cheek. "Thank you for that thing with my dad. I expect I'll be hearing all the details soon enough. For now, know that we all love you, okay? Erin says to tell you she'll be cupcake-ready in a few weeks."

"Tell her there's a red velvet with her name on it, when she's ready."

She hugged everyone one last time and headed out.

"Dad, what is your deal? Why did you come here if nothing has changed?"

Cope had wanted to run after Ella to check on her, to make sure she was all right, but damn it, his father needed dealing with too, and she'd gotten them more than halfway in a way he'd never expected.

It was hot, even as he was annoyed she'd hare off and challenge his father in a hospital parking lot like she was more than a bitty woman with more love in her heart than could be measured.

That she understood and accepted him, knew him better than the man he stood facing right then, was no small irony and no small amount of pain to admit. He'd spent all his life hoping his father would pay attention. All his life being measured against Ben and trying to do that, but failing because he wasn't Ben. And damn it, why it took him thirty-six years to discover that it wasn't supposed to be that way, he didn't know. To understand that he didn't have to be, because he was Andrew.

Ella knew that.

"I told you I came because your mother was upset. I promised to behave. It was your girlfriend who caused this mess. For fuck's sake, boy, you traffic with whores for years, and now you get this one hanging on you. Your mother says she had some violence in her past. Why do you and your brother sniff after damaged goods?"

He lunged forward, pinning his father to the wall just to the left of the elevator bank. "You shut your mouth about her and about Erin too. You don't know shit about it."

"Get off, or I'll knock you on your ass."

Cope snorted, stepping back. "You're full of it, old man. I've given you a pass because I love you. I will always love you because you're my father. But that man, the man who taught me how to carve, how to fit a joist, the guy who was there to take a picture the first time I hooked a trout, that man is not here today. You're half a man who's become obsessed over stuff that's just not his business. So you don't like it that Ben is in love with people you don't approve of. BFD. And? Do you run all your decisions past us? He's nearly forty with a baby on the way. He knows what he's doing. He's got a successful business, and I hate that you can't see how much he's loved."

"He's a deviant! Can't just be gay, oh no. He has to have two part-ners, or spouses, or whatever the hell you kids call it nowadays. Can't brag on the baby on the way because Dean already does. What am I supposed to say to that?"

Cope sighed heavily. "This isn't about you. Until you realize that, you're not welcome in my life or in Ben's. He only tolerated you here today because you promised to behave. And then lied. Far as I can see, he hasn't lied. He's trying to live his life as honestly as he can, given the unusual circumstances. But you? You're a piece of work. Just because you're my father and I love you does not mean I have to have you in my life."

He hit the elevator button. "I'm done with you. If you come back up, I'll call security. I'm not going to allow you to harm anyone else I love, and that includes Ella."

24

Ben was waiting for him when he got off the elevator.

"You all right? Do I need to send a nurse down there?"

Cope heaved a heavy sigh. "I don't know that this is ever going to be all right, Ben. I'm sorry."

His brother smiled at him and led him back into the adjacent waiting room. "Dude, is that what you think you need to do? Fix this?"

"He can't go on like this, ripping at you and Erin. We can't just not say anything."

"What about you? He rip at you? He tried to hit you, Andy. Just leave it be. I have enough to freak out about, and he can't be allowed to be part of that. I don't like it, but you know what? Fuck him. I'm not asking him to do anything more than accept my choices."

"Ella ripped him a new asshole." Despite his anger at his father, this made him smile. "Her hands shook a moment, but she never backed down."

Ben grinned. "Really? Not that I doubt it, she's been a good friend to us."

"Rest easy, he thinks she's damaged goods anyway." That hurt, but damn it, he wasn't going to let it bug him any more than he had to. "So fill me in. I know Erin has stabilized, and the baby is good. By the way, a son? Congratulations."

Ben's face cleared of worry and anger, replaced by total joy for a brief moment. "Thanks. I feel better that she's here so close to all the doctors. I just never imagined she'd have any problems. She's Erin; nothing slows her down."

Cope could hear the fear there in his brother's words. "She's going to be good, and you're going to be a dad. I know this is scary now, but she's Erin, and as you said, nothing slows her down."

"I don't know what I'd do if something happened to her. I don't know that I'd be able to get through it."

He watched his brother, sort of stunned to see this break in his very self-assured façade. Cope had simply always assumed Ben could handle anything, always felt his big brother was unshakable.

"You have Todd. You have me and mom and all our friends. And you have Erin. Nothing is going to happen to her. I researched pre-eclampsia and eclampsia. This is a good hospital; she's got great doctors watching over her. She's here close to operating rooms, and damn, dude, she's staying in a room that can be converted to a delivery room in minutes."

"I never imagined loving like this." Ben scrubbed hands over his face. "I never imagined the other side of the intensity and depth of my connection to Erin would be the bottomless pit of fear at the very idea of losing her. Andy, I'm so fucking scared every moment I'm awake."

He hugged his brother, trying to be strong, knowing that's what Ben needed. But it woke up those fears deep in his belly.

"She's everything I ever wanted, totally essential to me, and the thought of losing it leaves me in a cold sweat. And all I can think is how much Todd and I wanted a baby with her and if something happens it'll be our fault."

"She wants that too. She's been over the moon about this pregnancy and the baby. It's not your fault for wanting a family with her. And I imagine when Alexander comes home, that's going to scare you a few thousand times a day too. Just me here now, let it all out. Pinky swear I won't tell anyone." Cope sat back with a snort.

His brother needed to fall apart a little; he could see that clearly now. So he just sat with him, close, and let him. Ben didn't have to be strong in front of Cope, didn't need to hide his fear or his panic. Cope wouldn't judge him, and he understood it.

Adrian came out some minutes later, after Ben had begun to pull himself back together.

"Hey, you two, didn't expect to see you out here. Erin and I went for a walk around the perimeter a few dozen times, and she's back tucked into bed. Todd is with her, and I think they're talking dinner. She looks better. Alexander moved around a lot, which cheers Erin a lot I know. Anyway, I'm off to Brody and Elise's for movies and pizza. I figured I'd see you there." He looked to Cope.

"Ah, that's where they all went. I haven't checked my voice mail in a while. I think Ella and I had loose plans, so I'll check in with her."

"She's going over there too, I think. You okay, Ben?"

Ben took a deep breath and stood. "Yeah, I am now." He turned when Cope stood too. "Thanks. Now it's your turn to go to her, the woman who is your everything."

Cope smiled. "Yeah. Well. Give Erin a kiss for me, okay? I'll see you tomorrow morning. Let me know if you want me to bring breakfast in or something. I'll have my cell with me."

He stood in his front room, looking out the windows at the rain. This room smelled like Ella. She loved the overstuffed chair he'd put in near the window. She perched there often, reading, doing casework, whatever. He'd moved it closer to the window, had made sure the fireplace was working well, wanting her to be comfortable in his house, wanting her to choose to be there with him.

One of her cardigans hung on the back of the chair, a bright splash of blue against the paler green of the chair. He picked it up and breathed her in. Love filled him in a rush, flashing through him, leaving him weak in the knees.

In just a few months he'd taken a longtime crush and had tipped over into love so big and amazing he'd not bothered to fight it. Why would he?

He spent every spare moment he could get with her, thought about her when he wasn't with her. Saw a movie billboard and made a mental note to take her; saw a redheaded woman in a crowd, and an ache filled him as he wondered where she was and how her day was going.

Today she'd confronted his father in a way so fearless he'd been taken aback by it. She'd said the things he'd wanted to say, things he'd thought, and his normally macho father had stumbled a bit in the face of it.

He'd assumed she would still be so messed up by her past that a confrontation like that would not be something she'd be up to.

She'd left him a voice mail telling him of the plan to hang with everyone at Brody's. Only in her Ella way, she'd seen it as a way to comfort her friends and keep their minds off the scary stuff.

So why was he there? There looking out his window, frozen by his feelings for her? Why wasn't he with her, touching her, listening to her voice and letting the feel of her skin soothe the jangled nerves?

Fear.

It clawed at his insides. Seeing his hard-assed brother brought to tears from worry over his wife and child had shaken him harder than he'd imagined. Freaked him out, he supposed. Up until then he'd loved his family and slowly, those people they'd brought into their circle. He loved women in the same way he loved pistachio gelato and action movies. They made him feel better when he indulged, had given him a lot of pleasure.

But he didn't love them the way he loved her. Loved Ella Tipton so much that spot inside him he hadn't known was there yawned and freaked him the fuck out. He'd sort of assumed that when he fell in love he'd always get along with his wife. But he and Ella, well, she had a spark. His father had called her damaged goods, but so many people didn't get that she wasn't damaged at all. Bad things happened to her, and she survived them. Her skin was damaged, maybe her heart because she'd loved badly. But Ella Tipton was a survivor, a triumphant success story that his father could never understand, and more was the pity.

She'd become necessary to him.

That part wasn't scary. He liked that part. The scary part was imagining her sick or dying and being powerless to stop it. Stupid, he knew, but that fear of loss seemed so . . . big.

His phone rang, Foo Fighters' "Everlong." Ella.

"Hey."

"Did you get my message earlier? I was worried not to hear back. But Brody just called over to check in on Erin, and Ben said you'd left several hours before." Her voice lightened his heart, even as his stomach tightened.

"I was busy."

She paused. "All right. Are you coming over to Brody and Elise's? We're getting ready to play some Rock Band. Adrian is saying he should get to be the lead singer, God knows why. You'd think he was a rock star or something."

He heard laughter in the background.

"I don't think so. I have stuff to do here."

"Is there something wrong? Other than the obvious, I mean."

He sat in the chair he'd come to think of as hers. "No. I'm sorry I was short with you. It's just, it's been a long day. And this stuff with my dad. I need some time to process."

"I understand. I guess I'll see you later then."

"I'll most likely see you tomorrow."

"All righty then." She hung up, and he hadn't really expected her to. He hadn't told her he loved her, hadn't asked how she was. In short, he'd been sort of a dick, and now he felt even worse.

"He's not coming?" Elise looked taken aback.

He'd been in a snit; she could tell the difference in how he responded to her. That was the funny thing about having known him for so long. This wasn't some new guy she couldn't read. He was annoyed or maybe upset about something. He apologized for snapping at her, but he'd always told her he loved her when they hung up, and he'd held back that time. Then again, she had just hung up; maybe he'd been meaning to.

Ah well, she would not apologize for standing up to Cope and Ben's dad.

The nice thing was, it wasn't a big deal. He was short but not cutting or cruel. He needed some space, and she got that too. So he could have it.

"Guess not." She shrugged but didn't fail to notice the look on Brody's face. "No."

He burst out laughing. "What?"

"Don't interfere."

"*Pffft.*"

"I mean it. He doesn't feel up to company right now. Everyone is entitled to some space when they need it. And you"—she pointed at Adrian—"that goes for you too. Let's get this show on the road. Sing it, rock boy."

Brody laughed again, giving her a one-armed hug as he walked past.

She sang and danced and messed up every instrument they let her play. It was two in the morning when everyone wound down, and Adrian begged off to bed.

Ella stood, stretching. "I'm going to go home, I think. I'll see you all at the hospital in the morning. Or, later in the morning I should say, as it's already tomorrow."

"Honey, you're welcome to stay." Elise stood and followed her to the door. "Are you upset about Cope?"

She laughed. "No. I mean, he's upset, and I care about him." She paused. "That's not entirely true. I love him. Anyway, I'm not so fragile or deluded I ever imagined I'd never have tiffs with him. That comes with the territory. Erin and Todd fight all the time, you and Brody argue back and forth, and you're the sweetest couple I've ever seen. It happens, and I expect it to. I just want to be in my own bed tonight. Plus, dude, Rennie wakes up at dawn."

Elise hugged her. "You have a very good attitude. These men we've fallen for are bossy and they like to fix everything, even if you want to fix it yourself. But as we're all pretty strong ourselves, it can get heated."

"The makeup sex should be awesome." She winked as she headed out to her car. The night was quiet and cold, but the drive back to her place cleared her head.

Not bothering to do more than pull on sweats and a thermal shirt, she stumbled into her bed, smiling as Cope's spicy scent greeted her from his pillow. And fell asleep.

25

Cope hadn't slept well at all, so by the time he managed to accept reality and get up, he was already grumpy and agitated. He'd missed her in his bed, at his side. Had missed the sound of her puttering in his kitchen, missed her horrible, off-key singing while she showered. Missed the way her body felt when he slowly sank into her.

He'd slept alone, and he had no one to blame but himself. He hoped she hadn't been as lonely as he had. He laughed. Yes, yes he did, petty though it might be, he wanted to mean as much to her as she did to him.

He dialed the hospital and got Erin's room. Todd answered and told him Erin was doing well, but they were planning to keep her another day or two, just to keep a closer eye on her. He and Ben were going to trade off spending time at the hospital with Adrian and Brody because they were all, as Todd put it, getting on Erin's last nerve.

She was sleeping and they'd had an early breakfast, so they didn't want any visitors just yet. That would allow him time to head over to see Ella.

Time to pay the piper for not going over to Brody's the night before. He showered, got changed and picked up bagels, cream cheese, lox and other assorted goodies, including coffee, and headed over.

"She's not here." Elise looked him over when she opened the door. Rennie, still in her pajamas, saw him and squealed with delight.

"Cope!" She bounded over and hugged him, which soothed those nerves of his a bit.

"Brought bagels with all the fixings and coffee for the grown-ups. There are two cinnamon raisin for you in there. Tell Adrian hands off."

She grabbed the bag with a giggle, and he couldn't help but smile in response. "Thanks, Cope!" she called out, dashing toward the kitchen. "Cope brought bagels and coffee!"

"Where is she? Is she all right?" he asked Elise as they walked slowly toward the noise.

"Why don't you ask her yourself?"

"Stop busting his b-back," Brody said, quickly correcting from balls in Rennie's presence. Kid probably knew the term anyway.

"I wasn't. It's a fair question. Wouldn't *you* have called me first thing this morning?"

Adrian chuckled. "But he's perfect. None of us can be as awesome as Brody Brown."

"He is perfect. He's the best daddy ever and ever." Rennie beamed up at Brody, who smiled down, still looking totally surprised and touched by the things she said. Something tugged inside Cope, stirring up the maelstrom of fear he'd choked on the night before.

"Don't hate, Adrian, don't hate." Brody, grinning, picked Rennie up and hugged her before sitting down at the table with her ensconced in his lap.

"You Sorensons are easy for that guy." Adrian winked. "Cope, she's at her apartment, or that's where she headed when she left here last night. Don't be a jerk and mess it all up."

"Maybe I'll see her at the hospital. I haven't had this coffee yet. Or breakfast."

"Really? That's your answer?" Elise's brows flew up.

"Ren, honey, can you get me the sweatshirt I left on the bed? I'm a little chilly."

She hopped off Brody's lap. "Sure! Uncle Adrian, Cope says the cinnamon-raisin bagels are all mine. But since you're so nice and all, you can have one."

Once she was gone, Adrian stood up. "Let's walk, shall we? I think I left something in my car."

Cope groaned but grabbed a coffee and followed.

"Are you dumping her for the way she confronted your dad yesterday? Because if you are, first I will punch your face and then I will make a move on her myself. But since we're friends and you're obviously going through something, why don't you tell me what the fuck it is before I have to muss up that pretty face."

"I just didn't come over here last night. For fuck's sake! I'm not dumping her. I don't have to be with her every second of the day to be with her as her boyfriend. I'm not breaking up with her just because I needed some time alone."

"You're full of shit."

"I'm out of here. I don't want to have this conversation with you or with them. Did she talk about me last night? Say something bad? You're all overreacting." It had never occurred to him that she would, but they all seemed so judgy about him all the sudden.

"Do you really think Ella would do that? You're an asshole if you say yes, because we both know your girl adores you, dumb ass. She only says nice things about you, and I can't imagine her slagging you off in public, though she might private-like to Elise. That's what women do."

"Look, my brother is freaked, and it freaked me too. I'm human, for God's sake. Why do I have to apologize to people I'm not dating about it? Do you know what it's like? Huh?"

"Do I know what it's like to have my sister and nephew in the hospital? Um, yeah. I was there the first time, when she had Adele. Then

I was there when we had to claim Adele's body from the morgue and Erin was still laid up and on pain meds kept extra thick to control the hours upon hours of weeping over the murder of her child. So, um, yeah, yeah I do know."

Cope sighed. "I'm sorry, I didn't mean it like that. I worry about Erin too, and the baby."

"Then what are you talking about?"

"Have you ever been in love? Like really in love with a woman. So deeply that she's sort of like air, or food, you *need* her with all your heart and soul? She smiles and everything inside you settles down and admires because you know that smile is for you alone? You imagine her in your house, think about her round and pregnant with your children. The sound of her voice makes you happy. No other woman walks like her or sounds like her. No other beauty is like hers."

"I have liked women I've dated. I've enjoyed them, and if I'd stuck it out for a while longer, I suppose I could have fallen in love like that. But no. I haven't, and I'm damned glad to hear you have."

"So you get this thing that's like the best kind of high ever, this thing that fills you up, makes you whole and fuels you. You never expected it, you watched your friends find it, but what it looks like, no matter how good it looks from the outside, you can't understand just what it feels like to have it yourself. You get used to it. Find a rhythm that's totally natural. She fits me; I fit her."

Adrian nodded. "Yeah? So what's up your ass? This all sounds good to me. Did she dump *you*?"

Cope snorted. "No." At least he didn't think so. "What if I lost her? I've never been in a long-term relationship before. What if I fuck up, and she breaks up with me? What if I drive her away? What if we do stay together and she has problems with her pregnancy and I lose her and the baby both? What if she realizes I'm just a pretty face and no substance?"

"She told us about the house. We went over there, you know? You were at work. I went into the shop to get a touch-up, and we went to your house and peeked through your windows. She was right; you're so much more than what most people see. She gets that. She gets you. You're going to walk away from that now just in case she might die in a freak accident or you stick your dick into another woman for some unforeseen reason? Come on, Andrew, be real with yourself. She's solid, and you are too."

"I don't know what to do."

"Go to her. Talk to her. She looked very sad last night. She loves you, Andrew. Let yourself be loved."

Adrian turned and flipped him off as he walked back up to the house.

"Fuckin hippie," Cope called out.

"Whatever. Remember what I said: punch in the face, and then I will find out what it means to love the beautiful Ella Tipton."

"Just because you're a rock star doesn't mean I won't kick your ass." He got back in his car with a smile and headed toward Ella.

She woke up slowly, trying to ignore the way his absence felt. It wasn't like he'd spent every night with her. He hadn't. But they had at least spoken to each other, and last night had left her unsettled.

He'd been upset over the whole scene with his father, with her most likely, with Erin's health situation. She didn't like knowing he was upset and not having any real chance to help. Today she'd seek him out to talk, to work things through.

She started water for the French press and stumbled her way to the shower. She knew she'd need to check in at the hospital soon, but, as she washed her hair, she figured she'd give them some time to wake up. Hospitals were busiest first thing in the morning. She knew this because she'd been in one long enough to have the memory cemented into place.

So Erin would most likely con Todd or Ben to go grab her a real breakfast at one of the restaurants nearby. They'd assent and bring her back not the bacon, hash browns and two eggs she'd asked for, but something healthier and in line with the dietary restrictions she had due to the blood pressure problems.

She laughed to herself as she dried off and pulled on clothes. Those three were made for each other. Her men would be sure she took care of herself, and she'd do it for them, as well as for the baby. A boy.

Erin had this strong feeling the baby was a girl. Only Todd had known the gender, but the beans had been spilled the day before at the hospital. Ella's baby gift was that she'd made up three weeks of meals for the three of them, all now safely ensconced in the huge freezer at their apartment. Easy stuff to pop in the oven. She didn't have a lot of extra money, but she had the time, and she'd made them all in the larger kitchen of the café.

She'd babysit, of course, though she had a very strong feeling Erin wouldn't want to leave the baby much. After losing Adele, how else would she act?

It was brave.

Ella poured the hot water into the press and dropped bread into the toaster.

A few months back, Erin had told Ella she thought Ella was brave. But Erin had come to her after the attack. Erin, whose reasons for hospital aversion were far more devastating than Ella's had been. Erin, who'd opened herself up to love with Todd and then Ben. Erin, who'd been able to get past the loss and embrace the future with the baby she carried. Ella could only hope to be half that brave.

As she ate breakfast and sipped her coffee, she called and checked in. Erin had explained that they were going to keep her there a few more days, but that she still wasn't able to have visitors other than Ben, Todd and her brothers.

Ella insisted she'd stop by later to bring some books and magazines for her, and also said she'd check in on the café. Erin had tried to argue but in the end had thanked her, and they'd talked a bit more about the baby. Ella hadn't said anything about Ben and Cope's father; it wasn't necessary and it would only make Erin upset.

There was a buzz from the front door intercom, so she ended her call and found it was Andrew, who she let through. Most people would have left their front door ajar, but Ella wasn't most people. So she waited for him, opening the door when he got there.

Immediately he embraced her, and her worries fell away.

"Morning, Red. Mmmm, you smell good."

He kissed her, and she gave over to it, letting the way he tasted run riot through her.

"How are you this morning? I've got coffee. Want some?" She turned, leaving her hand in his, leading him to the kitchen.

"Busy. Spoke with Ben to check in on Erin. I suppose you've done that too?"

He sat, and she looked at him, liking how the light from the pale morning outside backlit his body.

"I did. She's in good spirits. Though she did tell me that after she gave birth she's sending someone out right away to get her a bacon, egg and cheese sandwich." She turned, smiling at the idea as she poured a cup of coffee for him.

"I'm sorry."

She sat next to him, tucking a leg beneath her, and sipped her own coffee. "For what?"

"If I told you I cheated on you last night, would you break up with me?"

She stood, spilling coffee on herself, cursing as she moved to clean it up. "What? Why? Why would you do that?" Her heart raced, and she felt like throwing up.

"I didn't. God, I'm sorry. I'm sorry I didn't mean to make you believe that. I was trying to make some other point, and now I see how stupid it was. I didn't cheat on you, Ella."

She wanted to throw the rest of the coffee in his face just then. Instead, she punched his arm and kicked her couch, which really hurt and made her even madder at him. "Why would you do that? Why would you say such a thing to me? If you want to break up, be a man and do it without mind-fucking me."

"I'm *scared*. All right?" He put his hands out, open palms facing her, and her heart softened. But she still didn't let him any closer.

"That you'll cheat on me?" Had she always wondered if she was enough? Maybe. She'd seen the way other women looked at him. Had watched him flirt hundreds of times. It came to him naturally. No, no that was stupid. He was different; he did love her, and doubts were stupid.

"I'm such a tool." He drew her to the couch and sat with her, and she put a pillow in between them. "I'm fucking this up and hurting your feelings."

"Yes! You are. Dear God, if you're going to break up with me, just do it! If you're scared of breaking up, I'm sorry, but you're ripping me to shreds here, Andrew."

"I love you. I don't want to cheat on you. I'm not worried I ever would. I know the difference between what I had before, what I did, who I was with those other women. And who I am now and what we are."

Where the hell was he going with all this?

"So why the fuck are you talking about cheating?"

"It was my stupid way of trying to make a point, and it sounded way better in my head than it does out loud. It was a stupid thing, and it has nothing to do with this." He sounded so miserable, she allowed him to take her hand. "I *am* worried I'm going to fuck up. I'm worried I'll be an asshole and drive you away and I won't have you. I don't know what I'd do without you."

Suddenly, everything inside her stilled, and she understood why he'd been so pissy, understood his comments about being afraid. He believed, on some level, all the shit his father had told him about being a shallow dumb fuck with a pretty face and no substance.

"Then stop acting like a dingus and just love me. I'm here, aren't I? Here waiting for you just like I was yesterday and the day before. Like I'll be tomorrow. I've never wanted anyone but you. Even before we were together, I had dates, I had someone I lived with even. But I didn't *want* any of them with the absolute certainty I have right now. I love you, Andrew."

"You do?"

She laughed. "Yes, dumb ass. I do. How could you think otherwise?"

"What if I do something stupid, Ella? I'm a stupid type of guy, you just said it yourself."

"I said you were a dumb ass, and you are." She took his hand. "But you're *my* dumb ass, and there's a universe between dumb ass and stupid. You just told me you were worried about things, but the one thing you weren't worried about was cheating on me. That's pretty much my big no-no. Other than hitting me. You planning on that?"

His eyes widened. "No! The only person I want to hit is your ex. Well, and my dad. I'd like to punch him right square in the face. But you're good and kind and, fuckall, Ella, you're soft and fragile and everything to me. What if you get sick when you're carrying our baby? What if you get into a car accident and die? What if I do something terrible and you hate me forever and I have to watch another man love you and make a life with you?"

She didn't bother replying; he clearly needed to say it all, cycle through it. His anguish was so clear she ached for him, even as she wanted to shake him and tell him there was nothing to worry about. So she held his hand, resting her head against the back of the couch, and listened.

"I watched my brother fall to pieces yesterday over the thought of

Erin dying. He's a stronger man than I am. If he's scared, what am I? I am not man enough, not brave enough to lose you."

She leaned in and kissed his temple. "You're the best man I know, Andrew. I wish you could see that. Ben is a lovely guy. He loves Erin, and she loves him back. He'd slay dragons for her, and that's great. For Erin. I don't love Ben. I love you. I love that you take pride in the beauty you've made with your hands at your house. I love that you read poetry. It makes me hot and tingly when you recite lines in Spanish when we're having sex. There's no one like you, Andrew Copeland."

"All this anxiety is choking me. I snap at you for doing what you do, for being strong with my dad. For taking care of our friends. You let it pass, and I wonder if I'm like him."

She burst out laughing at the very idea of Cope being a damned thing like Bill.

"I'm sorry, I'm not mocking you. But if I'd have confronted Bill's father, or anyone for that matter, he'd have belittled me until I felt like nothing. I wouldn't have been allowed to be at that hospital yesterday with Erin because he didn't approve of me having any friends at all. My time was his. That's how he saw our relationship, and I took it."

He started to speak, but she stopped him.

"No. I need to get this all out too. I took it, and I hated myself for that. It was that self-loathing that allowed him to control me all those years. It took me a long time to get to the place where I could accept responsibility for my part in the situation. And to admit to myself that I was manipulated and gamed into being nothing. Nothing is easy to shape into something else. And he did. And it was bad. But I am not her anymore."

She knew what she had to do, so she steeled herself against it. He needed to make the choice. He needed to be away from her and away from her apartment to look at the situation from a ways back and make his choice, out loud, on purpose and to himself, to stay despite the fear. If she let this go right now, how could she know for sure he really wanted to stay and take his chances with her and with fate? It would be there between them if they fought or if they hit a bad patch. She needed him to do this. For both of them.

So she knew she had to be honest and expose herself in the bargain.

"You are the reason. You're the reason I can say to myself that I deserve love and kindness and a normal relationship where I make decisions for myself and with my partner. When I was afraid, it was *you* who stepped up to give me the tools to combat that last hurdle. The last remnants of fear that held me back.

"On my last full day at the café, I went to buy coffee. The street was crowded, and I had a panic attack. Right there in the open like the freak I am."

"Why didn't you tell me?"

"Because I got through it. I went in, spoke with the clerk, paid money and walked out with my coffee. The other day, it was getting dark and I had to get back to my car, which I'd parked in the lot at the RJC in Kent. The courthouse," she added, to clarify. "It was creepy, and there wasn't anyone around until I heard footsteps, and the part of me he used to control got freaked out. But the part of me who you'd been training three times a week? Well, that part won. I kept an eye out, had my keys in my hand and I got to my car and drove away. I came up here and we had dinner at your house, and I was fine."

"You should have told me before now."

"I'm telling you now so you understand something very important. You gave me the tools to stand up and do the brave thing. I can't tell you I won't ever die. I can't promise that in some random chain of events I won't get killed in a freak accident or in labor or from a fucking infection from a scratch I get on the asphalt. I can't. You could lose me tomorrow. You could walk into a client's house and fall instantly in love with her. You could die in a plane crash. Nothing in life is certain. This used to keep me awake at night because I *needed* things to be certain.

"There are constants, though. You're the man I love. I can say this all to you now because no matter what happens, you will be the man I love. I will always love you, Andrew. It's my blessing to have that. It gives me the strength right now to tell you to go."

"What?"

"You need to work this through. I can take fighting with you. I'm not fragile, baby. Not at all. We can have an argument, and we will survive it. You seem to think I'm so broken that even having a tiff with me will damage me. I know you're not Bill. Couples fight. But people who love each other don't try to kill one another. Trust me, please, to understand the difference between what we've got and what I was before. You can be a total dick, Andrew. But so what? I can be a bitch. We're a good match." She grinned for a moment.

"So why are you kicking me out? I love you; you love me. End of story."

"Not really. Love isn't everything. It can't be. There's all the day-to-day stuff that fills in the rest. You're afraid, and I can't give you guarantees, not in the way you need. I can tell you I love you. I can tell you I'm committed to you, and the thought of me carrying our child fills me with so much joy I can't do it justice. But I can't promise not to die. I can't promise we'll be together forever. I can promise you I will work my ass off every single day for the rest of my life to keep our relationship working, to be the best person I can. What you need to figure out is if that's enough."

She had to pause to wrestle tears away.

"You need to figure out if that is enough for you to stay with me. Because while I respect your need for space to process stuff like this shit with your dad and all the hospital stuff, I don't plan to have this moment over and over. It's too much. I need assurances of my own. You need to figure out if your fear will choke you so much you can't give me all of yourself. I want it all. I want Andy, I want Cope and I want Andrew. The good, the bad, all of it. Because that's what I deserve and it's what you deserve. I'm giving you this gift because I love you. Go. Take the time and space you need to figure it out. Don't call me again until you're breaking up with me or telling me you're all mine."

She stood, and he did as well.

"I love you, Ella."

She nodded. "I know. I love you too. But that's not good enough for either of us. Take the time and come back to me."

He hugged her, his head hanging, and then he was gone and she was alone.

Alone enough to finally free the tears she'd been choking back the entire time she'd made the toughest decision of her entire life. If he didn't come back, she'd still love him, he'd still have changed her life for the better in so many ways she couldn't begin to add it all up. But boy, she sure hoped her inner voice was right and that he would figure it out and take the risk she'd asked for.

26

Walking out her door was the hardest thing he'd ever done. He had his own tears to shed as he stood there, just outside her apartment, heart aching as he heard the first sob from inside. He could go back in there right now and tell her to forget about it, that he loved her and didn't need any time to figure that out. He did love her, and she knew it.

But he knew she deserved more. Deserved all of him just as she'd asked, and he had to figure out if he could give it. So he turned and walked away, needing to bounce his situation off someone. But who?

Normally he'd seek out Ben, but Ben had enough problems just then. Adrian had been helpful, but he hadn't been where Cope was right now. He'd been helpful enough earlier that day, but Cope needed to talk with someone who was in a relationship that worked.

He drove around awhile, in the end, heading to the hospital because he needed to check in anyway.

And maybe because he knew there would be someone there who could help him find his way past this massive roadblock of fear that choked his fucking every thought.

He recognized Brody's truck in the lot across the way and found the big man talking with Todd in the waiting room.

"I say next time we meet we go for a place with better lighting." He plopped down next to Todd. "Here." Cope handed him a bag. "Thought Erin would appreciate something to do. It's a handheld system with some games."

Todd laughed. "She'll love it. Thanks."

"How is she?"

"The same pretty much. Bored out of her head. Grumpy. Scared. Her protein levels are better today. Alexander is right as rain. He's active and apparently happy in there."

"Good. Anything I can do?"

Todd sighed. "For now, no. Ella called earlier to say she'd check in at the café, but I told her Erin gave everyone the day off. She said she'd come in this morning to bring magazines and books. Erin says she's going to come out here so she can visit with everyone, though. If it wasn't raining so hard I'd take her out for a walk in the gardens in the back. She needs it."

"I figured Ella would come in with you." Brody gave him a once-over.

"It's complicated."

Both men goggled at him. "Complicated? What does that mean? You didn't cheat on her, did you?"

"Why would you think that? I'm not an ape, you know; I can keep my dick in my pants or in my girl. For the record, I have no desire to step out on Ella. What other woman could compare anyway?"

"So what makes it complicated?"

"Dude, your wife is in a hospital room right now. You have your own problems. Don't sweat it."

"Andy, we've been friends since before we had our permanent teeth. If that's not worth sweating over, I don't know what is. Erin is going to be fine. This is my mantra. I should have Brody ink it on my arm so I can look at it over and over. But she is, she will be and so will Alexander. Spill."

He took a deep breath and began to talk. "How do you get past the fear? Do you feel it?"

Brody nodded. "Hell yes. My god, when we didn't know if those fuckers would be successful at taking Rennie from Elise? I wanted to howl. I wanted to tear shit up. I wanted to fly to New York, find them, and beat them bloody. I knew Elise would fall apart if that happened, and I knew what my life would be like without that kid too. I knew what it would be to see this woman I adore lose that child. And I wondered if I would be enough if that were the case. Enough to keep her living with a purpose. And then I got sort of pissed about it, because why shouldn't I be first? Why wouldn't I be enough? Was I enough? Was I good enough? What if she looked at me really closely, what if she saw that I was so not worthy, and she left?"

Cope didn't know why, but hearing that made him feel better, even just a little bit. Maybe it was knowing he wasn't alone.

"During all that stuff, Raven was doing her thing. Being a bitch, but needing to be loved, and I'd been her friend forever and she was one of my people. But damn it, she was trying to mess with my girls, and I had to choose."

Brody stood and began to pace. "That's when I sort of knew I was fucked." He barked a laugh. "Because I did, and I would again. And because I did it knowing Elise would be first for me always, even if I messed up and she walked away. Rennie and Elise are mine. Mine in a way that comforts me, fills me up, thrills me and scares the ever living crap out of me. Jesus, these two ladies mean everything, and what if I mess it up? What would I do without them?"

"What if Erin dies on the delivery table? It would be my fault because I wanted a baby with her so bad. Ben and I wanted a family with Erin, wanted a child to fill the house with laughter. But we have laughter now. So in my greed, what if I've made the worst mistake in my life, and I lose them both?" Todd leaned back. "Christ, I want a cigarette."

"So is that what's making things complicated? You broke up with her because you're afraid she'll walk away?" Brody asked.

"We didn't break up. But this fear, seeing my brother who is the strongest guy I know reduced to tears because of how much he loves Erin, that hit me. I'm not that strong. Maybe it's a sign she and I aren't meant to be, if I can't take that last step. I told her this morning, essentially that I was freaked out and unsure. She told me to figure it out. Told me a lot more than that actually, but the gist is: *Don't call me again until you've got your shit together because I'm worth it.* And she's right. She is."

"So you're going to let a woman like Ella go because why? I'm not getting it. I mean, I get the fear part. That's what broke Erin and me up the first time. And we know how that turned out. Ten years of being unhappy and uncomfortable because I was meant to be with the one woman who challenged me on every level, even as she *got* me. Accepted all of me, the darkness, the broken stuff, the uneven edges. Do you know what that's worth, Andy? Fitting with someone in a way no one else will?

"I've seen you two together. Even before you finally manned up and asked her out. But since then you two fit. She's amazing. Beautiful. Strong. She works hard, and she looks at you and sees you. I've met the chicks you were with before. Not a single one saw the whole of you. Even I forget about it sometimes because you wear the smiling Cope façade so much."

"She told me she wanted all of me. Cope, Andy and Andrew. I suppose part of me has used Cope to hide behind. It's easier that way. She challenges me to be more. I have never been challenged this way. What if I fail? What if I give it my all and it still doesn't work and she walks away and I'm alone?"

"That's the rub isn't it? I mean, here we've got this awesome thing.

This woman who we'd give anything for, but the thing we have to give is, well everything. You have to figure out if she's worth the work. Because I can't lie and tell you it's easy to be with someone. Even someone you adore. Marriage is hard work. There's a balance there where things run on their own without much effort, but you have to do maintenance or it will break down. You have to expose yourself, ask someone else for their blood, sweat and tears and give your own. It leaves you laid bare and inside out, Andrew. And *that's* what makes it so good. That's love, man. That's love and part of what makes it so awesome is the level of real, true intimacy, and the risk you take by opening yourself up that way to someone who has the power to gut you."

Brody sat across from them. "That's it really, in a nutshell. So I guess the question here, Andrew Copeland, is do you have the balls? Because love is a go big or go home sort of thing. You can't sort of love someone. You can't caveat love. You do it, you make the effort and you live without a net sometimes. Thrilling and terrifying and I wouldn't have it any other way. "

Todd sat forward, clasping his hands between his knees. "I think the question is, can you live without her? Watch her fall in love with someone else? See her bring him to our events and stuff? She, Erin and Elise are tight, so the reality is, that's what will happen. You'll see some other dude get what *you* could have had. If the fear of some random thing happening in the future is bigger than the reality of her being with another guy, walk away now when it'll merely sort of kill you to do it. But you can't have this doubt between you. Man up. Love her the way she deserves it, or let another man do it."

That was the question.

He stood. "I gotta go. I'll talk to you later today to check back in. I'll have my cell if you need me. Thanks." He looked to both men who were friends who'd become his brothers as much as Ben was. "I mean it. I needed to get it all out there, and you helped me do that."

"Call if you need anything from us too, right?" Brody stood as well. "I'm going to call Elise and Rennie and then go in to hug my sister. Love, Andrew, love makes everything in the world seem doable."

He drove back to his place. Maybe working on the last part of the wainscoting in the formal dining room would help quiet his thoughts.

And there it was, in his mailbox. The envelope was manila, nothing fancy, her writing, the same beautiful script she'd used before, this time with forest green ink. It was not stamped, so she'd come by and tucked it into the box herself sometime between yesterday afternoon when he'd checked last and that morning.

He went into the house and sat in her chair, opening it up.

Inside was a photograph and a letter.

Andrew,

This is my great-grandfather and great-grandmother. When I look at them, I wonder what it would be like to be with you through our youth, into middle age and the waning days of our life together. I see a house filled with noisy Copland children, with grandbabies, dogs, the children and grandchildren of our friends. Our nieces and nephews. A happy life filled with vacations on the coast, with road trips and stolen kisses after we've put all the toys together, all ready for the morning when the kids wake up in the predawn hours and proclaim it Christmas.

You told me you loved me. I've always felt this from you, and I've carried it around inside and not really known it. It was just something I associated with you without being able to identify, really. This is what love means for me. Family. Fidelity. Faith in one another. And love.

I love you, and I want to spend every day until I am no longer breathing with you. I want to bear your children and open my eyes each day to see you there with me, beside me.

The writing changed, and more was added with a different pen.

I wrote the part above before Erin's pregnancy problems. I debated sending this to you. It's a big deal, and I haven't said any of this to you before. I may scare you off, or you may not feel the depth of love I do, and I'm running with something you hadn't intended.

I heard hesitation in your voice tonight when we spoke, and it scared me. It scared me because I realized I'd simply accepted your presence in my heart and in my life, accepted that you were mine.

I love you, and I want you to be happy. I hope that you want to be happy with me. All you need to do is give me the word and I'm yours.

Forever and always,
Ella

He put the envelope down and looked at the picture. He saw Ella in her great-grandmother's face. Though the picture was black and white and a bit yellowed with age, the spark between the couple leapt from the paper.

27

Ella sat back with a sigh. She'd scrubbed her bathroom floor with vicious intent. That grout would sparkle, damn it. She'd placed her obligatory and, as it happened, rather pleasant call to her parents. Had paid her bills online and tried to pretend the hours hadn't passed.

But they had, and he was not there. He had not called or come to her, and damn it, maybe he wouldn't. She pushed to to her feet and cleaned up. All on autopilot. She needed to get out and not wallow. She had to put her faith in him to figure out that she was worth the effort. They'd survive the fear. God knew she had her own.

Just a few days before, they'd been out and had run into not just one woman he used to sleep with, but two! Until that day, she'd met a few others in passing and had found herself wanting in some way. None of them were like her. They were all petite and tended toward blonde. Fake tans usually, lots of makeup. He had a type, clearly. And she was not it.

It made her insecure. Who wouldn't be?

But that day when they'd bumped into those two women, he barely saw them. He'd been friendly enough, not rude, but his attention had never really left Ella. She'd been his focus, and those women, pretty though they were, had not been her.

It had been a lightbulb moment and the time she'd let go of her own fear. Suddenly, she realized that she was his type in a way those others would never be. He'd chosen carbon copies of the same woman over and over, but they'd never gone anywhere. He'd never shown them his house, never shown them how to use a band saw.

She laughed at that, but the man was passionate about his tools, and it had been a big moment for her when he'd let her use it the first time without standing over her every moment.

As she walked toward the door to grab her coat and bag, she noticed the pale, cream-colored envelope someone had slid under her door.

She looked through the peephole and then carefully opened the door, but no one was there.

One glance at the front of the envelope, and she knew who it was from. She braced herself for the worst as she opened it up and pulled out the letter inside.

She unfolded the smooth, thick paper and smiled. The handwriting was typical of him, of his voice. Bold. Masculine. His words unfurled across the page as if he never doubted a thing he thought. She knew differently by then, of course, that Andrew Copeland was far more than what he appeared on the surface. But his letters had become essential. Part of the rhythm and play of their relationship, like foreplay. And this one could make or break that.

Dearest Ella,

Imagine my surprise when I opened my mailbox and found your letter and the picture. I looked at it and read your letter. Then I read it a dozen more times, railing against myself for not seeing the obvious.

I found this snippet in a journal I keep. A snippet I'd written intend-

ing to send you at some later date in a letter. But then I figured today was precisely the day I needed you to read it, because it's the truth.

As you slept, the rain fell outside and warm, I lay with you, naked, against your heart and body and you were mine. You are mine, and I don't think I know all the words to tell you just what that means. Only that when you breathe, I do, when you smile just for me everything inside me stills and knows it's found the key.

He'd sketched her on the paper, a quick pencil sketch of her shoulders and the top of her back, of the way her hair had swept forward over her face.

This is what I see. This is what I feel. This is what I want to feel every day for the rest of my life, and you're the only one who can make me this way. Let me love you, and I promise you all of me.

I love you,
Andrew, Cope and Andy

PS—Look out front when you're ready.

She read it twice more and, holding it to her heart, she went to her windows and looked outside. He stood there, looking up at her windows as he leaned against his truck, and when he saw her, his face lit with a smile so beautiful it nearly felled her.

Instead, she smiled back and waved.

He motioned up and managed to put a question on it, so she nodded.

And then she ran to the bathroom and tried to tame her hair, wished she had enough time for at least a bit of styling but opted for a quick, one-handed brush of her teeth while she buzzed him up.

She opened the door with a yank, not pretending she wasn't anxious.

He came into her arms just the way he was supposed to, and it felt so right she just gave in and began to cry.

"Shh. Ella, baby, please don't cry. I'm sorry for making you upset. I'm sorry I hurt you. I just want to be with you, and if that means realizing that something worth having is also something I'd be devastated at losing, then so be it."

He kissed her eyelids.

"I love you. When all this craziness with Erin and the baby and Brody and Elise's wedding is past, will you marry me? We can plan it for the anniversary of our first official date, though I can tell you the first day I saw you, May fifth, we can get married then too. Or tomorrow, or in two years. Whatever. I just want you. Every day forever."

"You have me. And yes, I'll marry you on the anniversary of that first date, though it makes me all smooshy inside to know you remembered the first day you met me. That was my third day at the café. I remember it too. I'd never seen anything like you before. You sort of scared me at first, still do I suppose, because I can't understand how you could want me. But it doesn't matter, because you do and I want you right back and those blonde skeezoids you were a boy skeezoid with can fuck right off."

He laughed as he angled her onto the bed, pulling her clothes off. "They're not skeezoids; they're just not you." At her look, he rolled his eyes. "Okay so one or two might be, probably the ones you have bumped into."

"Andrew, you are aware that no one should be that shade of orange unless they're an Oompa-Loompa, right?"

She was still laughing when he thrust into her body, choking off the sound, filling her and bringing a soft sigh of homecoming.

"I'm not wearing a condom," he said softly in her ear. "We'd sort of discussed this as the next step, but I wanted to be sure before I move again. Because this feels so good I might just blow if I pull out and push back in even once."

"Yes. Yes it's fine. More than fine, it's fabulous and beautiful, and you feel so good if you *don't* move soon, I'm going to pass out from frustration."

He nipped her neck and rolled them so she was on top. His favorite position and one she liked an awful lot too. "How can I resist all this masculine beauty spread out beneath me? How'd this happen, Andrew Copeland? How did I rate someone like you to love and to be loved by? Do you want to know what I think?"

"As long as you tell me while you're fucking me." He sent her a hopeful smile, and it was her turn to laugh. She circled her hips, keeping him deep, loving how it felt and that she knew it tortured him with pleasure.

"You make me feel like a siren. Did you know that?"

He slid his hands up from her hips to cup her breasts. "Red, you *are* a siren. Now tell me, oh holy shit, yep, like that. That's new, I like it."

She ground herself down onto him, moving her hips from side to side. "I like it too."

"There she is," he said when she'd sort of growled the last.

"I think that you're my blue ribbon. Not only because you look so good, and let's face it, Andrew Copeland, you look *fine*. Damn I have never seen a more beautiful man in my whole life. But you're my blue ribbon because you're good and kind, compassionate and you love me. Shelter me, protect me, trust me to protect myself and make my own choices. You are my blue ribbon for waiting and taking the hard way to get right here to this spot."

"Just when I think I can't love you any more, you prove me wrong."

"I made an appointment for later today. Raven is doing a piercing for me."

He stilled, his cock still deep within her. She leaned forward, bracing her hands on his shoulders to get better balance.

"Where?" he gasped out.

She dropped a kiss on his lips, meaning for it to be quick, but then falling into him the way she'd been unable to avoid every time she touched him. He took over the pace, lazily nipping at her bottom lip, sucking her tongue into his mouth until she writhed against him.

"My nipple," she whispered into his mouth. "You said you'd like it. I sure hope you do, because it looks like it hurts getting it done."

"It does for a few seconds. But I'll keep you feeling so much pleasure you won't notice the pain. Also?" He slid a hand down between them and found her clit. "Slick and hard, ready for me."

She had already been on edge emotionally, had needed him so much it only took a few brief touches before climax hit, sending her fully upright, her back bending as the shock of it hit, radiating pleasure through every part of her. So much she saw bursts of light behind closed eyes.

"Christ," he hissed as he began to come, pressing up as he held her down, even as she writhed still from her own orgasm.

Exhausted, she fell to the side in a heap of spent, jumping muscles, panting, not letting go of him for dear life.

"Can I risk telling you something really dirty?" he asked in that slow, sexy, lazy drawl of his.

"Duh. I want to hear all your something really dirty, any time it comes to mind, feel free to call me if I'm not around to hear it face-to-face."

He pulled her closer. "The idea of coming on your tits when you get the piercing gets me so hot."

She knew her full body blush would be impossible to miss. "Guh. That's, well, wow, I've read in books about clits pulsing, and I thought it was bullshit. But I'm pretty sure mine just did when you said that."

He laughed, rolling on top of her. "Sex will be a lot messier now that we don't use condoms. Your shower is very small. Mine is much bigger. This is my way of asking you to move into my house with me. To make it our home. You know, just in case you didn't know why the hell I brought that up."

"You're sure?"

He touched his forehead to hers. "This is go time, babe. I want you with me every day. When I want to talk to you, I want you to be there. I want your stamp on the house. Your cardigan is on the chair in the living room. I realized yesterday that I thought of it as your chair. I want it to be our house. I want to start our life. I know we've been dating for a relatively short period of time, but I know you. I've known you for six years. You know me. And I promise I will move heaven and earth to make you happy and keep you safe."

He had a two-headed shower in his bathroom. And a washer and dryer in his basement. His bed was big, and he had a fireplace in three rooms. Most of all, he was there, and he wanted her there too.

"We have to tell my parents together. First let's lead with the marriage part. And then the moving in part."

"We can tell them at dinner tomorrow. I was thinking of inviting my mom to come too if that's all right? I want her to know them, and I want them to realize I'm for real and forever and not anything like Bill. Your dad frowns at me a lot when he thinks I'm not looking. I want him to trust me with your heart."

She laughed. "All right then."

28

"Give that baby to me right now." Ella stood in front of Brody and gave him the look. "You've had him the last half hour. I was nice because it's your wedding day and all, but now it's my turn." She held her hands out, and with a disgruntled sigh, he kissed the top of Alexander's downy head and handed him over.

In the end, even after all the health-inspired madness Erin had suffered, Alexander had come easily and quietly a week after Erin had been discharged from the hospital the last time. Six weeks old already and he was big, healthy and adored by everyone in his life. Not a bad way to live..

"Five minutes. Not thirty, drama queen." Brody winked at her.

Alexander snuggled into her immediately and made a soft cooing sound. "Look at you. Already the handsomest boy in the whole wide world. Your mommy is looking for you. I think your dinner is ready."

He put a tiny fist into his mouth, sucking on it. "Yeah, I gotcha. We're moving."

Cope came around the corner, holding two glasses. "Hey, Red. I've been looking for you. Thought a glass of champagne would be a lovely way to end a great day."

"Thank you." She smiled at him, and they both looked down at Alexander again. "Hang on a sec. Alexander is hungry, and I need to get him to Erin."

"I'll come with you. Seeing you with him makes me simultaneously hot for you and tender about our future."

"There you are!" Erin called out from her place on a comfortable couch. Alexander heard his mother's voice and began to fuss until Ella handed him over. He turned immediately and latched on.

Erin settled back with her feet up, and Ben handed her the blanket she used to keep Alexander focused on eating and not looking around the room at all the people who wanted to give him love.

"Thanks for tracking Brody down. Man gets his mitts on my baby, and it's hell to get him back."

"Well, you're stingy with him. Sheesh, I got to hold him for all of two minutes before he threw me over for you and those giant boobs of yours."

Todd laughed. "Ella, I love you and all, but when it comes to a choice between food and boobs and a nice lady who snuggles you, you have to know the former will always win."

"Ella and I snuck away and got married last weekend," Andrew blurted.

"What?" Erin turned her gaze on Ella, who was just as surprised that he'd spilled the beans as Erin was. She shouldn't be surprised. He was like a kid at Christmas sometimes when it came to secrets.

"We were going to get married in the fall. You know, when we'd fully finished the house and all. But we were all in Vegas last week for pre-wedding stuff, so we snuck out and did it. Actually, I got her tipsy and convinced her we should do it. Hey, I'm not proud!"

"*Pffft.* I love you and I wanted to marry you. We didn't want to say anything just yet because we didn't want to take the focus off

Brody and Elise." Ella sent him a raised brow but he just laughed, unrepentant.

"Didn't want to take the focus off us for what?" Brody came in, Elise at his side wearing a red wedding dress, her hair styled in cascading curls with crystals tucked inside. She looked breathtakingly beautiful. But it was the love between them that made Ella choke up a bit.

Erin piped up. "Ella and Cope got married last week when we were all in Vegas."

"What the heck! You didn't tell me?" Elise hugged her. "Girl, I'm gonna kick your butt."

"It's your wedding day. You deserve every last bit of attention. It would have kept until next week."

"We want to try to get pregnant, and what better time to get married than when you're in Vegas."

She spun, ready to pinch him, but he danced out of her reach. "Oh my god! Andrew Copeland! You promised to hold off."

Moving to her, he kissed her hard. "You're my wife. The wedding is over, and we're in private with my brother and our friends. What better time to share? Anyway, now when we have our kiddo, he or she will know there wasn't a shotgun wedding or anything."

The man was absolutely incorrigible, but he was all hers, which was the very best part of every day. Her parents had been over the moon, though they'd been disappointed to have not been there, so they promised to throw a big party in a few months to announce it. Annalee had been likewise thrilled, and she had called Moira immediately to start planning the party.

"I just wanted to be his wife." She smiled at Elise, who grinned and then kissed Ella smack on the lips.

"We're pregnant. We told Rennie yesterday, and she gave us permission to tell you guys today."

"Holy cow!" There was much hugging and kissing, much commiserating and talking of dates.

"How awesome is this? Look at all this happily ever after." Adrian spoke from where he'd been perched on a couch arm.

Cope pulled her into his embrace, swaying to a tune only they could hear.

"I love you so much it's not funny," he murmured for her ears only. "Can't wait to get you home to show you."

He showed her every moment of every day, and she never quite got over the wonder of that. The beautiful normalcy of being loved so very fiercely by this man who wrote her poetry and brought her breakfast in bed after he'd kept her up all night making love.

"I do have a present for you now, though."

She let go, clapping her hands excitedly. "You're finally going to let me see?" Brody had given him a tattoo on his arm that Cope had been totally secretive about.

He'd kept it covered when she was around all during the time it had been healing.

Rolling up his shirtsleeve, she read the words scrolling down his right arm.

In your eyes of mourning, the land of dreams begin

"Oh." Tears welled up. It was her favorite line from Neruda's "In My Sky at Twilight."

"That's a good oh?"

She nodded, bending down to kiss his forearm. "It's beautiful. Thank you."

"You're my everything, Ella. Inside and out, the most beautiful creature to ever be. I adore you."

Life was very, very good.

AUTHOR'S NOTE

In this book, Ella makes her own special "Cope Playlist" and sends it to him in her own version of a mixtape.

"Everlong" — Foo Fighters
"Head First" — The Babys
"Still Remains" — Stone Temple Pilots
"Lost Without U" — Robin Thicke
"The Wait" — The Pretenders
"When It Don't Come Easy" — Patty Griffin
"Manhattan" — Kings of Leon
"Caligulove" — Them Crooked Vultures
"Birds" — Kate Nash
"Black Cherry" — Goldfrapp
"#1 Crush" — Garbage
"The First Taste" — Fiona Apple
"Mercy" — Duffy
"Ain't Nobody" — Chaka Khan
"No One's Gonna Love You" — Band of Horses
"Little Plastic Castle" — Ani DiFranco
"Gravel" — Ani DiFranco
"Fix You Up" — Tegan and Sara